Richard Brautigan

A Confederate General from Big Sur,
Dreaming of Babylon,
and
The Hawkline Monster

Books by Richard Brautigan

NOVELS

Trout Fishing in America
A Confederate General from Big Sur
In Watermelon Sugar
The Abortion: An Historical Romance 1966
The Hawkline Monster: A Gothic Western
Willard and His Bowling Trophies: A Perverse Mystery
Sombrero Fallout: A Japanese Novel
Dreaming of Babylon: A Private Eye Novel 1942
The Tokyo-Montana Express
So the Wind Won't Blow It All Away

POETRY

The Galilee Hitch-Hiker
Lay the Marble Tea
The Octopus Frontier
All Watched Over by Machines of Loving Grace
Please Plant This Book
The Pill *versus* the Springhill Mine Disaster
Rommel Drives on Deep into Egypt
Loading Mercury with a Pitchfork
June 30th, June 30th

SHORT STORIES

Revenge of the Lawn

Richard Brautigan

A Confederate General from Big Sur, Dreaming of Babylon, and The Hawkline Monster

(Three books in the manner of their original editions)

Houghton Mifflin/Seymour Lawrence

BOSTON

For information about permission to reproduce selections from
this book, write to Permissions, Houghton Mifflin Company,
2 Park Street, Boston, Massachusetts 02108.

Library of Congress Cataloging-in-Publication Data

Brautigan, Richard.
[Novels. Selections]
Richard Brautigan's A Confederate general from Big Sur, Dreaming
of Babylon, and The Hawkline monster : three books in the manner of
their original editions.
p.   cm.
ISBN 0-395-54703-2 (paper)
I. Title.   II. Title: Confederate general from Big Sur.
III. Title: Dreaming of Babylon.   IV. Title: Hawkline monster.
PS3503.R2736A6   1991   90-20524
813'.54—dc20   CIP

Printed in the United States of America

QUM 10 9

A Confederate General from Big Sur

by

Richard Brautigan

to my daughter
Ianthe

CONTENTS

Prologue

Attrition's Old Sweet Song

"THE RECORDS EXHIBIT that 425 individuals received appointment by the President to one of the four grades of general, of whom 299 were in grade at the end of the war. The attrition is accounted for as follows:

Killed in action or died of wounds	77
Resigned	19
Died by accident or from natural causes	15
Appointments cancelled	5
Declined appointment	3
Killed in "personal encounters"	2
Assassinated	1
Committed suicide	1
Dropped	1
Retired by reason of wounds	1
Reverted to rank of colonel	1
Total	**126**"

I Mean, What Do You Do Besides Being a Confederate General?

"Lawyers, jurists   129

"Lawyers, jurists	129
Professional soldiers	125
Businessmen (including bankers, manufacturers, and merchants)	55
Farmers, planters	42
Politicians	24
Educators	15
Civil engineers	13
Students	6
Doctors	4
Ministers	3
Frontiersmen, peace officers	3
Indian agents	2
Naval officers	2
Editor	1
Soldier of fortune	1
Total	425"

Part One

A Confederate General from Big Sur

A Confederate General from Big Sur

WHEN I FIRST HEARD about Big Sur I didn't know that it was a member of the Confederate States of America. I had always thought that Georgia, Arkansas, Mississippi, Florida, Alabama, Louisiana, South Carolina, Virginia, Tennessee, North Carolina and Texas were the Confederacy, and let it go at that. I had no idea that Big Sur was also a member.

Big Sur the twelfth member of the Confederate States of America? Frankly, it's hard to believe that those lonely stark mountains and clifflike beaches of California were rebels, that the redwood trees and the ticks and the cormorants waved a rebel flag along that narrow hundred miles of land that lies between Monterey and San Luis Obispo.

The Santa Lucia Mountains, that thousand-year-old flophouse for mountain lions and lilacs, a hotbed of Secession? The Pacific Ocean along there, that million-year-old skid row for abalone and kelp, sending representatives back to the Confederate Congress in Richmond, Virginia?

I've heard that the population of Big Sur in those Civil

War days was mostly just some Digger Indians. I've heard that the Digger Indians down there didn't wear any clothes. They didn't have any fire or shelter or culture. They didn't grow anything. They didn't hunt and they didn't fish. They didn't bury their dead or give birth to their children. They lived on roots and limpets and sat pleasantly out in the rain.

I can imagine the expression on General Robert E. Lee's face when this gang showed up, bearing strange gifts from the Pacific Ocean.

It was during the second day of the Battle of the Wilderness. A. P. Hill's brave but exhausted Confederate troops had been hit at daybreak by Union General Hancock's II Corps of 30,000 men. A. P. Hill's troops were shattered by the attack and fell back in defeat and confusion along the Orange Plank Road.

Twenty-eight-year-old Colonel William Poague, the South's fine artillery man, waited with sixteen guns in one of the few clearings in the Wilderness, Widow Tapp's farm. Colonel Poague had his guns loaded with antipersonnel ammunition and opened fire as soon as A. P. Hill's men had barely fled the Orange Plank Road.

The Union assault funneled itself right into a vision of sculptured artillery fire, and the Union troops suddenly found pieces of flying marble breaking their centers and breaking their edges. At the instant of contact, history transformed their bodies into statues. They didn't like it, and the assault began to back up along the Orange Plank Road. What a nice name for a road.

Colonel Poague and his men held their ground alone without any infantry support, and no way out, caring not for the name of the road. They were there forever and General Lee was right behind them in the drifting marble dust of their guns. He was waiting for General Longstreet's arrival with reinforcements. Longstreet's men were hours late.

Then the first of them arrived. Hood's old Texas Brigade led by John Gregg came on through the shattered forces of A. P. Hill, and these Texans were surprised because A. P. Hill's men were shock troops of the Confederate Army, and here they were in full rout.

"What troops are you, my boys?" Lee said.

"The Texans!" the men yelled and quickly formed into battle lines. There were less than a thousand of them and they started forward toward that abyss of Federal troops.

Lee was in motion with them, riding his beautiful gray horse, Traveller, a part of the wave. But they stopped him and shouted, "Lee to the rear! Lee to the rear!"

They turned him around and sent him back to spend the last years of his life quietly as the president of Washington College, later to be called Washington and Lee.

Then they went forward possessed only by animal fury, without any regard now for their human shadows. It was a little late for things like that.

The Texans suffered 50 per cent casualties in less than ten minutes, but they contained the Union. It was like putting your finger in the ocean and having it stop, but only briefly because Appomattox Courthouse waited less than a year away, resting now in its gentle anonymity.

When Lee got to the rear of the lines, there were the 8th Big Sur Volunteer Heavy Root Eaters reporting for duty. The air around them was filled with the smell of roots and limpets. The 8th Big Sur Volunteer Heavy Root Eaters reported like autumn to the Army of Northern Virginia.

They all gathered around Lee's horse and stared in amazement, for it was the first time that they had ever seen a horse. One of the Digger Indians offered Traveller a limpet to eat.

When I first heard about Big Sur I didn't know that it was part of the defunct Confederate States of America, a country that went out of style like an idea or a lampshade or some kind of food that people don't cook any more, once the favorite dish in thousands of homes.

It was only through a Lee-of-another-color, Lee Mellon, that I found out the truth about Big Sur. Lee Mellon who is the battle flags and the drums of this book. Lee Mellon: a Confederate general in ruins.

The Tide Teeth of Lee Mellon

It is important before I go any further in this military narrative to talk about the teeth of Lee Mellon. They need talking about. During these five years that I have known Lee Mellon, he has probably had 175 teeth in his mouth.

This is due to a truly gifted faculty for getting his teeth knocked out. It almost approaches genius. They say that John Stuart Mill could read Greek when he was three years old and had written a history of Rome at the age of six and a half.

But the amazing thing about Lee Mellon's teeth is their strange and constantly moving placement in the many and varied dentures those poor teeth briefly get to call home. I would meet him one day on Market Street and he would have just one upper left tooth in his face, and then I'd see him again, months later on Grant Avenue, and he'd have three lower right teeth and one upper right tooth.

I'd see him again just back from Big Sur, and he'd have four upper front teeth, and two lower left teeth, and then

19

after a few weeks in San Francisco, he'd be wearing the upper plate without any teeth in it at all, wearing the plate just so he would have a head start on gristle, and so that his cheeks wouldn't collapse in on his mouth.

I've adjusted to this teeth fantasia always happening to him, and so now everytime I see him, I have a good look at his mouth to see how things are going with him, to see if he has been working, what books he has been reading, whether Sara Teasdale or *Mein Kampf*, and whom he has been sleeping with: blondes or brunettes.

Lee Mellon told me that once in Modern Times, he'd had all his teeth in his mouth at the same time for a whole day. He was driving a tractor in Kansas, back and forth across a field of wheat, and his brand-new lower plate felt a little funny in his mouth, so he took it out and put it into his shirt pocket. The teeth fell out of his pocket, and he backed the tractor over them.

Lee Mellon told me rather sadly that after he had discovered that the teeth were gone from his shirt pocket, it took him almost an hour to find them, and when he found them, they weren't worth finding at all.

The First Time I Met Lee Mellon

I MET LEE MELLON five years ago in San Francisco. It was spring. He had just "hitch-hiked" up from Big Sur. Along the way a rich queer stopped and picked Lee Mellon up in a sports car. The rich queer offered Lee Mellon ten dollars to commit an act of oral outrage.

Lee Mellon said all right and they stopped at some lonely place where there were trees leading back into the mountains, joining up with a forest way back in there, and then the forest went over the top of the mountains.

"After you," Lee Mellon said, and they walked back into the trees, the rich queer leading the way. Lee Mellon picked up a rock and bashed the rich queer in the head with it.

"Ouch!" the rich queer said and fell on the ground. That hurt, and the rich queer began begging for his life.

"Spare me! Spare me! I'm just a lonely little rich queer who wanted to have some fun. I never hurt anyone."

"Stop blubbering," Lee Mellon said. "And give me all

your money and the keys to your car. That's all I want anyway, you rich queer."

The rich queer gave Lee Mellon $235.00 and the keys
to his car and his watch.

Lee Mellon hadn't said anything about the rich queer's
watch, but figuring that his birthday was coming up soon,
he'd be twenty-three, Lee Mellon took the watch and put it
in his pocket.

The rich queer was having the greatest time of his life.
A tall, young, good-looking, dashing, toothless raider was
taking all his money and his car and his watch away.

It would make a wonderful story to tell his other rich
queer friends. He could show the bump on his head and point
to the place where his watch had been.

The rich queer reached up and felt the bump on his
head. It was rising like a biscuit. The rich queer hoped the
bump wouldn't go away for a long time.

"I'm going now," Lee Mellon said. "And you sit right
where you are until tomorrow morning. If you move an inch,
I'll come back here and run over you a couple of times with
my car. I'm a desperate man, and I like nothing better in
this world than to run over rich queers."

"I won't move until tomorrow morning," the rich queer
said. This made sense to him. After all Lee Mellon did
appear to be quite a mean man, for all his good looks.

"I won't move an inch," the rich queer promised.

"That's a good rich queer," Lee Mellon said and
abandoned the car in Monterey and took a bus on into
San Francisco.

When I met the young raider for the first time, he had
been on a four-day drunk with his confiscated funds. He
bought a bottle of whiskey and we went into an alley to
drink it. Things are done like that in San Francisco.

Lee Mellon and I yakked up a storm and became close

friends immediately. He said he was looking for a place to live. He still had some of the rich queer's money left.

I said that there was a vacant room for rent under the attic where I lived over on Leavenworth Street, and Lee Mellon said, howdy neighbor.

Lee Mellon knew that there was no danger of the rich queer ever going to the police. "The rich queer's probably still sitting down there at Big Sur," Lee Mellon said. "I hope he doesn't starve to death."

Augustus Mellon, CSA

THE FIRST TIME I MET Lee Mellon the night went away with every totem drop of the whiskey. When dawn came we were down on the Embarcadero and it was raining. Seagulls started it all, that gray screeching, almost like banners, running with the light. There was a ship going someplace. It was a Norwegian ship.

Perhaps it was going back to Norway, carrying the hides of 163 cable cars, as part of the world commerce deal. Ah, trade: one country exchanging goods with another country, just like in grade school. They traded a rainy spring morning in Oslo for 163 cable car hides from San Francisco.

Lee Mellon looked at the sky. Sometimes when you meet people for the first time, they stare at the sky. He stared for a long time. "What?" I said, because I wanted to be his friend.

"Just seagulls," he said. "That one," and pointed at a seagull, but I couldn't tell which one it was for there were many, summoning their voices to the dawn. Then he said nothing for a while.

Yes, one could think of seagulls. We were awfully tired, hung over and still drunk. One could think of seagulls. It's really a very simple thing to do . . . seagulls: past, present and future passing almost like drums to the sky.

We stopped at a little cafe and got some coffee. The coffee was brought to us by the world's ugliest waitress. I gave her an imaginary name: Thelma. I do things like that.

My name is Jesse. Any attempt to describe her would be against my better judgment, but in her own way she seemed to belong in that cafe with steam rising like light out of our coffee.

Helen of Troy would have looked out of place. "What's Helen of Troy doing in here?" some longshoreman would have asked. He wouldn't have understood. So Thelma it was for the likes of us.

Lee Mellon told me that he was born in Meridian, Mississippi, and grew up in Florida, Virginia and North Carolina. "Near Asheville," he said. "That's Thomas Wolfe country."

"Yeah," I said.

Lee Mellon didn't have any Southern accent. "You don't have much of a Southern accent," I said.

"That's right, Jesse. I read a lot of Nietzsche, Schopenhauer and Kant when I was a kid," Lee Mellon said.

I guess in some strange way that was supposed to get rid of a Southern accent. Lee Mellon thought so, anyway. I couldn't argue because I had never tried a Southern accent against the German philosophers.

"When I was sixteen years old I stole into classes at the University of Chicago and lived with two highly cultured young Negro ladies who were freshmen," Lee Mellon said.

"We all slept in the same bed together. It helped me get rid of my Southern accent."

"Sounds like it might do the trick," I said, not knowing exactly what I was saying.

Thelma, the world's ugliest waitress, came over and asked us if we wanted some breakfast. The hotcakes were good and the bacon and eggs were good and would fill you up. "Hit the spot," Thelma said.

I had the hotcakes and Lee Mellon had the hotcakes and the bacon and eggs and some more hotcakes. He did not pay any attention to Thelma and continued to talk about the South.

He told me that he had lived on a farm near Spotsylvania, Virginia, and had spent a lot of time as a child going over the places where the Battle of the Wilderness had been fought.

"My great grandfather fought there," he said. "He was a general. A Confederate general and a damn good one, too. I was raised on stories of General Augustus Mellon, CSA. He died in 1910. The same year Mark Twain died. That was the year of Halley's Comet. He was a general. Have you ever heard of General Augustus Mellon?"

"No, but that's really something," I said. "A Confederate general . . . gee."

"Yeah, we Mellons have always been very proud of General Augustus Mellon. There's a statue of him some place, but we don't know where it is.

"My Uncle Benjamin spent two years trying to find the statue. He traveled all over the South in an old truck and slept in the back. That statue is probably in some park covered with vines. They don't pay enough respect to our honored dead. Our great heroes."

Our plates were empty now like orders for a battle not yet conceived, in a war not yet invented. I said farewell to the world's ugliest waitress, but Lee Mellon insisted on paying the check. He took a good look at Thelma.

Perhaps he was seeing her for the first time, and as I remember, he hadn't said anything about her while she was bringing the coffee and breakfast to us.

"I'll give you a dollar for a kiss," Lee Mellon said while she was giving him the change for ten dollars of the rich queer's rock-on-the-head money.

"Sure," she said, without smiling or being embarrassed or acting out of the way or anything. It was just as if the Dollar Lee Mellon Kissing Business were an integral part of her job.

Lee Mellon gave her a great big kiss. Neither one of them cracked, opened or celebrated a smile. He did not show in any manner that he was joking. I went along with him. The subject was never brought up by either one of us, so it *almost* stays there.

As we walked along the Embarcadero the sun came out like memory and began to recall the rain back to the sky and Lee Mellon said, "I know where we can get four pounds of muscatel for one dollar and fifteen cents."

We went there. It was an old Italian wineshop on Powell Street, just barely open. There was a row of wine barrels against the wall. The center of the shop led back into darkness. I believe the darkness came off the wine barrels smelling of Chianti, zinfandel and Burgundy.

"A half gallon of muscatel," Lee Mellon said.

The old man who ran the shop got the wine off a shelf behind him. He wiped some imaginary dust off the bottle. Like a strange plumber he was used to selling wine.

We left with the muscatel and went up to the Ina Coolbrith Park on Vallejo Street. She was a poet contemporary of Mark Twain and Brett Harte during that great San Francisco literary renaissance of the 1860s.

Then Ina Coolbrith was an Oakland librarian for thirty-two years and first delivered books into the hands of the child Jack London. She was born in 1841 and died in 1928: "Loved Laurel-Crowned Poet of California," and she was the same woman whose husband took a shot at her with a rifle in 1861. He missed.

"Here's to General Augustus Mellon, Flower of Southern Chivalry and Lion of the Battlefield!" Lee Mellon said, taking the cap off four pounds of muscatel.

We drank the four pounds of muscatel in the Ina Coolbrith Park, looking down Vallejo Street to San Francisco Bay and how the sunny morning was upon it and a barge of railroad cars going across to Marin County.

"What a warrior," Lee Mellon said, putting the last ⅓ ounce of muscatel, "the corner," in his mouth.

Having a slight interest in the Civil War and motivated by my new companion, I said, "I know a book that has all the Confederate generals in it. All 425 of them," I said. "It's down at the library. Let's go down and see what General Augustus Mellon pulled off in the war."

"Great idea, Jesse," Lee Mellon said. "He was my great grandfather. I want to know all about him. He was a Lion of the Battlefield. General Augustus Mellon! Hurray for the heroic deeds he performed in the War between the States! Hurray! Hurray! Hurray! HURRAY!"

Figure two pounds of muscatel apiece at twenty per cent alcohol: forty proof. We were still very rocky from a night of whiskey drinking. That's two pounds of muscatel multipled, squared and envisioned. This can all be worked out with computers.

The librarian looked at us when we came into the library and groped a volume off a shelf: *Generals in Gray* by Ezra J. Warner. The biographies of the 425 generals were in alphabetic order and we turned to where General Augustus

Mellon would be. The librarian was debating whether or not to call the police.

We found General Samuel Bell Maxey on the left flank and his story went something like this: *Samuel Bell Maxey was born at Tompkinsville, Kentucky, March 30, 1825. He was graduated from West Point in the class of 1846, and was brevetted for gallantry in the war with Mexico. In 1849 he resigned his commission to study law. In 1857 he and his father, who was also an attorney, moved to Texas, where they practiced in partnership until the outbreak of the Civil War. Resigning a seat in the Texas senate, the younger Maxey organized the 9th Texas Infantry, and with rank of colonel joined the forces of General Albert Sidney Johnston in Kentucky. He was promoted brigadier general to rank from March 4, 1862. He served in East Tennessee, at Port Hudson, and in the Vicksburg campaign, under General J. E. Johnston. In December 1863 Maxey was placed in command of Indian Territory, and for his effective reorganization of the troops there, with which he participated in the Red River campaign, he was assigned to duty as a major general by General Kirby Smith on April 18, 1864. He was not, however, subsequently appointed to that rank by the President. After the war General Maxey resumed the practice of law in Paris, Texas, and in 1873 declined appointment to the state bench. Two years later he was elected to the United States Senate, where he served two terms, being defeated for re-election in 1887. He died at Eureka Springs, Arkansas, August 16, 1895, and is buried in Paris, Texas.*

And on the right flank we found General Hugh Weedon Mercer and his story went something like this: *Hugh Weedon Mercer, a grandson of the Revolutionary General Hugh Mercer, was born at "The Sentry Box," Fredericksburg, Virginia, on November 27, 1808. He was graduated third in the class of 1828 at West Point, and was stationed for some time in Savannah, Georgia, where he married into a local family. He resigned his commission on April 30, 1835 and settled in Savannah. From 1841 until the outbreak of the Civil War he was cashier of the Planters' Bank there. Upon the secession of Georgia, Mercer entered Confederate service as colonel of the 1st Georgia Volunteers. He was promoted brigadier general on October 29, 1861. During the greater part of the war, with a brigade of three Georgia regiments, General Mercer commanded at Savannah, but he and his brigade took part in the Atlanta campaign of 1864, first in W. H. T. Walker's division and then in Cleburne's. On account of poor health he accompanied General Hardee to Savannah after the battle of Jonesboro, and saw no further field duty. Paroled at Macon, Georgia, May 13, 1865, General Mercer returned to banking in Savannah the following year. He moved to Baltimore in 1869, where he spent three years as a commission merchant. His health further declined, and he spent the last five years of his life in Baden-Baden, Germany. He died there on June 9, 1877. His remains were returned to Savannah for burial in Bonaventure Cemetery.*

But in the center of the line there was no General Augustus Mellon. There had obviously been a retreat during the night. Lee Mellon was crushed. The librarian was staring intently at us. Her eyes seemed to have grown a pair of glasses.

"It can't be," Lee Mellon said. "It just can't be."

"Maybe he was a colonel," I said. "There were a lot of Southern colonels. Being a colonel was a good thing. You know, Southern colonels and all. Colonel Something Fried Chicken." I was trying to make it easier for him. It's quite a thing to lose a Confederate general and gain a colonel instead.

Perhaps even a major or a lieutenant. Of course I didn't

say anything about the major or lieutenant business to him. That probably would have made him start crying. The librarian was looking at us.

"He fought in the Battle of the Wilderness. He was just great," Lee Mellon said. "He cut the head off a Yankee captain with one whack."

"That's quite something," I said. "They probably just overlooked him. A mistake was made. Some records were burned or something happened. There was a lot of confusion. That's probably it."

"You bet," Lee Mellon said. "I know there was a Confederate general in my family. There had to be a Mellon general fighting for his country . . . the beloved South."

"You bet," I said.

The librarian was beginning to pick up the telephone.

"Let's go," I said.

"OK," Lee Mellon said. "You believe there was a Confederate general in my family? Promise me you do. There was a Confederate general in my family!"

"I promise," I said.

I could read the lips of the librarian. She was saying Hello, police? Vaudeville, it was.

We stepped outside rather hurriedly and down the street to anonymous sanctuary among the buildings of San Francisco.

"Promise me till your dying day, you'll believe that a Mellon was a Confederate general. It's the truth. That God-damn book lies! There was a Confederate general in my family!"

"I promise," I said and it was a promise that I kept.

Headquarters

1

THE OLD HOUSE where I took Lee Mellon to live, provided, in its own strange way, lodging befitting a Confederate general from Big Sur, a general who had just successfully fought a small skirmish in the trees above the Pacific Ocean.

The house was owned by a very nice Chinese dentist, but it rained in the front hall. The rain came down through a broken skylight, flooding the hall and warping the hardwood floor.

Whenever the dentist visited the place, he put a pair of blue bib overalls on over his business suit. He kept the overalls in what he called his "tool room," but there weren't any tools there, only the blue overalls hanging on a hook.

He put the overalls on just to collect the rent. They were his uniform. Perhaps he had been a soldier at one time or another.

We showed him where the rain came from and the long puddle leading splash, splash down the hall to the community kitchen in the rear, but he refused to be moved by it.

"There it is," he said philosophically and went away peacefully to take off his overalls and hang them in his "tool room."

After all it was his building. He had pulled thousands of teeth to get the place. He obviously liked the puddle right where it was, and we could not argue with his cheap rent.

2

Even before Lee Mellon made the old place his official San Francisco headquarters in the spring of years ago, the building was already occupied by an interesting group of tenants. I lived alone in the attic.

There was a sixty-one-year-old retired music teacher who lived in the room right underneath the attic. He was Spanish and about him like a weathervane whirled the traditions and attitudes of the Old World.

And he was in his own way, the manager. He had appropriated the job like one would find some old clothes lying outside in the rain, and decide that they were the right size and after they had dried out, they would look quite fashionable.

The day after I moved into the attic, he came upstairs and told me that the noise was driving him crazy. He told me to pack my things quickly and go. He told me that he'd had no idea I had such heavy feet when he rented the place to me. He looked down at my feet and said, "They're too heavy. They'll have to go."

I had no idea either when I rented the attic from the old fart. It seems that the attic had been vacant for years. With all those years of peace and quiet, he probably thought that there was a meadow up there with a warm, gentle wind blowing through the wild flowers, and a bird getting hung up above the trees along the creek.

I bribed his hearing with a phonograph record of Mozart, something with horns, and that took care of him. "I love Mozart," he said, instantly reducing my burden of life.

I could feel my feet beginning to weigh less and less as he smiled at the phonograph record. It smiled back. I now weighed a trifle over seventeen pounds and danced like a giant dandelion in his meadow.

The week after Mozart, he left for a vacation in Spain. He said that he was only going to be gone for three months, but my feet must continue their paths of silence. He said he had ways of knowing, even when he wasn't there. It sounded pretty mysterious.

But his vacation turned out to be longer than he had anticipated because he died on his return to New York. He died on the gangplank, just a few feet away from America. He didn't quite make it. His hat did though. It rolled off his head and down the gangplank and landed, plop, on America.

Poor devil. I heard that it was his heart, but the way the Chinese dentist described the business, it could have been his teeth.

* * *

Though his physical appearance was months away, Lee Mellon's San Francisco headquarters were now secure. They took the old man's things away and the room was empty.

3

There were two other rooms on the second floor. One of them was occupied by a Montgomery Street secretary. She left early in the morning and returned late at night. You never saw her on the weekends.

I believe she was a member of a small acting group and spent most of her spare time rehearsing and performing. One might as well believe that as anything else because there was no way of knowing. She had long ingenue legs, so I'll go on believing she was an actress.

We all shared a bathroom on the second floor, but during the months I lived there, she passed.

4

The other room on the second floor was occupied by a man who always said hello in the morning and good evening at night. It was nice of him. One day in February he went down to the community kitchen and roasted a turkey.

He spent hours basting the bird and preparing a grand meal. Many chestnuts and mushrooms were in evidence. After he was finished he took the bird upstairs with him and never used the kitchen again.

Shortly after that, I believe it was Tuesday, he stopped ꞓaying hello in the morning and good evening at night.

5

The bottom floor had one room in the front of the house. Its windows opened on the street and the shades were always drawn. An old woman lived in that room. She was eighty-four and lived quite comfortably on a government pension of thirty-five cents a month.

She looked so old that she reminded me of a comic book hero of my childhood: The Heap. It was a World War I German pilot who was shot down and lay wounded for months in a bog and was slowly changed by mysterious juices into a ⅞ plant and ⅛ human thing.

The Heap walked around like a mound of moldy hay and performed good deeds, and of course bullets had no effect on it. The Heap killed the comic book villains by giving them a great big hug, then instead of riding classically away into the sunset like a Western, The Heap lumbered off into the bog. That's the way the old woman looked.

After she paid her rent out of the generous thirty-five-cent-a-month government pension, there was just enough money left over for her to buy bread, tea and celery roots, which were her main sustenance.

One day out of curiosity I looked up celery roots in a book called *Let's Eat Right to Keep Fit*, by that goddess of American grub, Adelle Davis, to see how you could keep alive on them. You can't.

One hundred grams of celery root contains no vitamins except 2 mg. of Vitamin C. For minerals, it contains 47 mg. of calcium, 71 mg. of phosphorous and 0.8 mg. of iron. It would take a lot of celery roots to make a battleship.

One hundred grams of celery root has for its grand

finale, in *Let's Eat Right to Keep Fit,* three grams of protein and the dramatic total of 38 calories.

The old woman had a little hotplate in her room. She did all her "cooking" in there and never used the community kitchen. A hotplate in a little room is the secret flower of millions of old people in this country. There's a poem by Jules Laforgue about the Luxembourg Gardens. The old woman's hotplate was not that poem.

But her father had been a wealthy doctor in the 19th century and had the first franchise in Italy and France for some wondrous American electrical device.

She could not remember what electrical device it was, but her father had been very proud of getting the franchise and watching the crates being unloaded off a ship.

Unfortunately, he lost all his money trying to sell the electrical devices. It seems that nobody else wanted to have the things in their houses. People were afraid of them, thought they would blow up.

She herself had once been a beautiful woman. There was a photograph of her wearing a dress with a decolletage. Her breasts, her long neck and her face were quite lovely.

Then she was a governess and a language instructor in Italian, French, Spanish and German, the border languages, but now, Heap-like senility covered her and there was only an occasional scrap of meat thrown in to break the celery root tyranny of her last days.

She had never married, but I always called her Mrs. I liked her and once gave her a glass of wine. It had been years. She had no friends or relatives left in the world, and drank the wine very slowly.

She said it was good wine, though it wasn't, and talked of her father's vineyard and the wine that came from those grapes until the thousands of unpurchased American electrical devices had withered the vines.

She told me that the vineyard had been on a hill above the sea, and she liked to go there in the late afternoon and walk down the shadowy rows of grapes. It was the Mediterranean Sea.

In her room she had trunks full of things from olden times. She showed me an illustrated book full of hospitals put out by the Italian Red Cross. There was a photograph of Mussolini in the front of the book. It was a little hard to recognize him because he was not hanging upside down from a light post. She told me that he was a great man, but that he had gone too far. "Never do business with the Germans," she said.

Often she wondered aloud what would happen to her things when she would be dead. Some old salt and pepper shakers with people on them. A bolt of faded cloth. There hadn't been time in 84 years to make a dress or some curtains out of the cloth.

They'll put them inside a celery root and then discover a way of making battleships out of celery roots and over the waves her things will travel.

6

The community kitchen was on the bottom floor in the rear of the house. There was a very large room attached by its own entrance to the kitchen. Before the retired music teacher went to Spain, there was a quiet, typical middle-aged woman who lived in the room, but she left the door from her room to the kitchen open all the time. It was as if the community kitchen were her kitchen and what were strangers doing in it. She was always coming and going and staring.

I liked to cook my meager bachelor meals in privacy, but she always watched. I didn't like it. Who wants to have a quiet, typical, middle-aged woman watching you boil a pathetic can of beef and noodle soup for dinner?

After all it was a community kitchen. When she was cooking in there, I thought it was perfectly natural for her to leave the door open, but when I was cooking in there I thought she should have kept the door closed, for after all it was a community kitchen.

While the music teacher was busy dropping dead in New York, the woman moved and three young girls took the room. One of the girls was quite pretty in a blonde athletic sort of way. The other two girls were uglies.

There were all sorts of men flocking around the pretty one, and because she couldn't handle them all, the other girls got a lot of attention.

I have noticed this pattern time and time again. A pretty girl living with an ugly. If you don't make the pretty one, you're aroused enough to take on the ugly. It throws a lot of action into the corner of the uglies.

That room off the kitchen became quite a hive. The girls had come from a small college somewhere in eastern Washington, and at first they allowed their attentions to be taken up by college and post-college types, mostly the clean-cuts.

Then as the girls grew more sophisticated, as they acclimated themselves to the throbbing pulse of a cosmopolitan city, their attentions naturally switched to bus drivers.

It was pretty funny because there were so many bus drivers hanging around, paying court in their uniforms, that the place looked like the car barn.

Sometimes I would have to cook a meal with four or five bus drivers sitting at the kitchen table, watching me fry a hamburger. One of them absentlymindedly clicking his transfer punch.

A Daring Cavalry Attack on PG&E

ONE MORNING AFTER LEE MELLON had been living below me on Leavenworth Street for a couple of weeks, I woke up and looked around me. The meadow was fading rapidly. The grass had turned brown. The creek was almost dry. The flowers were gone. The trees had fallen over on their sides. I hadn't seen a bird or an animal since the old man died. They all just left.

I decided to go down and wake Lee Mellon up. I got out of bed and put my clothes on. I went down to his room and knocked on the door. I thought we might have some coffee or something.

"Come on in," Lee Mellon said.

I opened the door and Lee Mellon was in the sack with a young girl. Their entwined feet were sticking out one end of the bed. Their heads were sticking out the other end. At first I thought they were fucking and then I could see that they weren't. But I hadn't been far behind. The room smelled like Cupid's gym.

41

I was standing there and then I closed the door.

"This is Susan," Lee Mellon said. "That's my buddy."

"Hello," she said.

The room was all yellow because the shades were pulled down and the sun was shining hard outside. There were all sorts of things thrown all over the room: books, clothes and bottles in cleverly planned disorder. They were maps of important battles to come.

I talked to them for a few minutes. We decided to go downstairs to the community kitchen and have some breakfast.

I stepped outside in the hall while they got dressed, and then we went downstairs together. The girl was tucking in her blouse. Lee Mellon hadn't bothered to tie his shoelaces. They flopped like angleworms all the way down the stairs.

The girl cooked breakfast. Funny, to this very day I remember what she cooked: scrambled eggs with scallions and cream cheese. She made some whole wheat toast and a pot of good coffee. She was very young and cheerful. She had a pretty face and body, though she was a little overweight. Buxom is the right term, but that was just baby fat.

She talked enthusiastically about *In Dubious Battle* by John Steinbeck. "Those poor fruit pickers," the girl said. Lee Mellon agreed with her. After breakfast they went upstairs to talk about their future.

I went downtown to see three movies in a Market Street flea palace. It was a bad habit of mine. From time to time I would get the desire to confuse my senses by watching large flat people crawl back and forth across a huge piece of light, like worms in the intestinal track of a tornado.

I would join the sailors who can't get laid, the old people who make those theaters their solariums, the immobile visionaries, and the poor sick people who come there for the outpatient treatment of watching a pair of Lusitanian mammary glands kiss a set of Titanic capped teeth.

I found three pictures that were the right flavors: a monster picturehelphelp, a cowboy picturebangbang and a dime store romance pictureIloveyou, and found a seat next to a man who was staring up at the ceiling.

The girl stayed for three days with Lee Mellon. She was sixteen years old and came from Los Angeles. She was a Jewess and her father was in the appliance business down in Los Angeles, and was known as the Freezer King of Sepulveda Boulevard.

He showed up at the end of the third day. It seems that the girl had run away from home, and when she had used up the last of her money, she called Poppa on the telephone and said that she was living with a man and they needed money and she gave her father the address where he could send the money.

Before the girl's father took her away, he had a little chat with Lee Mellon. He told Lee Mellon that he didn't want any trouble from this business and he made Lee Mellon promise never to see her again. He gave twenty dollars to Lee Mellon who said thanks.

The Freezer King said that he could build a fire under Lee Mellon if he wanted to, but he didn't want any scandal. "Just don't see her any more and everything will be all right."

"Sure," Lee Mellon said. "I can see your point."

"I don't want any trouble, and you don't want any trouble. We'll just leave it right there," her father said.

"Uh-huh," Lee Mellon said.

The Freezer King took his daughter back to Los Angeles. It had been a fine adventure even though her father had slapped her face in the car and called her a *schicksa*.

A little while after that Lee Mellon moved out of his room because he couldn't pay the rent and went over and lay siege to Oakland. It was a rather impoverished siege that went on for months and was marked by only one offensive maneuver, a daring cavalry attack on the Pacific Gas and Electric Company.

Lee Mellon lived in the abandoned house of a friend who was currently Class C Ping-Pong champion of a rustic California insane asylum. The classifications of A, B or C were determined by the number of shock treatments administered to the patients. The gas and electricity had been turned off in 1937 when the friend's mother had been tucked away for keeping chickens in the house.

Lee Mellon of course didn't have any money to get them turned back on again, so he tunneled his way to the main gas line and tapped it. Then he had a way to cook and heat the place, but he never quite got the energy to put the thing under complete control. Consequently, whenever he turned the gas on with a hastily improvised valve, and put a match to the gas, out jumped a six-foot-long blue flame.

He found an old kerosene lantern and that took care of his light. He had a card to the Oakland Public Library and that took care of his entertainment. He was reading the Russians with that certain heavy tone people put in their voices when they say, "I'm reading the Russians."

There wasn't much food because he had little money to buy it with. Lee Mellon didn't want to get a job. Laying siege to Oakland was difficult enough without going to work. So he went hungry most of the time, but he wouldn't give up his PG&E security. He had to scuffle for his chow: panhandling on the streets and going around to the back doors of restaurants, and walking around looking for money in the gutters.

During his extended siege he abstained from drink and

didn't show much interest in women. Once he said to me, "I haven't been laid in five months." He said it in a matter-of-fact way as if he were commenting on the weather.

Do you think it's going to rain?

No, why should it?

Susan arrived one morning over at Leavenworth Street and said, "I've got to see Lee Mellon. It's very important."

I could see that it was very important. She showed how important it was. The months had gathered at her waist.

"I don't know where he's living," I lied. "He just left one day without leaving a forwarding address," I lied. "I wonder where Lee Mellon is?" I lied.

"Have you seen him around town any?"

"No," I lied. "He's just vanished," I lied.

I couldn't tell her that he was living in Oakland in terrible poverty. His only comfort being that he had tunneled his way to the main gas line and was now enjoying the rather dubious fruit of his labor: a six-foot-long blue flame. And that his eyebrows were gone.

"He's just vanished," I lied. "Everybody wonders where he went," I lied.

"Well, if you see him any place, you tell him I've got to see him. It's very important. I'm staying at the San Geronimo Hotel on Columbus Avenue, Room 34."

She wrote it all down on a piece of paper and gave it to me. I put it in my pocket. She watched me put it in my pocket. Even after I had taken my hand out of my pocket, she was still watching the note, though it was in my pocket behind a comb, beside a wadded up candybar wrapper. I would have bet that she could have told me what kind of candybar wrapper it was.

I saw Lee Mellon the next day. He came over to the city. It had taken him nine hours to hitch-hike from Oakland to San Francisco. He looked pretty grubby. I told him about the Susan business, about the importance she had placed on seeing him. I told him that she acted and looked pregnant. Was, for my opinion.

"That's the way it goes." Lee Mellon said without any emotion. "I can't do anything about it. I'm hungry. Do you have anything to eat around here? A sandwich, an egg, some spaghetti or something? Anything?"

Lee Mellon never mentioned Susan to me again, and I of course never brought up the subject again. He stayed over in Oakland for a few more months.

He tried to pawn a stolen electric iron over there. He spent the whole day going from one hock shop to another hock shop. Nobody wanted it. Lee Mellon watched the iron slowly change into a one-legged moldy albatross. He left it on the bench at a bus stop. It was wrapped in newspaper and looked like some garbage.

Disillusionment over failing to pawn the iron finally ended his siege of Oakland. The next day he broke camp and marched back to Big Sur.

The girl continued living at the San Geronimo Hotel. Because she was so unhappy she kept getting bigger and bigger like a cross between a mushroom and a goiter.

Everytime she saw me she asked me anxiously if I had seen Lee Mellon, and I always lied, no. The disappearance had us all wondering. What else could I say? Poor girl. So I lied breathlessly . . . no.

I lied no again no no no no no no no no no no no no no no no no no no again. I again no no no no no no no no no no no no no no no no Lee Mellon. He has just vanished from the face of the earth.

Her father, the Freezer King of Sepulveda Boulevard, disowned her. He argued in the beginning for one of those Tijuana abortions that have a fancy office and an operating room clean as a Chevron station. She said no, that she was going to have the baby. He told her to get out and paid her a monthly stipend never to come back to Los Angeles. When the baby was born, she put it up for adoption.

At the age of seventeen she became quite a character in North Beach. She quickly gained over a hundred pounds. She became huge and grotesque, putting on layers and layers of fat like geological muck.

She decided that she was a painter and being intelligent she realized that it was much easier to talk about painting than to actually paint. So she went to the bars and talked about painters of genius like Van Gogh. There was another painter that she always talked about, but I have forgotten his name.

She also took up smoking cigars and became fanatically anti-German. She smoked cigars and said that all the German men should be castrated slowly, the children buried in snow, and the women set to work in the God-damn salt mines with no other tools than their tears.

Long after she'd had the baby, she would come up to me, waddle up to me is the right way of stating it, and ask if I ever saw Lee Mellon around. I would always say no, and after while it became a joke between us because she knew I had been lying, and by now she herself had seen Lee Mellon, found out the score, and didn't give a damn any more, but she still asked me, "Have you seen Lee Mellon around?" but now *she* was lying. Our positions had been reversed. "No. I haven't," I could say truthfully now.

She went on a kick of having babies for a few years. She turned herself into a baby factory. There's always someone who will go to bed with a fat broad. She gave the babies up for adoption as soon as they were born. It was something to do with her time, and then she grew tired of this, too.

I think by now she was twenty-one, prehistoric, and her fad as a character in North Beach had run its course. She had stopped going to the bars and talking about painters of genius and those bad Germans. She even gave up smoking cigars. She was attending movies all the time now.

She wheeled those by now comfortable layers of fat into the movies every day, taking four or five pounds of food in with her in case there should be a freak snowstorm inside the movie and the concession stand were to freeze solid like the Antarctic.

Once I was standing on a street corner talking to Lee Mellon and she came up to me. "Have you seen Lee Mellon?" she lied with a big smile on her face.

"No," I could say truthfully now.

Lee Mellon didn't show any interest at all in our little game. He said, "The light's changed." He was wearing a gray uniform and his sword rattled as we walked across the street.

Part Two

Campaigning with Lee Mellon
at Big Sur

The Letters of Arrival and Reply

The Letters of Arrival

1

Lee Mellon
General Delivery
Big Sur
California

Dear Lee Mellon,

How are things at Big Sur? Things in San Francisco are terrible. I have found out rather painfully that love moves mysteriously through the ways of the stomach, almost like bees, but the game has turned sour like the bees Isaac Babel writes about in *Red Cavalry*.

Those bees did not know what to do after their hives had been blown up by the soldiers. "The Sacred Republic of

51

the Bees" was reduced to nothing but anarchy and tatters.
The bees circled and died in the air.

That's what's happening in my stomach, a rather torn
landscape. I'm looking for a way out. Please excuse this
rather maudlin letter, but I'm in bad shape.

Yours,

Jesse

The Reply

1

Great! Why don't you come down here? I haven't got
any clothes on, and I just saw a whale. There's plenty of
room for everybody. Bring something to drink. Whiskey!
—— As always, Lee Mellon.

The Letters of Arrival

2

Lee Mellon
General Delivery
Big Sur
California

Dear Lee Mellon,

I'm in love with this girl and it is just plain hell with
onions on it. I certainly would like to go down to Big Sur.
I've never been there before.

What's this about your not having any clothes on, and
the whale?

Yours,

Jesse

The Reply

2

Just what I said—no clothes on and a God-damn whale! Can't you smell that sweet sagebrush-by-the-ocean air of Big Sur? Have you no feelings, sir? Do I have to draw you a nostril picture? Tell the broad to take a flying at the moon and come down here with that whiskey and let's catch some abalone and piss off a cliff. —— As always, Lee Mellon

The Letters of Arrival

3

Lee Mellon
General Delivery
Big Sur
California

Dear Lee Mellon,

I've got to get rid of this girl. It just isn't any good. She has drifted over from my stomach to attack my liver.

Is there any shelter down there against the elements? I mean, is there a roof over your head, fella?

Yours,

Jesse

The Reply

3

Oh, shit! Don't make a martyr out of yourself. You know what my philosophy about women is—fuckem/ shuckem. Sure there's God-damn shelter down here. What do you think I'm living in, a burrow? That business in Oakland was something else. A man needs the proper atmosphere to read the Russians. There are four houses down here and only one Lee Mellon. This morning I saw a coyote walking through the sagebrush right at the very edge of the ocean—next stop China. The coyote was acting like he was in New Mexico or Wyoming, except that there were whales passing below. That's what this country does for you. Come down to Big Sur and let your soul have some room to get outside its marrow. —— As always, Lee Mellon

The Letters of Arrival

4

Lee Mellon
General Delivery
Big Sur
California

Dear Lee Mellon,

There are no words to describe the grief this girl is causing me. She's been at it all week.

"The Sacred Republic of the Bees" flows off toward the sea.

I never thought this would happen to me. I feel hopelessly lost. Do any of those cabins have stoves in them?

Yours,

Jesse

The Reply

4

Sure they have stoves! Everyone of them has a dozen stoves. Make up your mind about that broad. Don't let her tan your balls and make a wallet out of them. Just tell her to take a flying at the moon, and tell her you're going down to Big Sur to let your soul rejoice in its freedom in the coyote camp. Tell her you're going to live in a cabin that has a dozen stoves that all burn whiskey until heaven freezes over. —— As always, Lee Mellon

The Letters of Arrival

5

Lee Mellon
General Delivery
Big Sur
California

Dear Lee Mellon,

The girl and I are patching things up. These last few days have been delightful. Perhaps I'll bring her down with me when I go to Big Sur.

Her name is Cynthia. I think you'd really like her.

By the way, your last letter shows strong evidence of a budding literary style.

Yours,

Jesse

The Reply

5

Literary style up your style! My stomach is full of deer steak, biscuits and gravy. Cynthia? Come off it, asshole! Cynthia? You've been writing these crybaby epistles about Cynthia? You really think I'd like Cynthia, huh? I can see it all now—Cynthia? Yes, Lee? It's your turn to slop the abalone. Is it really my turn, Lee? (Fear and disgust in her voice.) Yes, Cynthia, the abalone are calling. They need slopping. Oh, Lee! No! No! No! —— As always, Lee Mellon

The Letters of Arrival

6

Lee Mellon
General Delivery
Big Sur
California

Dear Lee Mellon,

I don't know why you are bitter about Cynthia. You've never even met her before. She is actually quite a girl and would easily adapt herself to any kind of life, besides, what's wrong with the name Cynthia? No kidding, I think you'd really like her.

Yours,

Jesse

The Reply

6

I'm positive I would like her! After all ¾ of the English teachers, ⅔ of the librarians and ½ of the society dames in America are named Cynthia. What's another Cynthia more or less, you poor fart-up. The frogs are croaking in the frog pond. I'm writing by lantern because there is no electricity down here. The wires stop five miles away and I think it's nice of them. Who needs electricity anyway? I did OK in Oakland without electricity. I read Dostoevsky, Turgenev, Gogol, Tolstoy—the Russians. Who needs electricity, but remember when you come down here don't forget to bring Cynthia. I can hardly wait to meet her. Does she have a small mustache? I met a librarian once who was from BM, Battle Mountain, Nevada, that is. She had a small mustache and her name was Cynthia. She came all the way to San Francisco on the bus to give her cherry to a genuine poet. She found one, too. Me! Who knows, it might be the same broad. Ask her something about Battle Mountain, to tell the secrets of BM, like *BM Anthology*. BM! BM! —— As always, Lee Mellon

The Letters of Arrival

7

Lee Mellon
General Delivery
Big Sur
California

Dear Lee Mellon,

The most horrible thing in my life has just happened.
I never thought that I would be saying this. Cynthia has
left me.
What am I going to do? She's gone for keeps this time.
She flew back to Ketchikan this morning.
I'm totally crushed. It just goes to prove that it's never
too late to learn. I wonder what that means?

Yours,

Jesse

The Reply

7

Cheer up, smarts! You've still got old Lee Mellon and
a cabin waiting for you down here at Big Sur. A good cabin.
It's on a cliff high over the Pacific. It has a stove and three
glass walls. You can lie in bed in the morning and watch
the sea otters making it. Very educational. It's the greatest
place in the world. What did I tell you about Cynthia? She
was probably from Battle Mountain by way of Ketchikan.
Weigh well the words of an old campaigner.—A Cynthia in

the library is better than two Cynthias in the sack. ——
As always, Lee Mellon

The Letters of Arrival

8

Lee Mellon
General Delivery
Big Sur
California

Dear Lee Mellon,

No word from Cynthia. All the bees in my stomach are
dead and getting used to it.
This is the end. So be it.
How do we keep alive at Big Sur? I've got a few bucks,
but is there any way to work down there, or what?

Yours,

Jesse

The Reply

8

I've got a garden that grows all year round! A 30:30
Winchester for deer, a .22 for rabbits and quail. I've got
some fishing tackle and *The Journal of Albion Moonlight.*
We can make it OK. What do you want, a fur-lined box of
Kleenex to absorb the sour of your true love Cynthia, the
Ketchikan and/or Battle Mountain cookie? Come to the
party and hurry down to Big Sur and don't forget to bring
some whiskey. I need whiskey!

"Want to put another log on the fire?" Lee Mellon said. "I think it could use another log. What do you think?"

I looked at the fire. I thought about it. Perhaps I thought about it a little too long. The days at Big Sur can do that to you. "Yeah, it looks like it could," I said, and went around to the other end of the cabin and walked through the hole in the kitchen wall and got a log from the pile.

The log was damp and buggy on the bottom. I came back through the hole in the kitchen wall and put the log in the fireplace.

Some bugs hurried to the top of the log and I banged my head hard on the ceiling. "It takes a little while to get used to that," Lee Mellon said, pointing at the 5' 1" ceiling. The bugs were standing there on the log and looking out at us through the fire.

Yes . . . yes, the ceiling. Lee Mellon had been responsible for the ceiling. I'd heard the story. Three bottles of gin and they built the cabin right off the side of the hill, so that one wall of the cabin was just dirt. The fireplace had been carved out of the hillside later and filled in with rocks brought up the cliff from the ocean.

It had been a hot day when they put the walls up and three bottles of gin and Lee Mellon kept putting it away and the other guy, a deeply disturbed religious sort of person, kept putting it away. It was of course his gin, his land, his building material, his mother, his inheritance, and Lee Mellon said, "We've dug the holes deep enough, but the posts are a little too long. I'll saw them off."

Then you begin to get the picture. Four words to be exact. I'll saw them off. But the guy said all right because he was deeply disturbed. Sun, gin, the blue sky and the reflection of the Pacific Ocean were spinning in his addled brain: *Sure, let old Lee Mellon saw them off. No use . . .*

anyway, it's too hot . . . can't fight it, and the cabin had a 5′ 1″ ceiling and no matter how small you were, BANG! you hit your head against the ceiling.

After a while it became amusing to watch people bang their heads against the ceiling. Even after you had been there for a long time, there was no way of getting used to the ceiling. It existed beyond human intelligence and coordination. The only victory came from moving around in there slowly so that when you did hit your head against the ceiling, the shock of the blow was reduced to minor significance. That must be some law of physics. It probably has a nice tongue-bottled name. *The bugs were standing there on the log looking out at us through the fire.*

Lee Mellon was sitting on a rather mangy-looking deer rug, leaning up against a board wall. It is important that one differentiate right now between the walls of the place, for the walls were of varied and dangerous materials.

There was the dirt wall of the hillside, and there was a wooden wall, and a glass wall and no wall, just a space of air that led out to a narrow catwalk that circled part of the frog pond and joined up with a deck that was cantilevered rather precariously, like a World War I airplane, out over a canyon.

Lee Mellon was leaning up against the wooden wall which was the only wall in the place to bet on. During the time that I spent down at Big Sur, I saw only one person lean up against the glass wall. That had been a girl who had an obsession with going around naked and we took her to the hospital in Monterey and while she was being sewed back together again we went down to a hardware store and got a new sheet of glass. *The bugs were standing there on the log and looking out at us through the fire.*

And I remember somebody leaning up against the dirt wall of the hillside, deriding William Carlos Williams, when suddenly there was a loud roaring, crunching noise and a chunk of the hill fell off and covered the person up to his neck.

The person, being a young classical poet fresh from NYU, began screaming that he was being buried alive. Fortunately, the landslide stopped and we dug him out and dusted him off. That was the last time he said anything against William Carlos Williams. The next day he began reading *Journey to Love* rather feverishly.

I've seen more than one person lean up against the wall that was but a space of air and fall into the frog pond. Usually strong spirits were in rabbit-like evidence whenever this happened.

So the wooden wall was the only safe wall in the place, and Lee Mellon was leaning up against that wall, sitting on a distorted deer rug. It looked as if it had never been tanned, as if after skinning the deer someone took the skin and a pound of garlic and put them together into an oven with a low temperature and left them there for a week or so . . . ugh!

Lee Mellon was rolling a cigarette very carefully. That and leaning up against the wooden wall were the only cautious traits Lee Mellon ever exhibited. *The bugs were standing there on the log and looking out at us through the fire. Bon voyage, bugs. Have a nice trip, little that they could see now.*

I walked out through the wall that was but a space of air to the narrow catwalk and stood there looking down at the frog pond. It was silent because a small amount of the day was still with us, but in a few hours the pond would be changed into the Inquisition. Auto-da-fé at Big Sur. Frogs wearing the robes, carrying the black candles——CROAK! CROAK! CROAK! CROAK!

The frogs would begin at twilight and go all night

long. God-damn them. Frogs, barely the size of quarters. Hundreds, thousands, millions, light years of frogs in that small pond could make enough noise to break one's soul like kindling.

Lee Mellon got up and stood beside me out there on the catwalk. "Soon it will be dark," he said. He stared down at the pond. It looked green and harmless. "I wish I had some dynamite," he said.

Breaking Bread at Big Sur

THE DINNER WE HAD that evening was not very good. How could it be when we were reduced to eating food that the cats would not touch? We had no money to buy anything edible and no prospects of getting any. We were just hanging on.

We had spent four or five days waiting for someone to come along and bring us food, a traveller or a friend, it made no difference. That strange compelling power that draws people to Big Sur had not been working for days.

The switch had been pulled and the Big Sur light turned off for us. That was kind of sad. There was, of course, the same meager traffic along Highway 1, but none of it stopped for us. Something caused them to fall short of us or to continue on beyond us.

I knew that if I ate abalone again I would die. If so much as one more bite of abalone were balanced in my mouth, I knew that my soul would slide out like toothpaste and be diminished for all time in the universe.

We had a little hope that morning but it was quickly

dissipated. Lee Mellon went hunting up on the plateau where the old house was. It was not that he was a bad shot, but that he was excitable. Sometimes there would be doves hanging around the house and quail near a spring where the old man had died years before. Lee Mellon took the last five bullets for the .22 with him. I implored him to take only three. We had quite a discussion about it.

"Save a couple," I said.

"I'm hungry," he said.

"Don't shoot them up in one thrill-crazed flurry," I said.

"I want a quail to eat," Lee Mellon said. "A dove or a big rabbit or a little deer or a pork chop. I'm hungry."

The bullets for the 30:30 had been gone for weeks and everyday, late in the afternoon, the deer would come out on the mountainside. Sometimes there would be twenty or thirty of them, fat and sassy, but we did not have any bullets for the Winchester.

Lee Mellon could not get close enough to do any appreciable damage with the .22. He shot a doe in the ass and the doe limped off into the lilac bushes and got away.

Anyway, I implored him to save a couple of the .22 bullets for a rainy day. "Maybe tomorrow morning we'll find a deer in the garden," I said. Lee Mellon would have none of it. I might as well have been talking about the poems of Sappho.

He went up the mountain to the plateau. There was an awkward dirt road. He kept getting smaller and smaller on the road and our five .22 bullets kept getting smaller and smaller, too. I imagined the bullets now to be about the size of undernourished amoebas. The road switched back behind a grove of redwood trees, and Lee Mellon was no more, taking with him all the bullets we had in the world.

Having nothing better to do, nowhere else to go, I sat

down on a rock beside the highway and waited for Lee
Mellon. I had a book with me, something about the soul.
The book said everything was all right if you didn't die
while you were reading the book, if your fingers maintained
life while turning the pages. I approached it as a mystery
novel.

Two cars came by. One of the cars had some young
people in it. The girl was attractive. I imagined that they
had left Monterey at daybreak after having eaten a great
big breakfast at the Greyhound bus depot. But that did not
quite make sense.

Why would they want to eat breakfast at the Greyhound bus depot? The more I thought about it, the more
it seemed unlikely. There were other places to eat breakfast
in Monterey. Perhaps some of them were fancier. Just
because I had eaten breakfast one morning at the Greyhound bus depot in Monterey did not necessarily mean that
everybody in the world ate there.

The second car was a chauffeur-driven Rolls Royce
with an old woman sitting in the back seat. She was drenched
in furs and diamonds as if wealth had been a sudden spring
shower that covered her with all these things instead of
rain. How fortunate she was.

She seemed a little surprised at seeing me sitting there
like a ground squirrel on a rock. She said something to the
chauffeur and his window drifted effortlessly down.

"How far is it to Los Angeles?" he said. His voice was
perfect.

Then her window drifted effortlessly down like the
neck of a transparent swan. "We're hours late," she said.
"But I always wanted to see Big Sur. How far is it to Los
Angeles, young man?"

"It's quite a ways to Los Angeles from here," I said.
"Hundreds of miles. The road goes slowly until you get to

San Luis Obispo. You should have taken 99 or 101 if you were in a hurry."

"It's too late," she said. "I'll just tell them what happened. They'll understand. Do you have a telephone?"

"No, I'm sorry," I said. "We don't even have electricity."

"It's just as well," she said. "Having them worry a little bit about Granny will be good for them. They've been taking me for granted about ten years now. It'll do them a world of good. I should have thought of it sooner."

I liked the way she said Granny, for the last thing in this world she looked like was somebody's granny.

Then she said thank you in a pleasant way and the windows drifted effortlessly up and the swans resumed their migration south. She waved good-bye and they went down the road and around a bend to the people waiting in Los Angeles, to the people getting more nervous with each passing moment. It probably would be a good thing if they worried about her some.

Where is she? Where is she? Should we call the police? No, let's wait five more minutes.

Five minutes later I heard the dim crack of the .22 and then I heard it again, and still a third time. What a terrible shame it was that we had a repeating rifle—again and again, and then silence.

I waited and Lee Mellon came down off the mountain. He followed the dirt road down and came across the highway. He was carrying the gun rather sloppily, as if it were reduced to the impotence of a stick.

"Well?" I said.

Toward the end of the afternoon Lee Mellon got up and stood beside me out there on the catwalk. "Soon it will be dark," he said. He stared down at the pond. It looked green and harmless. "I wish I had some dynamite," he said. Then he went up to the garden and cut some greens for the salad. When he came back down there was a sort of wistful expression on his face. "I saw a rabbit in the garden," he said.

With an enormous amount of self-control I drove the word Alice away from my mouth and finally out of my mind. I really wanted to say, "What's wrong, Alice, no guts?" but I forced myself to accept the fact that those five bullets were beyond recall.

The dinner we had that evening was not very good. Some salad made from greens and jack mackerel. The fellow who owned the place had brought the jack mackerel for the cats who hung around there, but the cats wouldn't eat it. The stuff was so bad that they would sooner go hungry. And they did.

Jack mackerel tears your system apart. Almost as soon as it hits your stomach, you begin to rumble and squeal and flap. Sounds made in a haunted house during an earthquake tear horizontally across your stomach. Then great farts and belches begin arriving out of your body. Jack mackerel almost comes out through the pores.

After a dinner of jack mackerel you sit around and your subjects of conversation are greatly limited. I have found it impossible to talk about poetry, esthetics or world peace after eating jack mackerel.

To make the meal a perfect gastronomical Hiroshima, we had some of Lee Mellon's bread for dessert. His bread fits perfectly the description of hardtack served to the soldiers of the Civil War. But that, of course, is no surprise.

I had learned to hold my face at absolute attention, my eyes saluting a silent flag, the flag of the one who does the cooking, when every few days, Lee Mellon would say, "I guess it's time to bake some more bread."

It had taken a little while, but I had gotten so I could eat it now: Hard as a rock, flavorless and an inch thick, like Betty Crocker gone to hell, or thousands of soldiers marching along a road in Virginia, taking up miles of the countryside.

Preparing for Ecclesiastes

A LITTLE WHILE AFTER DINNER, to avoid the sound of the frogs that were really laying it in now from the early color of the evening, I decided to take my farts and belches to the privacy of my cabin and read Ecclesiastes.

"I think I'm going to sit here and read frogs," Lee Mellon farted.

"What did you say, Lee? I can't hear you. The frogs. Yell louder," I farted.

Lee Mellon got up and threw a great big rock into the pond and screamed, "Campbell's Soup!" The frogs were instantly quiet. That would work for a few moments and then they would start in again. Lee Mellon had quite a pile of rocks in the room. The frogs would always begin with one croak, and then the second and then the 7,452nd frog would join in.

Funny thing though, about Lee Mellon's yelling "Campbell's Soup!" at the frogs while he was launching various missiles into the pond. He had yelled every kind of obscenity possible at them, and then he decided to experiment with nonsense syllables to see if they would have any effect, along with a well-aimed rock.

Lee Mellon had an inquiring mind and by the hit-or-miss method he came upon "Campbell's Soup!" as the phrase that struck the most fear into the frogs. So now, instead of yelling some boring obscenity, he yelled, "Campbell's Soup!" at the top of his voice in the Big Sur night.

"Now what did you say?" I farted.

"I think I'm going to sit here and read frogs. What's wrong, don't you like frogs?" Lee Mellon farted. "That's what I said. Where's your spirit of patriotism? After all, there's a frog on the American flag."

"I'm going to my cabin," I farted. "Read some Ecclesiastes."

"You've been reading a lot of Ecclesiastes lately," Lee Mellon farted. "And as I remember there's not that much to read. Better watch yourself, kid."

"Just putting in time," I said.

"I think dynamite's too good for these frogs," Lee Mellon said. "I'm working on something special. Dynamite's too fast. I'm getting a great idea."

Lee Mellon had tried various ways of silencing the frogs. He had thrown rocks at them. He had beaten the pond with a broom. He had thrown pans full of boiling water on them. He had thrown two gallons of sour red wine into the pond.

For a time he was catching the frogs when they first appeared at twilight and throwing them down the canyon. He caught a dozen or so every evening and vanquished them down the canyon. This went on for a week.

Lee Mellon suddenly got the idea that they were

crawling back up the canyon again. He said that it took them a couple of days. "God-damn them," he said. "It's a long pull up, but they're making it."

He'd gotten so mad that the next frog he caught he threw into the fireplace. The frog became black and stringy and then the frog became not at all. I looked at Lee Mellon. He looked at me. "You're right. I'll try something else."

He took a couple dozen rocks and spent an afternoon tying pieces of string to them, and then that evening when he caught the frogs, he tied them to the rocks and threw them down the canyon. "That ought to slow them down a little bit. Make it a little harder to get back up here," he said, but it did not work out for there were just too many frogs to fight effectively, and after another week he grew tired of this and went back to throwing rocks at the pond and shouting "Campbell's Soup!"

At least we never saw any frogs in the pond with rocks tied to their backs. That would have been too much.

There were a couple of little water snakes in the pond, but they could only eat a frog or two every day or so. The snakes weren't very much help. We needed anacondas. The snakes we had were more ornamental than functional.

"Well, I'll leave you to the frogs," I farted. The first one had just croaked and now they would all start up again and hell would come forth from that pond.

"Mark my words, Jesse. I got a plan going," Lee Mellon farted and then tapped his head with his finger in the fashion people do to see if a watermelon is ripe. It was. A shiver traveled down my spine.

"Good-night," I farted.

"Yes, indeed," Lee Mellon farted.

The Rivets in Ecclesiastes

I WENT UP to my cabin. I could hear the ocean below banging against the rocks. I passed the garden. It was covered with fishnets to keep the birds off.

As usual I stumbled over the motorcycle that was beside my bed. The motorcycle was one of Lee Mellon's pets. It was lying there in about forty-five parts.

A couple of times every week, Lee Mellon would say, "I think I'll put my motorcycle together. It's a four-hundred-dollar motorcycle." He always said that it was a four-hundred-dollar motorcycle, but nothing ever came of it.

I lit the lantern and was enclosed within the glass walls of the cabin. My place was furnished like all the other cabins down there. I did not have a table, any chairs or a bed.

I slept on the floor in a sleeping bag and used two white rocks for bookends. I used the engine block of the motorcycle to set the lantern on, so I could raise the light to make reading a little more comfortable.

The cabin had a very crude wood stove, Lee Mellon's

73

creation, that could warm the place up instantly on a cold night, but the moment you did not put another piece of wood in the stove, the cabin would be plunged right back into the cold.

I was, of course, reading Ecclesiastes at night in a very old Bible that had heavy pages. At first I read it over and over again every night, and then I read it once every night, and then I began reading just a few verses every night, and now I was just looking at the punctuation marks. Actually I was counting them, a chapter every night. I was putting the number of punctuation marks down in a notebook, in neat columns. I called the notebook "The Punctuation Marks in Ecclesiastes." I thought it was a nice title. I was doing it as a kind of study in engineering.

Certainly before they build a ship they know how many rivets it takes to hold the ship together and the various sizes of the rivets. I was curious about the number of rivets and the sizes of those rivets in Ecclesiastes, a dark and beautiful ship sailing on our waters.

A summary of my little columns would go something like this: the first chapter of Ecclesiastes has 57 punctuation marks and they are broken down into 22 commas, 8 semicolons, 8 colons, 2 question marks and 17 periods.

The second chapter of Ecclesiastes has 103 punctuation marks and they are broken down into 45 commas, 12 semicolons, 15 colons, 6 question marks and 25 periods.

The third chapter of Ecclesiastes has 77 punctuation marks and they are broken down into 33 commas, 21 semicolons, 8 colons, 3 question marks and 12 periods.

The fourth chapter of Ecclesiastes has 58 punctuation marks and they are broken down into 25 commas, 9 semicolons, 5 colons, 2 question marks and 17 periods.

The fifth chapter of Ecclesiastes has 67 punctuation

marks and they are broken down into 25 commas, 7 semi-colons, 15 colons, 3 question marks and 17 periods.

And this is what I was doing by lantern light at Big Sur, and I gained a pleasure and an appreciation by doing this. Personally I think the Bible gains by reading it with a lantern. I do not think the Bible has ever truly adjusted to electricity.

By lantern light, the Bible shows its best. I counted the punctuation marks in Ecclesiastes very carefully so as not to make a mistake, and then I blew the lantern out.

Begging for Their Lives

AROUND MIDNIGHT OR AN HOUR LATER—this is just a guess for we had no clocks at Big Sur—I heard some noises in my sleep. They came from the old truck we had parked up by the highway. The noises kept renewing themselves and then I could tell they were human sounds but there was a muttering and a strangeness to them and then a voice yelled, "For God's sake please don't shoot me!"

I unzipped myself from the sleeping bag and put my pants on very quickly. I found a small ax in the dark and wondered what the hell was happening out there. There was a lot of noise and none of it was pleasant. I went out carefully, moving with the shadows for I didn't want to just stumble out there and get fucked if that's what was happening out there. I was going to take it nice and easy, like they do in the Western movies.

I moved cautiously toward the sounds and the voices. A voice, the calmest one, belonged to Lee Mellon. There was a lantern on the ground and now I could see what was happening. I stopped in the shadows.

There were two guys on their knees in front of Lee Mellon. They were kids, probably teen-agers. Lee Mellon stood over them with the Winchester. He was holding it in an extremely businesslike manner.

"Please, for God's sake . . . please, please we didn't know, please," one of them said. They were both wearing very nice clothes. Lee Mellon stood there in front of them, wearing rags.

Lee Mellon was talking to them very quietly and calmly, perhaps as John Donne delivered his sermons in Elizabethan times. "I can shoot you fellas right through the heads like dogs and throw your bodies down there to the sharks and then drive your car down to Cambria. Wipe my fingerprints off. Leave the car there, and no one will ever know what happened to you. The sheriff's car will drive up and down the highway for a few days. The sheriff will stop here and ask some silly questions. I'll reply, 'No, I haven't seen them down this way, Sheriff.' Then they will drop the whole business, and you'll both be filed away permanently in the missing persons section in Salinas. I hope you fellas don't have any mothers, girl friends or pets because they're not going to see you for a long, long time."

One of them was crying very hard. He did not have the power of speech. The other one was crying too, but he could still talk. "Please, please, please, please, please," he said as if he were repeating a nursery rhyme.

It was then that I walked out of the shadows with the ax in my hand. I thought that they were both going to shit right there and ooze straight through to China.

"Howdy, Jesse," Lee Mellon said. "Look what I got here. A couple of smart fuckers, trying to syphon our gas. Guess what, Jesse?"

"What's up, Lee?" I said.

Do you see how perfect our names were, how the names
lent themselves to this kind of business? Our names were
made for us in another century.

"I think I'm going to kill them, Jesse," Lee Mellon
said calmly. "I've got to start someplace. This is the third
time in the last month somebody's come down here and
stolen our gas. I've got to start someplace. Can't let this go
on forever. Jesse, I think I'll take these two shit fuckers
for a down payment and shoot them."

Lee Mellon took the barrel of the empty Winchester
and placed it against the forehead of the one who could still
talk, and then he could not talk any more. The power of
speech had fled his mouth. He made all the motions of
talking, but there wasn't anything coming out.

"Wait a minute, Lee." I said. "Sure, these guys need
shooting. Steal a man's gas down here in the wilderness,
leave him up shit creek without even a pair of roller skates.
They deserve being shot, but they're only a couple of young
kids. Look, barely out of high school. See that peach fuzz."

Lee Mellon bent down and sort of looked at their chins.

"Yeah, Jesse," Lee Mellon said. "I know. But we got a
pregnant woman down there in the cabin. My wife, that's
my wife down there, and I love her. She's ready to have a
baby at any time. She's two weeks over. We'd come up here,
get in the truck to take her to Monterey so she could have
a doctor and a nice clean hospital, and then there wouldn't
be any gas in the truck and the baby would die.

"No, Jesse, no—no, no," Lee Mellon said. "For killing
my baby son, I think I'd better shoot them now. Hell, I
can make them put their heads together and use just one
bullet. I got a slow one here. Take about five minutes to go
through their heads. Hurt like hell."

The one who had never been able to say anything from

the moment Lee Mellon had stepped out there with the lantern and the gun, and told them if they moved one inch he would kill them, but they might as well move because he was going to kill them anyway, and liked a running target because it sharpened his eye—finally spoke, "I'm nineteen. We couldn't even find the gas tank. My sister lives in Santa Barbara." That was all he said, and his tongue was gone again. They were both crying very hard. The tears were coming down their cheeks and their noses were running.

"Yeah," Lee Mellon said. "They are young, Jesse. I guess a person should have a second chance before they get their fucking brains blown out for trying to steal gasoline from a baby that hasn't even been born yet." When he said that, they both started crying harder than ever, if that were possible.

"Well, Lee," I said. "No harm done. Nothing has really happened except that they tried to steal our last five gallons of gasoline."

"All right, Jesse," Lee Mellon said philosophically, though dragging his feet a little. "If they pay for all the gasoline they've been stealing from us this month, I might let them live. Just might. I once promised my mother, God bless her soul in heaven above, that if I ever had the chance to give a helping hand to some wayward boys, I would. How much money do you boys have?"

Both of them instantly, without saying anything, like a pair of mute Siamese twins, took out their wallets and gave Lee Mellon all of their money. They had about $6.72.

Lee Mellon took the money and put it in his pocket. "You boys have shown faith," he said. "You can live." One of them crawled forward and kissed Lee Mellon's boot.

"Come on, now," Lee Mellon said. "Don't slobber. Show some class." He marched them back to their car. They were the happiest kids in the world. Their car was a 1941

Ford with all those good things kids do that make them look nice.

The kids had probably been low on gas, taken the wrong road. They should have been over on 101. With no filling station for miles and miles, they decided that we wouldn't miss a few gallons of gas. They probably would have asked us if there had been a light on.

Lee Mellon waved good-bye with the Winchester as they drove off very slowly toward San Luis Obispo and the sister waiting in Santa Barbara. Yeah, it was probably just a mistake in navigation. They should have stayed over on 101.

Lee Mellon waved good-bye with the Winchester and at the same time, he pulled the trigger of the gun. They were, of course, too far away now to hear the gun go off. They were maybe fifty yards away, the car barely rolling forward, and they couldn't possibly have heard the click of the hammer as it hit against the empty chamber.

The Truck

THE NEXT MORNING we had cracked wheat for breakfast. We had a fifty-pound sack of it that had been bought in San Francisco at the old Crystal Palace Market. This was in the days before they tore that lovely building down and put a motel in there.

Cracked wheat was our lonesome breakfast when the food ran low. We had some powdered milk to go along with it, and some sugar and some of Lee Mellon's hardtack. There was no coffee, so we had some green tea.

"Well, we're rich," Lee Mellon said, taking the $6.72 out of his pocket. He put the money down on the floor in front of him like a coin collector looking at some rare specimens.

"We can get some food," I said naïvely. "And maybe some bullets for the guns."

"I wonder if those guys will ever get the stains out of their pants," Lee Mellon laughed. "It's for sure they won't take them to the cleaners."

"Ha-ha," I laughed.

One of the cats jumped down off the roof. We had about half-a-dozen cats. They were all starving. The cat came over and tried to eat a piece of Lee Mellon's hardtack. It took a few gnaws and decided that it wasn't worth the effort.

The cat went out on the deck and sat there in the weak sun, and watched a snake gliding pleasantly across the pond with a half-digested frog in its tummy.

"Let's take this money and get laid," Lee Mellon said. "I think that's more important than food or bullets. I did all right without bullets. We ought to move that truck a little closer to the highway. It might eventually lead to a good living."

"How do you get laid for $6.72?" I asked.

"We'll go up and see Elizabeth."

"I thought she only worked when she was in Los Angeles," I said.

"Yeah, that's the way she usually does it, but sometimes she doesn't mind. To be different. You have to catch her in the right mood. What she does down in Los Angeles is kind of weird stuff."

"A box of .22 bullets would be really sweet," I said. "A pound of coffee . . . both of us? A hundred dollar Los Angeles call girl for $6.72? You're awake, aren't you, fella?"

"Sure," he said. "I think it might be OK. Anyway, we haven't got anything to lose. Maybe she'll invite us for breakfast. Finish that slice of bread and let's get going."

What a wonderful sense of distortion Lee Mellon had. Finish that slice of bread. That thing I was holding in my hand had never had anything to do with a slice of bread. I put my hammer and chisel aside and we went up to the truck.

The truck looked just like a Civil War truck if they'd

had trucks back in those times. But the truck ran, even though it didn't have a gas tank.

There was an empty fifty-gallon gasoline drum on the bed of the truck with a smaller gasoline can on top of it, and there was a syphon leading from that can to the fuel line.

It worked like this. Lee Mellon drove and I stayed on the back of the truck and made sure everything went all right with the syphon, that it didn't get knocked out of kilter by the motion of the truck.

We looked kind of funny going down the highway. I'd never had the heart to ask Lee Mellon what happened to the gas tank. I figured it was best not to know.

In the Midst of Life

I HAD MET ELIZABETH only a couple of times, but I had been very impressed. She was beautiful and worked in Los Angeles three months out of the year. She hired somebody, usually a Mexican woman, to come to Big Sur and watch her children. Then she performed a fantastic change and did it with great skill.

At Big Sur she lived in a rough three-room shack with four children that were all reflections of herself as if she had hung mirrors on them. She wore her hair long and loose about her shoulders and on her feet she wore sandals and on her body she wore a rough shapeless dress and lived a life of physical and spiritual contemplation.

She had her garden and her canning and chopping wood and sewing and she did all the things that women have always done when there is not a man about the house and they live in the lonely reaches of the world, raising the children as best they can. She was very gentle and read a lot.

She lived this life for nine months out of the year, like

some strange pregnancy, and then she hired somebody to watch her children, and she went to Los Angeles and made the physical and spiritual transformation into a hundred dollar call girl who specialized in providing exotic pleasure for men who wanted a beautiful woman to put out with some weird action.

She did all the things that the men wanted her to do. They gave her the hundred dollars and sometimes more because she was very comfortable and did not make them feel self-conscious about what they wanted, not unless the men wanted to be made uncomfortable, of course, and then she would do this relentlessly and sometimes they paid her extra for making them feel so uncomfortable.

She was a highly paid technician who worked three months out of the year, saving the money. Then she went back to Big Sur and let her hair hang long and naturally about her neck and shoulders, and she lived a life of physical and spiritual contemplation and could not stand to kill a living thing.

She was a vegetarian. Eggs were her only vice. There were rattlesnakes around where her children played, but she would do nothing about it.

Her oldest child was eleven and her youngest six, and the rattlesnakes were in abundance. The snakes came and went like mice, but her children remained unaltered by them.

Her husband had been killed in Korea. That's all that anybody knew about him. She came to Big Sur after his death. She didn't care to talk about it.

We drove up to her place. It was about twelve miles away, and then off the highway a few miles up an obscure canyon. You had to watch carefully. It was easy to miss her road. Our maximum speed on the highway was twenty miles an hour. When we reached her place we stopped the truck and Lee Mellon got out and I got off. We made quite a team.

There was a long line of clothes between two trees. They hung perfectly still for there was no wind. We could see children's toys here and there, and we saw a game that the children had made themselves out of dirt, deer antlers and abalone shells, but the game was so strange that only children could tell what it was. Perhaps it wasn't a game at all, only the grave of a game.

Elizabeth's car was gone. Everything was quiet except for some chickens in a pen. A rooster was strutting around making a bunch of noise. Nobody was home.

Lee Mellon looked at the rooster. He decided to steal it, and then he decided to leave her some money for it along with a note on the kitchen table telling her that he had bought the chicken, and then he decided to hell with it. Let her keep the chicken. That was big of him. And all the time that this was going on, it was going on only in his mind, for he did not say a word.

Finally Lee Mellon did speak, saying, "Nobody's home," and that was right except for a rooster destined to live forever and the grave of a children's game.

The Extremity of $6.72

WHEN WE ARRIVED BACK at our place and Lee Mellon got out and I got off the truck, I could see that thirst had built itself a kind of shack in Lee Mellon's throat. Thoughts of strong drink crossed his eyes like birds in flight.

"I wish she had been home," Lee Mellon said, picking up a rock and throwing it at the Pacific Ocean. The rock did not quite reach the Pacific. It landed on a pile of about seven billion other rocks.

"Yeah," I said.

"Who knows what might have happened?" Lee Mellon said.

I was quite certain that nothing would have happened, but I said, "Yeah, if she had been home . . ."

The birds kept crossing his eyes, flocks of little drinky-winkies, their wings attached by glass to their bodies. A fog was building up on the ocean. It was not building up like a shack, but more like a grand hotel. The Grand Hotel of Big Sur. Soon it would start inward and curve up the slope of the canyon and everything would be lost in flocks of vaporous bellboys.

Lee Mellon was getting pretty nervous. "Let's hitchhike to Monterey and get drunk," he said.

"Only if I can fill my pockets with rice when we get there, and put a pound of hamburger in my wallet before we start drinking," I said. I used the word wallet like one uses the word mausoleum.

"OK," he said.

Eight hours later I was sitting in a small bar in Monterey with a young girl. She had a glass of red wine in front of her and I had a martini in front of me. Sometimes it just happens that way. There's no telling the future and little understanding of what's gone on before. Lee Mellon was passed out underneath the saloon. I had hosed the vomit off him and covered him with a large piece of cardboard so the police wouldn't find him.

There were a lot of other people in the bar. At first I could barely contain my amusement at human and public surroundings. I was pretending very hard that I was a human being and by doing so, I allowed myself to come on with the girl.

I had met her about an hour earlier when Lee Mellon had passed out on top of her. In subtracting him from her, a thing not taught in grade school arithmetic, we had struck up a casual conversation and it had flowered into us sitting opposite each other and having a drink together.

I held a sip of the cold martini in my mouth until the temperature of the drink was the same temperature as my body. The good old 98.6 fahrenheit—our only link with reality. That is if you want to consider a mouth full of martini as having anything to do with reality.

Elaine was the girl's name and the more I watched her the prettier she flowered out, which is a nice thing if one

can pull it off. It's hard. She could. That certain accelera-
tion that comes from within has always pleased me.

"What do you do?" she asked.

I had to think that one over. I could have said, "I live
with Lee Mellon and I am cursed like a dog." No, no, not
that. I could have said, "Do you like apples?" and she
would have answered yes, and then I could have said, "Let's
go to bed." No, no, that would be later. Finally I decided
on what I was going to say to her. I said quietly, but lined
with a gentle certainty, "I live in Big Sur."

"Oh, that's nice," she said. "I live in Pacific Grove.
What do you do?"

Not bad I thought. I'll try something else.

"I'm unemployed," I said.

"I'm unemployed, too," she said. "What do you do?"

This was a strong new part of her to be dealt with, but
I was ready to go now. Let me go! I looked at her very
shyly with a sort of religious awkwardness that was stacked
like palm branches about me. "I'm a minister," I said.

She looked at me just as shyly and said just as awkwardly, "I'm a nun. What do you do?"

There was a persistence there. We were beginning to
hit it off. I liked her. I've always been partial to clever
women. It is a weakness of mine, but it's too late to correct.

A little while later we were walking along the beach.
I had my arm under her sweater and around her waist and
my hand going sideways up to her breast and my fingers
doing things, reaching out with the intelligence of small
plants that were footloose and fancy-free.

Jesse's got a girl and Lee Mellon introduced her to him.
"When did you first decide to go into the nunnery?" I said.

"Oh, when I was about six," she said.

"I decided to be a minister when I was five," I said.

"I decided to be a nun when I was four."

"I decided to be a minister when I was three."

"That's nice. I decided to be a nun when I was two."

"I decided to be a minister when I was one."

"I decided to be a nun the day I was born. That very day. It's good to start your life out on the right foot," she said proudly.

"Well, I wasn't there when I was born so I couldn't make the decision. My mother was in Bombay. I was in Salinas. I think you're being very unfair," I said humbly.

This broke her up. It is pleasant when such silliness can lead to a girl's place. She closed the door and I glanced at her books, a very bad habit of mine. Hello, *Collected Poems* of Dylan Thomas. I looked over her place like a raccoon, another habit of mine but not as bad, though.

I have a great curiosity about the abodes where the young ladies live. I like the smells of where the young ladies live and the artifacts and the way the light falls upon things, especially the light upon the smells.

She made me a sandwich. I didn't eat it. I don't know why she made it. We got into bed. I put my hand between her legs. The blanket underneath her had a rodeo on it. Cowboys and horses and corrals. She forced her body hard against my hand.

Just before we went away with each other like small republics to join the United Nations, I had a cinematographic impression, about a dozen frames of Lee Mellon lying covered with cardboard underneath the saloon.

To Gettysburg! To Gettysburg!

AFTER A LONG PLEASANT WHILE I got up and sat on the edge of the bed. There was a small light in the room and an abstract painting coming out of the light. Elaine had a lamp with an abstract painted upon the shade. All right . . .

There was the old standby, that faithful servant of the walls: the Manolete bullfight poster you see again and again upon the wall of the young ladies. How well they like that poster and how it likes them. They take care of each other.

There was a guitar with the word LOVE written on the back, and the strings of the guitar were turned to the wall as if the wall should suddenly begin to plink out a little tune, a few snatches of "Greensleeves" or the "Midnight Special."

"What are you doing?" Elaine said, staring softly at me. Sexual satisfaction had puzzled her face. She was like a child that had just awakened from its nap, though she had never been asleep.

I was pleased with myself for it had been a long time

or seemed so, and pleased I was with myself again, and
again pleased to be pleased again.

"I've got to get Lee Mellon out from underneath that
saloon," I said. "I don't want the police to get him. He
wouldn't like that. Hates jail. Always has. The thrill of jail
was ruined for him when he was a child."

"What?" she said.

"Yeah," I said. "He did ten years for murdering his
parents."

She pulled the covers up over her body and lay there
smiling at me, who in turn was smiling. Then slowly she
drifted the covers down to the beginning of her breasts and
below them, a thing "infinitely gentle" moving . . . down.

"The police will get Lee Mellon," I said. I said it like
a slogan in a socialist country. GUARD AGAINST ELEC-
TRICAL WASTE AND TURN THE LIGHTS OUT
WHEN YOU LEAVE THE ROOM. THE POLICE WILL
GET LEE MELLON. It was all the same. "The police will
get Lee Mellon," I repeated.

Elaine smiled and then said all right. It was all right.
This life, how strange it is. Last night those two boys were
crawling in front of Lee Mellon's empty rifle, little realizing
as they begged for their imaginary lives that they were going
to finance all of this: I with a girl to the bed, Lee Mellon
under a saloon covered with cardboard.

Elaine got out of the bed. "I'll go with you. We can
bring him here and sober him up."

She pulled the sweater over the top of her head and
then she put her pants on. I was her appreciative Olympian
audience, watching things going away into clothes and then
appearing again with clothes on top of them. She put on a
pair of tennis shoes.

"Who are you?" asked I, the Horatio Alger of
Casanovas.

"My parents live in Carmel," she said.

Then she walked over and put her arms around me and kissed me on the mouth. I felt pretty good.

We found Lee Mellon right where I left him, cardboard still intact. He was like a box full of something and it certainly wasn't soap. A great big box full of Lee Mellon had arrived suddenly in America without any advertising campaign.

"Wake up, Lee Mellon," I said and began singing,

Way, hay, up she rises. Way, hay, up she rises,
Way, hay, up she rises earlye in the morning!

What will we do with the drunken general?
What will we do with the drunken general?
What will we do with the drunken general
earlye in the morning?

Why, send him off to Gettysburg!
Off to Gettysburg! To Gettysburg! O Gettysburg
earlye in the morning!

Elaine put her hand down the back of my pants and then slipped her fingers down past my shorts and let her hand go on down to the crack of my ass, and there her hand did rest like a bird upon the branch of a tree.

Lee Mellon slowly sat up. The cardboard fell away from him. He was unpacked. The world could now see him. The end product of American spirit, pride and the old know-how.

"What happened?" he said.

"Spiritus frumenti," Elaine said.

Great Day

THE NEXT MORNING WE DROVE down to Big Sur in Elaine's car. The back seat of the car was filled with sacks of food from the Safeway market in Monterey. There were two alligators in the trunk of the car. They were Elaine's idea.

Lee Mellon had blurted out in a flurry of drunken speech the trouble we'd had with the frogs, and Elaine just as fast but coherently said, "I'll get an alligator," and she did.

She went down to the pet shop and came back with two alligators. We asked her why she'd gotten two alligators, and she said they were on sale. Buy one at the regular price and you got another one for a penny. An alligator one cent sale. In its own way it made sense.

Happiness sagged out of Lee Mellon's bloodshot eyes as he drove while Elaine and I sat beside him in the front seat. I had my arm around her. We drove by Henry Miller's mailbox. He was waiting for his mail in that old Cadillac he had in those days.

"There's Henry Miller," I said.

"Oh," she said.

With every passing moment my liking for her flowered another time. Not that I had anything against Henry Miller, but like a storm of flowers remembered during a revolution I grew to like her more and more.

Lee Mellon was very impressed, too. She had bought fifty dollars worth of food and two alligators. Lee Mellon took his tongue and absentmindedly counted the teeth in his mouth. He found six in there and he divided the six teeth into the sacks of food in the back seat, and he was pleased with his mathematics for a smile like a ragged Parthenon appeared on his face.

"Great day!" Lee Mellon said. That was the first time I'd ever heard him say great day. I'd heard him say everything else but great day. He probably just said it to confuse me. He did.

"I've never been to Big Sur before," Elaine said, looking out the window at the passing country. "My parents moved to Carmel while I was going to college in the East."

"A college girl?" Lee Mellon said, turning suddenly to her as if she had announced that all the food in the back seat wasn't really food but cleverly designed wax.

"Oh, no!" she said triumphantly. "I failed all my courses and they blew up the college the day I left because I was so stupid. They felt the place couldn't be used for anything again."

"Good," Lee Mellon said, resuming visual control of the car.

There was a large bird in the sky. It went out over the ocean, and stayed there.

"This is beautiful," Elaine said.

"Great day!" Lee Mellon repeated to my consternation.

Motorcycle

WE NEARED OUR PLACE late in the afternoon. Half a mile away there was a wooden bridge and a creek that flashed below. I was holding Elaine's hand. Like a bottle of beer in a haze the sun was plying its ancient Egyptian trade toward the end of the sky, the beginning of the Pacific. Lee Mellon was holding the steering wheel of the car. We were all content.

Lee Mellon pulled off the highway and drove up to the old truck and stopped.

"What's that?" Elaine said.

"That's a truck," I said.

"Come off it," she said.

"I made it with my own hands," Lee Mellon said.

"That explains it," Elaine said. In an extraordinarily brief period of time she had grown to know, to understand what went on behind the surface of Lee Mellon. This pleased me.

"Well, here we are," Lee Mellon said. "The Homestead.

My grandpappy homesteaded this place. Fought Indians, drought, floods, cattlemen, varmints, the Southern Pacific, Frank Norris and strong drink. But do you know the worst thing we Mellons had to fight and still have to fight, the thing that finally gets us all?"

"No," Elaine said.

"The Mellon Curse. It comes in the form of a gigantic hound every decade. You know 'Twas not the track of man nor beast, but that of a gigantic Mellon Curse.' "

"Sounds reasonable," she said.

We got the groceries and took them through the hole in the kitchen wall. The cats darted into the brush like books into a library. It would take them a little while but hunger would return them to us like the classics: *Hamlet, Winesburg, Ohio.*

"What about the alligators?" Elaine said.

"Let's save them for tonight. They're OK in the car," Lee Mellon said, as if it were a perfectly natural thing for alligators to be in a car. "I've waited and dreamt of this for months. We'll show those frogs that man is the dominant creature on this shit pile, and they better believe it."

Elaine looked the place over and the light of Big Sur was upon her hair, and her hair was in perfect tune with California. "Very interesting," she said, and then hit her head on the ceiling. I comforted her, but it wasn't necessary. She hadn't hit her head very hard. It was only a love tap compared to some of the bone-crushing smashes I'd seen delivered against those beams.

"Who designed this place?" she said. "Frank Lloyd Wright?"

"No," I said. "Frank Lloyd Mellon."

"Oh, he's an architect, too."

Lee Mellon came over and inspected the ceiling from a kind of weird stoop. He was like a doctor taking the pulse

of a dead patient. I looked at myself. I was stooping the
same way and Elaine was, too. We were all joined together
in the famous Lee Mellon Indoor Stoop, a thing that would
have been copyrighted during the Inquisition.
    It's a little low," he said to Elaine.
    "Yes, it is," I said.
    "You'll get used to it," Lee Mellon said to Elaine.
    "I'm certain she will," I said.
    "I will," she said.
    Lee Mellon went and got a bottle of wine from the
groceries and we walked out onto the deck and toasted the
sundown. The sun broke like a beer bottle on the water. We
in a shallow sort of way reflected ourselves in the broken
glass of the Egyptians. Each piece of Ra went away with
a 60 horsepower Johnson outboard motor fastened to it.
    The wine was Wente Brothers gray riesling, soon gone.
    "Where do we stay?" Elaine said. I steered her back
up to the car and got her suitcase and took her to the glass
house, past the garden covered with fishnets.
    "What's that?" she said.
    "It's a garden covered with fishnets."
    We went inside the glass house and she looked at the
floor.
    "A motorcycle?" she said.
    "Sort of," I said.
    "Lee Mellon's," she said.
    "Yes."
    "Uh-huh," nodding her head.
    "This place is cosy," she said, dropping her hands to
her side. Then she saw the Bible. "You are a minister!"
    "Yes, I am. I attended the Moody Bible Institute and
studied to be a church janitor. I'm doing graduate work
now at Napa State Hospital. Soon I'll have a church of my

own. This is my vacation. I come here every year for the waters."

"Uh-huh," nodding her head.

Elaine sat down on the place where I slept and looked up at me, and then she lay carefully back upon the sleeping bag. "This is your bed," she said, not asking a question. There was no rodeo engraved upon my bed. No horses, no cowboys, no corrals. Nothing but sleeping bag. It seemed a little weird now as if all the places where people sleep in the world should have rodeos upon them.

I looked out the window and Lee Mellon was coming up the path to the house. I took my hand and waved him back. He paused, looked and cocked his head like a Confederate general, and turned around and went back down to the hole in the kitchen wall.

"What's that underneath the lantern?" Elaine said.

"Motorcycle," I said.

A Farewell to Frogs

ELAINE COOKED DINNER THAT EVENING. What a joy it was to have a woman behind the stove. She was our fair queen of grub as she fried up some pork chops. It was then I realized for the first time the extent of the damage Lee Mellon's cooking had done to my soul.

I don't believe I have ever fully healed spiritually from his cooking. I have built defensive mechanisms around those tragic memories, but the pain is still there. If I but for an instant diminish my defenses, the cloven hoof of his bad cooking prances again in all its dubious glory upon my palate.

Lee Mellon built a grandiose fire and we sat around the fire drinking cups of strong black coffee. Elaine had even bought some cat food. The cats were in there with us, stretched out like furry ferns in front of the fire. Everybody was nice and comfy. While the cats purred up from the depths of their prehistoric memories a rusty old plantlike purr—they were so little used to contentment—we engaged in dialogue.

"What do your parents do?" Lee Mellon said paternally. I choked on my coffee.

"I'm their daughter," Elaine said.

Lee Mellon stared blankly at her for a few seconds. "Sounds like a vaguely familiar story. Conan Doyle, I guess. *The Case of the Smart Ass Daughter*," Lee Mellon said.

He went and got one of our brand-new apples out of the kitchen. He began working on it with his six teeth. I knew the apples were crisp but there was no sound coming out of his mouth that would have indicated the presence of that quality.

"My father's a lawyer," Elaine said.

Lee Mellon nodded. There were hand grenade fragments of apple around the corners of his mouth.

Elaine reached over and put her hand on my thigh. I put my arm around her and leaned back against the wooden wall. Lee Mellon was enthroned upon his stale deer hide.

Night was coming on in, borrowing the light. It had started out borrowing just a few cents worth of the light, but now it was borrowing thousands of dollars worth of the light every second. The light would soon be gone, the bank closed, the tellers unemployed, the bank president a suicide.

We sat there quietly watching Lee Mellon valiantly attacking the world's longest apple, and then we were close to each other, and then we went back silently to Lee Mellon and the apple, and then back to ourselves and finally we were not watching the apple masquerade any more but were totally involved within our closeness to each other.

When Lee Mellon finished the apple he smacked his lips together like a pair of cymbals, and we heard the first frog.

"There it goes," Lee Mellon said, preparing immediately to send his cavalry in, dust rising in the valley, an excitment in the time of banners, in the time of drums.

We heard the second frog, and then we heard the first frog over again. A third frog joined in, and then they all had one good one together, and then a fourth frog came on through, and three other frogs popped like firecrackers, and Lee Mellon said, "I'll go get the alligators." He lit a lantern and walked through the hole in the kitchen wall and up the path to the car.

Elaine must have dozed off suddenly. She was lying on the floor with her head on my lap. She was a little startled. "Where's Lee Mellon?" she said. I barely heard her.

"He's gone to get the alligators," I said loudly.

"Are those the frogs?" she said loudly and pointing toward the noise that was beginning to boil all over the dark pond.

"Yes," I said loudly.

"Good," she said loudly.

Lee Mellon came back with the alligators. He had a nice six-toothed smile on his face. He put the box down and took one of the alligators out. The alligator was stunned to realize that he was not in the pet shop. He looked around for the puppies that had been in a wire cage next to his aquarium. The puppies were gone. The alligator wondered where the puppies were. Lee Mellon was holding the alligator in his hands.

"Hello, alligator!" Lee Mellon shouted. The alligator was still looking for the puppies. Where had they gone?

"You like frog legs?" Lee Mellon shouted to the alligator and put the alligator carefully down into the pond. The alligator lay there stationary like a toy boat. Lee Mellon gave him a little push and the alligator sailed out into the pond.

There was an instant silence over the pond as if the

pond had been dropped right into the heart of a cemetery. Lee Mellon took the second alligator out of the box.

The second alligator looked all around for the puppies. He couldn't find them either. Where had they gone to?

Lee Mellon stroked the back of the alligator and put it down into the pond and floated it away, and the silence in the pond was multiplied by two. Silence hung like mist over the pond.

"Well, that takes care of the frogs," Elaine whispered finally. We had been hypnotized by the silence.

Lee Mellon stood there staring incredulously at the dark watery silence. "They're gone," he said.

"Yeah," I said. "There's nothing in there now but alligators."

The Rites of Tobacco

NIGHT AND HOW PLEASANT it was to lie there in bed with Elaine curled about me like vines upon my shadow. She had outflanked the locusts of memory and that dismal plague with the equally dismal Cynthia. The way I felt about it now a salmon could fall oñ her in Ketchikan. I could see the headline in the Ketchikan newspaper: SALMON FALLS ON GIRL and a nice sub-headline: "Crushed Flatter than a Pancake."

My hand went over Elaine's face and found her mouth. Her lips were parted and I ran my fingers gently along her teeth and touched the sleeping tip of her tongue. I felt like a musician touching a darkened piano.

Before I fell asleep thoughts of Lee Mellon passed again in ordered columns carrying banners and drums down my mind. I thought about a distant and historical time called THREE DAYS BEFORE. I thought about Lee Mellon's Rites of Tobacco.

He had used up all his tobacco and was in desperate

need of a cigarette, so he took the inevitable trip to Gorda. A tobacco jaunt in the sun. It was his fifth or sixth time out since I had been there.

Lee Mellon's Rites of Tobacco went something like this: when he had no more tobacco and no more hope of getting any through the accepted tobacco channels of reality, he would take a hike to Gorda. Of course he had no money to buy any tobacco with, so he would walk along one side of the highway. Say first the side next to the Santa Lucia Mountains, and he would look along the edge of the highway for cigarette butts, and all that he found he would put in a paper bag.

Sometimes he would find a gathering of cigarette butts like a ring of mushrooms in an enchanted forest, but sometimes he would have to walk a mile for a cigarette butt. Then he would flash a six-toothed wonder when he finally found one. In other lands it might be called a smile.

Sometimes after he had walked a half a mile or so and hadn't found a cigarette butt, he would get very depressed and have a fantasy that he would never find another cigarette butt, that he would walk all the way to Seattle without finding one on the highway, and he would turn east and walk all the way to New York, looking carefully month after month along the highway for a cigarette butt without ever finding one. Not a damn one, and the end of an American dream.

It was five miles back to Gorda. Then Lee Mellon would turn around and walk back on the Pacific side of the highway. Down below the Pacific would be throwing its ashes upon the rocks and the shore. Cormorants would be tossing the air with their wings. Whales and pelicans, too, doing each to each the Pacific Ocean.

Like a kind of weird Balboa, Lee Mellon would look for cigarette butts on the shores of the Western World, and the

five miles back to our place, finding here and there an out-
cast of the tobacco kingdom.

When he got back home he would go and sit in front of
the fireplace and take out all the cigarette butts and break
them down until they were a pile of loose tobacco on a
newspaper. Then he would very carefully mix them all together and dividedividedivide the tobacco againagainagain
into itself and put the mixture into an empty tin can.

Lee Mellon's Rites of Tobacco had renewed themselves,
pleasure to be measured like great art, smoke to be counted
like famous paintings hanging in the lungs.

Lee Mellon was the last thing I remembered before I fell
asleep assumed in gentle and loving portions about Elaine.
Lee Mellon fell apart at the edges like tobacco crumbling.

Wilderness Again

I WOKE UP THE NEXT MORNING, sun shining through the glass, but Elaine was not under the sleeping bag with me. I was startled . . . where? Then I saw her bending over the motorcycle parts. She didn't have any clothes on and the sight of her butt renewed my faith in evolution.

"This motorcycle," she said aloud to herself. She sounded like a mother hen admonishing one of her chicks for falling apart.

"This motorcycle," she repeated. *You bad chick! Where's your head!*

"Hello," I said. "You got a nice keester."

She turned toward me and smiled. "I was just looking at this motorcycle. It needs something," she said.

"Yeah, an undertaker," I said. "A motorcycle coffin, a few good words said over it and then a slow majestic final ride out to Marbletown. You have nice breasts," I said.

The sun coming through the window made the room smell like hot motorcycle as if motorcycle were some kind of roast meat.

I'd like a slice of motorcycle on dark rye, please.

Anything to drink sir; gasoline?

No. No, I don't think so.

Elaine put her hands over her breasts. She looked coyish. "Guess who I am?"

"OK, who are you?"

She cocked her head and smiled.

I saw something approaching at the edge of my vision. It was Lee Mellon coming up the path. I waved for him to go back to the hole in the kitchen wall.

He was reluctant to go. He made the motions of eating breakfast, accompanied with facial expressions to show how good the food was. It was quite a breakfast with pork chops and eggs and fried potatoes and fresh fruit.

A rabbit ran behind Lee Mellon. He did not see it and the rabbit hid in the brush and stared out, ears flat against its head. Could Alice be far behind on this beautiful Big Sur morning?

"That's who you are?" I said to Elaine. She nodded her head . . . yes. Breakfast became even more obscure. The hands no longer over the breasts, the body tilted at an angle, slightly forward.

I gave Lee Mellon one HELL-OF-A-WAVE back and he retreated slowly to the hole in the kitchen wall, his inevitable Wilderness.

The Pork Chop Alligator

IT WAS JUST STARTING TO RAIN when we got down to breakfast. Light was tucked like artillery in and out of the clouds, and a warm rain was coming down off the light. Thirty degrees of the sky out over the Pacific was one great army: the Army of the Potomac with General Ulysses S. Grant, Commander in Chief. Lee Mellon was feeding a pork chop to one of the alligators. And Elizabeth was there.

"Nice alligators," she said, smiling with teeth born on the moon and the dark of her nostrils looked carved from jade.

"Have a pork chop," Lee Mellon said, stuffing a pork chop down the alligator's throat. The alligator was sitting on his lap. The alligator said, "GROWL!—opp/opp/opp/opp/opp/opp/opp/opp!" with the end of the pork chop sticking out of his mouth.

Elizabeth had an alligator on her lap. Her alligator didn't say anything. There was no pork chop sticking out of his mouth.

A beautiful gentleness glowed from her as if she had lanterns under her skin. Her beauty made me feel disconsolate.

"Hello," I said.

"Hello, Jesse."

She remembered me.

"This is Elaine," I said.

"Hello, Elaine."

"GROWL!—opp/opp/opp/opp/opp/opp/opp/opp!" the alligator said with the pork chop sticking out of his mouth.

Nothing Elizabeth's alligator said profoundly, for meek alligators shall inherit the earth.

"I'm hungry," I said.

"I'll bet," Lee Mellon said.

Elizabeth was wearing a plain white dress.

"What's for breakfast?" Elaine said.

"A museum," Lee Mellon answered.

"I've never seen any alligators down here before," Elizabeth said. "They're cute. What are they good for?"

"Frog baths," Elaine said.

"Companionship," Lee Mellon said. "I'm lonely. Our alligators could make beautiful music together."

His alligator said, "GROWL!—opp/opp/opp/opp/opp/opp/opp/opp!"

"Your alligator looks like a harp," Elizabeth said, as if she really meant it: with strings coming off her words.

"Your alligator looks like a handbag filled with harmonicas," Lee Mellon said, lying like a dog with dog whistles coming off his words.

"Up your alligator!" I said. "Is there any coffee?"

They both laughed. Elizabeth's voice had a door in it. When you opened that door you found another door, and that door opened yet another door. All the doors were nice and led out of her.

Elaine was looking at me.

"Let's make some coffee," I said.

"There is some coffee," Lee Mellon said. "You didn't hear me."

"I'll get it," Elaine said.

"I'll go with you."

"Good," she said.

That great dark cloud moved up a few degrees, a clock and a rush of wind came by the cabin. The wind made me think about the Battle of Agincourt for it moved like arrows about us, through the very air. Ah, Agincourt: the beauty is all in the saying.

"I'll put another log on the fire," I said. BANG! I hit my head. The coffee turned two white cups inside out, midnightly.

"I'll have a cup of coffee if there's enough," Elizabeth said. Make that a third white cup to the black inside out.

"Let's have some breakfast," somebody said. Perhaps it was me. I could very easily have said something like that for I was very hungry.

The pork chops and eggs were good, along with some fried potatoes and that good strawberry jam. Lee Mellon had a second breakfast with us.

He took the pork chop out of the alligator's mouth and used the alligator for a table to rest his plate on. "Fry this one up for me," Lee Mellon said. "It's tenderized now."

The alligator stopped saying, "GROWL!—opp/opp/opp/opp/opp/opp/opp/opp!" Tables should not say things like that.

The Wilderness Alligator Haiku

IT WAS NOW raining very hard and the wind roared like the Confederate army through the hole in the kitchen wall: Wilderness—thousands of soldiers taking up miles of the countryside—Wilderness!

Elizabeth and Lee Mellon had gone off to another cabin. They had to talk about something. Elaine and I were left holding the alligators. We didn't mind.

May 6, 1864. A lieutenant fell to the ground mortally wounded. Collapsing sideways into memory, marble of a classic gender began to grow on his fingerprints. As he lay there sublime in history, another bullet struck his body, causing it to jerk like a shadow in a motion picture. Perhaps Birth of a Nation.

112

He Usually Stays Over by the Garden

"Ouch!" Elizabeth said. "This ceiling." *The terror of it* and then sat down.

We put the alligators back into the pond. They both sank slowly to the bottom. It was now raining so hard on the pond that you could not see the bottom, nor wanted to.

Elizabeth was sitting there. The white dress was like a swan about her body. As she talked a lake flowed from the swan, answering for eternity that great question: Which came first the lake or the swan?

"I saw the ghost last night," she said. "He was out by the chicken house. I don't know what he was doing there. He usually stays over by the garden. In the corn."

"The ghost?" Elaine said.

"Yes, we have a ghost down here," Elizabeth said. "It's the ghost of an old man. That's his house up there on the plateau. The old man got so old that he had to go and live in Salinas, and they say he died there of a broken heart, and his ghost returned to Big Sur and sometimes he walks around at night. I don't know what he does during the daytime.

"I saw him last night. I don't know what he was doing by the chicken house. I opened the window and said, 'Hello, ghost. What are you doing out by the chicken house? You're usually by the garden. What's wrong?'

"Then the ghost yelled, 'Charge!' waved a large flag and ran into the woods."

"A flag?" Elaine said.

"That's right," Elizabeth said. "He was a veteran of the Spanish-American War."

"Oh. Does he frighten the children?"

"No," Elizabeth said. "They like company. This country is a little lonely for children. Ghosts are welcome. Besides he usually stays over by the garden." Elizabeth was now smiling.

The alligators bobbed to the top of the pond. It stopped raining. Elizabeth was wearing a white dress. Lee Mellon scratched his head. Night came. I said something to Elaine. The pond was quiet like the *Mona Lisa*.

❦

"*Where's Private Augustus Mellon?*" *the captain said.*

"*I don't know where he is. He was here just a minute ago,*" *the sergeant answered. He had a long yellow mustache.*

"*He's always here just a minute ago. He's never here now. Probably out stealing something as usual,*" *the captain said.*

That Chopping Sound

WE WENT UP TO THE CABIN and to bed. Elizabeth had to do something with Lee Mellon. Her children were in King City, visiting somebody. Elaine took off her clothes. I was very sleepy. I don't remember anything. I just closed my eyes or they closed themselves.

Then there was something moving me. Too nice to be an earthquake, but persistent in its motion, as if the sea had grown small and warm and human and beside me. Then the sea had a voice. "Wake up, wake up, Jesse," Elaine's voice: "Wake up, Jesse. Do you hear that chopping sound?"

"What is it, Elaine?" I said, rubbing the darkness because my eyes were darkness.

"It's a chopping sound, Jesse."

"No, say that again."

"A chopping sound. It's a chopping sound."

"All right," I said and stopped rubbing the darkness. *Let it be a chopping sound. Let it be a beautiful chopping sound,* and I started back down toward sleep.

"Wake up, Jesse!" she said. "It's a chopping sound!"

OK! and I was awake then and it was a chopping sound as if someone were chopping down a forest. Maybe a gang of them. "That's a chopping sound all right," I said. "I guess I'd better go find out what it is."

"That's what I've been trying to tell you," she said.

I lit the lantern: *oh, well, here we go again. The last time led to thee.* "What time is it?" I asked. I rolled over and looked down at Elaine. She looked nice.

"I'm not a clock," she said.

I put my clothes on.

"I'll stay here," Elaine said. "No, I'll go with you."

"It's up to you," I said. "That may be Paul Bunyan out there, desperate for a lay, but it's probably someone trying to steal gasoline with an ax."

"With an ax?"

"Yeah, they do it all the time. Sometimes they steal our gasoline with plows, shoehorns, kangaroo pouches, you know."

"What's so different about your gasoline?" Elaine said.

"It's here," I said.

I slipped a knife into my belt.

"What's that for? What are you trying to do? William-Bonney me?"

"No, no."

"It's up to you," she said. "If you want to go around looking like that."

"There might be a nut or something out there. Besides it's a vaudeville act that Lee Mellon and I perform. I do all the cutting. He does the shooting. Damn good job, too," I said, touching softly her hair: *O gun-gathered lady of my heart!*

The night was cool and the stars were clear like fluid: twinkle, twinkle, little martini star, the same star that led me to thee. Is somebody using an ax to steal our gasoline with? 163 axes full of gasoline.

We'll find out, little star. We have no other choice, being the dominant creature on this shit pile. We have to look after ourselves.

That chopping sound came from the other side of the highway, up along that ragged road. It came loud and unabetted in its hackEty/wackEty: CHOP!

We used the darkness for a light and Elaine held close to me as I found our way along the road like a spoon probing carefully through a blindman's soup, looking for alphabets.

"Why didn't you bring a light?" Elaine said.

"I don't want anybody to know we are here."

"We're not," she said.

We saw a strange light in front of us, coming from the middle of that chopping sound.

"I wonder what it is," Elaine whispered.

"It ain't a time warp," I said, as we approached until we were there and saw a pair of car headlights turned like visionary hooks into the mountain, and a little man with a large ax chopping down trees and piling them on top of his car.

The car looked like a forest now, light coming out as if the moon were somewhere in there or fireworks of it.

"Good morning," I said.

The man stopped and looked at me. He was startled. "Is that you, Amigo Mellon?" he said.

"No," I said.

"Yes, it is," Lee Mellon said and there he was suddenly standing beside us. Elaine jumped like a fish against my arm.

"Good morning, Amigo Mellon," the man said. He looked kind of frenzied standing there with an ax in his hand and a forest stacked on top of his car.

"What are you up to, sport?" Lee Mellon said, now standing in front of me, looking curiously concentrated.

"Covering my car up with trees so they won't find me. They're looking for me. The cops. I'm on the lam. I just paid a two hundred dollar speeding ticket. Can I use this place for a hideout, Amigo Mellon?"

"Sure, just stop chopping down trees."

"Who's that with you? They're not the law, are they? Is that woman a detective?"

"No, this is my buddy and his lady friend."

"Are they married?"

"Yeah."

"Good. I hate the law."

And then he started chopping down another tree. A redwood tree about four feet in diameter. "Hold it, sport," Lee Mellon said.

"What's up, Amigo Mellon?"

"I think you've chopped down enough trees for today."

"I don't want them to find the car."

"You've already got a forest on it," Lee Mellon said. "What kind of car is that, anyway?"

It looked like a sort of sports car all covered with trees, certainly not like the way they do it at the Grand Prix.

"That's my Bentley Bomb, Amigo Mellon."

"Well, I think you've chopped down enough trees. Why don't you turn the lights out. The police won't find you if you keep your lights out."

"Good idea," the man said.

He took some of the trees off the car and got the door of the car open and doused the lights. Then he closed the door and piled the trees back on top of the car.

He picked up a paper bag that was in the brush. Instinctively he knew where it was in the sudden darkness. There seemed to be bottles in the bag.

"Hide me out, Amigo Mellon," he said. The man sort of looked like Humphrey Bogart in *High Sierra*, except that he was short, fat, bald-headed and looked like a guilty businessman because somewhere he had also found a briefcase and had it cemented under his arm.

"Let's go, Roy Earle," Lee Mellon said, touching the same ether that I was touching: the character Humphrey Bogart played in *High Sierra*.

And we walked down from High Sur now, the four of us together, engendered by the fates, Roy Earle and Lee Mellon gradually taking the lead.

❦

A fragment off a cannon ball shattered the branch of a tree and it fell into a spring. The impact of water and branch together was almost like a newspaper headline: WHERE'S AUGUSTUS MELLON? as black mud churned up from the bottom.

A horse lay smoldering in the brush. A great din of rifle fire almost stirred the horse into flames immediate as the year 1864.

A Short History of America
After the War Between the States

ELIZABETH WAS SITTING beside the fireplace when we came down through the hole in the kitchen wall. She did not have her white dress on. She had a gray blanket wrapped around herself like a ragged Confederate uniform. She was staring into the fire. She hardly looked up when we came in.

"Is that a detective?" Roy Earle said, jumping around and shifting the bag. "She looks like a detective. One of those lady-purse-snatching detectives. With a tear gas fountain pen in her purse."

Elizabeth of course had stopped looking into the fire by this time and was staring incredulously at Roy Earle who was really beginning to dance around.

"Who are you?" she asked as if she were addressing a bug.

"I'm Johnston Wade," he said. "I'm head cheese of the Johnston Wade Insurance Company in San Jose. What do you mean who am I? I'm a big shot. I've got a $100,000 in this briefcase, and two bottles of Jim Beam in this sack, and some cheese, too, and a pomegranate."

"This is Roy Earle," Lee Mellon said, introducing the stranger to Elizabeth. "He's crazy and on the lam."

"You don't think this is a $100,000?" Roy Earle said, taking a $100,000 out of the briefcase, and all put together in neat $100 bundles.

And then he dropped down on his knees beside Elizabeth. He looked her hard in the eye and said, "You're passable. I'll give you $3,500 to sleep with me. Cash on the barrel head."

Elizabeth drew the gray uniform closer about her shoulders. She looked away into the fire. A log was burning there, but there were no bugs staring out at her, no bon voyage, no have a nice trip.

"We don't want to hear any of that," Lee Mellon said like the gallant Confederate general he was.

Roy Earle looked at Elaine. Frenzy dripped off him like a flood of detergent soapsuds roaring through the Carlsbad Caverns. "I'll give you $2,000," he said.

"Get rid of him," I said.

"I'll handle this, Jesse. I know this bird." Lee Mellon turned and looked very concentrated at Roy Earle. "Shut up, sport," he said. "Sit down over there and keep your lips flat on your face."

Roy Earle went over and sat down against the wooden wall. He put the $100,000 back into the briefcase. He put the briefcase on the floor and then he put his feet on the briefcase. He sat there with his feet on his briefcase and took a bottle of Jim Beam out of the paper bag.

He broke the seal on the bottle, unscrewed the cap and poured a big slug of whiskey into his mouth. He swallowed it down with a hairy gulp. Strange, for as I said before: he was bald.

He went UMMM-good, smacked his lips and rolled his eyes like the octopus ride in a cheap carnival. He put the bottle back into the paper bag, and then looked innocent as a newborn baby.

That made Lee Mellon mad.

"Hold it, sport."

"What's up, Amigo Mellon?"

"The sauce is up, sport."

"The sauce?"

"Yeah, the King James Version of the Bible you got there in that sack, sport."

"Oh, you want a drink?"

"I don't want a lifesaver."

"That's very funny." Roy Earle started laughing like hell and took his feet off his money, rolled back onto the floor and began kicking his feet in the air like mashed potatoes. Then he sat back up and put his feet down on his money.

He stared straight ahead at us, and suddenly it was as if he were not there at all. He was just sitting there smiling, but it was terrible. False teeth showed in a light that dangled like an illuminated grave off them. He really looked in bad shape, hardly human any more.

Lee Mellon looked at him, shook his head slowly, walked over and took the paper bag out of his hand, opened it up, removed the bottle of Jim Beam, took a big slug of it, handed it to Elizabeth, who did likewise, wrapped in the Confederate uniform.

Elizabeth handed it to me. I handed it to Elaine. She took a medium slug out of it, and handed it back.

BANG! I hit my God-damn head on the ceiling and

took some of the whiskey to stop the pain. It did. With Roy Earle smiling all the time.

"Let's go have a talk, Roy," Lee Mellon said.

"My name is Johnston Wade. I run the Johnston Wade Insurance Company in San Jose. My wife wants to put me in the nuthouse because I bought a new car: my Bentley Bomb. She wants all my money and so does my son who goes to Stanford and my daughter who goes to Mills College.

"They want to lock Pop up, put Pop away in the nuthouse. Well, I got a surprise for them. I just paid a $200 speeding ticket and they can all go to hell.

"What do you think about that, huh? Pop's too smart for them. I went down to the bank and I got all the money and the stocks and bonds and deeds and jewelry, and I got a pomegranate, too."

He reached into the bag and took out the pomegranate. He held it up as if he were a magician showing off the end product of a trick.

"I bought it in Watsonville," he said. "For a dime. The best dime I ever spent in my life. That cunt in Mills College learning arithmetic and modern dance and how to screw her dear old dad out of everything he earned, she won't get that dime.

"That asshole son at Stanford, learning to be a doctor, he won't get that dime out of his dear old pop's gullet. Ha-ha.

"That bridge-playing psychopath, my wife, who's trying to lock me up because I want a Bentley Bomb. That pomegranate dime's gone. She won't spend that dime on her lover in Morgan Hill.

"I run the Johnston Wade Insurance Company in San Jose. I am Johnston Wade. Just because I'm fifty-three years old and want a sports car, they think they're going to lock me up, put me away. They got another think coming. Fuck 'em.

"My lawyer told me to get every cent I got and run for cover, go on the lam. They won't find me down here. Will they, Amigo Mellon?

"My lawyer's going to send me a telegram down at my hidden hunting lodge in San Diego. Near where I got my moose and my Kodiak bear.

"He's going to send me a telegram when everything is all clear, when he's put the kibosh on their plans. That's right. Ain't it, Amigo Mellon?"

Then he was instantly quiet. He stared at us with that same stupid smile on his face. He said all these things to us as if he were a prisoner of war, giving his name, rank and serial number.

❧

A crow had somehow grown webs about itself, driven by the fear of the Wilderness. Other creatures: mice, beetles, rabbits had also grown webs about themselves, usurping the spiders that were now long and slender and like worms in the ground, waiting for the entrance of graves.

A boy of sixteen, uniform torn awry like a playground in an earthquake, lay dead next to an old man of fifty-nine, uniform solemn as a church, complete, closed, dead.

Lee Mellon's San Jose Sartorious

WE WERE STUNNED. Lee Mellon led him away. He was
totally shattered. Nobody said anything. We couldn't and
the stars were silent out over the sea. They had to be.

Elizabeth went back to staring into the fire. Elaine sat
down. We waited for Lee Mellon. The stars waited. Elizabeth waited. Elaine waited. I, and even waiting itself waited,
second only to the stars because they had been at it a longer
time.

"HURRAY FOR AMIGO MELLON!" Roy Earle
yelled from the next cabin down.

"SHUT UP, YOU NUT!"

"HURRAY FOR AMIGO MELLON!"

"NUT! NUT!"

Then silence again, the stars out over us . . . Elizabeth
silence. "Coffee?" Elaine said, trying to make reality out of
what we had to deal with. It made me think of a French
cook trying to work with a two-headed dragon onion.

"That would be good," I said, trying to help out a little

for I wanted reality to be there. What we had wasn't worth it. Reality would be better.

Elaine made some coffee. It didn't help at all.

I had a vision of Lee Mellon as the world's only Confederate psychiatrist: Zurich-trained, battleflag-draped, Maryland!-My-Maryland! psychiatrist into Big Sur, into dreams, and this reality into here.

Elizabeth was staring into the fire, and Elaine's coffee had become a nervous trait. She fidgeted with it.

"YOU NUT!" Amigo Mellon's voice cut through the darkness. Yes, psychiatry in action, another mind being led to the path of light by our gallant laurel-crowned, laurel-gathered psychiatrist.

"He seems to be having trouble," Elizabeth said.

The stars didn't say anything. They waited. My cup of coffee changed into an albino polar bear: I mean, cold and black. I threw it into the pond.

Then Lee Mellon appeared. He looked tired. He had the whiskey with him, a bottle in each hand. He offered us all a drink, spreading the whiskey about like martial music. "You might as well leave him with a loaded gun," Lee Mellon said. "The guy's out of it. The only way you can treat him is like a nut. He responds to it because he is a nut."

"He's pretty far out," I said.

"Yes," the women said.

The whiskey went well. I wish I could have offered the stars a drink. Looking down upon mortals, they probably need a drink from time to time, certainly on a night like this. We got drunk.

"Who is he?" I said.

"He came down here six months ago," Lee Mellon said. "He had the same story. Stayed three days. Crazy as a rattlesnake in dog days, a real dingo. He took me up to his place in San Jose. On the way we honky-tonked at Nepenthe for a couple of days. He spent $2,000 and we went up to his place in San Jose.

"His family shit when they saw me. They're just like he described them. Bad news.

"He was going to give me a truck he had in the garage. His layout was really something: three stories high, lots of lawns and flowers around. A jap gardener. You know, up in those fancy hills back of San Jose where the big money subdivides.

"I stayed with him for a month. God, did that cunt family of his have no use for me. And all I wanted was the fucking truck.

"I stayed around his place drinking that good wine he bought by the case, and listening to records on his hi-fi. He took me around to all the fancy San Jose eats. Wined and dined me, he did. He didn't come on with me at all, didn't put the make on me.

"I must have drunk ten cases of the good stuff. I bugged the shit out of his family. The hi-fi had about a hundred speakers. I turned the hi-fi up so loud that I reduced that house to tears. And all I wanted was the God-damn fucking truck.

"Roy put a couple thousand dollars worth of fancy camping equipment and wine and canned lobster and shit in the truck. He gave me everything but the fucking keys.

"I used to go out to the garage all the time and look at the truck. God, it sure looked purty. The guy was completely out of his mind. Just nutty. Almost as bad as he is now. The only way you can treat him is just like a nut, tell him to shut up, sit down, when to pee, etc.

"It really bugged the daughter when I yelled, 'SHUT UP, YOU NUT!' to her father. One morning I was lying in a puddle of wine when suddenly I was awakened by the wife.

And she said, 'It's time to leave now. I've already called the police. You've got about sixty seconds to be on your way, you sponge.'

"I took a quick look around for Roy. He was of course gone. I think they had him under observation, so I had to light out: no truck, nothing.

"I was so drunkied up that I even forgot my shoes. I arrived back here with no shoes. Hard as hell hitch-hiking, too. Finally got a ride on the back of a fertilizer truck, sitting on the shit.

"I haven't heard from him since. Thought they had him locked up. He's in a lockup way, but he really is a big shot. Still smart, too.

"While I was down there at the other cabin he slipped away and buried that briefcase full of money some place. He came back covered all over with dirt, looked like he was waylayed and raped by a gravedigger."

❦

WHERE's AUGUSTUS MELLON? on the front page of the Wilderness Bugle. *Turn to page 17 for Robert E. Lee. Turn to page 100 for an interesting story about alligators.*

The Camp-fires of Big Sur

I see before me now a traveling army halting,
Below a fertile valley spread, with barns and the
orchards of summer,
Behind, the terraced sides of a mountain, abrupt,
in places rising high,
Broken, with rocks, with clinging cedars, with tall
shapes dingily seen,
The numerous camp-fires scatter'd near and far,
some away up on the mountain;
The shadowy forms of men and horses, looming,
large-sized, flickering,
And over all the sky—the sky! far, far out of
reach, studded, breaking out, the eternal stars.

—WHITMAN

WE KILLED THE WHISKEY in that hour before dawn. It lay
like the prophecy of a battle at our feet. The stars did late
things in the sky and were fastened by picture wire above
our future. Then we saw a fire just a ways down the coast,

perhaps three or four hundred yards. The fire loomed up and grew in momentum and speed and importance.

Lee Mellon took out running and I was running after him, stumbling. We got there just in time for the fire was only a moment away from being out of control.

While we were putting out the fire, beating and whacking and clawing at the flames with dirt and branches, throwing fire on fire to put out fire, Roy Earle was saying, "Ha-ha fire."

I thought Lee Mellon was going to slug him, but all Lee Mellon did was sit him down and tell him to cover his eyes with his hands, and he did so, but he kept saying, "Ha-ha fire." And then there wasn't any fire.

"I hope they didn't see that down at the lighthouse," Lee Mellon said. "It's twenty-five miles away, but they see real good, and I don't want them to come up here and poke around. It wouldn't make sense."

We were both smoky and sweating and blackened and inflamed with exhaustion. We didn't look very good, like an advanced case of Smokey Bear leukemia.

Roy Earle sat there cool as a cucumber with his hands over his eyes: See no evil, hear no evil, speak no evil, except for ha-ha fire, and above all, suddenly, the great transcendental fire department of American history, Walt Whitman, fire chief, with the stars like fire engines hanging in the air and streams of light coming from their hoses.

❦

Private Augustus Mellon thirty-seven-year-old former slave trader in residence at a famous Southern university ran for his life among the casual but chess-like deaths in the Wilderness. Fear gripped every stitch of his clothing and would have gripped his boots if he'd had a pair.

He ran barefooted through a spring with a shattered branch lying in it, and he saw a horse smoldering in the brush, and a crow covered with spider webs, and two dead soldiers lying next to each other, and he could almost hear his own name, Augustus Mellon, searching for himself.

The Discovery of Laurel

WE ALL WENT TO BED AFTER THAT. Elaine and I to the
glass house. There were some quail at the edge of the garden
and they flew away back up the mountain.

Lee Mellon did something with Roy Earle. I don't
know what he did, but he said that Roy Earle wouldn't
start any more fires while they got some sleep: the Confederate general and his lady.

"I'm very tired," Elaine said as we lay down.

"You know something?" I said.

"No, what?"

"The next time you hear a chopping sound, do me a
favor and forget about it."

"All right," and we cradled together. It grew cloudy
again and we were able to sleep without the hot sun coming
in through the window.

We woke up in the middle of the afternoon. "I want
to be layed," Elaine said.

All right. I layed her but my mind was elsewhere. I don't know where it was at.

When we got down to the cabin Elizabeth was there. She looked beautiful. "Good morning," she said.

"Hi, and good morning," we said.

"Where's Lee?" I said.

"He's gone to get Roy."

"Where's Roy at?"

"I don't know. Lee put him some place."

"I wonder where he put him?" Elaine said.

"I don't know but Lee said he wouldn't start any more fires. Roy had obviously been there before because he said, 'I don't want to go.' But Lee told him it wouldn't be as bad this time as it was before. Lee said he could have a blanket. Does this make any sense?" Elizabeth said.

"I wonder where that is?" I said. "There aren't too many places you can put somebody down here."

"I don't know," she said. "But here they come."

Lee Mellon and Roy Earle were talking as they came up the path from the lower cabin.

"You were right, Amigo Mellon," Roy Earle said. "It wasn't as bad this time as it was before. That blanket really helped out."

"I told you so, didn't I?" Lee Mellon said.

"Yeah, but I didn't believe it."

"You've got to have more faith," Lee Mellon said.

"It's pretty hard to have faith when everybody is trying to lock you up," Roy Earle said.

Then they were with us.

"Good morning," Roy Earle said cheerfully. He was acting as if his muscles were a little cramped, but he seemed to be in a lot better mental shape.

"Howdy," Lee Mellon said. He went over and kissed

Elizabeth on the mouth. They put their arms around each other.

I looked down at the alligators in the pond. 75 per cent of their eyes were staring back at me.

We had breakfast.

Roy Earle ate a great big breakfast along with us and then he began to go insane again. Food seemed to abet his madness.

"Nobody's going to find my money," Roy Earle said. "I buried it."

"Fuck your money," somebody said: me.

Roy began rooting around the rocks in the fireplace and he found something stuffed behind one of the rocks. It was wrapped in plastic.

Roy unwrapped it, looked at it very carefully, smelled it and then said, "This looks like marijuana."

Lee Mellon walked over. "Let me look at that." He took a look at it. "It's oregano," he told Roy Earle.

"Looks like marijuana to me."

"It's oregano."

"I'll bet you a $1,000 it's dope," Roy Earle said.

"No, it's oregano. Very good in spaghetti," Lee Mellon said. "I'll put it in the kitchen. The next time we make spaghetti we can use it."

Lee Mellon went and put the dope in the kitchen. Roy Earle shrugged his shoulders. The rest of the day passed quietly. Elizabeth looked beautiful. Elaine was nervous. Roy Earle got deeply involved in watching the alligators.

He looked at them and smiled and was quietly amused for the rest of the day until about sundown. SUDDENLY he stared at the pond and said in a voice filled with earthquakes, pestilence and apocalypse, "MY GOD, THEY ARE ALLIGATORS!"

Lee Mellon led him away. He was totally shattered.

"They are alligators. They are alligators. They are alligators," he kept saying over and over again until we could not hear his voice any more.

Lee Mellon took him and put him away where he kept him. I don't know where that could have been. I don't even want to think about it: a Confederate flag over Zurich.

❧

He saw some Union soldiers coming through a thicket. He dove forward onto the ground and pretended that he was dead, though it would not have made any difference if he had been dead and pretended to be alive. The Union soldiers were so scared that they did not see him. None of them had guns, anyway. They had thrown their guns away and were looking for a Confederate to surrender to. Of course Augustus Mellon did not know this, lying there as he was, eyes pretending to be closed forever, breath silenced for all time.

Lee Mellon, Roll Away! You Rolling River

LEE MELLON CAME BACK without Roy Earle. "He's cosy as a bug in a rug."

"Where are you putting him?" I said.

"Don't worry about it. He's OK and has a lovely view of the ocean. After all he's a nut. We can't let him run around and turn Big Sur into a torch. He's OK. Don't worry."

"Analytical psychology à la Jung, huh?" I said.

"Don't be so funny," Lee Mellon said. "He's OK. I'm taking good care of him."

"All right," I said. "You're in residence here."

"Then do I have your permission to go and get the dope?" Lee Mellon said. "I don't know about you but I feel like turning on. Getting a little dopey. OK?"

"Yeah, that sounds OK."

Lee Mellon went into the kitchen and got the dope out of where we kept the spices.

"That's really marijuana that Roy found there in the fireplace?" Elaine whispered to me.

"Yeah," I said.

"Lee Mellon's pretty fast, isn't he?"

"Yeah, I guess he is. Have you ever turned on?"

"No," she said.

"Ah, dope," Lee Mellon said, coming out of the kitchen, carrying the little plastic package in his hand.

"Ah, dreaded narcotics. The evil root. The bad-bad," he said. "I was church people until I discovered this shit. Let's turn on."

"I've never turned on before," Elaine said. "What's it like?"

"Hurry! Hurry!" Lee Mellon said, coming on like a carnival barker. "Dope tours! Dope tours! Get your fresh dope tours! Read all about it! World-renowned eighty-nine-year-old philosopher arrested in jazz musician dope den! Said he thought it was tuna fish! Read all about it! Tangier! Tangier! Albania!"

Elaine was breaking up. Elizabeth was smiling. I was casually memorizing everything and Lee Mellon got a piece of newspaper and put the dope on it, and began to manicure it: to separate the stems and seeds and work the dope up until it was delicate in nature.

"Ah, dope," Lee Mellon kept repeating over and over again. "It's dope. It's dope. Mamma warned me against it. My minister said it would rot the bones in my brain cells. My papa put me over his knee and said, 'Stop turning the barnyard stock on, son. One of the cows laid an egg this morning and one of the rabbits tried to put a saddle on.' Ah, dope. It's dope."

I had never turned on with Lee Mellon before and it looked as if it would be different. The young dope fiend seemed to know what he was up to.

He rolled a surgical joint, lit it up and gave it to his young Confederate lady who inhaled deeply and passed it on to Elaine. She didn't know quite what to do with it. "Breathe it into your lungs," I said. "And hold it down as long as you can."

"All right," she said.

She did what I told her. Good girl and passed the joint to me. I stoked my lungs with the dope smoke and passed it back to Lee Mellon, and it went around and around and around and around and around until we were there: higher than kites.

Lee Mellon started laughing after about the fifth joint and he continued laughing and he didn't say anything.

"This is pretty good," Elaine said. "But I certainly don't feel any different. Not like a revolution." All the time she said this to me, she was just staring at the fire.

Elizabeth acted like an infinite swan. I mean, that quality advanced beyond the limits of her body and hovered there in the room. "I feel good," she said.

Lee Mellon was just laughing away like hell, then he took all the roach-ends of the dreaded dope sticks and he began to break them down and he ate each piece of charred paper very carefully until they were gone, and then like shuffling a deck of cards he took the little survivors of those dope sticks and rolled them all together into a B-17 bomber, and he lit that one up, like antiaircraft fire over Berlin and sent everybody higher.

Elaine took up permanently staring at the fire. Elizabeth played with her hair while she watched Lee Mellon, who was still laughing away like hell.

He did not seem to have the power of speech any more, so I began pacing back and forth and saying things like, "Hummm, hummm, you seem to have lost the power of speech," and Lee Mellon would laugh even harder than ever.

"Can't talk, huh?"

Lee Mellon shook his head no.

"Can you hear?"

Lee Mellon held up two fingers.

"Good," I said. "The power of speech is obviously gone, but the man can still hear. That's good."

Lee Mellon flashed the two fingers like bombs falling on a city.

"Good. Good. Communication," I said. "That good old yes or no. Contact with the land of the living. You may not be able to speak, to carry on a healthy conversation about politics, but you can flash those two fingers yes and shake that head no. Let's try that again. Flash those fingers for yes, and shake that head for no."

He did it laughing like seven hyenas turned inside out and covered with chicken feathers.

"Yes. Yes, that looks good. After careful examination I say this man is under the influence of narcotics."

Lee Mellon flashed two fingers like Winston Churchill's V for victory.

"Yes, yes, this man reminds me of David Copperfield and those sordid adventures of Mr. Dick and his erotic, neurotic, bubonic kites.

"This man is obviously a fly-by-nighter. Probably never pays his rent, steals goofy shoes, paints the town, has a pair of stuffed seal flippers in his suitcase.

"Yes, this man is definitely under the influence of narcotics. Probably has a Thomas De Quincey costume in his suitcase, along with those stuffed seal flippers."

Lee Mellon beat his hands on the floor like a seal and began making seal sounds. To think that less than an hour before he had been taking care of Roy Earle, and now he needed a keeper himself.

Elizabeth was very amused by the whole scene but she didn't say anything except, "Lee's pretty high."

Elaine was hung up on the fire. She didn't take her eyes off the fire. It was as if for the first time in her life she was seeing fire. It was the fire for her.

"Come off it, Mellon," I said. "Jack London threw that plot away as being too corny. Let's have something a little more original."

Lee Mellon continued to beat his hands on the floor like a seal. Obviously he thought the plot was pretty good. Then I got hung up on Elizabeth's hair. It almost began to move in the light. I was pretty far out myself. Like a marriage.

"Dope's all right," Elaine said finally.

Lee Mellon held up two fingers and Elizabeth's hair affirmed it.

❦

After the Union soldiers had fled in panic, Augustus Mellon waited a while before trying out life again. An ant crawled across his hand. The ant moved as if it had a passport to rheumatism. Augustus Mellon rang forth a tintinnabulation of silent curses, being dead was one thing, this was another.

Alligators Minus Pork Chops

AFTER ABOUT TWO HOURS of speechless laughter Lee Mellon
got up and jumped into the pond, and began splashing
alligators out of the dark water.

"GROWL!—opp/opp/opp/opp/opp/opp/opp/opp!"
They appeared and disappeared from his hands like a sloppy
reptile magician performing incoherent alligator tricks.

It took him about fifteen minutes before he caught one
of them. He still could not talk and was laughing all the
time. What a vision!

Then he made a grand Confederate general gesture and
gave the alligator to Elizabeth. She accepted the alligator
with a twinkling solemnness. She returned a kiss for it. It
was all very touching.

Lee Mellon jumped back into the pond, fell is a better
word, I guess. He fell face first into the pond, making a
great splash.

At that precise instant Roy Earle appeared at the edge

of the firelight. He was chained to a log he had dragged from God knows where. It was just horrible.

"What's Amigo Mellon up to?" he said, asking a question about his Confederate psychiatrist who was splashing to the surface, laughter coming out of the water.

"Alligators," I said.

"OH, GOD, NO! NO! NO!" Roy Earle screamed, picking up his log and dragging it away into the night. He had appeared as a specter and disappeared as a specter. There was nothing of us in his coming and going. He was just another specter, chained to a log, fleeing alligators at Big Sur.

Lee Mellon came up out of the water with an alligator fastened by its teeth to the collar of his shirt. Lee Mellon stalked out of the water and back into the room, the alligator hanging like a medallion from his neck.

❦

He came upon a Union captain lying headless among the flowers. With no eyes and no mouth, only flowers on top of the neck, the captain looked like a vase. But this did not distract Augustus Mellon to the point of not seeing the captain's boots. Though the captain's head was absent from this world, his boots were not, and they entertained the barefoot fantasies of Augustus Mellon's feet, and then replaced those fantasies with leather. Private Augustus Mellon left the captain even more deficient, even more unable to cope with reality.

Four Couples: An American Sequence

BEFORE WE WENT TO BED, Elaine got so she really liked dope. I don't know what happened to Elizabeth. She went away with Lee Mellon.

They had the alligators with them. I don't know if Lee Mellon was talking or not. Elizabeth said she could drive.

I looked around for Roy Earle. I didn't want him to get up on the highway, chained to that log. It might attract the wrong attention. I do not know what the right attention would be in a case like that. Everything was very strange.

Roy Earle where are you at? I looked all around, carrying a lantern. I left Elaine sitting in front of the fire. She was really hung up on it. She said there was something of all of us in the fire, and I said yeah, and take care of yourself.

"Roy Earle? Roy-baby? Roy?" I looked all around and everywhere and worked my way down to the last cabin. "Roy, everything is all right. The alligators are gone.

Everything's OK. You can come out now. Johnston Wade?
Mr. Wade? Wade Insurance Company?"

"In here," a rather calm voice said. "The Wade Insurance Company is in here. In the cabin." It did not sound like
Roy Earle, but who else could it be?

I opened the cabin door and brought the lantern in,
and there was Mr. Johnston Wade in a double sleeping bag.
There was somebody else in the bag with him. For a second
I thought that it was Elizabeth, but of course it wasn't,
couldn't be. Why should I think that?

"Who's that with you?" I said.

"That's the log," Johnston Wade said. "I couldn't get
it off, so I put it in the sack with me."

"Are you all right?" I said.

"Yeah," he said. "But I'm crazy most of the time. I
don't know what I'm saying or where I'm at. Where am
I and who are you?"

"At Big Sur. I'm Jesse."

"Hello, Jesse."

I turned the lantern away from him and there was a
moment of silence after that, and then he said out of the
silence, "Just as well. Please go away. I'm very tired."

"Want me to help you get that chain off?" I said.

"No," he said. "It's all right. Actually, I kind of like
it. Reminds me of my wife. Good night."

"Good night," I said. I went back and rescued Elaine
from the fire. I felt like some weird kind of Saint Bernard
dog saving a skier lost in fire.

"It really looks pretty," she said. "You know that we
are all in there."

"Yeah," I said. "Let's go to bed."

We passed through the hole in the kitchen wall, effortlessly.

"Where are Lee and Elizabeth?" she said.

"They've gone some place in her car. They took the alligators with them. I don't know where they've gone."

"I saw them in the fire," she said.

❦

Private Augustus Mellon was up and moving. All around him were the sounds of war as if placed under a magnifying glass. Then in the midst of the great rifle fusilade, he heard the unlimbering of artillery like new muscles being used in the Wilderness.

Awaken to the Drums!

I DON'T KNOW HOW LONG we were asleep—I had a dream about Alfred Hitchcock; he said the Civil War was all right —before Elaine began stirring me again: *Oh, no.*

I would not fight it this time. There was no reason ever to fight it again. I opened my eyes. It was early in the morning, and the morning seemed as strange to me as any of the recent events. It was cloudy and cool and the air seemed dead through the glass.

"What's up?" I said.

"Drums," she said. Her voice was tired. "Hear them?"

Yup, I heard them. Drums. They were drums all right, not as violent as Walt Whitman's drums but they certainly were there.

Perhaps the Confederate army was getting ready to move, a new invasion of the North. Who knows? I didn't. Drums.

"Stay here."

I got dressed and went out to see what was up. I

146

expected to see thousands of ragged Confederate troops going by on Highway 1, with cavalry dashing through and scattering the ranks, and hundreds of wagons filled with ammunition and supplies, and artillery going by, their horses moving at a good pace.

I expected to see a Confederate invasion of Monterey, California, drums and banners going by on Highway 1, but all I saw was Roy Earle, free of his wife, sitting by the hole in the kitchen wall, beating on an overturned washtub.

"What's up?" I said.

"Nothing. I was just trying to drum somebody up," he said rather sanely. "I didn't know where everybody had gone to."

"You did," I said.

❦

Augustus Mellon stumbled into a clearing that had a de luxe muscle building course of artillery at one end of it, and then a furious assault by Texas troops, Hood's old boys against the Union army, and General Robert E. Lee tried to get into it, but those Texans wouldn't allow it, and then the 8th Big Sur Volunteer Heavy Root Eaters arrived and one of them offered Traveller a limpet to eat, and Private Augustus Mellon had a new pair of boots, and then the 8th Big Sur Volunteer Heavy Root Eaters began dancing in a circle, the general and his horse in the middle, while all around them waged the American Civil War, the last good time this country ever had.

Bye Now, Roy Earle,
Take Care of Yourself

ROY EARLE was in fairly good shape when Lee Mellon and Elizabeth drove up in her car. "That's Lee Mellon," Roy Earle said. "That's my amigo, Amigo Mellon."

"Yeah," I said. "Amigo Mellon."

"How did he get loose?" Lee Mellon said, speech having been restored to his mouth like birds to the sky.

"I don't know," I said. "Why did you chain him to a log? Couldn't you have done something else, Dr. Jung?"

"I know how to take care of him," Lee Mellon said.

"Yeah," I said. "Sure, he was running around here last night with a log chained to him. Didn't you see him last night when you were playing Hamlet?"

"Don't worry about it," Lee Mellon said. "Everything's under control now."

"I guess it's all right," I said, feeling a sudden wave

148

of vacancy go over me, like a hotel being abandoned by its guests for an obvious reason.

While breakfast moved along, Roy Earle was strangely quiet and his features calculated themselves and before breakfast was over, he looked and acted again as he did last night when I went down to the cabin and found him asleep with a log, covered by a green sleeping bag, like a man sticking out of a meadow.

When we finished breakfast, he said, "It's time for me to go now. This is Wednesday, isn't it?"

"Yes, it is," Elizabeth said.

"I have to meet a client in Compton," he said. "I guess I'll be going shortly. It's been very nice meeting you people. You must come up and visit me sometime in San Jose."

"Yes," Lee Mellon said.

Mr. Johnston Wade looked perfectly sane, except of course for his clothes and body that were rather disheveled with Big Sur grime.

"Yes, I have an appointment and must be going now."

"Are you all right?" Elaine said.

"Yes, I am, young lady," he said. "I guess my car's up on that road by those trees."

"Do you have your money?" Elaine said, casting an inquisitional glance toward Lee Mellon: notorious for thought and deed.

"I have my briefcase," Mr. Johnston Wade said and went over and lifted up that horrible deer rug that looked like a toupee for Frankenstein. "Here it is," he said. "I got it this morning."

"Good," I said.

Lee Mellon stared at the pond. It was different without frogs or alligators. I was going to ask Lee Mellon where the alligators were, but I figured it would be better to save that question until Mr. Johnston Wade was on his way to his insurance appointment in Compton.

He took the trees off his car and we said good-bye to him. "Do visit me in San Jose," he yelled out the window as he backed the sports car down the road.

"Yes," Lee Mellon said.

Bon voyage, Roy. Have a nice trip. Bye now, Roy Earle, take care of yourself, but I didn't feel very good at all. More rooms were being vacated. The elevator was jammed with suitcases.

Crowned with Laurel and Our
Banners Before Us We Descend!

WE WENT BACK DOWN to the cabin. The sun came out and a nice sweet smell rose like small invisible birds from the sagebrush and circled about us in the air and followed us down, with a great light on the ocean.

"Well, that takes care of Roy Earle," Lee Mellon said. "You must stop at San Jose and visit him sometime, but I'd bring an extra pair of shoes with you and a getaway car. It's a lot of fun while it lasts.

"I recommend the hi-fi wine. Speaking of hi-fi wine: Let's go down to the Pacific and turn on and go with the waves. They're great on dope.

"I like the way they crack like eggs against the Grand Grill of North America. You like that, huh? You're supposed to be literary."

"Ah, fuck it. Where are the alligators?" I said.

"I'd like to turn on," Elaine said.

"Down at Hearstville," Lee Mellon said.

"Hearseville?"

"No, Hearstville. San Simeon."

"Oh, God, what are they doing down there?"

"We threw them in the pond. You know, Citizen-Kane chess. It seemed like the thing to do," Lee Mellon said. "The frogs are gone. They'll never come back.

"They've probably committed themselves to some place like Norwalk. They're all in psycho-fucking-alligator shock. Bad medicine.

"We thought the alligators should live out the rest of their days peacefully in swell digs. In tune with the Greek temples and the good life. Not like social security."

"All right," I said. "Sounds reasonable."

I was really gone. My mind was beginning to take a vacation from my senses. I felt it continuing to go while Lee Mellon got the dope.

Elizabeth was as usual. Somewhere she had gotten a scarlet sash and Lee Mellon tied it around her waist. We started down the steep rocky path to the Pacific. It looked like a Confererate flag tied about her.

We were strung out behind her like fish in a net. Three whales came by, spouting high and clear. I looked from Elizabeth's waist to the whales. I expected Confederate flags to be flying from their spouts.

To a Pomegranate Ending,
Then 186,000 Endings Per Second

THE PACIFIC OCEAN rolled to its inevitable course: our bodies at the edge with Lee Mellon rolling dope. He handed some to Elaine. She really went at it, and then she handed it to me. I gave it to Elizabeth, who was like a Greek dance, forgotten in Modern Times.

We smoked five or six chunks of dope and then the ocean began to come in on us in a different manner: I mean, slow and light itself.

I looked over at Elizabeth. She was sitting on a white rock, the wind lighting the end of her red banner. She stared out at the ocean with her head in her hands. Lee Mellon was lying flat on his back, sprawled flung out on the rough sand.

Elaine stared at the waves that were breaking like ice cube trays out of a monk's tooth or something like that. Who knows? I don't know.

153

I was staring at the three of them, high on their earthly presence and my relationship to the presence. I felt very strange and confused inside.

The last week's activities had been a little too much for me, I think. A little bit too much of life had been thrown at me, and I couldn't put it all together. I stared at Elizabeth.

She was beautiful and seagulls flew over the ocean, fastened by harp strings to the surface, Bach and Mozart broke on the foam. We sat there. Four people poleaxed by dope.

Elizabeth was beautiful and the wind got in her hair and lifted up the hem of her white dress and the Confederate banner was curling in its red hair. Elaine sat there alone.

Then she came over to me and said, "Let's take a walk."

"All right," I said. That was my voice, wasn't it? Yes, it was. We walked down a ways, maybe fifty years, and Elaine suddenly put her arms about me and kissed me very hard on the mouth and she put her hand between my legs.

There was nothing girlish about the gesture. She meant it. My, how she had come along. "I want," she said, like a child.

She put her mouth inside my mouth, but I felt very strange. It had been such a long hard week. I felt things slipping in my mind.

"I'll undress you," Elaine said.

I sat down on a place where there was rough sand and small white pebbles and many flies in the air. The flies kept landing on me and Elaine took off my shoes, and then she took off my pants and she noticed that I didn't have an erection.

"We'll get something down there," she said. "Right away." She took off my shorts. I must have put them on when I woke up, but I didn't remember doing so. It really wasn't very important, but it surprised me. Things like that should not surprise a person.

"Off with your shirt," she said. "Now look at you. You don't have any clothes on." She was very pleased with herself, but she seemed awfully strange to me, almost as if she were somebody else.

I wondered what Elizabeth was doing, and things were slipping in my mind. I slapped at a fly on my leg. The flies came from a lot of kelp that had been thrown up on the beach after the storm. Was it really just a couple days before? Must have been.

"I still have my clothes on," Elaine said, and kicked off her shoes. She was really on an erotic thing. I could only look at it like somebody watches a pinball machine.

She took off her shirt and the ocean blew against her and the surf cracked behind her like white marble castles against glasses of Rhine wine.

She was exploiting the maximum amount of drama out of taking off her clothes. It made me think of *Hamlet,* some kind of weird *Hamlet* where maybe Ophelia would take her clothes off like Elaine was doing.

Her breasts tensed up at the shock of the cold. Her nipples hardened like stones in the mind. The surface of her skin acted cinematographically to the cold.

She was wearing a pair of jeans. Strange, I hadn't noticed that all day. She pulled them down slowly, floated them down her hips like statues coming down a river on rafts.

Why would anyone want to do something like that? I didn't have an erection.

I didn't feel any desire. I looked between my legs and there were small white pebbles, just a little bit larger than sand. I looked at them and a fly landed on my shoulder. I shrugged him off.

Elaine stopped her jeans right in the middle of her vagina. It looked strange to me. I didn't know what to think about it.

I couldn't get an erection. Maybe it would come later. Strange, maybe she could help me out with it. I didn't feel very good.

Of course she would help me out. This was just a little thing.

She stepped out of her jeans and moved toward me like a rhythm. She got down on her knees in front of me. I looked at the white rocks under my penis and the shadow of her head came over the top of them and put them entirely in the shade.

But nothing worked and the flies crawled on us. I got on top of her, hoping that might do it, but the flies crawled all over us and nothing happened. Nothing happened for a long time.

Who said we were the dominant creature on this shit pile? The flies were teaching an advanced seminar in philosophy as they crawled up the crack of my ass.

After a while it was apparent to everybody: Elaine the sky, Elaine the Pacific Ocean, Elaine the sand, Elaine the sun, Elaine, Elaine, Elaine . . .

"It's all right," she said. "It's all right." That was really a very nice sound. There should be a bird that does that: that sings when you are impotent.

"You poor dear," she said. "You're so high you can't make it." She kissed me sweetly upon the mouth. "That's what your trouble is, you're a dope fiend."

We lay there for a while, just holding on to each other. Somehow I had forgotten about how Elaine could be. I had been distracted, but I guess that's nothing unusual for me. "How do you feel? Don't feel bad," she said.

* * *

A seagull flew over us. We got dressed and went back to Lee Mellon and Elizabeth. They were looking for something and Roy Earle was there looking for something with them. It was good that I was not surprised.

"Lose something?" Elaine said.

"Yeah," Roy Earle said. "Forgot my pomegranate. I remember putting it down here somewhere. Right around here."

"It must be some place," Elizabeth said.

Lee Mellon was looking under a rock.

"I spent a dime for that pomegranate," Roy Earle said. "It means a lot to me. I bought it in Watsonville."

"We'll look over here," I said. There was nothing else to do, for after all this was the destiny of our lives. A long time ago this was our future, looking now for a lost pomegranate at Big Sur.

"What are you going to do with that pomegranate?" Lee Mellon said.

"It's going to Los Angeles with me. Big Business."

Elizabeth looked up and smiled. Lee Mellon put the rock back in place so you couldn't tell it had been moved.

A SECOND ENDING

A seagull flew over us. We got dressed and went back to Lee Mellon and Elizabeth. They were just as we had left them.

Elizabeth was sitting on a white rock and Lee Mellon

was lying flat on his back, sprawled flung out on the rough sand.

Nothing had changed. They were exactly the same.

They looked like photographs in an old album. They didn't say anything and we sat down beside them. That's where you've seen us before.

A THIRD ENDING

A seagull flew over us, its voice running with the light, its voice passing historically through songs of gentle color. We closed our eyes and the bird's shadow was in our ears.

A FOURTH ENDING

A seagull flew over us. We got dressed and went back to Lee Mellon and Elizabeth. Roy Earle was there with them. It was good that I was not surprised.

They were all standing together in the surf and throwing Roy Earle's money into the Pacific Ocean. Hundred dollar bills scattered off their hands.

"What are you doing?" I said.

Lee Mellon turned toward me, hundred dollar bills still falling off his hands, floating down onto the water.

"Roy Earle doesn't want his money any more, and we're helping him throw it in the ocean."

"We don't want it either," Elizabeth said.

"All this money ever did was bring me here," Roy Earle volunteered as the hundred dollar bills fluttered like birds onto the sea.

"You can have it," he said, addressing the waves. "Take it on home with you."

And they did.

A FIFTH ENDING

A seagull flew over us. I reached up and ran my hand along his beautiful soft white feathers, feeling the arch and rhythm of his flight. He slipped off my fingers away into the sky.

186,000 ENDINGS PER SECOND

Then there are more and more endings: the sixth, the 53rd, the 131st, the 9,435th ending, endings going faster and faster, more and more endings, faster and faster until this book is having 186,000 endings per second.

RICHARD BRAUTIGAN

DREAMING OF BABYLON

A Private Eye Novel 1942

*This one is for Helen Brann
with love from Richard.*

I guess one of the reasons
that I've never been
a very good private detective
is that I spend too much time
dreaming of Babylon.

What Happened to C. Card in Early 1942:

Good News,
Bad News

January 2, 1942 had some good news and some
bad news.

First, the good news: I found out that I was 4F and wasn't
going off to World War II to be a soldier boy. I didn't feel
unpatriotic at all because I had fought my World War II five
years before in Spain and had a couple of bullet holes in my
ass to prove it.

I'll never figure out why I got shot in the ass. Anyway, it
made a lousy war story. People don't look up to you as a hero
when you tell them you were shot in the ass. They don't take
you seriously but that wasn't my problem any more at all.
The war that was starting for the rest of America was over
for me.

Now for the bad news: I didn't have any bullets for my gun. I had just gotten a case that I needed my gun for but I was fresh out of bullets. The client that I was going to meet later on in the day for the first time wanted me to show up with a gun and I knew that an empty gun was not what they had in mind.

What was I going to do? I didn't have a cent to my name and my credit in San Francisco wasn't worth two bits. I had to give up my office in September, though it only cost eight bucks a month, and now I was just working out of the pay telephone in the front hall of the cheap apartment building I was living in on Nob Hill where I was two months behind in my rent. I couldn't even come up with thirty bucks a month.

My landlady was a bigger threat to me than the Japanese. Everybody was waiting for the Japanese to show up in San Francisco and start taking cable cars up and down the hills, but believe me I would have taken on a division of them to get my landlady off my back.

"Where in the hell is my rent, you deadbeat!" she'd yell at me from the top of the stairs where her apartment was. She was always wearing a loose bathrobe that covered up a body that would have won first prize in a beauty contest for cement blocks.

"The country's at war and you don't even pay your God-damn rent!"

She had a voice that made Pearl Harbor seem like a lullaby.

"Tomorrow," I'd lie to her.

"Tomorrow your ass!" she'd yell back.

She was about sixty and had been married five times and

widowed five times: the lucky sons-of-bitches. That's how she'd come to own the apartment building. One of them left it to her. God had done him a favor when He stalled his car one rainy night on some railroad tracks just outside of Merced. He had been a travelling salesman: brushes. After the train hit his car they couldn't tell the difference between him and his brushes. I think they buried him with some of his brushes in the coffin, believing they were part of him.

In those ancient long-ago days when I paid my rent, she was very friendly to me and used to invite me into her apartment for coffee and doughnuts. She loved to talk about her dead husbands, especially one of them who'd been a plumber. She liked to talk about how good he was at fixing hot water heaters. Her other four husbands were always out of focus when she talked about them. It was as if the marriages had taken place in murky aquariums. Even her husband who'd been hit by the train didn't merit much comment from her, but she couldn't say enough about the guy who could fix the hot water heaters. I think he was pretty good at fixing her hot water heater, too.

The coffee she served was always very weak and the doughnuts slightly stale because she bought day-old stuff at a bakery a few blocks away on California Street.

I'd have coffee with her sometimes because I didn't have much to do, anyway. Things were just as slow then as they are now except for the case I just got but I had saved up a little money that I'd gotten from being in an automobile accident and settling out of court, so I could still pay my rent, though I'd given up my office a few months before.

In April 1941 I had to let my secretary go. I hated to do that. I spent the five months she worked for me trying to

3

get her in the sack. She was friendly but I barely got to first base with her. We did some kissing at the office but that was about it.

After I had to let her go, she told me to buzz off.

I called her up one night and her parting shot at me over the telephone went something like this: "... and besides not being a good kisser, you're a lousy detective. You should try another line of work. Bellboy would suit you perfectly."

CLICK

Oh, well . . .

She had a lard ass, anyway. The only reason I hired her was because she would work for the lowest wages this side of Chinatown.

I sold my car in July.

Anyway, here I was with no bullets for my gun and no money to get any and no credit and nothing left to pawn. I was sitting in my cheap little apartment on Leavenworth Street in San Francisco thinking this over when suddenly hunger started working my stomach over like Joe Louis. Three good right hooks to my gut and I was on my way over to the refrigerator.

That was a big mistake.

I looked inside and then hurriedly closed the door when the jungle foliage inside tried to escape. I don't know how people can live the way I do. My apartment is so dirty that recently I replaced all the seventy-five-watt bulbs with twenty-five-watters, so I wouldn't have to see it. It was a luxury but I had to do it. Fortunately, the apartment didn't have any windows or I might have really been in trouble.

My apartment was so dim that it looked like the shadow of an apartment. I wonder if I always lived like this. I mean,

I had to have had a mother, somebody to tell me to clean up, take care of myself, change my socks. I did, too, but I guess I was kind of slow when I was a kid and didn't catch on. There had to be a reason.

I stood there beside the refrigerator wondering what to do next when I got a great idea. What did I have to lose? I didn't have any money for bullets and I was hungry. I needed something to eat.

I went upstairs to my landlady's apartment.

I rang the doorbell.

This would be the last thing in the world that she would expect because I'd spent over a month now trying to elude her like an eel but always being caught in a net of curses.

When she answered the door she couldn't believe that I was standing there. She looked as if her doorknob had been electrified. She was actually speechless. I took full advantage of it.

"Eureka!" I yelled into her face. "I can pay the rent! I can buy the building! How much do you want for it? Twenty thousand cash! My ship has come in! Oil! Oil!"

She was so confused that she beckoned me to come into her apartment and pointed out a chair for me to sit down in. She still hadn't said a word. I was really cooking. I could hardly believe myself.

I went into the apartment.

"Oil! Oil!" I continued yelling, and then I started making motions like oil gushing from the ground. I turned into an oil well right in front of her eyes.

I sat down.

She sat down opposite me.

Her mouth was still glued shut.

"My uncle discovered oil in Rhode Island!" I yelled across at her. "I own half of it. I'm rich. Twenty thousand cash for this pile of shit you call an apartment building! Twenty-five thousand!" I yelled. "I want to marry you and raise a whole family of little apartment buildings! I want our wedding certificate printed on a No VACANCY sign!"

It worked.

She believed me.

Five minutes later I had a cup of very weak coffee in my hand and I was munching on a stale doughnut and she was telling me how happy she was for me. I told her that I would buy the building from her next week when the first million dollars' worth of oil royalties arrived.

When I left her apartment with hunger abated and another week's housing assured, she shook my hand and said, "You're a good boy. Oil in Rhode Island."

"That's right," I said. "Near Hartford."

I was going to ask her for five dollars so that I could buy some bullets for my gun but I figured I'd better let well enough alone.

Ha-ha.

Get the joke?

Babylon

Uh-oh, I started dreaming of Babylon as I walked back down the stairs to my apartment. It was very important that I not dream of Babylon just as I was starting to get some things worked out. If I got started on Babylon whole hours would pass without my knowing it.

I could sit down in my apartment and suddenly it would be midnight and I would have lost the edge on getting my life back together again whose immediate need was some bullets for my gun.

The last thing in the world that I needed right now was to start dreaming of Babylon.

I had to hold Babylon back for a while, long enough for me to get some bullets. I made an heroic effort as I walked down the stairs of the musty, seedy, tomb-like smelling apartment building to keep Babylon at arm's reach.

It was touch and go there for a few seconds and then Babylon floated back into the shadows, away from me.

I felt a little sad.

I didn't want Babylon to go.

Oklahoma

I went into my apartment and got my gun. *I should clean this thing someday,* I thought, as I put it into my coat pocket. Also, I should probably get a shoulder holster. That would be an authentic touch that might help me get more cases.

When I left my apartment to go out into San Francisco to hustle some bullets, my landlady was standing at the top of the stairs, waiting for me.

Oh, God, I thought. *She's come to her senses.* I waited for a huge tirade of curses to bombard my ears and bring my life back to hell on earth again, but it didn't happen. She just stood there watching me as I walked out of the building with a frozen smile on my face.

Just as I was opening the front door, she spoke. Her voice was almost child-like. "Why not oil wells in Oklahoma?" she said. "There's a lot of oil in Oklahoma."

"Too close to Texas," I said. "Salt water flows under the highway."

That finished her off.

There was no reply.

She looked like Alice in Wonderland.

Cactus Fog

There was no place that I was going to get any money to buy bullets, so I decided to go where there are always bullets: a police station.

I walked down to the Hall of Justice on Kearny Street to see a detective that I knew down there and once had been very good friends with to see if I could borrow some bullets from him.

Maybe he would loan me six until I met my client and got an advance. I was supposed to meet them in front of a radio station down on Powell Street. It was now 2 P.M. I had four hours to get some bullets. I hadn't the slightest idea who my client was or what they wanted done except that I was to meet them in front of the radio station at six and then they would tell me what they wanted done and I'd try to get an advance from them.

Then I'd give my landlady a few bucks and tell her that an armored car bringing me the million dollars had gotten lost in a cactus fog near Phoenix, Arizona, but she shouldn't worry because the fog was guaranteed to lift any day now and then the money would be on its way.

If she asked me what a cactus fog was, I'd tell her it was the worst kind of fog because it had sharp spines on it. It made moving around in it a very dangerous proposition. It was best to stay where you were at and just wait until it went away.

The million dollars is waiting for the fog to pass.

My Girlfriend

It was a fast hike down to the Hall of Justice. I'd gotten used to walking in San Francisco and could move around at a good clip.

I started 1941 off with a car and now a year later, here I was totally relying on my feet. Life has its ups and downs. The only place my life could go now was up. The only thing lower than me was a dead man.

It was a cold windy day in San Francisco but I enjoyed the walk down Nob Hill to the Hall of Justice.

I started to think about Babylon as I neared Chinatown but was able to change the marquee in my mind just in time. I saw some Chinese kids playing in the street. I tried to figure out what kind of game they were playing. By concentrating on the kids, I was able to avoid Babylon rolling toward me like a freight train.

Whenever I was trying to get something done and Babylon started coming upon me I'd try to focus on anything that could keep it away. It was always very hard because I really like to dream of Babylon and I have a beautiful girlfriend there. This is a hard thing to admit but I like her better than real girls. I've always wanted to meet a girl that interested me as much as my friend in Babylon.

I don't know.

Maybe someday.

Maybe never.

Sergeant Rink

After the Chinese kids' game I thought about my detective friend to keep Babylon away. He was a sergeant and his name was Rink. He was a very tough cop. I think he held the world's record for being tough. He had perfected a slap across the face that left an exact hand print on it like a temporary brand. That slap was just a friendly greeting from Sergeant Rink compared to how things got later on if you weren't very, very cooperative.

I met Rink when we were both trying out for the force back in '36. I wanted to be a cop. We were very good friends back then. We might be on the force together right now, partners solving murders, if only I had managed to pass the final examination. My score was close, though. I was just five points away from being a cop.

Dreaming of Babylon got the best of me. I would have been a good cop, too. If only I had been able to stop dreaming of Babylon. Babylon has been such a delight to me and at the same time such a curse.

I didn't answer the last twenty questions of the test. That's why I failed. I just sat there dreaming of Babylon while everybody else answered the questions and became policemen.

The Hall of Justice

I never really cared about the way the Hall of
Justice looks. It's a huge, tomb-like gloomy-looking building
and inside it always smells like rotten marble.
I don't know.
Maybe it's just me.
Probably.
One interesting thing, though, is: I've been in the Hall
of Justice a couple of hundred times at least and I never
think about Babylon when I'm there, so it does serve some
purpose for me.
I took the elevator up to the fourth floor and found my
detective friend sitting at his desk in the homicide department. My friend resembles exactly what he is: a very tough

cop who's interested in solving murder cases. The only thing he likes better than a nice juicy homicide is a sirloin steak smothered with onions. He was in his early thirties and built like a Dodge pickup.

The first thing I noticed was his shoulder holster with a nice-looking .38 police special resting comfortably in it. I was particularly attracted to the bullets in the gun. I would have liked all six of them but settled for three.

Sergeant Rink was very carefully examining a letter opener.

He looked up.

"A sight for sore eyes," he said.

"What do you need a letter opener for?" I said, slipping into the genre. "You know that reading isn't one of your gifts."

"Still selling dirty pictures?" he said, smiling. "Tijuana valentines? The ones for dog lovers?"

"No," I said. "Too many cops kept asking for samples. They cleaned me out."

The private detective business was very slow one time when the Worlds Fair was going on over at Treasure Island in '40, so I supplemented my income by selling a few "art" photographs to the tourists.

Sergeant Rink always liked to kid me about them.

I've done a lot of things in my life that I haven't been proud of, but the worst thing I ever did was getting as poor as I was now.

"This is a murder weapon," Rink said, dropping the letter opener on his desk. "It was found in a prostitute's back early this morning. No clues. Only her body in a doorway and this."

"The murderer was confused," I said. "Somebody should have taken them to a stationery store and pointed out the difference between an envelope and a whore."

"Oh, boy," Rink said, shaking his head.

He picked up the letter opener again.

He turned it very slowly over in his hand. Watching him play with a murder weapon wasn't getting me any closer to some bullets for my gun.

"What do you want?" he said, staring at the letter opener, not bothering to look up at me. "You know the last time I loaned you a buck I said that was it, so what do you want? What can I do for you except give you directions to the Golden Gate Bridge and a few basics on how to jump? When are you going to give up this silly notion of you being a private detective and get a paying job and out of my hair? There's a war going on. They need everybody. There must be something you can do."

"I need your help," I said.

"Ah, shit," he said, finally looking up. He put the letter opener down and reached into his pocket and took out a handful of change. He very carefully selected two quarters, two dimes and a nickel. He put them down on the desk and then pushed them toward me.

"That's it," he said. "Last year you were worth five bucks, then you dropped to one. Now you're a seventy-five-center. Get a job. For Christ's sake. There must be something you can do. I know one thing for sure: detective work isn't it. Not many people want to hire a detective who's only wearing one sock. You could probably count them on your hand."

I was hoping that Rink wouldn't notice that, but of course

he had. I was thinking about Babylon in the morning when I got dressed and didn't notice that I was only wearing one sock until I walked into the Hall of Justice.

I was going to tell Rink that I didn't need the seventy-five cents, which of course I did, but what I really wanted was some bullets for my gun.

I tried to size up the situation.

I had limited options.

I could take the seventy-five cents and be ahead of the game or I could say: No, I don't want the money. What I want is some bullets for my gun.

If I took the seventy-five cents and then asked him for the bullets, he might really blow his stack. I had to be very careful because as I said earlier: He was one of my friends. You can imagine what the people who didn't like me were like.

I looked at the seventy-five cents on his desk.

Then I remembered a minor criminal I knew who lived in North Beach. As I remembered he had a gun once. Maybe he still had it and I could get some bullets for my gun from him.

I picked up the seventy-five cents.

"Thank you," I said.

Rink sighed.

"Get your ass out of here," he said. "The next time I see you I want to be looking at an employed man who's eager to repay eighty-three dollars and seventy-five cents to his old friend Rink. If I see anything that resembles you the way you are now, I'll vag you and make sure you get thirty days. Pull yourself together and get the fuck out of here."

I left him playing with the letter opener.

Maybe it would give him an idea for a lead that would solve the case of the murdered prostitute.

Also, maybe, he could take it and shove it up his ass.

Adolf Hitler

I left the Hall of Justice and walked up to North Beach to see if I could get some bullets out of the minor criminal I knew who lived on Telegraph Hill.

He lived in an apartment on Green Street.

Just my luck the minor crook wasn't home. His mother answered the door. I had never met her before but I knew it was his mother because he had talked a lot about her. She took one look at me and said, "He's gone straight. Go away. He's a good boy now. Find somebody else to break into places with."

"What?" I said.

"You know what," she said. "He doesn't want to have

anything to do with guys like you. He goes to church now. Six o'clock Mass."

She was a little old Italian lady about sixty. She was wearing a white apron. I think she misunderstood what type of person I was.

"He's gone down to join the Army," she said. "He can, you know. He never got into any real trouble. Just little things. Guys like you made him do it. He's going to fight Adolf Hitler. Show that son-of-a-bitch what's what."

Then she started to close the door.

"Get out of here!" she yelled. "Go join the Army! Make something of yourself! It's not too late! The recruiting office is open right now! They'll take you if you haven't been in the pen!"

"I don't think you know who I am. I'm a private—"

SLAM!

It was an obvious misunderstanding.

Amazing.

She thought I was a crook.

I'd just come there to borrow a few bullets.

Mustard

Still no bullets, and I was getting hungry. The nutrition from the stale doughnut I had cadged from my landlady was rapidly becoming a thing of the past.

I went into a little Italian delicatessen on Columbus Avenue and got a salami and Swiss cheese sandwich on a French roll with lots of mustard.

I like it that way: lots and lots of mustard.

It put a forty-five-cent dent in my seventy-five cents.

I was now a thirty-cent private detective.

The old Italian who made the sandwich for me was very interesting looking. Anyway, I made him look interesting because I started to think about Babylon, and I couldn't afford to if I was going to earn some money from my first client since October 13, 1941.

Jesus, what a dry spell!

That had been a divorce case.

A three-hundred-pound husband wanted the goods on his three-hundred-pound wife. He thought that she was fooling around and she was: with a three-hundred-pound automobile mechanic. Some case. She used to go down to his garage every Wednesday afternoon and he'd fuck her over the hood of a car. I got some terrific photographs. That was before I had to pawn my camera. You should have seen the expression on their faces when I jumped out from behind a Buick and started snapping away. When he pulled out of her she rolled right over onto the floor and made a sound like an elevator falling on an elephant.

"Put a little more mustard on it," I said.

"You sure likea the mustard," the old Italian said. "You shoulda ordera plain mustard sandwich." He laughed when he said that.

"Maybe your next customer won't want any," I said. "He might be a mustard hater. Can't stand the stuff. Would sooner go to China."

"I surea hope so," he said. "I go outa business. No more sandwiches."

The old Italian looked just like Rudolph Valentino if Rudolph Valentino had been an old Italian making sandwiches and complaining about people having too much mustard on their sandwiches.

What's wrong with liking mustard?

I could like six-year-old girls.

Bela Lugosi

I walked back down Columbus Avenue, eating my sandwich and headed toward the morgue. I had remembered another place where I might get some bullets. It was a long shot but everything I did these days was a long shot, starting off when I woke up in the morning. The odds were 50–1 against me taking my morning piss without getting half a bladder on my foot, if you know what I mean.

I had a friend who worked at the morgue. He kept a gun in his desk. I thought it was sort of strange when I first got to know the guy. I mean, what in the hell do you need a gun for in a place filled with dead bodies? The chances are very slim that Bela Lugosi and some of his friends, like Igor, are going to break into the place and make off with some stiffs to bring back to life.

One day I asked my friend about the gun.

He didn't say anything for a few minutes.

He was really thinking about it.

"They brought in this dead ax murderer," he said, finally. "Who'd been shot by the police after beheading all the participants of a card game that he held every Friday night for twenty years in his basement. He was running around in the street waving his ax when the police pumped eight bullets into him. When the police brought him in here, he sure looked dead to me, but it didn't quite work out that way. I was putting him in the cooler when suddenly he sat up and tried to chop my head off with his hand. He still thought he had an ax in it. I hit him over the head with an autopsy pan and that quieted him down. He was really dead by the time the police got here after I called them.

"That caused an embarrassing situation because they didn't believe me. They thought I'd had a drink or two and imagined the whole thing.

" 'No,' I said. 'You guys brought somebody in here who wasn't dead. I mean, this son-of-a-bitch was still kicking.'

"Then your friend Rink who was with them said, 'Peg-leg, let me ask you a question.'

" 'Sure,' I said.

" 'And I want you to answer this question as truthfully as you can. OK?'

" 'OK,' I said. 'Shoot.'

" 'Do you see a lot of bullet holes in this bastard?'

" 'Yeah,' I said.

27

" 'Is he dead now?'

"We were all standing around the body. He had so many bullet holes in him that it was ridiculous.

" 'Yeah,' I said.

" 'Are you sure he's dead?'

" 'Positive,' I said.

" 'Positive?' Rink said.

" 'Positive,' I said.

" 'Then forget about it,' he said.

" 'You don't believe me?' I said.

" 'We believe you,' he said. 'But don't tell anybody else. I wouldn't even tell your wife.'

" 'I'm not married,' I said.

" 'Even a better reason not to.'

"Then they left.

"They all took a good long look at me before they left. I got the message but still that son-of-a-bitch had been alive, so I didn't want to take any more chances with all the dead murderers, bank robbers and maniacs that come in here. You never know when they're not dead, when they're just playacting or unconscious or something and they might suddenly attack you, so I got the gun I keep here in the desk. I'm prepared now. The next time: BANG!"

That's where I'd borrow the bullets I needed.

I'd get them from my friend Peg-leg who works at the morgue and keeps a gun around to shoot dead people.

1934

Suddenly I remembered that earlier in the day I was supposed to make a phone call but I didn't have a nickel then, but now I did, thanks to Sergeant Rink, so I stopped at a telephone booth and made the call.

The person I was supposed to call wasn't home and the telephone didn't return my nickel. I hit it a half-a-dozen times with my fist and called it a son-of-a-bitch. That didn't work either. Then I noticed some mustard on the receiver and I felt a little better.

I'd have to call again later on and my original seventy-five cents was busy wasting away. This could be very funny if it was a laughing matter.

Anyway, I wasn't hungry, any more.

Got to keep looking at the bright side.

Can't let it get to me.

If it really gets to me I start thinking about Babylon and then it only gets worse because I'd sooner think about Babylon than anything else and when I start thinking about Babylon I can't do anything but think about Babylon and my whole life falls to pieces.

Anyway, that's what it's been doing for the last eight years, ever since 1934, which was when I started thinking about Babylon.

The Blonde

When I walked into the morgue just behind
the Hall of Justice on Merchant Street, a young woman was
walking out crying. She was wearing a fur coat. She looked
like a very fancy dame. She had short blonde hair, a long
nose and a mouth that looked so good that my lips started
aching.
I hadn't kissed anyone in a long time. It's hard to find
people to kiss when you haven't got any money in your
pocket and you're as big a fuckup as I am.
I hadn't kissed anybody since the day before Pearl Harbor. That was Mabel. I'll go into my love life later on when
nothing else is happening. I mean, absolutely nothing: zero.
The blonde looked at me as she came down the stairs. She

looked at me as if she knew me but she didn't say anything. She just continued crying.

I looked over my shoulder to see if there was somebody else behind me that she might be looking at, but I was the only person going into the morgue, so it had to be me. That was strange.

I turned around and watched her walk away.

She stopped at the curb and a chauffeur-driven 16-cylinder black Cadillac LaSalle limousine pulled up beside her and she got in. The car seemed to come out of nowhere. It wasn't there and then it was there. She was staring out the window at me as the car drove away.

Her chauffeur was a very large and mean-looking gent. He had a Jack Dempsey–type face and a huge neck. He looked as if he'd get a lot of pleasure out of going ten rounds with your grandmother and making sure she went the whole distance. Afterwards you could take her home in a gallon jar.

As the limousine drove away he turned and gave me a big smile as if we shared a secret: old buddies or something.

I'd never seen him before.

"Eye"

I found my morgue pal Peg-leg back in the
autopsy room staring at the dead breasts of a lady corpse
lying on a stone table, obviously waiting to get her very own
autopsy. You only get one in this world.

He was thoroughly engrossed in staring at her tits.

She was a good-looking woman but she was dead.

"Aren't you a little old for that?" I said.

"Oh, 'Eye,' " Peg-leg said. "Haven't you starved to death
yet? I've been waiting to get your body."

Peg-leg always called me "Eye." That was short for private eye.

"My luck's changing," I said. "I got a client."

"That's funny," Peg-leg said. "I read the paper this morning and I didn't see anything about any inmates escaping from the local asylums. Why did the person choose you? They've got real detectives in San Francisco. They're in the phone book."

I looked at Peg-leg and then at the corpse of the young woman. She had been very beautiful in life. Dead, she looked dead.

"I think if I'd come in here a few minutes from now, you'd be humping your girlfriend there," I said. "You ought to try a live one sometime. You don't catch a cold everytime you fuck them."

Peg-leg smiled and continued admiring the dead broad.

"A perfect body," he said, sighing. "The only flaw is a five-inch-deep hole in her back. Somebody stuck a letter opener in her. A real shame."

"She was stabbed with a letter opener?" I asked. That rang a bell but I couldn't place it. Somehow it was familiar.

"Yeah, she was a lady of the night. They found her in a doorway. What a waste of talent."

"Have you ever gone to bed with a living woman?" I said. "What would your mother think if she knew you were doing things like this?"

"My mother doesn't think. She's still living with my father. What do you want, 'Eye?' You know your credit isn't any good but if you want a place to sleep, there's an empty bunk downstairs in cold storage, waiting for you, or I can tuck you in up here." He motioned his head toward an eerie-looking refrigerator built into the wall that had enough space for four dead bodies.

Most of the bodies were kept downstairs in "cold storage," but they kept a few special ones in the autopsy room.

"Thanks, but I don't want any perverts staring at me while I'm sleeping."

"How about some coffee, then?" Peg-leg asked.

"Sure," I said.

We went over to his desk that was in the corner of the autopsy room. He had a hot plate on the desk. We poured ourselves some coffee from a pot and sat down.

"OK, 'Eye,' spill it. You didn't come down here because you wanted to pay back the fifty bucks you borrowed from me. Right? Right," he answered himself.

I took a sip of coffee. It tasted like he got it out of the asshole of one of his corpse friends. I was going to say that but I changed my mind.

"I need some bullets," I said.

"Oh, boy," Peg-leg said. "Repeat that."

"I've got a case, a client, cash money, but the job requires that I pack a piece."

"You carry a gun?" he said. "Isn't that kind of dangerous?"

"I was in the war," I said. "I was a soldier. I got wounded. I'm a hero."

"Bullshit! You fought for those fucking Communists in Spain and got shot in the ass. It serves you right, too. How did you get shot in the ass?"

I returned the conversation to its original subject. I didn't have all day to spend with this joker.

"I need six bullets," I said. "My gun's empty. I don't think my client would want to hire a private detective who carries an empty gun. Don't you have a gun you keep here in case stiffs get up and and start chasing you with axes?"

"Not so loud," Peg-leg said, looking around, though there

35

wasn't anybody else in the room. He had taken Sergeant Rink's advice about not telling people about the ax-murderer incident very seriously. I was one of the few people that he had told about it. We were pretty close friends until I started borrowing money from him and couldn't repay it. We were still friends but he wanted his money, so there was kind of like a short wall between us. It wasn't serious but it was there.

"Well?" I said.

"Yeah, I've still got it here. You never know."

"Will you loan me some bullets, then? Six would do fine."

"First, you start out borrowing tens, then you switch to fives, then it's ones and now you want the bullets from my fucking gun. You take the cake. You are a loser. A real loser."

"I know that," I said. "But I need some bullets. How can I ever pay you back if you don't loan me enough ammunition so that I can go to work?"

Peg-leg looked slightly disgusted.

"Oh, shit," he said. "But I'm not going to give them all to you. I'm going to keep three of them for myself just in case something weird happens around here again."

"You still think that was real, huh?" I said.

"Watch it, 'Eye,' " Peg-leg said.

He took another look around the room. We were still alone. He pulled the drawer of his desk out very cautiously and removed a revolver. He opened up the cylinder and took out three bullets and gave them to me. Then he put the revolver away.

"Deadbeat," he said.

I looked at the cartridges in my hand. Actually, I was staring at them.

"What's wrong?" he said.

"What caliber are these?" I said.

".32s," he said.

"Ah, shit!" I said.

.38

"You've got a .38, right?" Peg-leg said.

"How did you guess?"

"Knowing you it wasn't hard."

"What am I going to do?" I said.

"Why don't you get a job?" Peg-leg said. "A lot of people work. It's not like leprosy."

"But I've got a client," I said. "A real client."

"You've had clients before and you've been fired before. Face it, pal. You're not any good at this private detective business. If my wife was cheating I'd hire Donald Duck to find out who she was doing it with before I'd hire you, and I'm not even married. Why don't you buy some bullets for your God-damn gun?"

"I don't have any money," I said.

"Not even enough to buy some bullets? Hell, they only cost a dollar or so."

"I've fallen on hard times," I said.

"I think the only good times I ever saw you have was when you got hit by a car last year," Peg-leg said. "And some people don't consider being hit by a car and breaking both your legs good luck."

"What am I going to do?" I said.

Peg-leg shook his head and smiled painfully.

He opened the desk drawer and took out his gun and handed it to me.

"If some dead stranger comes back to life and throttles me while I'm trying to wash their face, it'll be your fucking fault and I'll come back and haunt you. You'll never get a decent night's sleep again. I'll be flapping my sheet right up your asshole. You'll be sorry."

I put the gun in my coat pocket that didn't already have a gun in it.

"Thanks a lot, Peg-leg," I said. "You're a true-blue pal."

"You're a total fuckup," Peg-leg said. "I want to see that gun back here tomorrow morning."

"Thank you," I said, feeling like a real private detective with a loaded gun in my pocket. My luck was definitely changing. I was on my way up.

The Morning Mail

Peg-leg walked me out to the front door. He moved quickly and gracefully for a man with a peg-leg. Did I mention that before? I don't think I did. I should have. It's kind of interesting: a man with a peg-leg taking care of dead people.

Then I remembered something that I was going to ask him.

"Hey, Peg-leg," I said. "Did you see that blonde who came out of here a little while ago? She had short hair, a fur coat, real good-looking."

"Yeah," he said. "She was here visiting one of my clients: the good-looker that somebody used as a substitute because they couldn't wait to open their morning mail."

"What?" I said.

"The letter-opener job."

"Did you say a letter opener?" I asked.

"Yeah, the girl who was killed with the letter opener. The blonde saw her. She said she thought the girl might be her sister. She read about it in the newspaper but it turned out she was the wrong girl."

"That's funny," I said. "She was crying when she went out the door."

"I don't know anything about that but she wasn't crying when she left me. She was very unemotional. A cold fish," Peg-leg said.

The letter opener!

Now I remembered.

Sergeant Rink was playing with the letter opener that killed the girl I had just seen Peg-leg drooling over. I knew when Peg-leg first mentioned a letter opener that it rang some kind of bell and this was it. The letter opener was the murder weapon.

A bunch of amateur coincidences for no particular reason, I thought, *but they don't have anything to do with me.*

"Good-bye," I said.

"Don't forget to bring the gun back tomorrow morning," Peg-leg said, peg-legging it back into the morgue.

The Boss

Hurray, I had a loaded gun! In a few hours I would be able to meet my client with confidence in my step. I wondered what they wanted me to do that required a gun. Oh, well, beggars can't be choosers. I really needed the money.

I was going to ask for fifty dollars expense money. That would go a long way in changing my circumstances. I could get the landlady off my back with a few bucks. I didn't think that story I fed her about oil wells in Rhode Island had much longevity. I figured by the time I got back to the apartment, she'd be howling away like a banshee.

I had some time to kill, so I walked up the street to

Portsmouth Square and sat down on a bench near the statue dedicated to Robert Louis Stevenson.

A lot of Chinese were coming and going in the park. I watched them for a while. Interesting people. Very energetic. I wondered if anyone had ever told them that they looked just like Japanese and it was not a good time to look like Japanese.

That didn't have anything to do with me any more because my war was over, so I thought, sitting there on a park bench in San Francisco, letting the world go by. I had a loaded gun in my pocket and a client that was willing to pay for my services.

The world wasn't such a bad place, so I started thinking about Babylon. Why not? I didn't have anything else to do for a couple of hours. It couldn't hurt. I'd just have to be very careful about dreaming of Babylon. I wouldn't let it get the best of me. I'd stay on top of it. That's what I would do.

I'd show Babylon who was boss.

The Front Door
to Babylon

I guess I should give you a little background about my involvement with Babylon. I was out of high school and looking around for something to do with my life. I'd been a pretty fair baseball player in high school. I lettered two years in a row and hit .320 in my senior year, including four home runs, so I decided to try my hand at professional baseball.

I tried out one afternoon for a semi-pro team and figured that it was the beginning of a career that would take me to the New York Yankees. I was a first baseman, so the Yankees would have to get rid of Lou Gehrig who was playing first base for them, then, but I figured that the better man would win out and that was of course me.

When I arrived at the ball park to try out for the team, the first thing the manager said to me was, "You don't look like a first baseman."

"Looks are deceiving. Watch me play. I'm the best."

The manager shook his head.

"I don't think I've even seen a baseball player that looks like you. Are you sure you've played first base?"

"Put a bat in my hand and I'll show you who I am."

"OK," the manager said. "But you'd better not waste my time. We're in second place, just a game out of first."

I didn't know what that had to do with me but I pretended that I appreciated the significance of this achievement.

"You'll be five games in first place after I take over first base," I said, humoring the son-of-a-bitch.

There were about a dozen halfwit-looking baseball players standing around playing catch and shooting the breeze with each other.

The manager motioned toward one of them.

"Hey, Sam!" he yelled. "Come over here and throw a few balls at this guy. He thinks he's Lou Gehrig."

"How'd you know?" I said.

"If you're wasting my time, I'll personally toss your ass out of this ball park," the manager said.

I could see that him and me were never going to be friends, but I'd show the bastard. He'd be eating his own words soon enough.

I picked up a baseball bat and walked up to home plate. I felt very confident.

Sam, the pitcher, took his place on the mound. He was a very unimpressive-looking pitcher. He was about twenty-five and had a slight build hanging awkwardly on a six-foot frame. I don't think he weighed over a 130 soaking wet with a bowling ball in his lap.

"Is that the best you've got!" I yelled at the manager.

"Sam!" the manager yelled. "Put some smoke on it for this kid!"

Sam smiled.

He was never going to make it in the movies. He had a pair of buckteeth that made him look like the first cousin of a walrus.

I took some practice swings. Then Sam very slowly wound up. He took the longest time to wind up. He was like a snake uncoiling. The smile never left his face.

That's the last thing I remembered before being in Babylon.

President Roosevelt

It was really beautiful in Babylon. I went for a long walk beside the Euphrates River. There was a girl with me. She was very beautiful and wearing a gown that I could see her body through. She had on an emerald necklace.

We talked about President Roosevelt. She was a Democrat, too. The fact that she had large firm breasts and was a Democrat made her the perfect woman for me.

"I wish that President Roosevelt was my father," she said in a husky voice like honey. "If President Roosevelt was my dad, I'd cook breakfast for him every morning. I make a very good waffle."

What a gal!
What a gal!
By the banks of the Euphrates in Babylon
What a gal!

It was just like a song being played on the radio in my
mind.

A Babylonian
Sand Watch

"How do you make your waffles?" I said.

"I use two eggs," she said, and then suddenly looked at her watch. It was a Babylonian sand watch. It had twelve little hourglasses in it and told the time by sand.

"It's almost twelve," she said. "Time to go out to the ball park. The game starts at one."

"Thanks," I said. "I'd forgotten about the time. When you started talking about President Roosevelt and waffles, my mind couldn't think of anything else. Two eggs. Those sound like great waffles. You'll have to make them for me sometime."

"Tonight, hero," she said. "Tonight."
I wished that tonight were here right now.
I wanted some waffles and to hear her talk some more about President Roosevelt.

Nebuchadnezzar

When we arrived at the ball park, there were
fifty thousand people waiting for me. They all stood up and
started cheering when they saw me come into the park.
Nebuchadnezzar had three extra units of cavalry there to
keep the fans under control. There had been a near riot the
day before and some people had been injured, so old "Neb"
was taking no chances with today's game.

The cavalry looked very smart in their armor.
I think they were glad to be at the ball game watching me
hit home runs. It certainly was a lot better than going to war.

I went down to the locker room and the girl went with
me. Her name was Nana-dirat. When I walked into the
locker room all the players stopped talking and watched as

I walked through and went into my own private dressing room. There was hushed silence. Nobody knew what to say. I don't blame them. After all, what do you say to somebody who has hit twenty-three home runs in their last twenty-three times at bat?

The team and I had gone far beyond small talk.

I was like a god to them.

They worshiped at the shrine of my bat.

The 596 B.C.
Baseball Season

The walls of my dressing room were covered
with tapestries of my baseball feats woven in gold and covered with precious stones.

There was a tapestry of me beheading a pitcher with a line
drive. Another tapestry showed a group of opposing players
standing around a huge hole in the infield between second
and third base. They never did find that ball. Still another
tapestry showed me accepting a bowlful of jewels from
Nebuchadnezzar for finishing the 596 B.C. season with an
.890 batting average.

Nana-dirat took off my clothes and I lay down upon a solid
gold dressing table and she gave me a pre-game massage

53

with rare and exotic oils. Her hands were so gentle they felt like swans making love on a full moon night.

After massaging me Nana-dirat dressed me in my baseball uniform. It took her five minutes to put the uniform on. She did it very sensually. I had an erection by the time she finished with the uniform and I almost came when she put my shoes on. She ended by giving my spikes a delicate and loving caress.

Ah, paradise! There can be paradise on earth if you're a Babylonian baseball star.

First Base Hotel

"OK, asshole, wake up!" a voice came grinding into my ears like somebody deliberately stepping on an old lady's glasses. "You've had your beauty sleep! Wake up! This isn't a hotel! It's a baseball team!" the voice kept grinding. My head felt as if a safe had dropped on it.

I opened my eyes and there was the manager and Sam standing above me, staring down. The manager really looked pissed off. Sam was smiling like a puppy with his buckteeth leading the way. I was lying on the grass beside first base.

The team was having batting practice. They kept looking over at me and making jokes. Everybody was having a good time except the manager and me.

"I knew you weren't a baseball player," he said. "You

don't look like a baseball player. I don't think you ever saw a baseball before."

"What happened?" I said.

"Listen to that, Sam," the manager said. "Did you get that? This punk asked me what happened. What in the fuck do you think happened? Run down the possibilities and then tell me what you think might have happened. What could have happened?" Then he started yelling again, "You got hit in the head! You just stood there like some kind of lamebrain and got hit in the head! You didn't even move! I don't think you even saw the baseball! You stood there like you were waiting to catch a bus!"

Then he reached down and grabbed me by the collar and started dragging me across the grass toward the street.

"Hey, stop it!" I said. "Stop it! My head is killing me. What are you doing?"

My words didn't have any effect on him. He just kept dragging me along. He left me lying out on the sidewalk. I lay there for a long time, first thinking that perhaps I wasn't cut out to be a professional baseball player. Then I thought about the dream I'd had of Babylon and how very pleasant it was.

Babylon . . . what a nice place.

That's how it started.

I've been going back ever since.

A Cowboy in Babylon

Getting hit in the head with a baseball on June
20, 1933 was my ticket to Babylon. Anyway, I had a few
hours to kill before I had to meet my first client in over three
months, so I'd walked up from the morgue to Portsmouth
Square on the edge of Chinatown and was sitting on a bench
watching Chinese people come and go through the park.

Then I decided to do a little daydreaming about Babylon.
I had everything under control: a loaded gun, some spare
time, so I went to Babylon.

My latest adventures in Babylon concerned me having a
big detective agency. I was the most famous private eye in
Babylon. I had a fancy office just down from the Hanging
Gardens. There were three very skillful operatives working

for me and my secretary was a knockout, a real looker: Nana-dirat. She had become a permanent part of my adventures in Babylon. She was the perfect female counterpart for everything that I did there.

When I was a cowboy in Babylon, she was a school teacher who was kidnapped by the bad guys and I rescued her. We almost got married that time, but something came up, so it didn't happen.

During my military career when I was a general in Babylon, she was a nurse and nursed me back to health after I had suffered some terrible wounds in battle. She'd bathed my face with cool water as I lay suffering and delirious through hot nights in Babylon.

I just couldn't get enough of Nana-dirat.

She was always waiting for me in Babylon.

She of the long black hair and lissome body and breasts that were made to addle my senses. Just think: I never would have met her if I hadn't been hit in the head with a baseball.

Terry and the Pirates

Sometimes I played around with the form of my adventures in Babylon. They would be done as books that I could see in my mind what I was reading, but most often they were done as movies, though once I did them as a play with me being a Babylonian Hamlet and Nana-dirat being both Gertrude and Ophelia. I abandoned the play halfway through the second act. Someday I must return and pick it up where I left off. It will have a different ending from the way Shakespeare ended it. My *Hamlet* will have a happy ending.

Nana-dirat and I will take off in an airplane of my own invention built out of palm fronds and propelled by an engine that burns honey. We will fly to Egypt to have supper on a golden barge floating down the Nile with the Pharaoh.

Yes, I will have to pick that one up soon.

I had also done half-a-dozen adventures in Babylon in the form of comic strips. It was a lot of fun to do them that way. They were modelled after the style of *Terry and the Pirates*. Nana-dirat looked great as a comic-strip character.

I had just finished doing a private-eye mystery in detective magazine form like a short novel in *Dime Detective*. As I read the novel paragraph after paragraph, page following page, I translated the words into pictures that I could see and move rapidly forward in my mind like having a dream.

The mystery ended with me breaking the butler's arm as he tried to stab me with the same knife that he had used to murder the old dowager who'd been my client, having hired me to look into the matter of some stolen paintings.

"See," I said, turning triumphantly to Nana-dirat, leaving the murderous wretch to writhe in pain on the floor, the down payment for a life of thievery, betrayal and murder. "The butler did do it!"

"Ohhhhhhhhhh!" the butler moaned up from the floor.

"You didn't believe me," I said to Nana-dirat. "You said that the butler couldn't have done it, but I knew better and now the swine will pay for his crimes."

I gave him a good kick in the stomach. This caused him to stop concentrating on the pain in his arm and start thinking about his stomach.

Not only was I the most famous detective in Babylon but I was also the most hard-boiled just like a rock. I had no use for lawbreakers and could be very brutal with them.

"Darling," Nana-dirat said. "You're so wonderful, but did you have to kick him in the stomach?"

"Yes," I said.

Nana-dirat threw her arms around me and pressed her beautiful body up close to mine. Then she looked up into my cold steel eyes and smiled. "Oh, well," she said. "Nobody's perfect, you big lug."

"Mercy," the butler said.

Case closed!

Ming the Merciless

Sitting there on the park bench with the United States of America freshly at war with Japan, Germany and Italy, I decided to do my next adventure as a private eye in Babylon in the form of a serial that would have fifteen chapters.

I of course would be the hero and Nana-dirat the heroine, my faithful and loving secretary. I decided to borrow Ming the Merciless from *Flash Gordon* to be the villain.

I had to change his name and alter his character slightly to fit my needs. That wouldn't be hard. Actually, it would be an immense amount of pleasure for me. I had spent a very pleasant part of eight years making up situations and characters in Babylon, unfortunately to the point of being a detriment to my real life, such as it was.

I'd much rather be in ancient Babylon than in the Twentieth Century trying to put two bits together for a hamburger and I love Nana-dirat more than any woman I've ever met in the flesh.

First, what to do with Ming the Merciless? Change his name. That was the first thing that had to be done. In my serial he would be Dr. Abdul Forsythe, publicly known as one of the most generous and kindest men in Babylon but secretly he had a laboratory under the clinic that he used to provide free medical services for the poor. In the laboratory he was constructing a powerful and evil ray that he was going to conquer the world with.

The ray changed people into shadow robots that were totally subservient to Dr. Forsythe and would do his evil work, responding to his slightest beckoning.

He had a plan for creating artificial night composed of his shadow robots that would move during the real night from town to town conquering unsuspecting citizens and changing them into more shadow robots.

It was an ingenious plan and he had already changed thousands of unsuspecting and helpless poor people that came to his clinic seeking free medical help into shadow robots.

They came to be helped by Dr. Forsythe and then disappeared from the face of the earth. Their absence was hardly noticed in Babylon because they were poor. Sometimes relatives or friends would come by and inquire into their disappearance. Often, they, too, would disappear.

The fiend!

He needed only one more ingredient to put his plan into action. After he changed them into shadow robots, he stacked them like newspapers in a hidden warehouse nearby, waiting for the time to come when he could turn them loose on the world as artificial night.

The Magician

Escitybrell. Escitybrell.
I heard a sound in the distance that was directed toward
me but I couldn't make it out.
"Excuse me. Excuse me."
The sound was words.
Babylon fell over on its side and lay there.
"Excuse me, C. Card, is that you?"
I looked up, totally returned to the so-called real world.
The voice belonged to an old comrade in arms from the
Spanish Civil War. I hadn't seen him in years.
"Well, I'll be," I said. "Sam Herschberger. Those nights
in Madrid. Those were the days."
I stood up and we shook hands. I had to shake his left

hand because his right hand wasn't there. I remembered when he'd gotten it blown off. It had not been a good day for him because he was a professional juggler and magician. When he looked at his blown-off hand lying on the ground nearby, all he could say was, "This is one trick I'll never be able to duplicate."

"You seemed a million miles away," he said, now years later in San Francisco.

"I was daydreaming," I said.

"Just like the good old days," he said. "I think half the time I knew you in Spain you weren't even there."

I decided to change the subject.

"What are you up to these days?" I said.

"I'm working just as much as all the other one-armed jugglers and magicians are."

"That bad, huh?"

"No, I can't complain. I married a woman who owns a beauty parlor and she's got a thing for people with missing limbs. Sometimes she hints that I would be twice as sexy as I am now if I only had one leg, but that's the way it goes. It beats working for a living."

"What about the Party?" I said. "I thought they loved you."

"With two arms they loved me," he said. "I wasn't much use to them with only one. They used me as a warm-up act for recruiting farm workers over in the valley. They'd gather around to watch me juggle and do tricks and then they'd hear about Karl Marx and how great Soviet Russia was and Lenin. Oh, well, that was a long time ago. A guy's got to keep moving. If you don't the grass will grow on you. What have you been doing? The last time I saw you, you had a

66

couple of bullet holes in your ass and you were going to be a doctor. How'd you get shot in the ass, anyway? As I remember the Fascists were on our left flank and there was nobody behind us and you were in a trench. Where did the bullets come from that got you? That's always been a mystery to me."

I wasn't going to tell him that I slipped while I was taking a shit and sat down on my pistol causing it to go off and blow a couple of holes clean through both cheeks of my ass.

"Water under the bridge," I said. "It hurts just to think about it."

"I know what you mean," he said, looking down at the place where his right hand used to be.

"Anyway, did you become a doctor?"

"No," I said. "That didn't work out the way I planned it."

"What are you doing, then?"

"I'm a private eye," I said.

"A private eye?" he said.

67

Barcelona

The last time I'd seen Sam had been in Barcelona in '38. He had been a hell-of-a-good juggler and magician. Too bad about his arm, but it sounded to me as if he was using its absence to best advantage. A guy's got to make do.

We shared some Spanish Civil War memories and then I hit him up for five bucks. I try not to let a chance go by.

"By the way," I said. "Did you ever repay me that five you borrowed in Barcelona?"

"What five?" he said.

"You don't remember?" I said.

"No," he said.

"Then forget it," I said. "No big deal." Then I started to change the subject—

"Wait a minute," he said. He had always been an unscrupulously honest person. "I don't remember borrowing five dollars from you. When was that?"

"In Barcelona. A week before we left, but forget it. It's OK. If you don't remember it, I don't want to bring it up. It's the past. Forget it," and I started to change the subject again.

A few moments later, after he had given me the five bucks, with a curious expression on his face he walked up Washington Street and out of my life.

The Abraham
Lincoln Brigade

The Spanish Civil War was a long way off but
I was glad that it was able to yield five dollars years later. I
hadn't really been a political enthusiast. That wasn't the
reason that I joined the Abraham Lincoln Brigade. I went
to Spain because I thought it might resemble Babylon. I
don't know where I got that idea. I get a lot of ideas about
Babylon. Some of them are right on the money and others
are half-baked. The only trouble is that it's hard to tell which
are which, but it always works itself out in the end. Anyway,
it does for me when I'm dreaming of Babylon.

Then I remembered that I still had to make that phone
call, but for a few seconds I didn't know whether I was

supposed to call Babylon or my mother out in the Mission
District.

It was my mother.

I promised her a call and I knew that she'd be upset if I
didn't call her soon, though we didn't have anything to talk
about because we couldn't stand each other and always got
into the same arguments.

She didn't like the idea of me being a private eye.

Yes, I'd better call Mom. She'd be angrier than she normally was if I didn't call her today. I hated to do it but if
I didn't I'd have hell to pay for it. I called her once a week
and we always had the same conversation. I don't think we
even bothered to change the words. I think we used the
same words all the time.

It would go just like this:

"Hello?" my mother would say when she answered the
telephone.

"Hi, Mom. It's me."

"Hello? who is this speaking? Hello?"

"*Mom.*"

"This can't be my son calling. Hello?"

"*Mom,*" I'd always whine.

"It sounds like my son," she'd always say. "But he
wouldn't have the nerve to call if he was still a private
detective. He just wouldn't have the nerve. He still has some
self-respect left. If this is my son, then he must have given
up his private-eye nonsense and now he has a decent job.
He's a working stiff who can hold his head up high and he
wants to pay back the eight hundred dollars that he owes his
mother. Good boy."

Then after she finished speaking, there would always be a long pause and I'd say, "This is your son and I'm still a private detective. I've got a case. I'm going to pay back some of the money I owe you soon."

I'd always tell her that I had a case even if I didn't have one. It was part of the routine.

"You've broken your mother's heart," she'd always say then and I'd answer, "Don't say that, Mom, just because I'm a private detective. I still love you."

"What about the eight hundred dollars?" she'd say. "My son's love can't pay for a quart of milk or a loaf of bread. Who do you think you are, anyway? Breaking my heart. Never having a decent job. Owing me eight hundred dollars. Being a private detective. Never getting married. No grandchildren. What am I going to do? Why did I have to be cursed with a son who is an idiot?"

"*Mom,* don't say things like that," I'd whine on cue. That whining used to be able to spring a five spot or ten dollars out of her but nothing these days, nothing at all. It was just plain whining but if I didn't call her it made things worse, so I'd call her because I didn't want things to get any worse than what they were.

My father died years ago.

My mother still hadn't gotten over it.

"Your poor father," she'd say and then would start crying. "It's your fault that I'm a widow."

My mother blamed me for my father's death and in a way it was my fault, even if I was only four years old at the time. She'd always bring it up on the telephone. "Brat!" she'd yell. "Evil brat!"

"*Mom,*" I'd whine.

Then she'd stop crying and say, "I shouldn't blame you.
You were only four at the time. It's not your fault. But why
did you have to throw your ball out in the street? Why
couldn't you have just bounced it on the sidewalk like any
other kid who still has a father?"

"You know I'm sorry, Mom."

"I know you're sorry, son, but why are you a private
detective? I hate those magazines and books. They're so
seamy. I don't like the long black shadows those people have
on the covers. They frighten me."

"Those aren't the real thing, Mom," I'd always say, and
she'd answer, "Then why do they sell them at the newsstand
for everyone in the world to see and buy. Answer that one
if you can, Smart Guy. Come on and answer it, Mr. Private
Eye. I dare you. Come on! Come on! This is your mother!"

I couldn't answer it.

I couldn't tell my mother that people wanted to read
stories about people who had long black ominous shadows.
She just wouldn't have understood. Her thinking didn't run
along those lines.

She would end the conversation by saying, "Son . . . ,"
pausing for a long time, ". . . why a private detective?"

We'd been having the same conversation now for six
months.

I sure wish I hadn't run out of money, trying to be a
private detective and had to borrow so much from my
mother and all my friends.

Well, anyway, my luck was going to turn today.

I had a client and some bullets for my gun.

Everything was going to turn out OK in the end.

That's what counts.

It would be a turning point.

I'd get lots of clients, pay back all my debts, have an office, a secretary and a car again, but this time I would have a secretary that would fuck my ears off. Then I'd take a vacation to Mexico and just sit there on the beach, dreaming of Babylon. Nana-dirat would be right beside me, looking great in a bathing suit, but right now I'd better call my mother.

Loving Uncle Sam

I went into a nearby bar on Kearny Street to use their pay telephone. The place was empty except for the bartender and a fat lady who was on the phone. She wasn't talking. She was just standing there, nodding her head to the person on the other end of the line.

I decided to have a quick beer from my new five dollar bill while she finished her call. I sat down on a stool and the bartender walked down the bar to me. He was so ordinary looking that he was almost invisible.

"What will you have?" he said.

"Just a beer," I said.

"Better drink it in a hurry," the bartender said. "The

Japanese might be here by dark." Somehow he thought that this was very funny and laughed heartily at his "joke."

"The Japanese love beer," he said, continuing to laugh. "They're going to drink every drop in California when they get here."

I looked over at the fat lady nodding her head up and down like a duck. There was a huge smile on her face. She looked as if she were at the beginning of a telephone conversation that might take years to finish.

"Forget the beer," I said to the bartender and got up from my stool and headed toward the door. I hadn't had a beer in weeks and I didn't want it ruined by a bartender who didn't make any sense.

I think he had a few nuts and bolts loose in his head. No wonder the bar was empty except for the fat woman who was having a love affair with a pay phone.

I now pronounce you telephone and wife.

"Every drop," the bartender laughed as I went through the door and back out onto Kearny Street, almost knocking a Chinaman over as I stepped outside. He was walking by on the street and I stepped through the door right into him. We were both very surprised but he was more surprised than I was.

He had a package under his arm when we collided. He juggled it briefly and managed to keep it from falling on the sidewalk. He was very ruffled by the incident.

"Not Japanese," he said, turning to me as he started to hurry away. "Chinese-American. Love flag. Love Uncle Sam. No trouble. Chinese. Not Japanese. Loyal. Pay taxes. Keep nose clean."

Bus Throne

Things were starting to get too complicated. I'd better call my mother later on when things got a little simpler. I didn't want to push my luck while I was ahead of the game, so I decided to go home and take a shower before I met my client.

Maybe I had a shirt that resembled something clean in the closet. I wanted to look my best for my client. I'd even brush my teeth.

I walked down Kearny to Sacramento Street and waited for the bus to take me up Sacramento to Nob Hill and my apartment. I didn't have to wait long. The bus was only a few blocks away coming up Sacramento toward my stop.

See: Luck was running my way.

I think that luck is like the tide.

When it comes in, it comes in.

I was really going to enjoy the luxury of the bus trip. I had been hoofing it around San Francisco for weeks. This was the poorest I'd ever been but those days were over now.

I got onto the bus, paid my nickel and sat down as if I were a king enjoying a brand-new throne. I sighed with pleasure as the bus started up Sacramento. I think I sighed a little too loudly because a young woman who was sitting with her legs crossed in a seat opposite me, uncrossed her legs and turned her head uncomfortably the other way.

She'd probably had a bus seat every God-damn day of her life. She may even have been born on a bus and had a lifetime ticket, and when she died, they'd take her coffin on a bus to the cemetery. It would be painted black of course and all the seats filled with flowers like crazy passengers.

Some people don't appreciate how good they've got it.

Drums of
Fu Manchu

The short trip on the bus up the hill was a good time to do a little thinking about my private-eye serial in Babylon. I settled back and Babylon took over my mind like warm maple syrup being poured over piping hot pancakes.

. . . ummmmm good.

. . . ummmmm Babylon.

I had to have a name for my serial.

What was I going to call it?

Let's see.

Then I thought about the names of serials I'd seen in the last few years. I'm really quite a movie fan:

Mandrake the Magician
The Phantom Creeps
Adventures of Captain Marvel
Mysterious Dr. Satan
The Shadow
Drums of Fu Manchu
and The Iron Claw.

Those were all good titles and I needed one just as good for my serial. As the bus travelled toward the top of Nob Hill, stopping and starting, picking up passengers and letting passengers off, I ran a hundred titles through my mind. The best ones I came up with were:

The Horror of Dr. Abdul Forsythe
Adventures of a Private Eye in Babylon
The Shadow Robots Creep.

Yes, this was going to be fun. I had a lot of possibilities to work with, but I had to be careful not to let things run away with themselves. Even with a tight rein on Babylon, I still went two stops past my stop and had to walk back a couple of blocks.

I had to watch myself very carefully, especially because I had a client, not to let Babylon get the best of me again.

Friday's Grave

I saw a pay telephone.

Maybe I'd better call my mother and get it over with. The sooner I called her, the sooner I wouldn't have to call her again. It would be taken care of for another week.

I dropped a nickel in the slot and dialed.

I let the phone ring ten times before I hung up.

I wondered where she was.

Then I remembered that it was Friday and she was at the cemetery putting flowers on my father's grave. She did that every Friday. It was a ritual with her, rain or shine, she visited his grave every Friday.

Maybe today wasn't the day to call her.

It would only remind her that I had killed him when I was four years old.

No, I'd better call tomorrow.

That would be a smart move on my part.

I started to think about the day I killed my father. I got as far as remembering that it was a Sunday and a very warm day and a brand-new Model T sedan was parked in the street in front of our house and I had walked over to it earlier and had smelled how new the car was. I was a kid then and just walked right over and put my nose directly down on a fender and gave it a big sniff.

I think the best perfume in this world is the smell of something brand-new. It can be clothes or furniture or radios or cars, even appliances like toasters or electric irons. They all smell good to me when they're brand-new.

Anyway, I was remembering back to the morning that I killed my father. I had gotten as far as having my nose on the fender of a brand-new Model T when I suddenly rerouted my thinking. I didn't want to think about killing my father, so I just changed the subject in my mind.

I couldn't think about Babylon or I might blow it, so I thought about my client.

Who was my client?

What did they look like?

What did they want done?

Why did I have to have a gun?

Were they going to ask me to do something illegal?

If they did, of course, I would do it, short of killing somebody. Beggars can't be choosers. A man in my boat has to row where he's told to except that I wasn't going to kill anybody. That was the only thing I wouldn't do. I was really desperate. I needed the God-damn money.

I didn't know whether my client was a man or a woman. All I knew was that I was supposed to meet somebody in front of a radio station at 6 P.M. They already knew what I looked like, so I didn't have to know what they looked like. It only made sense if you were as broke as I was, and it made a lot of sense to me.

Smith

Thinking about the fact that I didn't know the name or sex of my client somehow returned me to Babylon and my serial.

Sometimes Babylon just happens like that.

What was I doing trying to think up a title for the serial when I hadn't even given all my main characters names yet? There was of course a name for the villain: Dr. Abdul Forsythe, but I didn't even have a name for myself.

Oh, boy, where was my noggin? I'd better get a name for me. I might want to use it in the title.

I had used the name Ace Stag for my name in the detective novel about Babylon that I had just finished living, but I didn't like to use the same name for myself in my Babylonian adventures. I liked to change my name. For instance, when I was a baseball hero in Babylon, I used the name Samson Ruth, but enough of that. I needed a new name for myself in the serial.

I tried out a few names as I backtracked the two blocks to my intended bus stop. I like the name Smith. I don't know why but I've always liked that name. Some people consider it ordinary. I don't.

Smith . . .

I ran some variations of Smith through my mind:

Errol Smith
Cary Smith
Humphrey Smith
George Smith (as in Raft)
Wallace Smith
Pancho Smith
Lee Smith
Morgan Smith
"Gunboat" Smith
"Red" Smith
Carter Smith
Rex Smith
Cody Smith
Flint Smith
Terry Smith
Laughing Smith
Major Smith (I liked that one a lot.)
"Oklahoma Jimmy" Smith
F.D.R. Smith

There certainly are a lot of possibilities when you use the name Smith.

Some of the names were good but so far I hadn't come up with one that was perfect and I wouldn't settle for less than a perfect Smith.

Why should I?

Lobotomy

Ah, shit!

I walked two blocks beyond my stop the other way, past the street that I lived on, thinking about having the name Smith for a private eye in Babylon, so I had to turn around and walk back again and felt like a fool because I couldn't afford to do things like that when I was just a few hours away from my first client in months.

Thinking about Babylon can be a dangerous thing for me.

I had to watch my ass.

I walked back down Sacramento Street *very* carefully not thinking about Babylon. As I walked along, I pretended that I had a prefrontal lobotomy.

The Milkmen

I felt a certain sense of triumph when I arrived
at Leavenworth Street and walked half a block to the brok-
en-down apartment building I was living in. I hadn't
thought about Babylon once.

The morgue wagon was parked in front of the apartment
house. Somebody had died in the building. I tried to imagine one of the tenants being dead but I couldn't imagine
anyone being dead in that place. Why bother when paying
your rent there was a form of death?

I certainly was going to be surprised when I found out
who it was.

The morgue wagon was a converted panel Mack truck

with enough corpse room to accommodate four brand-new ex-taxpayers.

I walked up the steps and opened the front door and stepped into the dark musty hall of the building that some called home but I called shit.

Though I had cooled the rent business with the landlady, I involuntarily looked up the stairs to the second floor and her apartment. The door was open and two morgue attendants were carrying her body out. It was lying on a stretcher covered with a sheet. There were some tenants cluttered around the door. They acted like amateur, just-drafted mourners.

I stood at the bottom of the landing and watched the attendants bring her body down the stairs. They did it very smoothly, almost effortlessly, like olive oil pouring out of a bottle.

They didn't say anything as they came down the stairs. I knew a lot of guys who worked at the morgue but I didn't know these guys.

The tenant mourners stood in a very small crowd at the top of the stairs whispering and mourning amateurishly. They weren't very good at it. Of course how good can you be at mourning a landlady who had a shrill temper and was a big snoop? She had a bad habit of peeking out a crack in the door to her apartment and scrutinizing everybody who came and went in the building. She had incredible hearing. I think there was a bat somewhere in her family tree.

Well, those days were over for her.

She was now taking a trip down to my peg-legged friend who'd be putting her on ice shortly. I wondered if he would do any sight-seeing on her naked body. No, I don't think so. She was too old and had eaten too many stale doughnuts. She couldn't hold a candle to that prostitute who was keeping him company now, the one who'd been opened up with a letter opener. For a few seconds, I saw her dead body in my mind. She was a real looker. Then I thought about the beautiful blonde that I'd met leaving the morgue and how she'd been crying when I saw her but had pretended to be very aloof and distant to Peg-leg when she'd looked at the body of the dead whore. That line of thought led to a flash of her chauffeur smiling at me as they drove away up the street, almost as if he knew me, that we were old friends who didn't have time to talk right now but we'd see each other soon.

I mentally returned to the business at hand, watching the attendants complete getting the dead landlady's body down the stairs. They sure were good at it. Of course that was their occupation but I had to admire it. I think there's an art to doing everything and they were proving my theory by moving that old bag's carcass just like she was an angel or at least a millionaire.

"The landlady?" I said as they finished getting her down the stairs. Saying that made me sound like a private detective. I like to keep in shape.

"Yup," one of them said.

"What was it?" I said.

"Ticker," the other one said.

The amateur mourners followed down the stairs and watched the attendants finish carting her out of the building. They slid her body into the back of the morgue wagon. There was already another corpse in there, so she'd have some company on her trip downtown to the morgue. I guess it beats going by yourself.

The attendants closed the door behind her and her new-found friend. They walked slowly around and got into the front seat. There was a very offhand casualness to their demeanor. They had about the same attitude toward dead bodies as a milkman does toward empty bottles. You just pick them up and take them away.

My Day

After the landlady was gone I walked down the hall to my apartment and suddenly the bright side of the situation came into focus. The old landlady owned the building and she was a widow and she didn't have any relatives or friends. Her estate would be in a complete mess. It would take months to sort out, so nobody would be bothering me about my overdue rent.

What a break!

This was really my day.

I hadn't had a day like this since that car ran over me a couple years ago and broke both my legs. I got a nice settlement out of that. Even though I was in traction for three months, it beat working for a living and oh, what times I had! dreaming of Babylon there in the hospital.

I almost hated to leave.

I guess I showed it.

The nurses made some jokes about it.

"Why so gloomy?" one of them said.

"You look as if you're going to a funeral," another one said.

They didn't know how comfortable the hospital was, just to lie there and have all my wants taken care of, with practically nothing to do except dream of Babylon.

The second I went out the front door of that hospital on my crutches everything started downhill. From then on it just kept spiralling down until today, and what a day it had been so far: a client! Bullets for my gun! Five dollars! And best of all, a dead landlady!

Who could ask for anything more?

Christmas Carols

The dank grubbiness of my apartment hadn't changed while I was gone. What a rock bottom hole . . . Jesus, how could I live the way I was living? It was a little frightening. I stepped over some unidentified objects lying on the floor. I deliberately didn't look at them very hard. I didn't want to know what they were. I also avoided looking at my bed.

My bed resembled something that belonged in the violent ward of an insane asylum. I had never really been much of a bedmaker even when I had been inspired to do so in days long gone past.

My mother used to yell at me all the time, "Why don't

you make your bed! Do I have to do everything for you!"
After I made my bed, she'd yell, "Why can't you make
your bed right! Look at those sheets! They look like nooses.
I don't know what I'm going to do! Mercy, Lord, please
mercy!" And now I owed her eight hundred dollars and my
bed looked like the gallows they hanged the people who'd
assassinated Abraham Lincoln from, and I hadn't called my
mother this week.

I needed a shower to impress my client, so I took my
clothes off and was just about to turn the shower on when
I realized that I didn't have any soap. I'd used up the last
little scrap a few days before. Also, my razor possessed a
blade so dull that you couldn't shave a pear with it.

I thought about putting my clothes back on and going out
and getting some soap and some razor blades, but then I
remembered that there wasn't a store within a mile of the
place that I didn't owe money to. If I flashed that five dollar
bill in front of a store owner, he'd tear me limb from limb.

No, sir . . .

What was I to do?

I couldn't borrow some soap or a razor blade from any of
the tenants in the building because there wasn't a single one
that I hadn't borrowed down like a forest fire. They wouldn't
loan me a Band-Aid if my throat was cut.

I thought it all over very carefully.

My thinking went something like this: Water is more
important than soap. I mean, what is soap without water?
Nothing. That's what it is. So logically water could handle
the situation by itself, and also it was better than nothing,
if you know what I mean.

Having convinced myself of this logic, I turned the water on and stepped into the shower. I immediately stepped back out.

"YEOWWWWWWWWWWWWWWWWW!" I yelled, jumping around in agony.

The water had been scalding hot and I was paying for it. Too bad my thinking had not been carried to the point of adjusting the temperature of the water so that a human being could stand it.

Oh, well . . .

It was just an oversight on my part. As soon as the pain stopped, I adjusted the hot and cold faucets so that they combined to create an acceptable environment for a shower without soap.

Normally, I sing in the shower, so I started singing in the shower:

"O come, all ye faithful, Joyful and triumphant,
O come ye, O come ye to Bethlehem.
Come and behold Him, Born the King of angels . . ."

I always sing Christmas carols in the shower.

A few years ago a woman spent the night with me when I was living in a fancier apartment. She was the secretary to a used-car dealer. I really liked her. I had hopes that we might get something heavy going between us and maybe a few bucks off a used car.

We'd gone out on a few dates together but this was our first time together in bed and we did pretty good at it, anyway, I thought so. Those were the days when I had soap, so in the morning I went in to take a shower. She was still lying in bed when I left the room. I got into the shower and started singing:

> "It came upon a midnight clear that glorious song of old . . ."

I sang away . . .

When I finished my shower I returned to the bedroom and she was gone. She'd gotten up, dressed and left without saying a word, but she'd left a note on the table beside my bed.

The note read:

Dear Mr. Card,

Thanks for a nice time. Please don't call me again.

Yours sincerely,
Dottie Jones

I guess some people don't want to hear Christmas carols in July.

A World Renowned Expert on Socks

I finished my personal hygienic orgy by throwing the world's least effective shave on my face, thanks to the dullness of the razor blade, the sharpest one I had.

Then I sorted through various piles of my clothes and put together the cleanest wardrobe I could under the conditions brought about by months of extreme poverty, and also I made sure that I had two socks on. They of course didn't match but they were close enough, not unless you were a world renowned expert on socks.

Thank God all of that was going to be taken care of by my new client. They'd get me out of this hell I was in.

I looked over at the clock on the table beside my bed.

Its face barely peeked out from a thousand bits of hopeless clutter. The clock didn't look too happy. I think it would have preferred to have been in the house of a banker or a spinster schoolteacher instead of a San Francisco private eye down on his luck. The hands of the demoralized clock said 5:15. I had forty-five minutes before I was to meet my client in front of the radio station on Powell Street.

I hoped that whatever my client wanted me to do would take place in the radio station because I'd never been in a radio station before and I liked to listen to the radio. I had a lot of favorite programs.

Well, now I was "showered," "shaved," "clean," and "clothed." It was about time I headed downtown. I decided to walk because I was so used to it, but those days were over. My client's fat fee would end that routine, so this walk downtown was a sort of farewell to walking all over the place.

I put the coat back on that had a gun in each pocket: one loaded and one empty. Looking back on it now, I wish I had taken the empty gun out of my pocket, but you can't go back and redo the past. You just have to live with it.

Before leaving the apartment I looked around to see if I had forgotten anything. I of course hadn't. I had so little stuff in this world what in the hell did I have to forget?

A watch, no, a signet ring with a huge diamond, no, a good-luck rabbit's foot, nope. I had eaten that long ago. So just standing there with the two guns in my pockets, I was as ready to leave as I was ever going to be.

The only thing that was nagging my mind was the fact that I still had to call my mother and have the same conversation all over again and take my week's abuse.

Oh, well . . . if they wanted life to be perfect they would have made it that way in the first place and I'm not talking about the Garden of Eden.

Good-bye, Oil Wells
in Rhode Island

The amateur landlady mourners were not at the top of the stairs when I left the building. They certainly had been a ridiculous crew drafted into a pathetic opera of mourning, but now they had all gone back to their ratholes and the landlady was only dead.

I thought about her as I left the place.

I had certainly done a good con job on her when I had gotten a reprieve on my rent by telling her that my uncle had struck it rich with oil wells in Rhode Island. That was a great inspiration, right out of left field, and she bought it. I could have been a great politician if Babylon hadn't gotten in my way.

As I went down the front stairs, I had a vision of the

landlady thinking about oil wells in Rhode Island just as her ticker stopped. I could hear her saying outloud to herself, "I never heard of oil wells in Rhode Island before. Somehow that doesn't sound right to me. I know there are a lot of oil wells in Oklahoma and Texas, and I've seen them in Southern California, but oil wells in Rhode Island?" Then her heart stopped.
Good.

Pretty Pictures

I was walking down Leavenworth Street, very carefully not thinking about Babylon, when suddenly a young man in his early twenties spotted me from across the street and started waving his arms at me.

I had never seen him before.

I didn't know who he was.

I wondered what was up.

He was very anxious to get across the street to me but the light was red and he stood there waiting for it to change. While he waited he kept waving his arms in the air like a crazy windmill.

When the light changed he ran across the street to me.

"Hello, hello," he said like a long-lost brother.

His face was covered with acne and his eyes suffered from character weakness. Who was this bozo?

"Do you remember me?" he said.

I didn't and even if I did, I didn't want to, but as I said I didn't.

"No, I don't remember you," I said.

His clothes were a mess.

He looked as bad as I did.

When I said that I didn't know him, he looked very disheartened as if we had been very good friends and I had forgotten all about him.

Where in the hell did this guy come from?

He was now staring at his feet like a freshly-disciplined puppy.

"Who are you?" I said.

"You don't remember me," he said, sadly.

"Tell me who you are and maybe I'll remember you," I said.

He was now shaking his head dejectedly.

"Well, come on," I said. "Spill the beans. Who are you?"

He continued shaking his head.

I started to walk past him.

He reached out and touched my coat with his hand, so as to stop me from walking away. That gave me two reasons now to have my coat cleaned.

"You sold me some pictures," he said, slowly.

"Pictures?" I said.

"Yeah, pictures of lady women with no clothes on. They were pretty pictures. I took them home. Remember Treasure Island? The Worlds Fair? I took the pictures home with me."

Oh, shit! I bet he took the pictures home with him.

"I need some more pictures," he said. "Those pictures are old."

I had a vision of what those pictures looked like now and shuddered.

"Do you have some more I can buy?" he said. "I need new pictures."

"That was a long time ago," I said. "I'm not doing that any more. That was just a one-time thing."

"No, it was 1940," he said. "That was only two years ago. Don't you have just a few left over? I'll pay you good for them."

He was now staring at me with dog-like pleading eyes. He was desperate for pornography. I'd seen that look before, but those days of selling dirty pictures were behind me now.

"Fuck you, pervert!" I said and continued on down Leavenworth Street toward the radio station.

I had better things to do than stand on a street corner talking to asshole sex perverts. I shuddered again thinking about how those pictures I sold him at the Worlds Fair in 1940 got old.

Pedro and
His Five Romantics

I walked a few more blocks down Leavenworth Street toward meeting my client and then remembered the dream I'd had last night. I dreamt that I was a famous chef from South of the Border and I opened up a Mexican restaurant in Babylon specializing in chiles rellenos and cheese enchiladas.

It became the most famous restaurant in Babylon.

It was near the Hanging Gardens and the finest people in Babylon ate there. Nebuchadnezzar came there often, but he didn't care for the house specialties. He preferred tacos. Sometimes he would be sitting there with one in each hand.

What a character, making jokes all the time and gesturing at people with his tacos.

Nana-dirat worked there as a dancer.

The place had a stage with a small mariachi band: Pedro and His Five Romantics.

They could play up a storm and when Nana-dirat danced everybody ordered more beer to cool themselves off. She was a Mexican firecracker dancing in old Babylon.

Uh-oh, suddenly I realized as I was walking down the street toward my client that I was thinking about Babylon again. Big mistake.

I stopped it immediately.

I slammed on the brakes.

Got to be careful. Can't let Babylon get me. I had too many things going for me. Later for Babylon. So I rearranged my thought patterns to concentrate on something else and the thing I chose to think about was my shoes. I needed a new pair. The ones I was wearing were worn out.

Smith Smith

I was a block away from the radio station, busy thinking about my shoes, when the name Smith Smith flashed into my mind and I blurted out, "Great!" The whole world could have heard me but fortunately there was nobody around. That block of Powell Street was quiet. There were a few people at each end of the block but I was alone in the middle of the block.

Luck was still with me.

Smith Smith, I thought, *that's the name for my private eye in Babylon.* He'll be called Smith Smith.

I'd come up with the perfect variation of the name Smith. I'd combined it with a second Smith. I was really proud of myself. Too bad I didn't have anybody to share my accomplishment with but I knew if I told anybody about Smith Smith it would be good cause for an involuntary trip to the nuthouse, which was where I wasn't interested in going. I'd keep Smith Smith to myself. I went back to thinking about my shoes.

Roast Turkey
and Dressing

I arrived at the radio station at ten of six. I wanted to be on time to show that I was a responsible private detective who had better things to do than think about Babylon all the time.

There was nobody else in front of the radio station. My client whoever they were hadn't arrived yet.

I was very curious about who would show up.

I didn't know whether it would be a man or a woman. If it was a woman I hoped that she would be very rich and beautiful and she would fall madly in love with me and want me to retire from the private-eye business and live a life of luxury, and I'd spend half my time fucking her, the other half dreaming of Babylon.

It would be a good life.

I could hardly wait to get started.

Then I thought about what would happen if a Sydney Greenstreet–type client showed up who wanted me to tail a Filipino cook who was having a love affair with his wife, and I'd have to spend a lot of time sitting at the counter of the café that he cooked in, watching him cook.

The case would take a month.

Every week I'd meet with Sydney Greenstreet in his huge Pacific Heights apartment and describe in detail to him everything the Filipino cook had done that week. He was very interested in everything the Filipino cook did, even to the point of wanting to know what the menu was on Wednesday in the restaurant the cook worked at.

I'd be sitting opposite Sydney Greenstreet in this fantastic apartment filled with rare art works. The apartment would have a tremendous view of San Francisco, and I'd have a glass of fifty-year-old sherry in my hand that was constantly being refilled by Peter Lorre who was the butler.

Peter Lorre would project an illusion of poised disinterest in our conversation when he was in the room with us, but later I would see him hovering near the door to the room, eavesdropping.

"What was the menu on Wednesday?" Sydney Greenstreet would say with his huge fleshy hand incongruously wrapped around a delicate sherry glass.

Peter Lorre would be hovering on the other side of the open living room door, pretending that he was dusting a large vase but actually listening very carefully to what we were saying.

111

"The soup was rice tomato," I'd say. "The salad was a Waldorf salad."

"I'm not interested in the soup," Sydney Greenstreet would say. "Or the salad. I want to know what the entrées were."

"I'm sorry," I'd say. After all, it was his money. He was paying the bill. "The entrées were:

Fried Prawns
Grilled Sea Bass with Lemon Butter
Filet of Sole with Tartar Sauce
Veal Fricassee with Vegetables
Corned Beef Hash with Egg
Grilled Pork Chop and Apple Sauce
Grilled Baby Beef Liver and Onions
Chicken Croquettes
Ham Croquettes with Pineapple Sauce
Breaded Veal Cutlet with Brown Sauce
Fried Unjointed Spring Chicken
Baked Virginia Ham with Sweet Potatoes
Roast Turkey and Dressing
Corn-fed Steer Beef Club Sirloin Steak
French Lamb Chops and Green Peas
New York Cut Sirloin."

"Did you try one of the entrées?" he'd ask.

"Yes," I'd say. "I had the roast turkey and dressing."

"How was it?" he would ask, leaning anxiously toward me in his chair.

"Terrible," I'd say.

"Good," he'd say, with a great deal of relish, smacking his

lips with pleasure. "I don't understand what she sees in him. They're both swine. They deserve each other."

Then he would pause and lean back comfortably in his chair and take an appreciative sip of sherry. He would look at me with contentment in his lazy tropical eyes.

"The roast turkey and dressing were terrible?" he'd ask.

"Were they really that bad?" with almost a smile on his face.

"The dressing was the worst I ever tasted," I'd say. "I think it was made out of dog shit. I don't know how anyone could eat it. I took one taste and that was enough for me."

"How interesting," Sydney Greenstreet would say. "How very interesting."

I'd look over at Peter Lorre who'd be pretending to dust a large green vase with Chinamen riding horses on it.

He would also think my comments on the roast turkey and dressing were interesting, too.

Cinderella
of the Airways

I was standing there in front of radio station WXYZ "Cinderella of the Airways" thinking about Sydney Greenstreet and Peter Lorre, roast turkey and dressing, when the Cadillac limousine that had driven by me earlier in the day when I was going into the morgue pulled up in front of me and the rear door opened effortlessly toward me. The beautiful blonde I'd seen leaving the morgue was sitting in the back seat of the limousine.

She gestured with her eyes for me to get in.

It was a blue gesture.

I got in beside her.

She was wearing a fur coat that was worth more than all

the people I know put together and multiplied twice. She smiled. "What a coincidence," she said. "We saw each other at the morgue. It's a small world."

"It sure is," I said. "I take it that you're my—"

"Client," she said. "Do you have a gun?"

"Yes," I said. "I've got one."

"Good," she said. "That's very good. I think we're going to be friends. Close friends."

"Why do you need somebody with a gun? What am I supposed to do?" I said.

"I've seen all the movies," she said, smiling. She had perfect teeth. They were so perfect that they made me feel self-conscious about my teeth. I felt as if I had a mouth full of broken glass.

The same chauffeur who'd been driving her earlier in the day was in the front seat behind the wheel. He had a very powerful-looking neck. He hadn't looked back once since I'd gotten into the car. He just kept staring straight ahead. His neck looked as if it could dent an ax.

"Cozy?" the rich blonde said.

"Sure," I said, having seen this movie before.

"Mr. Cleveland," she said, addressing the chauffeur who answered her with a twitch of his neck.

The car started slowly down the street.

"Where are we off to?" I said, offhandedly.

"Sausalito to have a beer," she said.

That seemed strange.

The last thing in the world that she looked like was a beer drinker.

"Surprised?" she said.

"No," I said, lying.

"You're not being truthful," she said, smiling at me. Those teeth were really something.

"OK, a little," I said. She had all the money. I'd play any game she wanted me to.

"People are always surprised when I say I want a beer. They naturally assume that I'm a champagne-type lady because of the way I look and dress, but looks can be deceiving."

When she'd said the word champagne, the chauffeur's neck twitched violently.

"Mr. Card?" she said.

"Oh," I said, looking from the chauffeur's neck back to her.

"Don't you think so?" she said. "Or are you a person who's taken in by looks?"

As I said, it was her money and I wanted some.

"To be honest with you, lady, I'm surprised that you're a beer drinker."

"Call me Miss Ann," she said.

"OK, Miss Ann, I'm surprised that you prefer beer to champagne."

The chauffeur's neck twitched violently again.

What in the hell was happening?

"Are you a champagne man?" she said, and as soon as she said the word champagne the chauffeur's neck twitched again. It was a twitch that looked powerful enough to break your thumb if you were touching his neck when the twitch went off. This guy's neck was something to be reckoned with.

"Mr. Card, did you hear me?" she said. "Are you a champagne man? Do you like champagne?"

The neck went off again like a gorilla rattling the bars of its cage.

"No, I like bourbon," I said. "Old Crow on the rocks."

The chauffeur's neck stopped twitching.

"How droll," she said. "We're going to have a wonderful time together."

"What are we going to do?" I said.

"Don't worry," she said. "There's plenty of time for that."

The chauffeur's neck remained quiet as we drove through San Francisco toward the Golden Gate Bridge. I could see that his neck had the potential for providing trouble in the future. I thought of what might happen if you crossed that neck. I didn't like that idea at all. I was going to keep on the good side of the neck. That neck and I were going to be close buddies if I had my way about it.

The neck didn't like the word champagne.

I would be very careful to avoid using that word in the future.

The neck liked the word bourbon, so that was a word that the neck was going to hear a lot of.

What in the hell was I getting myself into?

We drove down Lombard Street toward the Golden Gate Bridge and what I was going to get myself into.

Smith Smith Versus the Shadow Robots

Halfway across the Golden Gate Bridge, sitting beside a beautiful rich dame with a gigantic and very unstable neck driving the car, it came to me: the name for my serial about a private eye in Babylon. I would call it *Smith Smith Versus the Shadow Robots*. What a great title! I was almost beside myself with joy.

"What is it?" my client said who hadn't spoken in a couple of minutes as we drove along.

I started to say outloud the title of my serial. It was involuntary but I was able to stop it after the first word blurted itself out.

"Smith—" I said, stopping the rest of the words by sitting a mental elephant down on my tongue.

"Smith?" my client said.

The neck of the chauffeur looked as if it were about to twitch. I sure as hell didn't want that.

"I just remembered that a friend of mine's birthday was yesterday and I forgot all about it," I said. "I was going to give him a present. His name is Smith. A wonderful guy. A fisherman. He's got a boat down on the wharf. I grew up with his son. We went to Galileo High School together."

"Oh," my rich blonde client said with a slightly bored tone to her voice. She didn't want to hear about a fisherman named Smith. I wondered how she would have reacted if I had finished what I started out to say: *Smith Smith Versus the Shadow Robots.*

I would have found it very interesting to see how she would have handled that one. Thank God I only said the word Smith. I might have been out a client or even worse that neck might have gone into action.

The neck was relaxed now, just driving the car across the bridge.

A freighter was going out on the tide.

Its lights floated on the water.

"I want you to steal a dead body," my client said.

The Morning Paper

"What?" I said because a what was certainly needed at this time and nothing else but a what would be adequate for the situation.

"I want you to steal a body from the morgue."

She didn't say anything else.

She had very blue eyes. Even in the semidarkness of the car the blue was easy to see. Her eyes were staring at me. They waited for me to respond.

The neck waited, too.

"Sure," I said. "If the money's interesting enough I'll have Abraham Lincoln's body on your doorstep tomorrow with the morning paper."

That was exactly what she wanted to hear.

The neck wanted to hear it, too.

"How does a thousand dollars sound?" she said.

"For a thousand dollars," I said, "I'll bring you a whole cemetery."

Beer Tastes on a Champagne Budget

The lights of San Francisco looked beautiful shining across the bay from where we were sitting in a little bar in Sausalito.

My client was enjoying a beer.

She took a great deal of pleasure from drinking it. She didn't drink the way you'd expect her to. There was nothing lady-like the way she handled her beer. She drank beer like a longshoreman on payday.

She'd taken her fur coat off and underneath she was wearing a dress that showed off a knockout figure. This whole thing was just like a pulp detective story. I couldn't believe it.

The neck was out in the car, waiting for us, so I felt a little more relaxed around her. If I wanted to I could use the word champagne without fear of the unknown. The world sure is a strange place. No wonder I spend so much time dreaming of Babylon. It's safer.

"Where is the body you want stolen?" I said, watching this delicate-looking rich dame belt down a gulp of beer. Then belch. "You really enjoy your beer, don't you?" I said.

"I have beer tastes on a champagne budget," she said. When she said champagne I involuntarily looked around for the neck. Thank God it was in the car.

"Now about this body you want," I said.

"Where do they keep bodies?" she said as if I were a little slow.

"A lot of places," I said. "But mostly in the ground. Do I need a shovel for this job?"

"No, silly," she said. "The body's in the morgue. Isn't that a logical place to keep one?"

"Yeah," I said. "It'll do."

She took another huge gulp of beer.

I motioned to the cocktail waitress to bring us some more beer. While I did this my client finished off the one that was in front of her. I think she'd just set the world record for a rich woman drinking a beer. I don't think Johnny Weissmuller could have gone through a beer any faster.

The waitress put another beer down in front of her.

I was still dabbling in an Old Crow on the rocks that I had ordered when we first came into the place. It would be my only drink. I wasn't much of a drinking person: a drink now and then, and one was my limit.

She went at the second beer with the same relish she had applied to the first beer. She was right when she said that she was a beer drinker.

"Do you think you can handle stealing a body from the morgue?" she said.

"Yeah, I can handle it," I said.

Then something popped up like a shooting gallery rabbit in my mind. Peg-leg had told me that she'd looked at the body of the dead prostitute for possible identification as a relative but said it wasn't the right person and she'd been very cold about the whole thing as if looking at dead bodies was a normal part of her day.

I thought about her crying when she left the morgue.

This was getting interesting.

Playing it casual, I said, "Who's the body you want me to steal from the morgue?"

"Who it is isn't important," she said. "That's my business. I just want you to get the body for me. It's the body of a young woman. She's upstairs in the autopsy room. There's a four-unit storage space for corpses built into the wall. She's on the top left side. She's got a Jane Doe tag on her big toe. Get her for me."

"OK," I said. "Where do you want the body after I get it?"

"I want you to take it to a cemetery," she said.

"That's simple enough," I said. "That's where bodies end up, anyway."

I ordered her another beer. She had already finished the second one. I had never seen a glass of beer look so empty, so fast before in my life. She practically breathed beer.

"Thank you," she said.

"When do you want the body?" I said.

"Tonight," she said. "Holy Rest Cemetery."

"That sounds soon enough," I said.

"May I ask what you're going to do with it?" I said.

"Come on, bright boy," she said. "What do you do with bodies in a cemetery?"

"OK," I said. "I get the picture. Do you want me to bring along a shovel?"

"No," she said. "You just bring the body to the cemetery and we'll take care of the rest. All we want from you is the body."

When she said we, I assumed what it took to make a we was the neck.

I ordered her another beer.

Earthquake in
an Anvil Factory

"It's now seven-thirty," she said as we were sitting in the back seat of the limousine being driven back to San Francisco by the neck.

"I want the body at the cemetery at one A.M.," she said very succinctly, not showing in the slightest the effects of the six beers she'd put away in record time.

"OK," I said. "But if I'm late you can start without me."

The neck twitched in the front seat.

"Just kidding," I said.

"It's very important that the body be there at one A.M.," she said. She was sitting close to me and her breath hadn't the slightest scent of beer to it. Also, after finishing the six beers she got directly back into the car without going to the toilet. I wondered where in the hell the beer had gone to. "Don't worry," I said. "I'll have the body there on time." "Good," she said.

I paused before I spoke again. I wanted the words that I was going to use to be the right ones. I didn't want any sloppy or inadequate words to come out of my mouth.

"I'll need half my fee up front," I said. "And also, I'll need three hundred dollars expense money. Some palms are going to have to be greased. I think you can appreciate the fact that stealing a body from the morgue is not your every-day run-of-the-mill thing. The city doesn't particularly like to lose bodies. People are prone to ask questions. It takes money to provide the answers."

"I understand," she said.

I looked over at her.

Where in the hell was that beer?

"Mr. Cleveland," she said to the neck driving the car. The neck reached into his coat pocket and took out a roll of bills and handed them back to me. The roll contained exactly eight hundred dollars in one hundred dollar bills. It was as if they had read my mind.

"Is that satisfactory?" she said.

I almost fainted when the money was handed to me. It had been a long time like light-years to the nearest star. I hadn't seen this much money since I'd gotten paid off for my automobile accident.

This was definitely the start of an upward trend in my life. I couldn't have been happier as I sat there driving across the Golden Gate Bridge and all I had to do to earn the money was to steal a corpse.

Then the neck spoke for the first time. A voice that

sounded like an earthquake in an anvil factory came from the front of the neck that didn't bother to turn its head toward me.

"Don't fuck up," the neck said. "We want that body."

The Private Detectives of San Francisco

I didn't take the neck seriously. Stealing that body would not be a difficult task at all. There would be nothing to it. It was as good as in the cemetery right now.

I felt wonderful as we went through the tollgate.

I was on top of the world.

Money again!

I'd be able to get some of my debts off my back and be able to have an office again and maybe even a part-time secretary. I could even afford an old car to get around in.

Things couldn't have looked better for me at that time. I was looking at the world through rose-colored glasses. It didn't even bother me that I couldn't figure out where six glasses of beer had disappeared to in my fancy client. They were there someplace. That's all I needed to know.

Something crossed my contented mind.

I couldn't resist asking about it.

"By the way," I said. "How did you hear about me? I mean, there are a lot more well-known private detectives in San Francisco. Why did you choose me?"

"You're the only one we could trust to steal a body for us," the rich blonde said. "The other detectives might have some scruples. You don't have any."

It was of course true.

I wasn't offended at all.

I didn't have anything to hide.

"Where did you hear about me?" I said.

"I have my sources," she said.

"Don't fuck up," the neck said.

Future Practice

I had them let me off at a fancy apartment building with a doorman a few blocks away from where I lived. I told them that's where I lived.

They pulled up in front of the place and let me out.

The doorman looked curiously at me.

"Thanks for taking me home," I said.

The neck turned toward me as I got out of the car and it spoke. "Why do you want to get out here?" it said. "You don't live here. You live in a rat-trap a couple of blocks away. But maybe you need the exercise. We don't care where you live. We just want that body at the south gate of Holy Rest Cemetery at one A.M. Sharp."

I stood there not being able to think of anything to say.

Who were these people? How did they know so much about me? I didn't think I was that popular.

"I'm practicing," I said, finally. "Someday I'll live here."

The neck started to speak again, "Don't—"

"I know," I said. "Fuck up."

"See you later, Mr. Card," the fancy blonde said to me with six glasses of beer hidden somewhere in her beautiful body.

The car drove slowly away.

I watched it until it turned a corner and was gone.

The doorman started sweeping the sidewalk. He was sweeping very close to me. I moved on.

C. Card,
Private Investigator

I still hadn't called my mother.

She was back from the cemetery by now.

I'd better get that done with. Also, I'd be able to tell her that I could repay some of the money that I had borrowed from her. Of course I wouldn't tell her the size of my fee because she'd want more money than I wanted to repay her.

I was very much interested now in getting an office, a secretary and a car. My mother could wait. She was used to it. She wouldn't do anything but put the money in the bank, and that's the last place in this world where I wanted my money.

I needed an office that had

C. Card
Private Investigator

in gold on the door, and I needed a gorgeous secretary taking dictation.

Dear Mr. Cupertino,

Thank you very much for the five-hundred-dollar bonus for finding your daughter. It's a pleasure to do business with a gentleman. If you ever lose her again, you know where to find me, and the next time it's on the house.

> Yours sincerely,
> C. Card

And I needed a car so I could get around town without wearing holes in my shoes. There's something about a private detective walking or taking the bus that lacks class.

It makes clients uncomfortable to meet a private detective who has a bus transfer sticking out of his shirt pocket.

But right now I'd better call my mother.

I walked a couple of blocks to a phone booth.

I dropped a nickel in and then put the receiver up to my ear. There was no dial tone. I pressed the coin return but my nickel stayed inside the telephone. I clicked the telephone hook. Silence continued inside the receiver, and it was not golden. It was my fucking nickel.

God-damn it!

I was out a nickel.

Big business had fucked me over again.

I hit the telephone a couple of times with my fist to make

the point that some people won't take being robbed without putting up a fight.

I left the phone booth and walked half a block.

I turned around and looked angrily back at the telephone. An old man was standing inside the booth. He had the receiver in his hand and he was talking to somebody on the telephone.

You just can't win.

I wondered if the old man was using his nickel or perhaps in some totally unjust way he had managed to make his call as the result of my nickel.

The only revenge I got out of the situation was the thought that if he was making that call with my nickel, I hoped that he was calling his doctor to get some relief from a hideous attack of hemorrhoids.

That was the only way that I was going to come out on top of this bad deal.

I turned around and walked to the bus stop on Clay Street. I was going to take the bus down to the morgue. I could have gotten a cab but I decided to take the bus as a sort of farewell bus trip because I was never going to have to ride a bus again.

This was the last time.

A young woman was waiting for the bus.

She was kind of good looking, so I decided to try out my new affluence by giving her a big smile and saying good evening.

She didn't return the smile and she didn't say good evening.

She nervously turned her back on me.

Suddenly the bus loomed up a block away.

A minute later I was sitting on the bus heading back down to the morgue. I got on the bus first and when I sat down in a front seat, the young woman went to the back of the bus.

I've just never been a lady's man but that was all going to change as soon as I stole that body and got the rest of my fee and became the most famous private detective in San Francisco, make that California, no, let's make it America. Why settle for less than the whole God-damn country?

I already had a foolproof plan to steal the body.

Nothing could go wrong.

It was perfect.

So I settled back in my seat and started dreaming of Babylon. My mind slipped effortlessly back into the past. I was no longer on the bus. I was in Babylon.

Chapter 1 /
Smith Smith Versus
the Shadow Robots

Deep in the hidden recesses of his cellar laboratory hidden under the clinic that he used to lure unsuspecting sick people into only to change them into shadow robots, Dr. Abdul Forsythe was removing a person who had been changed into a shadow from his diabolical transformation chamber.

"This is a good one," he said, examining the texture of the shadow.

"You're a genius," his henchman Rotha said, standing beside the doctor, looking at the shadow. After admiring his handiwork, Dr. Abdul Forsythe gave the shadow to Rotha who took it over and put it on top of a six-foot pile of shadows. There were a thousand shadows in the pile. There were a dozen or so piles in the laboratory.

Dr. Forsythe had enough shadows to create an artificial night large enough to take over a small town. He only lacked one thing to put his plot into action. That one ingredient was the mercury crystals that had just been invented by Dr. Francis, a humanitarian doctor who had devoted his life to good works in Babylon. He lived near the Ishtar Gate with his beautiful daughter Cynthia who had a half-sister named Nana-dirat.

Dr. Francis had invented the mercury crystals to power a rocket ship that he was constructing to fly to the moon with.

After Rotha had put the shadow of an unfortunate sandal maker, who'd come to the clinic to have a sore looked at but had stayed to end up as a shadow and part of a diabolical plan, on the pile, he returned to the side of his evil master.

"Now what, boss?" Rotha said.

"The mercury crystals," Dr. Abdul Forsythe said. "Then we're in business." They both laughed fiendishly. You could tell by the way they laughed that the business they were involved in did not have retirement benefits. There was no pension for what they were doing.

Quickdraw Artist

Suddenly I realized where I was at and like a quickdraw artist in a cowboy movie my hand flew up and pulled the cord to stop the bus. I got it just in time.

Another few seconds and I would have missed my stop.

Dreaming of Babylon is a tricky business.

One miscalculation and you're blocks beyond your stop.

Fortunately, this was my last bus trip and I wouldn't have to worry about missing my stop any more. Thank God. Once I went all the way to the end of the line dreaming of Babylon and I didn't have enough money to get back and the driver wouldn't let me ride for free, even after I had explained to him that I didn't have any money and told a lie to him, that I had fallen asleep.

"I hear stories like this all the time," he said, with a remarkable lack of concern for my plight. "You can't ride my bus with stories for a fare. I want a nickel. If you don't have a nickel, get off my bus. I don't make the rules. It costs a nickel to ride. I'm just a working stiff, so get off my bus."

I didn't like the way the son-of-a-bitch kept saying "my bus" as if he owned the God-damn thing.

"Do you own this bus?" I said.

"What do you mean?" he said.

"I mean, do you own this bus? You keep saying 'my bus' so I thought maybe you owned the fucking bus and you take it home with you and sleep with it. Maybe you're even married to it. This bus is your wife."

I didn't get to say anything else because the bus driver knocked me unconscious with one blow right there from his seat. It was lights out. I came to about ten minutes later, sitting on the sidewalk, leaning up against the front of a drugstore.

To have the perfect ending for a bus trip was what woke me up. It was a dog peeing on me. Maybe he thought that I looked like a fire hydrant. Anyway, those days were over. I had eight hundred bucks in my pocket and this had been my last bus trip.

When I got off the bus, I turned around and yelled "Fuck you!" at the driver. He looked bewildered. It served him right. No more dogs were going to pee on me.

Ghouls

As I walked into the morgue two guys were walking out carrying a large bag between them. You couldn't tell what was in the bag but it was heavy. They seemed to be in quite a hurry. There was a car double-parked in front of the morgue and the trunk was open. They put the bag in the trunk, closed it and drove off. They were in such a hurry that the rear tires screeched when they drove away.

I wondered briefly what was in the bag. It was kind of late to be taking things out of the morgue but obviously they had a reason because that's what they had just done. I walked back into the morgue, looking for Peg-leg but I couldn't find him. He wasn't in the autopsy room or downstairs in "cold storage" with his beloved stiffs. I walked back out into the front hall and there was Peg-leg coming in the door. He had a paper bag in his hand. He pegged down the hall toward me.

"Well," he said. "If it isn't a sight for poor eyes. What are you doing back here? Looking for a partner who's as bad a dancer as you are? Well, we got 'em. Dead people dance almost as badly as you do, 'Eye.' "

That was a joke that Peg-leg liked to repeat as often as he could. We'd once gone dancing together on a double-date with a couple of stenographers. I've always been a terrible dancer. He thought it was really funny watching me try to dance with a dumb redhead.

Peg-leg of course is a great dancer. It always amazes people. Often a whole dance hall will come to a complete stop with everybody standing there watching Peg-leg dance. They can't believe it. When I dance nobody cares.

People have even suggested seriously that Peg-leg open up a dance studio like Arthur Murray.

I'd like to see that.

"What have you got in the bag?" I said, changing the subject away from my dancing.

"A sandwich and you can't have any. It's my dinner. What are you doing here, anyway, 'Eye?' Returning my gun and paying back the fifty you owe me? I sure hope so, but I don't think my heart could take it."

"No," I said. "I've got a business proposition for you."

"You're too broke to have a business proposition," Peg-leg said. "So what do you really want?"

"I'm not kidding," I said. "I've got a bona fide proposition and some money to back it up."

"Money?" he said. "You?"

"Yeah, my bad-luck streak is over. I'm on my way to the top. Nothing can stop me."

"I know you're not a drinking man, 'Eye,' so you've got to be sober. Jesus. First, Pearl Harbor and now you've got a business proposition. What next? Let's go back to my office and talk about this, but you'd better not be pulling my leg because if you do you're going to get some splinters in your hand."

Peg-leg's "office" was a desk in the autopsy room.

I walked behind Peg-leg who was agilely moving along on his wooden stem.

"Hey," I said, suddenly remembering the two men and the bag they were carrying. "Did you have something picked up here a few minutes ago?"

"What do you mean?" Peg-leg said.

"Two men walked out of here with a large bag full of something."

"No," Peg-leg said. "Nobody was supposed to pick up anything here. It's too late for pickups. I think the City and County of San Francisco just got robbed. I wonder what they took. What in the hell can you steal from a morgue? We've only got one thing here. I mean, this isn't a grocery store." When he said that, he stopped talking and looked very seriously at me. Then he scratched his chin and sighed.

"As I said," he said. "We've only got one thing here and I think we're probably one less now."

"Are you thinking what I'm starting to think?" I said, starting to think it.

"Yup," he said. "Ghouls."

143

Cold Heartless Cash

We walked back to Peg-leg's "office"—the autopsy room.

When we got there Peg-leg stood for a few seconds in front of a small icebox for dead people that was built into one wall. It was a mini-refrigerator that had enough space for four corpses. The rest of the stiffs were kept downstairs in a big cold storage room. The ones they kept upstairs were special. I don't know why. I never asked. I didn't care.

I thought that Peg-leg was going to check the icebox to see if anybody was missing from there but instead he walked over to his desk and sat down and took his sandwich out of the paper bag. He motioned toward the coffee pot that was on a hot plate on the desk beside him. "Get yourself a cup," he said, then motioning toward an autopsy sink that had some cups beside it. "Pour me some while you're at it. I'm going to eat my sandwich while it's still hot."

"What about the missing body?" I said, going over to the autopsy sink and getting the cups.

"It's still going to be gone by the time my sandwich cools off. I didn't get a hot sandwich to eat it cold. Do you know what I mean?"

"Yeah," I said. "I understand. I just wondered who would steal a body from the morgue."

"I told you," Peg-leg said, taking a bite out of a bacon, lettuce and tomato sandwich, the old BLT. His words became entangled with the sandwich but I could still make them out. "Ghouls," he said. "But why in the hell couldn't they get a body from the cemetery? Why did they want one of mine?"

"Maybe they wanted a fresh one instead of a stale one," I said.

"That sounds logical," Peg-leg said. "Sort of. I guess."

I poured two cups of Peg-leg's coffee and took a sip of mine. I grimaced as the fluid hit my taste buds. His coffee had the same effect as being whacked in the mouth with a baseball bat.

"You could raise the dead with this coffee," I said.

"Don't think I haven't thought about it," Peg-leg said. "Especially that little whore they brought in this morning."

"You mean the one you were getting ready to fuck when I came by earlier?" I said.

"I wasn't going to fuck her," Peg-leg said. "I don't know where you get ideas like that. Just say I'm a fan of the human body. I like its contours and lines."

"That's a different way of putting it," I said. "From where I was standing you looked about five seconds away from humping her."

"Hey, what are you doing down here again?" Peg-leg said, changing the subject.

"I told you," I said. "I've got a business proposition for you. You can make some money."

"What do you mean *make* some money?" Peg-leg said. "You already *owe* me some money. When are you going to pay up? That's the cash I'm interested in."

"Right now," I said and reached into my pocket. I knew that I was going to have to repay him the money I owed him before I could get on with my business transaction.

"Here's a hundred," I said, liking this part a lot. "Now you owe me some money, Keeper of Dead People."

Peg-leg couldn't believe the hundred dollar bill in his clammy hand. He stared at it as if it were a miracle. He was suddenly a very happy Peg-leg.

"It must be real. I know it's not a mirage because I can feel it in my hand. What's the business proposition?" Peg-leg said. "I want more of this stuff. I know exactly where to spend it."

"There's two hundred dollars more where that came from," I said.

"Hurray!" Peg-leg said. "What do I have to do?"

"You have a car, don't you?" I said.

"Yeah, an old Plymouth," Peg-leg said. "You know the car. Why?"

"I want to borrow it," I said.

"Consider it yours, old pal," Peg-leg said. "Where's

the two hundred? This is the easiest money I've ever made."

"That's not all I want," I said. "There's something else. I want to put it in the trunk."

"I'll help," Peg-leg said. "Where are the C notes?"

"Don't you want to know what I want you to help me put in the trunk?" I said.

"For two hundred dollars I don't care what you're going to put in the trunk," Peg-leg said. "I'll help. I'm your man. Where's it at?" He was staring happily at the hundred dollar bill in his hand.

"Here," I said.

"What?" Peg-leg said, looking up.

"You've got what I want to put in the trunk right here," I said.

Peg-leg looked puzzled. He was mulling it over in his mind. It didn't take him long. I could see that he was mentally approaching what I wanted. Then he was there.

"What in the hell is going on? You're not thinking what I think you're thinking?" Peg-leg said. "No, not two of them in the same night. Tell me I'm wrong."

"You're right," I said. "It's a strange world. I've been hired to steal a stiff and you've got the body the people want right here."

"What do they want a dead body for?" Peg-leg said.

"Lonely, I guess. I don't know," I said. "It's their business and I don't care just as long as I see some long green looking up at me from my palm. Are you still interested in the two hundred?"

"Sure," Peg-leg said. "I don't care. I'm already out one

corpse today and I didn't get a cent for it or even a thank you. It's just as easy to explain the absence of two bodies as it is one. I'm your man. Let me see the two hundred and take your pick."

I gave him the two hundred.

He was ecstatic.

"Take your pick," Peg-leg said, making a grandiose circle in the air with the hand that contained the money. "Take your pick. You can have anyone you want."

"I'm sorry but I'm going to have to break up your romance," I said. "I hope I don't break your heart but somebody will come along to replace her. Women are dying all the time."

"Oh, no," Peg-leg said. "Not her. She's my favorite."

"I'm sorry, pal," I said.

He shook his head.

"I'll get her for you," Peg-leg said.

"I'm surprised at you," I said. "Selling your sweetie for cold heartless cash. How can you do it?"

"Easy," Peg-leg said. "She's heartless, too. We did an autopsy on her while you were gone."

Time Heals
All Wounds

Peg-leg finished eating his BLT.

"Let's get your body for you," he said. "I hate to see her go. She's the prettiest corpse I've had here in years."

"You'll get over it," I said. "Time heals all wounds."

"No," Peg-leg said. "Two hundred bucks does."

"Where's she at?" I said, pretending that I didn't already know. Don't ask me why.

Peg-leg pointed over at the four-corpse refrigerator in the autopsy room. "Top left," he said.

I walked over to the refrigerator, opened the top left door and started to pull the tray out.

"No, it's the top right," Peg-leg said. "I forgot. I moved her. She's in the top right."

"I know. There's nobody in here," I said. I was going to tell Peg-leg but he told me first.

"What?" Peg-leg said and walked over to the refrigerator. "There should be a corpse in there. I put one in there a few hours ago. What in the hell is going on?" He looked inside as if the corpse were hiding in there and he was going to find it. "God-damn it! There was a divorcée in here when I went out to get my sandwich and now she's gone. She killed herself this afternoon. Climbed into an oven with the gas on. Where did she go? I mean, she was dead."

"That's your problem," I said. "I just paid you two hundred dollars for the body of a dead whore, and I want her. She's over here on the left, huh? Are you sure?"

"Yeah," Peg-leg said, shaking his head over the absence of the divorcée's corpse. "Over here." He pulled out the tray, lifted up the sheet and there she was. "See, two hundred dollars' worth. But where did that other body go? It was here a couple of hours ago. Now it's gone. What in the hell is going on in this place?"

Suddenly a thought came to my mind.

Thank God it wasn't about Babylon.

"Wait a minute," I said. "I'll bet you anything she was the body the two guys stole from here a little while ago."

"I think you're right, 'Eye,' " Peg-leg said. "You are right. That's the only thing that could have happened. They stole the divorcée. Why would anyone want her body? She was real ugly. A wino. I don't know why anyone would want her. She was a total mess. I think she did herself and the world a favor by getting in the oven."

Interesting, I thought. There seemed to be more to this than met the eye. I wondered if perhaps those two guys had gotten the wrong body, and the body they had intended to steal was the one I was looking at.

This was starting to get complicated.

Maybe this wasn't going to be as easy as it had looked in the beginning. Suddenly I was very glad that I had a gun in my pocket with some bullets in it. Who knows? That gun might come in handy.

Yeah, the night had the possibility of being a long one and I'd better keep on my toes. The first thing I had to do was to get the body I was being paid to steal out of the morgue. When those guys found out that they had the wrong body they might come back looking for the right one and they might not be nice about it.

The
Jack Benny Show

"Let's get this thing out of here," I said.

"Listen, 'Eye,'" Peg-leg said. "Don't talk like that about her. She doesn't like being dead any more than you would. OK?"

I'd gotten Peg-leg's dandruff up.

"I'm sorry," I said, though I wasn't sorry at all. I just wanted to get on with it.

"I'll find something to put her into," Peg-leg said, pacified.

"Where's your car?" I said.

"Parked across the street," Peg-leg said. "I always park it across the street."

He pegged over and opened up a closet door. There was a pile of corpse-dirty laundry beside a full laundry bag. "God-damn it! The bastards stole my laundry bag," Peg-leg said, opening up the other laundry bag and dumping its contents on top of the other pile. "This makes two of them they stole," he said. "Anyway, that's what I'm going to tell the police after you give me a punch on the jaw, so I can have a good alibi for this caper. I'll tell them that two body snatchers raided the icebox. I put up a good fight but they knocked me out. Maybe I'll even get a medal and the mayor will shake my cold, cold hand."

We put the young prostitute's body in the laundry bag. Peg-leg did a good job of folding her up.

"You're pretty good at this kind of business," I said.

"I should be," Peg-leg said. "I got a gold watch last year for my ten thousandth corpse." He gave her a little pat on the head before pulling the strings that closed the top of the laundry bag over her head.

"Good-bye, baby," Peg-leg said. "I'll miss you."

"Don't worry," I said. "You'll catch up with her later on."

"Funny man," Peg-leg said. "You should be on the *Jack Benny Show.*"

A Strange Cup of
Sugar from Oakland

Peg-leg helped me carry her out to his car.

I was smiling as we toted her along.

Peg-leg looked curiously at me. "Let me in on it," he said.

"I was just thinking," I said. "There sure are a lot of bodies going out of this place in laundry bags. If it keeps up at this rate, you'll be out of bodies by the end of the week, and to be a respectable big-city morgue, you'll have to borrow some from Oakland."

"I wish I hadn't asked," Peg-leg said.

We were now halfway across the street carrying the body between us.

Peg-leg opened up the trunk of his car and we put the body in. He closed the lid and handed me the keys.

"Hey, what about my gun?" Peg-leg said. "When are you going to return it? With body thieves running all over the God-damn place, present company included, I need my cannon. I don't know what in the hell is going to happen in there next." He motioned with his head toward the morgue that was running out of bodies at a very fast clip.

"The gun's part of the two hundred," I said. "I'll return it tomorrow with your car."

"You strike a hard bargain," Peg-leg said.

"Do you want your body back?" I said.

"Nope."

"You always were a fickle one with the ladies," I said. "Are you sure you don't want her back?"

"She's yours," Peg-leg said. "I'll take the two hundred and buy a piece of ass from a live one." He started back across the street, then he stopped in his tracks, one of which was wooden. "Hey," he said. "You forgot to hit me on the jaw. My alibi. Remember?"

"Sure," I said. "Bring your jaw back here."

I hit him on the jaw.

His head snapped back four inches.

"Does that do it?" I said.

Peg-leg was rubbing his jaw.

"Yeah, that does it. Thanks, 'Eye.' "

"Don't mention it."

He pegged back into the morgue.

Warner Brothers

I got into the front seat of the car and put the key into the ignition. All I had to do now was drive around for a few hours and kill some time until 1 A.M. and body-delivery time at Holy Rest Cemetery.

Before I could get the car started, another car pulled up opposite me and two guys got out. They looked very angry. They seemed familiar. Then I recognized them. They were the same guys who had stolen the body of the divorcée a little while ago.

They were really pissed off.

There was a third guy in the driver's seat.

When they got out of the car, he drove off.

The guys walked very business-like, as if they were characters in a Warner Brothers' gangster movie, into the morgue. They weren't fooling around.

One of the guys was very large with a square build. He looked like a ham with legs.

Peg-leg was really going to earn his two hundred and fifty dollars.

I drove off.

The Babylon-Orion Express

A morgue scene would be a very good one to include in Smith Smith Versus the Shadow Robots, *I* thought as I drove down Columbus Avenue with the girl's body safely in the trunk.

I envisioned Nana-dirat and I going into the city morgue of Babylon to identify a body. It was night and foggy in Babylon as we walked down the street to the morgue. We were a block away.

"You don't have to do this," I said. "It might be a little grizzly. The guy was hit by a train. There's very little left to identify. You might want to wait outside for me."

"No," she said. "I want to go with you. I don't like to have you out of my sight if I can help it. You know how stuck on you I am. You're my guy, you big lug. I don't care if that guy was hit by three Babylon-Orion Expresses."

Nana-dirat really had a crush on me.

"OK," I said. "But remember I warned you."

"Make that six Babylon-Orion Expresses," Nana-dirat said.

What a gal!

A private eye couldn't have a better secretary in Babylon.

Partners in Mayhem

Ah, shit . . . good-bye, Babylon.

I turned the car around at Union Street and drove back to the morgue. Try as I could, I just couldn't leave old Peg-leg to provide amusement for those goons.

Peg-leg's parking place was available right across the street from the morgue, so I pulled in there. I looked around for the goons' car but it was nowhere in sight. I slipped out of the car like the shadow of a banana peeling and walked quickly but almost anonymously into the morgue.

I had my hand in my coat pocket, fingering the loaded pistol. I was ready for business and I wanted some answers to why in the hell these guys were stealing bodies from the morgue. I was going to find out what was happening.

That's what private detectives are supposed to do and if I had to get a little rough it was totally acceptable in the tradition.

I was halfway down the hall toward the autopsy room when I heard a crash and a moan. Those bastards were already working poor Peg-leg over.

They would pay for it.

I stood outside the closed door with the gun in my hand, ready to spring inside and give those guys quite a surprise. I heard another moan and then another crash. There was silence for a few seconds and then a horrible scream—

AAAHHHHHHHHHHHHHHHHHH!

A sound from hell was the cue to my grand entrance.

I sprung into the autopsy room and there was quite a sight waiting for me like some kind of strange greeting card. First of all, Peg-leg was sitting at his desk with a cup of coffee in his hand. He was as relaxed and cool as a cucumber. He wasn't even startled as I flew into the room.

"Welcome to the party," he said like a host, motioning toward the activities that were going on in the room. There was another blood-curdling scream, "AAAHHHHHHHH-HHHHH! Don't put me back in here! For God's sake! AAAHHHHHHHHHHHH! AAAHHHHHHHHHHHHHH!"

In the corner of the autopsy room was the body of one of the hoods. He was very unconscious. He looked as if he were going to hibernate for the winter.

Sergeant Rink was standing beside the open door of one of the death icebox trays. The second hood was lying hand-cuffed on the tray. He was the one who was doing all the screaming. He had been pushed about ninety percent of the way into the refrigerator for dead people and he didn't care for that at all. All you could see of him was his face that was totally terrified to the point of almost going mad.

"AAAHHHHHHHHHHHHHHHH!" he screamed.

"One more time," Sergeant Rink said. "What in the fuck are you up to going around stealing dead bodies and trying to beat up morgue attendants who happen to be my friends?"

"I'll tell you anything just don't put me in here with the dead people," the hood said. He had a good point. It was not a pleasant place to be. I certainly would not have wanted to be in his shoes which were now growing cold.

Sergeant Rink pulled him out a ways, so that you could see his belt buckle.

"Is that better?" he said to the hood.

"Yes, thank you," the goon responded with a sudden, joyous look of relief on his face.

"OK, insect, spill it."

Sergeant Rink had a reputation of being a very tough cop and it was a reputation that he lived up to 100%. I really had to admire him. Too bad Babylon had gotten the best of me when I was going to the police academy with him. We might have turned out to be partners together. I liked that idea a lot.

Oh, well, I also liked Babylon a lot, too. Even though things had been a bit hard, I had no regrets about dreaming of Babylon all the time.

Sergeant Rink had been so involved with interrogating the goon that he hadn't responded to me running into the autopsy room with a gun in my hand or he had recognized that it was me and I didn't require that much immediate attention.

But now he was looking at me.

He had diverted his attention from the gorilla who had just become a canary.

"I was hired—" the goon started to say.

"Shut up, roach," Sergeant Rink said, diverting his attention to me. The "roach" shut up. He didn't want to spend the night in the freezer with what few bodies were left in the morgue that somehow had avoided being stolen that night.

"Hi, Card," Rink said. "Why the pistola? and what in the hell are you doing here, anyway?"

"I came to visit Peg-leg and I heard some loud activity going on in here," I said. "I knew that something had to be up because they keep dead people in here and they aren't famous for causing a commotion, so I came in prepared for action. What's up?" I said, praying to God that Peg-leg hadn't spilled the beans on me being one of the people who had taken a fresh body from the place and happily put it in the trunk of a car.

"Caught some ghouls here," Sergeant Rink said. "They stole two bodies from Peg-leg and then they came back and tried to work him over while they stole some more. Sons-of-bitches. I've been giving them a little lesson in crime doesn't pay."

He casually pushed the hood back into the refrigerator until only his eyes were staring out at us.

"AAAHHHHHHHHHHHHHH!" the hood responded to being pushed back into the refrigerator.

"See, crime doesn't pay," Rink said to the hood as he pushed the tray all the way in and then closed the door. We could hear the muffled screams of the man coming from the refrigerator.

"aaahhhhhhhhhhhh . . . aaahhhhhhhhh . . . aaahhhhhhhhhhh . . ."

Sergeant Rink walked over and poured himself a cup of morgue coffee. "I'll leave him in there for a little while. Let him cool his heels. He won't be stealing any more bodies when I'm through with that bastard."

Rink took a sip of coffee.

He didn't even grimace.

He was one hell-of-a tough cop.

Muffled screams kept coming from the freezer.

"aaahhhhhhhhhhhhhhhh . . ."

. . . on and on.

It didn't seem to bother Peg-leg or Rink, so I didn't let it bother me.

Today
Is My Lucky Day

I got a cup and joined Peg-leg and Sergeant Rink in some coffee while the goon continued screaming, tucked away on his tray in the city refrigerator.

"I told Sergeant Rink just before you jumped in here, 'Eye,' which I appreciate a lot, shit, if the sergeant hadn't come along you'd be my hero, that these guys stole two bodies from me today," Peg-leg said. "I don't know what in the hell they wanted two bodies for. They were just getting ready to work me over again when the sergeant came by. What a break. Today is my lucky day."

Peg-leg was looking directly into my eyes when he said, "Lucky day." I appreciated it. Of course two hundred and fifty bucks in your pocket isn't exactly a horse laugh.

"I'll find out why these guys stole those bodies," Sergeant Rink said. "I'll let our friend stay in the cooler until we finish our coffee. He'll be ready to talk by then and I don't think he'll want to steal any more bodies. He'll be reformed, the fucking desecrater."

His screams continued to work their way out of the cooler. They never stopped. The guy sounded as if he were going insane in there.

"You have no idea why these guys wanted to steal those bodies, huh?" Sergeant Rink said to Peg-leg.

"None," Peg-leg said. "I think they're just a pair of fucking ghouls. Bela Lugosi would be proud to know these jerks."

"What bodies did they take?" Rink said.

"Two women," Peg-leg said. "A suicide divorcée, no loss, and the body of that murdered whore you brought in earlier."

"Her, huh?" the sergeant said. "She was a good-looking woman. Too bad. So those creeps stole her body. This is getting a little more interesting."

The ghoul hood continued screaming from the icebox.

"I think he's almost ready," Rink said. "I don't think I'm going to have any trouble getting the truth out of him."

The other hood continued to hibernate on the floor in the corner. He sure was unconscious. When Rink puts them out, they stay out.

"*aaahhhhhhhhh . . . aaahhhhhhhhh . . . aaahhhhhhhhh*"
. . . continued to come from the refrigerator.

Sergeant Rink took another sip of coffee.

The Sahara Desert

Just about that time the third hood came
strolling into the autopsy room, looking for his amigos in
body theft. He was greeted by the sight of one of his buddies
lying in a very unconscious heap in the corner and he could
hear the muffled screams of his other partner coming from
the icebox.

The hood turned white as a sheet.

"Wrong room," he said. The words were very dry when
they came out of his mouth. He sounded like the Sahara
Desert talking.

"Excuse me," he said, turning around with great difficulty
and heading unevenly toward the sanctuary of the door
which must have seemed like a million miles away to him.

167

He had just been turned from a living, breathing hood to a cardboard cutout of a hood.

"Wait a minute, citizen," Sergeant Rink said, and then took a casual sip of his coffee. "Where in the fuck do you think you're going?"

The hood stopped dead in his tracks which was very appropriate for the place that he was at.

"I've got the wrong address," he said, Sahara-ily.

Sergeant Rink shook his head very slowly.

"Do you mean this is the right address?" the hood said, not knowing what he was saying, his brain hypnotized by fear.

Sergeant Rink nodded his head, yes, this was the right place.

"Sit down, fuckball," the sergeant said, motioning toward a chair on the far side of the room right beside the body of the sleeping bear-like hood.

"Fuckball" started to say something but Sergeant Rink shook his head, no. The hood let out a huge sigh that could have filled a clipper sail. He started walking very unsure of himself as if on a stormy deck toward the chair.

The screams continued coming from the refrigerator.

"*aaahhhhhhhhhhhhh . . . aaahhhhhhhh . . . aaahhhhhhhhhh*"

"Wait a minute," Rink said to the hood. "Do you have a heater?"

The hood stopped in his tracks and stood there as if he were frozen. He was staring at the icebox where the screams were coming from. He looked as if he were in a dream. He slowly nodded his head that he had a gun.

"That's not a nice boy," Sergeant Rink said fatherly, but

he sounded like a father whose business was a pitchfork factory in hell. "I bet you don't have a permit either."

The gunsel shook his head that he didn't have a permit. Then he spoke with great difficulty. "Why's he in there?" he said.

"Do you want to join him?"

"NO!" the crook yelled.

He was very emphatic about not wanting to get into the refrigerator with his comrade.

"Then be a good boy and I won't put you in with the dead people."

The hood nodded his head very emphatically that he wanted to be a good boy.

"Take the gun slowly out of your pocket and don't point it at anybody. Guns sometimes go off accidentally and we wouldn't want that to happen because somebody might get hurt and then somebody would spend their school vacation in the refrigerator with the dead people."

The crook took a .45 so slowly out of his pocket that he reminded me of trying to get very cold maple syrup out of a bottle.

The sergeant just sat there with the cup of coffee in his hand. He was a very cool customer and I could have been his partner if Babylon hadn't gotten the best of me.

"Bring the gun over here," the sergeant said.

The crook brought the gun over to the sergeant.

He was carrying the .45 as if he were a girl scout with a box of cookies in his hand.

"Hand me the gun."

He handed the gun to the sergeant.

"Now go put your ass down on that chair and I don't want

to hear anything out of you," Rink said. "I want you to become a statue. Do you understand?"

"Yes."

It was a yes that sounded as if it really wanted to go and sit down and become a living statue.

The hood took the yes over to the chair beside his sleeping chum and sat down. He did just what the sergeant said and became a statue of failed criminality. He had pointed himself marbly in the direction of the icebox. He sat there staring at it and listening to the screams coming from it.

"aaahhhh ! ! ! aaahhhhh ! ! ! aaahhhhh ! ! ! aaahhhh!!!"

. . . coming now in short gasps.

"Just like the Shadow says," Sergeant Rink said. " 'Crime doesn't pay.' "

"aaahhhh ! ! ! aaahhhh ! ! ! ahhhh ! ! ! aaahhhh ! ! !"

"I think this fucker is ready to sing now," Rink said. "I'm going to get to the bottom of this. Morgues shouldn't be this exciting. The city of San Francisco can't afford to have its corpses pickpocketed. It gives the town a bad reputation among dead people."

"aaahhhh ! ! ! aaahhhh ! ! ! aaahhhh ! ! ! aaahhhh !!!"

. . . continuing to come from the refrigerator.

"Any operas you guys want to hear?" the sergeant said.

"La Traviata," I said.

"Madam Butterfly," Peg-leg said.

"Coming up," Rink said.

The Edgar Allan Poe Hotfoot

There are no words to describe the expression on the hood's face when Sergeant Rink pulled him out of the refrigerator. He opened it up just a crack at first. You could only see the guy's eyes. They looked as if Edgar Allan Poe had given them both hotfoots.

He was screaming as the tray was slowly pulled out.

"AAAHHHHHHH! AAAHHHHHHH! AAAHHH-HHH! AAAHHHHHHHHH!"

. . . with those eyes looking wildly at us.

"Shut up," Rink said.

"AAAH—" The hood shut totally up as if an invisible Mount Everest had been dropped on his mouth.

The expression in his eyes changed from Poe-esque terror

to an unbelievable dimension of silent pleading. He looked as if he were asking the Pope for a miracle.

"Would you like to come out a little further into the world of the living?" Rink said.

The hood nodded his head and tears started flowing from his eyes.

The sergeant pulled the tray out until his entire face was visible. He pulled it out very slowly. Then he stopped and stood there, staring down at the destroyed hood. A benevolent smile crept its way onto Rink's features. He patted the terrified hood on the cheek affectionately with his hand. Mother Rink.

"Ready to sing?"

The hood nodded his head.

"I want it all, right from the top or back in you go and I might not take you out the next time. Also, I'm not above embalming a cheap rat like you alive. Get the picture?" *Mother Rink.*

The hood nodded his head again.

"OK, tell me all about it."

"I don't know where she put all the beer," the hood started talking hysterically. "She had ten beers and she didn't go to the toilet. She just kept drinking beer and not going to the toilet. She was so skinny. There was no place for the beer to go inside her body but she just kept packing it away. She had at least ten beers. There was no room for the beer!" he screamed. "No room!"

"Who was that?" the sergeant said.

"The woman who hired us to steal the body. She was a beer drinker. God, I never saw anything like it. The beer just kept disappearing."

"Who was she?" Rink said.

"She didn't tell us. She just wanted the body. No questions asked. Good money. We didn't know this was going to happen. She was a rich dame. My father told me never to get involved with rich dames. Look at me. I'm in a cooler full of dead people. I can smell them. They're dead. Why in the hell didn't I listen to him?"

"You should have listened to your father," Rink said.

Just then the hood lying in the corner started coming to. The sergeant looked over at the statue of a hood sitting in a chair above him.

"Your friend's coming to," he said to the hood. "Kick him in the head for me. He needs some more rest."

The hood in the chair, without standing up because he hadn't been told to stand up, kicked the other hood in the head. He went back to sleep.

"Thank you," Rink said and then went back to grilling the hood handcuffed on the tray. "Do you have any idea why she wanted the body?"

"No, she just drank beer all the time. The money was good. I didn't know this was going to happen. We were just going to steal a body."

"Was she alone?" Rink said.

"No, she had a bodyguard chauffeur-type with a big neck like a fire hydrant. We came here and got a body but it was the wrong one, so we came back for the right one but it wasn't here. We weren't really going to hurt your one-legged pal. We were just going to rough him up a little bit, so we could get the right body."

"What body were you going for?" Rink said.

"The whore who got knocked off today."

"Did you kill her?"

"No! No, oh, God, no!" the hood said. He didn't like that question at all.

"Don't use the word God around here, you little prick, or I'll stick you back in the freezer."

The sergeant was an Irish Catholic who went to Mass every Sunday.

"I'm sorry! I'm sorry," the hood said. "Don't put me back in there."

"That's better," Rink said. "How many bodies did you guys take from here?"

"Only one. The wrong one. Some lady. We got her instead of the whore, so we came back to get the right one but she was gone. We weren't going to hurt your friend. That's all I know. I promise."

"You're sure you're not keeping anything from me?" Rink said.

"No, I promise. I wouldn't lie," the hood said.

"You guys only took one body, huh?"

"Yeah, some dead lady. The wrong one."

"There are two bodies missing," the sergeant said. "Who took the body of the whore?"

"If we were paid to take the body of the whore and we got her out of here, do you think we'd be so stupid as to come back to get her body if we already had it?" the hood said, making a mistake.

Rink didn't like his attitude.

He slid him about six inches back into the cooler.

That stimulated a predictable response.

"AAAHHHHHHHHH! NO! NO! NO!" the cheap

crook started screaming. "I'm telling the truth! We only took one body! You can have it back!"

"This is interesting," the sergeant said. "There seems to be an epidemic of body theft going on in San Francisco."

"Are you sure this guy's telling the truth about not stealing both bodies?" Peg-leg said, adding his two cents. "Because who else would come in here on the same night and steal a body? I've been working here since 1925 and this is the first time anybody has taken a body and the chances are a million to one that two bodies would be stolen by different people on the same night. Put the son-of-a-bitch back in there and get the truth out of him."

"AAAHHHHHHHHHH!" was the hood's response to that remark.

"No, he's telling the truth," Rink said. "I know the truth when I hear it and this bastard's not lying. Look at him. Do you think there's a lie left in this quivering mass of bullshit? No, I've got him telling the truth for the first time in his life."

"Then I don't know what in the hell is happening," Peg-leg said, pretending to be angry. "Maybe there's another nut loose in San Francisco. All I know is I'm short two bodies and I want you to put it in your report that I want them back."

"OK, Peg-leg," Rink said. "Calm down. These guys have got the divorcée's body, so I've already got one of them back for you."

"You're right," Peg-leg said. "Getting one of them back is better than having both of them gone. I need dead bodies, so I can make a living."

"I know. I know," the sergeant said, walking over to the desk and getting some more coffee. He just left the hood lying there on the tray with half of his face out in the light. The hood didn't say a word about his condition. He didn't want to ruin a good thing and find himself all by his lonesome back in the dark with the dead people for company. He was going to let well enough alone.

Sergeant Rink took a sip of coffee.

"There's no reason why anybody would want to short you some bodies, is there?" Rink said to Peg-leg. "You haven't noticed anything suspicious going on around here, have you?"

"Fuck no," Peg-leg said. "This place is filled with corpses and I want that dead whore back."

"OK, OK," Sergeant Rink said. "I'll see what I can do."

He turned casually toward me.

"Do you know anything about this?" he said.

"How in the hell would I know anything about this? I just dropped by to say hello and have a cup of coffee with my old friend Peg-leg," I said.

The hood lying in the corner started to come to again. He began fluttering like a drunken butterfly.

"You didn't kick him hard enough," Rink said to the statue of a hood sitting next to him.

The statue obediently kicked him very hard in the head. The butterfly hood became unconscious again.

"Thank you," Sergeant Rink said.

The
Labrador Retriever
of Dead People

I started thinking about my involvement with all of this and did a quick little summary of where I was at, taking into consideration the answers Sergeant Rink had gotten from the hood on the tray.

In other words, I was thinking about my client: the beautiful rich woman who could put away the beer. She'd hired these cheap hoods to do the same thing that I was hired to do, to snatch that body. It didn't make any sense. We'd practically fallen over each other stealing a corpse, and the guy lying handcuffed on the tray had certainly gotten more than he had bargained for.

Rink returned to the slab to do a little more grilling.

"Comfortable?" he said in a motherly tone.

"Yes," the hood said, sonlike.

What else could he say?

"Here, let me make you feel a little better," Mother Rink said.

The sergeant pulled the tray out, so that you could see the hood's chest.

"Comfy?"

The hood nodded his head slowly.

"Now, what were you supposed to do with the body of that God-damn whore? What did the rich dame want done with it?"

"We were supposed to call a bar at ten o'clock and ask for a Mr. Jones and he'd tell us what we were supposed to do, then," the hood sang like a choir boy.

"Who's Mr. Jones?" Rink said.

"The guy with the fire-hydrant neck," the hood said.

"Good boy," the sergeant said. "What's the name of the bar?"

"The Oasis Club on Eddy Street."

"It's eleven now," Rink said.

He walked over to a telephone on the desk where Peg-leg was sitting. He dialed information and then he dialed the Oasis Club. "I'd like to speak to Mr. Jones." He waited for a moment and then he said, "Thank you," and hung up the telephone. He walked back over to the refrigerator.

"There's no Mr. Jones there. You're not looking for a little more time with the dead people are you?"

"No! No," the hood said. "Maybe he got tired of waiting. He said if we didn't call him then the deal was off and he'd assume that we hadn't been able to get the body. He also said something else."

"What was that?" Rink said.

"He said, 'Don't fuck up.' He really meant it."

"You should have listened to him because you guys fucked up."

"We tried. How did we know that we were taking the wrong body? They told us what slab it was on and everything. I mean, how could we go wrong?"

"Easy," Rink said. "I wouldn't hire you clowns to walk a dog."

Then Rink turned to Peg-leg.

"I wonder how the employers of these goons knew which tray the body was on," he said.

"Obviously they didn't," Peg-leg said. "Because the wrong body was snatched. Speaking of the wrong body: I want that suicide wino divorcée back and pronto."

"Where's the body?" Rink said to the hood sitting on the chair beside his freshly-unconscious friend.

"Can I speak?" the hood said. He didn't want to do anything that would get the sergeant excited. He wanted things to stay the way they were because he wasn't hand-cuffed on a tray or lying unconscious on the floor.

"You're talking right now," Rink said. "You just answered me."

"Oh, that's right," the hood said, surprised to hear his own voice speaking. "What do you want?" he said, trying it out again.

"Besides stupidity, deafness runs in your family, too, huh? I want to know where the body is, you asshole," Rink said.

"In the trunk of our car."

"Where's the car?"

"Parked around the corner," the hood said.

"Go and get the body," Rink said.

"Sure, then what?"

"What do you mean then what? Bring it back here, stupid," the sergeant said.

"You're going to let me walk out of here by myself?" the hood said, dumbfoundedly. He couldn't believe his ears.

"Why not?" Rink said. "Go and get it. You're stupid but I don't think you're crazy enough to try and take a powder on me. I'm a mean man. You want to stay on the good side of me. I'm beginning to take a liking to you, so go and get that fucking body right now."

"OK," the hood said apologetically. I don't know why he was apologetic but he was. Human behavior is hard to bet on.

A few moments later he came back lugging the laundry bag with the dead divorcée in it. He bore a great resemblance to a Labrador Retriever bringing back a duck to its master.

"You're a swell guy," Rink said. "Give that body to Peg-leg and set your ass back down."

"Thanks, boss," the hood said.

"There's one body for you, Peg-leg," Rink said. "Said case solved."

Dancing Time

Peg-leg was holding up his end of the deal perfectly. What a pal. Of course two hundred and fifty dollars cash money helps. A one-legged man can get a lot of dancing time out of that in San Francisco.

"Well, I've got to be on my way," I said. "This has been very interesting but I've got to make a living."

"That's a joke," Sergeant Rink said, then he kind of sighed. "You could have been a good detective, Card, if you hadn't spent so much time daydreaming. Oh, well . . ."

He let it drop.

I'd always been a major disappointment to him.

Rink didn't know that I was living part of my life in Babylon. To him I was just a daydreaming fuckup. I let him think that. I knew that he wouldn't be able to understand Babylon if I told him about it. He just didn't have that kind of mind, so I let it pass. I was his fuckup and that was all right. Babylon was a lot better than being a cop and having to wage the war against crime on time.

I started toward the door. I had a body out in the car that needed to be delivered, and I'd have to drive around for a while first and think about it. Things had gotten a little complicated with the entrance of the three hoods. I needed some time to think it all over. I had to make the right move.

"See you later, 'Eye,' " Peg-leg said.

"Keep your nose clean and stop being a fuckup," Rink said.

I looked over at the hood handcuffed on the slab.

He was just lying there staring up at the ceiling.

This had not been a good day for him.

The hood in the chair sat there looking as if he'd been caught with his pants down at a nuns' picnic.

The third hood lay beside him on the floor.

The electric company had turned off his lights for not paying the bill.

I think when he came to he would think twice about continuing the profession of being a hood, not unless he liked to sleep on morgue floors.

The Blindman

The car was waiting for me parked across the street from the morgue with the body of the murdered whore in the trunk. That body was my ticket to five hundred more bucks but things had gotten a little complicated.

Why had the beer-drinking rich dame hired these three hoods to steal the same body that I had been hired to steal? It didn't make sense. By doing that this whole business had been turned into a Bowery Boys' comedy with everybody falling all over everybody else, but the results hadn't been too amusing for those hoods back in the morgue.

Sergeant Rink had turned their lives into hell on earth. I shuddered when I thought about that poor son-of-a-bitch who'd been put alive into the cooler. I don't think that was his idea of fun. I think he would have preferred watching a baseball game or doing something else.

But I had spent enough time thinking about those jerks. I had more important things on my mind. What was I going to do with this God-damn body? The hoods were supposed to get in touch with the neck at a bar at ten, but he wasn't there when Sergeant Rink had called.

My appointment with the rich beer drinker and the neck was at Holy Rest Cemetery at 1 A.M. Now I had to figure out what I was going to do next. Should I keep the rendez-vous?

That was my only chance to get the five hundred bucks and be able to afford an office, a secretary, a car, and be able to change the style of my life. They'd already paid me five hundred dollars for half my fee and given me three hundred dollars expense money. I still had the five hundred bucks and so I was ahead of the game anyway you looked at it.

Maybe I should just take the body and dump it in the bay and forget about meeting the people and consider myself five hundred bucks closer to having some human dignity. I could probably afford some kind of office, secretary, and car for that if I counted my pennies and made each one of them run a mile. It wouldn't be a fancy operation but at least it would be.

I didn't know what kind of weird business might happen if I kept the appointment with them. Normal people don't hire two different sets of men to steal a corpse from the morgue. That didn't make any sense at all and I had no way of anticipating what would happen if I went out to the cemetery and kept my appointment with them.

They might not even be there.

They might be in China right now for all that I knew, but if they did keep the appointment I had a gun to put a dent in any weird business they might try. That neck was a frightening human being. I'd hate to tangle with him but I did have six pieces of lead to throw at him. I wasn't a bad shot and he'd be hard to miss.

Those were my options: a sure five hundred dollars or a gamble for five hundred more with some very strange citizens, a beer-vanishing rich woman and a chauffeur with a neck the size of a herd of buffaloes.

At least I had some options.

A couple of days ago I'd been reduced to bumping into a blind beggar and knocking the cup out of his hand. I picked the money up off the sidewalk for him and he was fifty cents short when I handed his cup back to him. I think he was a very perceptive blindman because he started yelling at me, "Where's the rest of the money! It's not all here! Give me my money back, you God-damn thief!"

I had to take a quick powder.

So what I was thinking about now was a lot more interesting than the things I had been thinking about.

There are only so many blind beggars in San Francisco and the word gets around.

BABY

What in the fuck do I have to lose? I thought as I turned the key in the ignition. I'd made up my mind. I was going to deliver the body. It was now a little after eleven and I had some time to kill before I was due at Holy Rest Cemetery, so I decided to drive around for a little while. I had been without a car for a long time. I looked at the gas gauge. The tank was 3/4's full. This would be fun. I started up the engine and was off.

I headed for the Marina.

I turned the radio on.

In no time at all I was humming along to some popular song that I'd never heard before. I have a very good ear for music. I pick up tunes fast. It's one of my talents. Too bad

I never learned how to sing or play a musical instrument. I might have gone far, all the way to the top if I'd done that.

I was feeling very good.

I'd made up my mind.

I was listening to some good music.

And I had the body of a dead whore in the trunk.

What more could a man want in these troubled times? I mean, the world was at war but everything was going OK for me. I didn't have any complaints. This was my day.

As I drove up Columbus Avenue toward the Marina, I thought about being a big bandleader in Babylon with my own radio station.

"Hello, out there. This is station BABY from high atop the Hanging Gardens of Babylon. We're very happy to bring you tonight C. Card and His Big Band," the announcer would say. "And here's C. Card . . ."

"Hello, swinging cats of Babylon!" I would say. "This is your servant of sound C. Card playing music to light your dreams by, and we'll start out with Miss Nana-dirat, our songbird of forbidden pleasure, singing 'When Irish Eyes Are Smiling.' "

I was really getting the maximum amount of pleasure out of the radio. That is, until I noticed that a car was following me.

Stew Meat

The car was a 1937 black Plymouth Sedan with four black guys in it. They were very, very black and all wearing dark suits. The car looked like a piece of coal with headlights and it was definitely following me.

Who were these guys?

How had they gotten into the picture?

My few moments of radio bliss had been totally shattered. Why can't life be as simple as it could be?

There was a red light at the next intersection. I stopped and waited for it to change.

The black Plymouth filled with black men pulled up along side me and the front window next to me was rolled down. One of the black men leaned out and said in a voice deep enough to be on the *Amos 'n' Andy Show*, "We want that body. Pull over and give it to us or we'll razor you into stew meat."

"You've made a big mistake," I said through my partially rolled down window. "I don't know what you're talking about. I'm an insurance salesman for Hartford of New York."

"Don't be funny, Stew Meat," the black man said.

The light turned green and the chase was on.

It was the first car chase I'd ever been in.

I'd seen a lot of them in the movies but I'd never been in one before. It was a lot different from the ones I'd seen in the movies. First of all, I've never really been a very good driver and their driver was topnotch. Also, in the movies the car chases go on for miles. This one didn't. I made a turn a few blocks away on Lombard and crashed my car into a parked station wagon. That brought an abrupt end to the car chase. It had been interesting. Too bad it had been so short.

Fortunately, I hadn't hurt myself.

I was shaken up a little but I was OK.

The car full of black guys pulled up behind me and they jumped out. True to their promise they each had a razor, but I had a gun in my pocket, so things were not going to be as uneven as they appeared.

I slowly got out of the car. It's good to do things slowly when you've got a .38 in your pocket ready for action. I had all the time in the world.

"Where's that body, Stew Meat?" the one who had spoken before said. He was a very tough-looking hombre and so were his three dusky muchachos.

I pulled the gun out of my pocket and pointed it in their

189

general direction. The shoe was on a different foot now. They froze in their tracks.

"And I don't like to be called stew meat," I said, enjoying the situation. "Drop those razors."

There was the sound of four razors hitting the street. I was really ahead of the game. That is, until an old woman rushed out onto the front porch of her house and inquired into why we had ruined her car. She introduced her inquiry by screaming at the top of her lungs, "My station wagon! My station wagon! I just finished paying for it yesterday. I sent the last check in."

A dozen or so of her neighbors had poured out onto their front porches and were rapidly taking sides with the woman whose station wagon wasn't any more.

Nobody was interested in my viewpoint. I wasn't able to get a word in.

I figured the only way I could get some respite from them was to fire my gun into the air. That would drive them back into their houses and give me a minute or two to take command of the situation and do something because I sure had to do something and quick.

I aimed the gun in the air and pulled the trigger.

click

WHAT!

click click click, I kept clicking away.

IT WAS THE WRONG FUCKING GUN!

It was my gun, the empty one. The four black men went to the street for their razors. The woman was still yelling, "My station wagon! My station wagon!" The neighbors were busy joining in. The whole situation had suddenly turned into Bedlam on one of its bad days.

The black men had re-razored themselves and were coming at me. I reached into my other pocket and took out Peg-leg's gun: the one with the bullets.

"Stop!" I said to the black guys.

They looked meaner than hell except for one of them who was smiling. He was the one who'd called me "stew meat." He had a huge smile that went ear-to-ear like a pearl necklace. It sent a chill down my spine. He should meet the neck. They'd be great friends together. They had so much in common.

I could hear somebody making the introduction:

"Smile, meet Neck."

"Glad ta meetcha."

If I'd been there I would have been introduced as Stew Meat:

"Stew Meat, this is Neck."

"Hi-ya, Neck."

"My friend Smile."

"A friend of Neck's is a friend of mine."

Then I was jerked back to reality by the real voice of Smile saying, "Stew Meat, you just run outa luck."

"I'm warning you," I said.

"Hee-hee," Smile said.

He was still smiling when I shot him in the leg. That sent the woman who owned the smashed station wagon and all of her neighbors running screaming into their houses.

The smile didn't leave Smile's face but it changed from an ear-to-ear smile to a soft smile that resembled an old man getting a little Christmas present from a child. The razor dropped gently out of his hand. There was a small bloody patch on his leg that was getting bigger and bigger. The

191

bullet had gone right through his leg about six inches above the knee. It just punched a hole in him.

The other three black men dropped their razors, too.

"Shit, Stew Meat, you just shoot me with an empty pistol," Smile said. "This ain't worth no fifty bucks. They say you just give us the body if we show you our razors. Shit, a bullet just went through my leg."

I didn't have time to console him.

I had to get out of there before the police came and brought an end to all of this. Well, my car wasn't working any more, so that left one car that was working: theirs.

"Enough of this," I said. "All of you take deep breaths right now and don't move. I'll tell you when to exhale."

They all took deep breaths and held them in.

I stepped back to Peg-leg's wrecked car and got the keys out of the ignition.

"Keep that breath in there," I warned them, waving the gun at them. I stepped around to the back of the car. I could see that the four black gentlemen were having trouble keeping their breaths in. I opened up the trunk.

"OK," I said.

They all exhaled.

"Shit," Smile said. "Shit."

"Get this body out of here," I said. I motioned toward them again with the gun and they stepped forward and removed the body. "Put it in the back seat of your car," I said. "And on the double. I don't have all day."

Smile was still smiling. It had grown a little fainter but it could still be classified as a smile. The closest description that I can think of would be to say that it was now philosophical.

"Shit," he said. "First, he shoot me with an empty gun, then he make me hold my breath until I get dizzy and now he steal my car."

I could still see him smiling as I drove away.

The Lone Eagle

I was about a block away when suddenly I made a left and drove the car around the block, returning to the scene of Peg-leg's wrecked car and the four bad black men. I came up behind them. They were standing there staring in the direction I had driven away.

I honked and they turned around.

I'll never forget the expression on their faces when they saw me. The three unwounded men had picked up their razors again. When they saw me the razors dropped effortlessly out of their hands and back down onto the street that was rapidly becoming their home. It seemed at this point impossible for those razors ever to make stew meat again or even come up with a shave.

They had seen their day.

The black man with the bullet hole in his leg flashed me a huge smile when he saw me. "Shit!" he said. "It's Stew Meat again. What happened this time? You come back for our pants?"

The other three black men thought that was pretty funny and they started laughing. It was pretty funny. I couldn't help from smiling myself. Except for their wanting to carve me up, these were good guys.

"No, keep your pants," I said.

"You Santa Claus," Smile said.

"Who paid you to get this body from me?" I said. "That's all I want to know."

"Why didn't you say so?" Smile said. "Shit! that's an easy one. A guy with a neck like a trunk and a flashy white doll who drank beer but didn't go piss. Where'd she put all that beer? Them da boss, but you da boss now."

"Thanks," I said.

"Shit, Stew Meat," Smile said. "Anytime, but don't shoot me no more. I'm getting too old for bullets. You don't need any partners, do ya?"

"No," I said. "I'm a lone eagle."

This time they all waved as I drove off in their car.

A Funny Building

Now what was I going to do?

When you're hired to steal a body from the city morgue, that's very strange in itself, but when the people who hire you hire other people to steal the same body from the morgue and then hire some more people to steal the body from you after you manage to steal it, you've got a lot of weirdness going on.

Why did it have to get more complicated after I'd made up my mind to go to the cemetery and see if I could get the remaining five hundred of my fee from them?

What was my next move going to be?

I still had some time before I was to keep my appointment with those people, but I'd be a fool if I did. They definitely were not to be trusted. The only thing they had going for them was the possibility of five hundred bucks.

But of course I had something they wanted very much in their weird way. I had the dead whore's body in the back seat of the just commandeered automobile of four bad black men.

Maybe I should start playing my cards a little differently. I had been playing things too much their way.

I think I'll raise the ante, I thought to myself, *and introduce a new game.* I was going to need more money than five hundred dollars. I knew that Peg-leg was going to have a very adverse reaction to my cracking his car up. I think he was going to want a new car.

No, seeing how things were developing, five hundred was chicken feed now. If those people wanted that body, and they certainly seemed to be showing a lot of inclination in that direction, they were going to have to pay through the nose to get it.

I made a quick stop at my apartment house.

I took the body out of the back seat and slung it over my shoulder and carried it into the building. I pretended that it was a bag of laundry. My pretending didn't make any difference because nobody was there to see me. Thank God that the landlady had croaked that day. Maybe my luck wasn't so bad after all. I might come out of this with a lot more money than I had anticipated.

I smiled as I carried the dead whore's body past the stairs that led up to the apartment of the dead landlady. I thought about her body being carried down the stairs a little while earlier in the day, and now here I was carrying another dead body back into the building.

This was really a funny building.

It would make a nice little extension to add onto the morgue. Bodies were coming and going in here like letters in the post office.

I took the dead whore down the hall and into my apartment. I put her body down on the kitchen floor next to the refrigerator and then I opened the refrigerator and took all the moldy food and unidentifiable objects off the shelves. Ugh . . .

Then I took the shelves out.

Why not?

It was the perfect place to keep her and the last place anyone would look.

The Five-hundred-dollar Foot

I was back in the car driving south out of San Francisco toward Holy Rest Cemetery and my "appointment" with the neck and his beer-drinking mistress. This was going to be an interesting meeting but it wasn't going to be the way they had planned it. We were going to play by my rules now and I had a feeling that corpse back in my refrigerator was worth a lot more than five hundred bucks.

I had the feeling that I now owned a ten-thousand-dollar dead body. I had stolen it and it was mine and I intended to get paid every dollar that it was worth and the sum of ten thousand dollars seemed just right to me.

I saw the light of a telephone booth ahead of me along the road. I remembered that I still hadn't called my mother and gotten that out of the way. I'd better take care of that before I got onto more serious business. I didn't want it preying on my mind as I was getting ready to pull off the biggest caper of my life and be put permanently on Easy Street.

I pulled over and got out.

I dropped a nickel in and dialed her number.

It rang a dozen times.

God-damn it! I didn't get to hear her answer the phone with, "Hello?" and then I'd say, "Hi, Mom. It's me," and then she'd say, "Hello? who is this speaking? Hello?" and, "*Mom,*" I'd whine, followed by, "This can't be my son calling. Hello?" continuing with me whining, "*Mom,*" and her saying, "It sounds like my son, but he wouldn't have the nerve to call if he was still a private detective."

By her not being home I was spared all that.

Where was she?

It was Friday and she'd gone to the cemetery to see my father that I'd killed when I was four, but I knew she was back from the cemetery by now.

Where was she?

I got back in the car and continued on my way to the cemetery. It was only about ten minutes away. Then the shit would hit the fan. I had the idea that the neck and his rich boss weren't going to like the new change in plans and my brand-new price for the body.

Yes, they were in for an unpleasant surprise and I couldn't think of two nicer people for it to happen to. I was very glad that I had five bullets left. That was enough to turn the neck into a little finger.

Then I remembered something.

I reached into my pocket and took out the empty revolver and put it down on the seat beside me. I wasn't going to make that mistake again. How embarrassing. That could have backfired on me if I hadn't regained control of the situation the way I did by shooting Smile in the leg.

I'd been lucky.

Shit. Smile might have been sitting where I was sitting right now at the steering wheel of his own car with his three friends in the car, joking and laughing, the whore's body in the trunk, and I could be lying in the street as part of an unfinished recipe. All you would need to finish it would be some onions, potatoes, carrots and a bay leaf.

I didn't like the idea of being stew.

The Night
Is Always Darker

It was really a dark night as I drove toward
Holy Rest Cemetery. It was so dark that I thought about my
serial *Smith Smith Versus the Shadow Robots.* When Professor Abdul Forsythe got the mercury crystals and was able
to activate his piles of poor unfortunate shadow victims and
set them marching upon the world, the results would look
like this.

The Professor-Abdul-Forsythe artificial night would resemble the kind of night that I was driving through to get
to the cemetery.

Then another thought crossed my mind jerking me back
from Babylon. Perhaps the night is always darker when

you're on your way to a cemetery in it. That was something to think about, but not for long because my mind was immediately returned to Babylon.

BZZZZZZZZZZZZZZZZZZ

It was my beautiful eternal secretary Nana-dirat on the intercom.

"Hello, doll," I said. "What's up?"

"It's for you, lover," she said in her breathless voice.

"Who is it?" I said.

"It's Dr. Francis, the famous humanitarian."

"What does he want?"

"He won't tell me. He says that he can only speak to you."

"OK, doll," I said. "Put him on."

"Hello, Mr. Smith Smith," Dr. Francis said. "I'm Dr. Francis."

"I know who you are," I said. "What do you want? Time is money."

"Excuse me?" the doctor said.

"I'm a busy man," I said. "Give it to me straight. I can't waste my time."

"I want to hire you."

"That's what I was waiting to hear," I said. "My fee is one pound of gold a day plus expenses."

"That sounds reasonable for a man of your reputation as a private investigator," Dr. Francis said.

"You've heard of me?" I said, playing it coy.

"All of Babylon has heard of you," he said.

I of course knew that. I just wanted to hear him say it. I had a delightful ego problem.

"Now what can I do for you?" I said. There was a pause at the other end of the line. "Dr. Francis?" I said.

"Is it all right for me to speak freely over the telephone?" he said. "I mean, nobody could be listening in?"

"Don't worry," I said. "If anybody does any telephone tapping in Babylon it's usually me. Tell me what your problem is."

Little did I know that the diabolical Professor Abdul Forsythe was listening to our conversation. I had been a little too glib with my telephone-tapping joke and it was to cause me a lot of trouble later on.

"Well, Mr. Smith Smith," Dr. Francis said.

"Just call me Smith," I said. "Everybody does."

"Smith, I have reason to believe that somebody is trying to steal my latest invention and use it for evil purposes."

"What's your invention?" I said.

"I've invented mercury crystals," Dr. Francis said.

"I'll be right over," I said.

I had been afraid this was going to happen: that somebody would come along and invent mercury crystals. I frankly didn't think the world was ready for it yet. After all, this was the year 596 B.C. and the world had a lot of growing up to do.

Smiley's Genuine
Louisiana Barbecue

SSSCCCRRREEEEEECCCHHH!!!

I slammed on the brakes.

Babylon almost caused me to drive right past the ceme-tery. I pulled over and stopped and turned my lights out. I didn't see any other cars there. If anyone was coming I'd arrived first. I didn't even know if the neck and its beer-drinking keeper were going to show up, but I had a hunch they would. That's why I was there. Now I'd just wait and see what happened. You don't get a chance at ten thousand dollars every day.

Suddenly I was curious about something.

I reached into my pocket and took out a match.

I lit it and read the registration on the steering wheel: Smiley's Genuine Louisiana Barbecue.

That figured.

I'd have to stop in and visit Smiley someday and try some of his barbecue. It would really be worth it to see the expression on his face when he saw me coming through the door.

I blew out the match and waited in the dark for a while.

I started to think about Babylon but I was able to wrestle it out of my mind by carefully not being impressed by how dark it was. That could lead me very easily back to Babylon. If I thought about the darkness, I'd soon be thinking about the shadow robots, and that wouldn't do at all.

I didn't want Babylon to put me behind the eight ball again. I was lucky that I saw the cemetery. I could have driven halfway to Los Angeles and be on Chapter Seven of *Smith Smith Versus the Shadow Robots*. Then I never would have had a chance at finding my client and getting ten thousand dollars. All I would have ended up with was a dead whore in my refrigerator.

That's what you would hardly call the successful conclusion of a case.

Into the Cemetery We Will Go

I had been sitting there—I don't know how long—when a car came down the road. It was the only traffic that I had seen. The car was driving very slowly. It looked as if its destination was the cemetery.

It was too far away to tell what kind of car it was. Anyway, I couldn't tell. I wondered if it was the Cadillac limousine. The car stopped two hundred yards down the road from me. The headlights went black and some people got out of the car. They had a flashlight but I couldn't make out who they were. It could be the neck and blonde company or just some plain ordinary grave robbers.

I had no way of knowing until I got out of the car and became a stealthful confident private eye starting to conclude the biggest deal of his life, so that's what I did. I got out of the car.

I was lacking only one thing: a flashlight.

Then I got an idea.

I got back into the car and opened up the glove compartment.

Bonanza!

A flashlight!

This was a sign from heaven.

Everything was going to work out OK.

I was supposed to meet the neck and Our Lady of the Limitless Bladder by a monument to some fallen soldiers of the Spanish-American War. The monument was about three hundred yards into the cemetery. It was only a little ways away from my father's grave.

I had passed that monument many times visiting his grave. I sure wish I hadn't killed him. Perhaps if everything worked out with this case, I might have a few moments left over at the end of it to do a little mourning for him. Why did I throw that ball out into the street? I wish I had never seen that ball!

With the flashlight in one hand, I didn't have it on, but it was ready to stab a ray of light if I should need it, and the loaded gun in my other hand, I slipped into the cemetery and made my way among the graves toward the Spanish-American War monument.

I moved with a great deal of caution.

Surprise was a very important element in this situation and I wanted it on my side. I had to cut through a grove of trees to get to the monument. It was just on the other side of the trees. I had to be careful going through the trees. It was very dark and I didn't want to fall down and make a lot of noise. When I got into the trees, I measured every step as if it were my last.

I was halfway through the trees, moving like a shadow, when I heard voices coming from the direction of the monument about fifty yards in front of me.

I couldn't quite make out what they were saying but there were three of them: two men and a woman. I was too far away to recognize them. The trees muffled their sound.

I took ten more very careful steps forward and then stopped for a few seconds and collected my thoughts and tried to make out what they were saying and who it was but they were still too far away.

I had a haunted feeling that this case was rapidly coming to a close. Something was not right. I started moving forward again. Every step was an eternity. I wished I was in Babylon, holding hands with Nana-dirat.

The Surprise

This is what I saw when finally I was positioned in the trees to see what was happening at the monument: The first thing I saw was Sergeant Rink standing there, holding a flashlight in his hand.

I stood in the trees out of sight staring at him.

He was the last person in the world I expected to see there. I was dumbfounded. What in the hell was happening?

The next thing I saw was the neck and its beer-guzzling mistress standing there, fastened together by a pair of handcuffs. The neck looked very unhappy. The rich blonde looked as if she needed a beer really bad, which in her case meant a case.

Rink was in full control of the situation.

He was talking to them.

"All I want to know is why did you murder the girl and then try to steal her body from the morgue? When you killed her you could have taken the body away with you. It doesn't make any sense. I can't figure it out. Stealing that body is what caused you to be caught."

"We have nothing to say," the neck said.

"Who said I wanted to hear from you?" Rink said. "I'm talking to the lady here. She's the one who ran this show, so you keep your mouth zipped or I'll take care of it for you."

The neck started to say something and then changed his mind. Sergeant Rink's presence could cause that.

"Well, lady, tell me the truth and I can make it easier on you. Nobody really cares about a murdered whore. At the most it can only cost you a few years if you level with me."

Rink waited.

Finally she spoke, wetting her lips first.

"Listen, fat cop," she said. "First, these handcuffs are too tight. Second, I want a beer. Third, I'm rich and it's already easy for me. And fourth, you can't prove a thing. All you've got is a chain of circumstantial evidence that my lawyers will blow away like a summer breeze. After they get you on the stand and are through with you, the police department will retire you as a mental defective. Either that or your next case will be cleaning up after the horses at the police stables. Are things a little clearer now?"

Nobody had ever called Sergeant Rink a fat cop before.

He stood there unable to believe it.

He had made his bet and he had been called.

"Think it over," she said. Then she looked down at her

handcuffed wrist with a very sophisticated expression of exasperation. After that she looked into the sergeant's eyes. She did not look away.

I just stood there like somebody in a movie theater watching it all happen in front of my eyes. The price of admission was only a trip to the cemetery at midnight in a stolen car after having shot a Negro in the leg and then stopping at my apartment and putting the body of a murdered prostitute in my refrigerator.

That's all.

"I think you're bluffing," Sergeant Rink said.

"You can't be as stupid as you look," the rich blonde said. "Do you know what twenty-five years of horse shit looks like?"

The sergeant had to think that one over. Rink was a very smart detective but he had met his match. He didn't have any more cards up his sleeve.

Too bad I had been out of earshot when Sergeant Rink was telling them his evidence. That would have given me some idea of what was going on. Right now I hadn't the slightest idea. I was totally in the dark.

I was still stunned to see Sergeant Rink there. How in the hell had he found out where we were to meet? It baffled the imagination. I had expected the possibility of seeing the neck and its rich pal, but the sergeant never.

Then Rink shook his head slowly and reached into his pocket for the key to the handcuffs. He walked over and released the neck and the blonde. The sergeant didn't look too happy.

The rich woman rubbed her wrist and then looked at the sergeant sort of sympathetically. "It was a nice try," she said.

The neck started to growl.

It liked having the upper hand now.

"Shut up, Mr. Cleveland," she said.

The neck stopped growling and changed from a bear into a lamb.

"Well," Sergeant Rink said. "You can't win them all. At least if I'm going to lose, I like losing to some class." The socialite smiled at the servant of the law.

The neck trying to please its owner smiled, too. But it failed miserably. Its smile resembled a movie marquee advertising a horror film.

"How about a beer, Sergeant?" she said, smiling. "There's a tavern back down the road." She held out her hand toward him. Rink looked at it for a few seconds and then gave it a good friendly shake.

"Sure," he said. "Let's go have a beer."

Boy, did he have a surprise coming.

Good-bye, $10,000

After they had gone to get a beer, I just stood there for a few moments. There went my prospects for wealth. Good-bye, $10,000. That body in my refrigerator wasn't worth a penny now.

I walked out of the trees over to the monument dedicated to those who had fallen in the Spanish-American War. I felt as if I were one of them.

Oh, well, I still had five hundred bucks in my pocket.

I wouldn't be able to have all the things that I had envisioned like a fine office and a beautiful secretary and a good car, so I'd have to compromise. I'd have a small office, a plain secretary and a Model A.

I was standing by the monument, lost in thought, thinking about all of this when I was rudely surprised by the sudden appearance of four black men all carrying razors.

"Hi, Stew Meat," Smiley said, who was limping at the head of them. He had a tie wrapped around his leg just above the bullet hole.

Where in the hell did they come from?

"We thought we'd pick up our car and get a nice thank you for da loan of it," he said. Smiley had a huge smile on his face. He had something up the sleeve of that smile. "Also, Stew Meat. We need dat money in your pocket for expenses and don't reach for dat gun you shot me with or we cut you real bad, Stew Meat."

Ah, shit. I didn't care any more. Everything had gotten to be a little bit too much for me. I reached toward my pocket.

"Careful now," Smiley said, still smiling. "I sorta like you even if you did shoot me in the leg. Don't disappoint me now."

I very slowly reached in my pocket and took out the money. It was a nice roll: a few dreams. I flipped it to him.

"Good, Stew Meat," Smiley said.

He looked at the money.

"Five C's," he said.

"What about the girl's body?" I said. "Still want it?"

"Naa, you can have it, Stew Meat."

"What now?" I said, expecting some wear and tear on my body from the four black men. After all, I had shot their head man in the leg and I had stolen their car. Some people take offence at things like that.

"This is enough, Stew Meat. I like you," Smiley said. "We got da money. We got paid. The bullet didn't break the bone. Just went clean through. We leave you alone. Bygones be da bygones."

"You're OK, Smiley," I said. "How's your barbecue?"

"Da best," Smiley smiled. "Stop by. I'll give you some ribs. On the house."

And off they went.

It's Midnight.
It's Dark.

I was standing beside the monument to the fallen of the Spanish-American War, alone again, having watched my little office, plain secretary and Model A vanish into thin air.

Thank God I still had a wonderful office with a sunken marble bath, the most beautiful woman in the world, and a golden chariot in Babylon.

That was the consolation prize.

"Son!" I heard a voice yell coming toward me from behind some tombstones. "Son!" I recognized the voice. It was my mother. She came hurrying up to me, almost out of breath.

"What are you doing here?" I said in a numb voice.

217

"You know this is the day I always visit the father and husband you murdered. You know that. Why do you ask that?"

"It's midnight," I said. "It's dark."

"I know that," she said. "But do the dead know that? No, they don't. I just stayed a little longer than usual. But why are you here? You never visit your father any more."

"It's a long story."

"Are you still being that private detective, chasing people with bad shadows? When are you going to pay the money you owe me? You bastard!"

Sometimes Mother liked to call me a bastard.

I was used to it.

"Now that you're here, go say something to the man you murdered. Ask him forgiveness," she said, marching me over to his grave.

I stood there in front of his grave, wishing at the age of four I hadn't thrown a red rubber ball out into the street while playing with him on a Sunday afternoon in 1918 and he hadn't run after it, right into the front of a car and stuck to the grill. The undertaker had to peel him off.

"I'm sorry, Daddy," I said.

"You should be," my mother said. "What a naughty boy. Your daddy's probably a skeleton now."

Good Luck

My mother and I walked back across the cemetery to the other side where her car was parked.

We didn't say anything as we walked along.

That was good.

It gave me some time to think about Babylon. I picked up where I left off in my serial *Smith Smith Versus the Shadow Robots*. After I'd finished talking to the good Dr. Francis, I gave my secretary a passionate kiss on the mouth.

"What's that for?" she said, a little breathless afterward.

"Good luck," I said.

"Whatever happened to the good old rabbit's foot?" she said.

I took a long lustful look at her moist delicious mouth.

"Are you kidding?" I said.

"I guess not," she said. "If that's replaced rabbits' feet for luck, I want some more."

"Sorry, babe," I said. "But I've got work to do. Somebody has invented mercury crystals."

"Oh, no," she said, the expression on her face changing to apprehension.

I put my sword shoulder holster on underneath my toga.

"Watch out, son!" my mother said as I almost walked straight into an open, freshly-dug grave. Her voice jerked me back from Babylon like pulling a tooth out of my mouth without any Novocaine.

I avoided the grave.

"Be careful," she said. "Or I'll have to visit both of you out here. That would make Friday a very crowded day for me."

"OK, Mom, I'll watch my step."

I had to, seeing that I was right back where I started, the only difference being that when I woke up this morning, I didn't have a dead body in my refrigerator.

THE END

The Hawkline Monster
A Gothic Western

Richard Brautigan

This novel is for the Montana Gang.

Book 1

· Hawaii ·

· The Riding Lesson ·

They crouched with their rifles in the pineapple field, watching a man teach his son how to ride a horse. It was the summer of 1902 in Hawaii.

They hadn't said anything for a long time. They just crouched there watching the man and the boy and the horse. What they saw did not make them happy.

"I can't do it," Greer said.

"It's a bastard all right," Cameron said.

"I can't shoot a man when he's teaching his kid how to ride a horse." Greer said. "I'm not made that way."

Greer and Cameron were not at home in the pineapple field. They looked out of place in Hawaii. They were both dressed in cowboy clothes, clothes that belonged to Eastern Oregon.

Greer had his favorite gun: a 30:40 Krag, and Cameron had a 25:35 Winchester. Greer liked to kid Cameron about his gun. Greer always used to say, "Why do you keep that rabbit rifle around when you can get a real gun like this Krag here?"

They stared intently at the riding lesson.

"Well, there goes 1,000 dollars apiece," Cameron said. "And that God-damn trip on that God-damn boat was for nothing. I thought I was going to puke forever and now I'm going to have to do it all over again with only the change in my pockets."

Greer nodded.

The voyage from San Francisco to Hawaii had been the most terrifying experience Greer and Cameron had ever gone through, even more terrible than the time they shot a deputy sheriff in Idaho ten times and he wouldn't die and Greer finally had to say to the deputy sheriff, "Please die because we don't want to shoot you again." And the deputy sheriff had said, "OK, I'll die, but don't shoot me again."

"We won't shoot you again," Cameron had said.

"OK, I'm dead," and he was.

The man and the boy and the horse were in the front yard of a big white house shaded by coconut trees. It was like a shining island in the pineapple fields. There was piano music coming from the house. It drifted lazily across the warm afternoon.

Then a woman came out onto the front porch. She carried herself like a wife and a mother. She was wearing a long white dress with a high starched collar. "Dinner's ready!" she yelled. "Come and get it, you cowboys!"

"God-damn!" Cameron said. "It's sure as hell gone now. 1,000 dollars. By all rights, he should be dead and halfway through being laid out in the front parlor, but there he goes into the house to have some lunch."

"Let's get off this God-damn Hawaii," Greer said.

· Back to San Francisco ·

Cameron was a counter. He vomited nineteen times to San Francisco. He liked to count everything that he did. This had made Greer a little nervous when he first met up with Cameron years ago, but he'd gotten used to it by now. He had to or it might have driven him crazy.

People would sometimes wonder what Cameron was doing and Greer would say, "He's counting something," and people would ask, "What's he counting?" and Greer would say, "What difference does it make?" and the people would say, "Oh."

People usually wouldn't go into it any further because Greer and Cameron were very self-assured in that big relaxed casual kind of way that makes people nervous.

Greer and Cameron had an aura about them that they could handle any situation that came up with a minimum amount of effort resulting in a maximum amount of effect.

They did not look tough or mean. They looked like a relaxed essence distilled from these two qualities. They acted as if they were very intimate with something going on that nobody else could see.

In other words, they had the goods. You didn't want to fuck with them, even if Cameron was always counting things and he counted nineteen vomits back to San Francisco. Their living was killing people.

And one time during the voyage, Greer asked, "How many times is that?"

And Cameron said, "12."

"How many times coming over?"

"20."

"How's it working out?" Greer said.

"About even."

· Miss Hawkline ·

Even now Miss Hawkline waited for them in that huge very cold yellow house . . . in Eastern Oregon . . . as they were picking up some travelling money in San Francisco's Chinatown by killing a Chinaman that a bunch of other Chinamen thought needed killing.

He was a real tough Chinaman and they offered Greer and Cameron seventy-five dollars to kill him.

Miss Hawkline sat naked on the floor of a room filled with musical instruments and kerosene lamps that were burning low. She was sitting next to a harpsichord. There was an unusual light on the keys of the harpsichord and there was a shadow to that light.

Coyotes were howling outside.

The lamp-distorted shadows of musical instruments made exotic patterns on her body and there was a large wood fire burning in the fireplace. The fire seemed almost out of proportion but its size was needed because the house was very cold.

There was a knock at the door of the room.

Miss Hawkline turned her head.

"Yes?" she said.

"Dinner will be served in a few moments," came the voice of an old man through the door. The man did not attempt to come into the room. He stood outside the door.

"Thank you, Mr. Morgan," she replied.

Then there was the sound of huge footsteps walking down the hall away from the door and eventually disappearing behind the closing of another door.

The coyotes were close to the house. They sounded as if they were on the front porch.

"We give you seventy-five dollars. You kill," the head Chinaman said.

There were five or six other Chinaman sitting in the small dark booth with them. The place was filled with the smell of bad Chinese cooking.

When Greer and Cameron heard the price of seventy-five dollars they smiled in that relaxed way they had that usually changed things very rapidly.

"Two hundred dollars," the head Chinaman said, without changing the expression on his face. He was a smart Chinaman. That's why he was their leader.

"Two hundred and fifty dollars. Where's he at?" Greer said.

"Next door," the head Chinaman said.

Greer and Cameron went next door and killed him. They never did find out how tough the Chinaman was because they didn't give him a chance. That's the way they did their work. They didn't put any lace on their killings.

While they were taking care of the Chinaman, Miss Hawkline continued to wait for them, naked on the floor of a room filled with the shadows of musical instruments. Lamp-aided, the shadows played over her body in that huge house in Eastern Oregon.

There was also something else in that room. It was watching her and took pleasure in her naked body. She did not know that it was there. She also did not know that she was naked. If she had known that she was naked she would have been very shocked. She was a proper young lady except for the colorful language that she had picked up from her father.

Miss Hawkline was thinking about Greer and Cameron, though she had never met them or even heard about them, but she waited eternally for them to come as they were always destined to come, for she was part of their gothic future.

Greer and Cameron caught the train to Portland, Oregon, the next morning. It was a beautiful day. They were happy because they liked riding the train to Portland.

"How many times now?" Greer asked.

"8 times straight through and 6 times we got off," Cameron said.

· Magic Child ·

They had been whoring for two days when the Indian girl found them. They always liked to whore for a week or so in Portland before they settled down to thinking about work.

The Indian girl found them in their favorite whorehouse. She had never seen them before or heard about them either but the moment she saw them, she knew they were the men Miss Hawkline wanted.

She had spent three months in Portland, looking for the right men. Her name was Magic Child. She thought that she was fifteen years old. She had gone into this whorehouse by accident. She was actually looking for a whorehouse on the next block.

"What do you want?" Greer said. There was a pretty blonde girl about fourteen years old, sitting on his lap. She didn't have any clothes on.

"Is that an Indian?" she said. "How did she get in here?"

"Shut up," Greer said.

Cameron was starting to fuck a little brunette girl. He stopped what he was doing and looked back over his shoulder at Magic Child.

He didn't know whether to go on and fuck the girl or find out what the Indian girl was about.

Magic Child stood there without saying anything.

The little whore said, "Stick it in."

"Wait a minute," Cameron said. He started to shift out of the love position. He had made up his mind.

The Indian girl reached into her pocket and took out a photograph. It was the photograph of a very beautiful young woman. She wasn't wearing any clothes in the photograph. She was sitting on the floor in a room filled with musical instruments.

Magic Child showed the photograph to Greer.

"What's this?" Greer said.

Magic Child walked over and showed the photograph to Cameron.

"Interesting," Cameron said.

The two little whores didn't know what was happening. They had never seen anything like this before and they had seen a lot of things. The brunette suddenly covered up her vagina because she was embarrassed.

The blonde stared silently on with disbelieving blue eyes. Whenever a man told her to shut up, she always shut up. She had been a farm girl before she went into whoring.

Then Magic Child reached into the pocket of her Indian

dress and took out five thousand dollars in hundred dollar bills. She took the money out as if she'd been doing it all her life.

She gave Greer twenty-five of them and then she walked over and gave Cameron twenty-five of them. After she gave them the money, she stood there looking silently at them. She still hadn't said a word since she'd come into the room.

Greer sat there with the blonde whore still on his lap. He looked at the Indian girl and nodded OK very slowly. Cameron had a half-smile on his face, lying beside the brunette who was covering up her vagina with her hand.

· Indian ·

Greer and Cameron left Portland the next morning on the train up the Columbia River, travelling toward Central County in Eastern Oregon.

They enjoyed their seats because they liked to travel on trains.

The Indian girl travelled with them. They spent a great deal of time looking at her because she was very pretty.

She was tall and slender and had long straight black hair. Her features were delicately voluptuous. They were both interested in her mouth.

She sat there exquisitely, looking at the Columbia River as the train travelled up the river toward Eastern Oregon. She saw things that interested her.

Greer and Cameron started talking with Magic Child after they were three or four hours out of Portland. They were curious as to what it was all about.

The girl hadn't said more than a hundred words since she had walked into the whorehouse and started to change their lives. None of the words were about what they were supposed to do except go to Central County and meet a Miss Hawkline who would then tell them what she would pay them five thousand dollars to do.

"Why are we going to Central County?" Greer said.

"You kill people, don't you?" Magic Child said. Her voice was gentle and precise. They were surprised by the sound of her voice. They didn't expect it to sound that way when she said that.

"Sometimes," Greer said.

"They got a lot of sheep trouble over that way," Cameron said. "I heard there was some killings there. 4 men killed last week and 9 during the month. I know 3 Portland gunmen who went up there a few days ago. Good men, too."

"Real good," Greer said. "Probably the best three men going I know of except for maybe two more. Take a lot to put those boys away. They went up there to work for the cattlemen. Which side is your bosslady on or does she want some personal work done?"

"Miss Hawkline will tell you what she wants done," Magic Child said.

"Can't even get a hint out of you, huh?" Greer said, smiling.

Magic Child looked out the window at the Columbia River. There was a small boat on the river. Two people were sitting in the boat. She couldn't tell what they were doing. One of the people was holding an umbrella, though it wasn't raining and the sun wasn't shining either.

Greer and Cameron gave up trying to find out what they were supposed to do but they were curious about Magic Child. They had been surprised by her voice because she didn't sound like an Indian. She sounded like an Eastern woman who'd had a lot of booklearning.

They'd also taken a closer look at her and had seen that she wasn't an Indian.

They didn't say anything about it. They had the money and that's what counted for them. They figured if she wanted to be an Indian that was her business.

·Gompville·

The train only went as far as Gompville, which was the county seat of Morning County and fifty miles away by stage-coach to Billy. It was a cold clear dawn with half-a-dozen sleepy dogs standing there barking at the train engine.

"Gompville," Cameron said.

Gompville was the headquarters of the Morning County Sheepshooters Association that had a president, a vice-president, a secretary, a sergeant at arms and bylaws that said it was all right to shoot sheep.

The people who owned the sheep didn't particularly care for that, so both sides had brought in gunmen from

Portland and the attitude toward killings had become very casual in those parts.

"We're running it tight," Greer said to Magic Child as they walked over to the stagecoach line. The stage to Billy left in just a few moments.

Cameron was carrying a long narrow trunk over his shoulder. The trunk contained a sawed-off twelve-gauge pump shotgun, a 25:35 Winchester rifle, a 30:40 Krag, two .38 caliber revolvers and an automatic .38 caliber pistol that Cameron had bought from a soldier in Hawaii who was just back from the Philippines where he had been fighting the rebels for two years.

"What kind of pistol is that?" Cameron had asked the soldier. They had been in a bar having some drinks in Honolulu.

"This gun is for killing Filipino motherfuckers," the soldier had said. "It kills one of those bastards so dead that you need two graves to bury him in."

After a bottle of whiskey and a lot of talk about women, Cameron had bought the gun from the soldier who was very glad to be on his way home to America and not have to use that gun any more.

· Central County Ways ·

Central County was a big rangy county with mountains to the north and mountains to the south and a vast loneliness in between. The mountains were filled with trees and creeks.

The loneliness was called the Dead Hills.

They were thirty miles wide. There were thousands of hills out there: yellow and barren in the summer with lots of juniper brush in the draws and a few pine trees here and there, acting as if they had wandered away like stray sheep from the mountains and out into the Dead Hills and had gotten lost and had never been able to find their way back.

. . . poor trees . . .

The population of Central County was around eleven

hundred people: give or take a death here and a birth there or a few strangers deciding to make a new life or old-time residents to move away and never to return or come back soon because they were homesick.

Just like a short history of man, there were two towns in the county.

One of the towns was close to the northern range of mountains. That town was called Brooks. The other town was close to the southern range of mountains. It was called Billy.

The towns were named for Billy and Brooks Paterson: two brothers who had pioneered the county forty years before and had killed each other in a gunfight one September afternoon over the ownership of five chickens.

That fatal chicken argument occurred in 1881 but there was still a lot of strong feeling in the county in 1902 over who those chickens belonged to and who was to fault for the gunfight that killed both brothers and left two widows and nine fatherless children.

Brooks was the county seat but the people who lived in Billy always said, "Fuck Brooks."

· In the Early Winds of Morning ·

Just outside of Gompville a man was hanging from the bridge across the river. There was a look of disbelief on his face as if he still couldn't believe that he was dead. He just refused to believe that he was dead. He wouldn't believe he was dead until they buried him. His body swayed gently in the early winds of morning.

There was a barbed-wire drummer riding in the stagecoach with Greer and Cameron and Magic Child. The drummer looked like a fifty-year-old child with long skinny fingers and cold-white nails. He was going to Billy, then onto Brooks to sell barbed wire.

Business was good.

"There's a lot of that going on around here now," he said, pointing at the body. "It's those gunmen from Portland. It's their work."

He was the only one talking. Nobody else had anything to say out loud. Greer and Cameron said what they had to say inside their minds.

Magic Child looked so calm you would have thought that she had been raised in a land where bodies hung everywhere like flowers.

The stagecoach drove across the bridge without stopping. It sounded like a minor thunderstorm on the bridge. The wind turned the body, so that it was watching the stagecoach drive up the road along the river and then disappear into a turn of dusty green trees.

· "Coffee" with the Widow ·

A couple of hours later, the stagecoach stopped at Widow Jane's house. The driver always liked to have a cup of "coffee" with the widow on his way to Billy.

What he meant by a cup of coffee wasn't really a cup of coffee. He had a romance going with the widow and he'd stop the stagecoach at her house and just parade all the passengers in. The widow would give everybody a cup of coffee and there was always a big platter of homemade doughnuts on the kitchen table.

Widow Jane was a very thin but jolly woman in her early fifties.

Then the driver, carrying a ceremonial cup of coffee in

his hand, and the widow would go upstairs. All the passengers would sit downstairs in the kitchen, drinking coffee and eating doughnuts while the driver would be upstairs with the widow in her bedroom having his "coffee."

The squeaking of the bedsprings shook the house like mechanical rain.

· Cora ·

Cameron had brought the trunk full of guns into the house with him. He didn't want to leave the guns unattended in the stagecoach. Greer and Cameron never carried guns on their persons not unless they intended to kill somebody. Then they carried guns. The rest of the time the guns stayed in the trunk.

The barbed-wire drummer sat there in the kitchen with a cup of coffee in his hand and from time to time he would look down at the trunk that was beside Cameron, but he never said anything about it.

He was curious enough, though, about Magic Child to ask her what her name was.

"Magic Child," Magic Child said.

"That's a pretty name," he said. "And if you don't mind me saying so, you're quite a pretty girl."

"Thank you."

Then, to be polite, he asked Greer what his name was.

"Greer," Greer said.

"That's an interesting name," he said.

Then he asked Cameron what his name was.

"Cameron," Cameron said.

"Everybody here's got an interesting name," he said. "My name is Marvin Cora Jones. You don't come across many men who's middle name is Cora. Anyway, I haven't and I've been to a lot of places, including England."

"Cora is a different kind of middle name for a man," Cameron said.

Magic Child got up and went over to the stove and got some more coffee for Greer and Cameron. She also poured some for the barbed-wire drummer. She was smiling. There was a huge platter of doughnuts on the table and everybody was eating them. Widow Jane was a good cook.

Like a mirror the house continued to reflect the motion of the bed upstairs.

Greer and Cameron each had a glass of milk, too, from a beautiful porcelain pitcher on the table. They liked a glass of milk now and then. They also liked the smile on Magic Child's face. It had been the first time that Magic Child had smiled.

"They named me Cora for my great-grandmother. I don't mind. She met George Washington at a party. She said that he was really a nice man but he was a little shorter than what she had expected," the barbed-wire drummer said. "I meet a lot of interesting people by telling them that my middle name is Cora. It's something that gets people's curiosity up. It's kind of funny, too. I don't mind people laughing because it is sort of funny for a man to have the name of Cora."

· Against the Dust ·

The driver and the widow came down the stairs with their arms in sweet affection around each other. "It certainly was nice of you to show that to me," the driver said.

The widow's face was twinkling like a star.

The driver acted mischievously solemn but you could tell that he was just playing around.

"It's good to stop and have some coffee," the driver said to everybody sitting at the table. "It makes travelling a little easier and those doughnuts are a lot better than having a mule kick you in the head."

There was no argument there.

· Thoughts of July 12, 1902 ·

About noon the stagecoach was rattling through the mountains. It was hot and boring. Cora, the barbed-wire drummer, had dozed off. He looked like a sleeping fence.

Greer was staring at the graceful billowing of Magic Child's breasts against her long and simple dress. Cameron was thinking about the man who had been hanging from the bridge. He was thinking that he had once gotten drunk with him in Billings, Montana, at the turn of the century.

Cameron wasn't totally certain but the man hanging from the bridge looked an awful lot like the guy he had gotten drunk with in Billings. If he wasn't that man, he was his twin brother.

Magic Child was watching Greer stare at her breasts. She was imagining Greer touching them with his casually powerful-looking hands. She was excited and pleased inside of herself, knowing that she would be fucking Greer before the day was gone.

While Cameron was thinking about the dead man on the bridge, *perhaps it was Denver where they had gotten drunk together,* Magic Child was thinking about fucking him, too.

· Binoculars ·

Suddenly the stagecoach stopped on top of a ridge that had a meadow curving down from it. There was an Old Testament quantity of vultures circling and landing and rising again in the meadow. They were like flesh angels summoned to worship at a large spread-out temple of many small white formerly-living things.

"Sheep!" the driver yelled. "Thousands of them!"

He was looking down on the meadow through a pair of binoculars. The driver had once been an officer, a second lieutenant in the cavalry during the Indian Wars, so he carried a pair of binoculars with him when he was driving the stagecoach.

He had gotten out of the cavalry because he didn't like to kill Indians.

"The Morning County Sheepshooters Association has been working out this way," he said.

Everybody in the stagecoach looked out the windows and then got out as the driver climbed down from his seat. They stretched and tried to unwind the coils of travel while they watched the vultures eating sheep down below in the meadow.

Fortunately, the wind was blowing in an opposite manner so as not to bring them the smell of death. They could watch death while not having to be intimate with it.

"Those sheepshooters really know how to shoot sheep," the driver said.

"All you need is a gun," Cameron said.

· Billy ·

They crossed the Shadow Creek bridge at suppertime. *There's nobody hanging from this bridge:* Cameron thought as the stagecoach drove into Billy.

There was an expression of pleasure on Magic Child's face. She was happy to be home. She had been gone for months, doing what Miss Hawkline had sent her to do, and they sat beside her. She looked forward to seeing Miss Hawkline. They would have many things to talk about. She would tell Miss Hawkline about Portland.

Magic Child's breathing had noticeably changed in sexual anticipation for the bodies of Greer and Cameron. They of course didn't know that Magic Child would soon be fucking them.

They could see that her breathing had changed but they

didn't know what it meant. They thought she was happy to be home or something.

Billy was noisy because it was suppertime. The smell of meat and potatoes was heavy on the wind. All the doors and windows in Billy were open. It had been a very hot day and you could hear people eating and talking.

Billy was about sixty or seventy houses, buildings and shacks built on both sides of a creek that flowed through a canyon whose slopes were covered with juniper brush that gave a sweet fresh smell to things.

Billy had three bars, a cafe, a big mercantile store, a blacksmith, and a church. It didn't have a hotel, a bank or a doctor.

There was a town marshal but there wasn't a jail. He didn't need one. His name was Jack Williams and he could be a mean motherfucker. He thought putting somebody in jail was a waste of time. If you caused any trouble in Billy, he'd punch you in the mouth and throw you in the creek. The rest of the time he ran a very friendly saloon, The Jack Williams House, and would buy a drink every morning for the town drunk.

There was a graveyard behind the church and the minister, a Fredrick Calms, was always trying to raise enough money to put a fence around the graveyard because the deer got in there and ate the flowers and stuff off the graves.

For some strange reason, it made the minister mad whenever he saw some deer among the graves and he'd start cursing up a storm, but nobody ever took putting a fence up around the graveyard very seriously.

The people just didn't give a shit.

"So a few deer get in there. That's no big thing. The minister is kind of crazy, anyway," was their general reaction to putting a fence around the graveyard in Billy.

· The Governor of Oregon ·

Greer, Cameron and Magic Child went over to the black-smith's shop to get some horses for the ride out to Miss Hawkline's in the morning. They wanted to make sure the horses would be ready when they left at dawn.

The blacksmith had a collection of strange horses that he would rent out sometimes if he knew you or liked your looks. He'd had a bucket of beer along with his dinner that evening, so he was very friendly.

"Magic Child," he said. "Ain't seen you around for a while. You been someplace? Hear they're killing people over Gompville way. My name is Pills," holding out his beer-friendly hand to Greer and Cameron. "I take care of the horses around here."

"We need some horses in the morning," Magic Child said. "We're going out to Miss Hawkline's."

"I think I can do you up with some horses. Maybe one of them will get that far: if you're lucky."

Pills liked to joke about his horses. He was famous in those parts for having the worst bunch of horses ever assembled in a corral.

He had a horse that was so swaybacked that it looked like an October quarter moon. He called that horse Cairo. "This is an Egyptian horse," he used to tell people.

He had another horse that didn't have any ears. A drunken cowboy had bitten them off for a fifty-cent bet.

"I bet you fifty cents I'm so drunk I'd bite a horse's ears off!"

"God-damn, I don't think you're that drunk!"

And he had another horse that actually drank whiskey. They'd put a quart of whiskey in his bucket and he'd drink it all down and then he'd fall over on his side and everybody would laugh.

But the prize of his collection was a horse that had a wooden foot. The horse was born without a right rear foot, so somebody had carved him a wooden one, but the person had gotten confused in his carving, he wasn't really right in the head, anyway, and the wooden foot looked more like a duck's foot than a horse's foot. It really looked strange to see that horse walking around with a wooden duck foot.

A politician once came all the way from La Grande to look at those horses. It was even rumored that the governor of Oregon had heard about them.

· Jack Williams ·

On their way over to Ma Smith's Cafe to have some dinner,
Jack Williams, the town marshal, strolled out of his saloon.
He was going someplace else but when he saw Magic Child,
whom he liked a lot, and two strange men with her, he
walked over to Magic Child and her friends to say hello and
find out what was happening.

"Magic Child! God-damn!" he said and threw his arms
around her and gave her a big hug.

He could tell that the two men did not work for a living
and in appearance there was nothing about them that one
would ever remember. They both looked about the same

except they had different features and different builds. It was the way they handled themselves that was memorable.

One of them was taller than the other one but once you turned your back on them you wouldn't be able to remember which one it was.

Jack Williams had seen men similar to these before. Instinctively, without even bothering with an intellectual process, he knew that these men could mean trouble. One of them was carrying a long narrow trunk on his shoulder. He carried the trunk easily as if it were part of his shoulder.

Jack Williams was a big man: over six feet tall and weighed in excess of two hundred pounds. His toughness was legendary in that part of Eastern Oregon. Men with evil thoughts on their minds generally stayed clear of Billy.

Jack Williams wore a shoulder holster with a big shiny .38 in it. He didn't like to wear a regular gun belt around his waist. He always joked that he didn't like to have all that iron hanging so close to his cock.

He was forty-one years old and in the prime of health.

"Magic Child! God-damn!" he said and threw his arms around her and gave her a big hug.

"Jack," she said. "You big man!"

"I've missed you, Magic Child," he said. He and Magic Child had fucked a few times and he had a tremendous respect for her quick lean body.

He liked her a lot but sometimes he was a little awe-struck and disturbed by how much she looked like Miss Hawkline. They looked so much alike that they could have been twins. Everybody in town noticed it but there was nothing they could do about it, so they just let it be.

"These are my friends," she said, making the introductions. "I want you to meet them. This is Greer and this is

· 44 ·

Cameron. I want you to meet Jack Williams. He's the town marshal."

Greer and Cameron were smiling softly at the intensity of Magic Child's and Jack Williams' greeting.

"Howdy," Jack Williams said, shaking their hands. "What are you boys up to?"

"Come on now," Magic Child said. "These are my friends."

"I'm sorry," Jack Williams said, laughing. "I'm sorry, boys. I own a saloon here. Any time you want there's a drink waiting over there for you and it's on me."

He was a fair man and people respected him for it.

Greer and Cameron liked him immediately.

They liked people who had strong character. They didn't like to kill people like Jack Williams. Sometimes it made them feel bad afterwards and Greer would always say, "I liked him." and Cameron would always answer, "Yeah, he was a good man." and they wouldn't say anything more about it after that.

Just then some gunshots rang out in the hills above Billy. Jack Williams paid no attention to the shots.

"5, 6," Cameron said.

"What's that?" Jack Williams said.

"He was counting the gunshots," Greer said.

"Oh, that. Oh, yeah," Jack Williams said. "They're up there probably killing themselves or killing off their animals. Frankly, I don't give a fuck. Excuse me, Magic Child, I'm sorry. I've got a tongue that was hatched on an outhouse seat. I'm saving it for my old age. Instead of whittling, I'll stop cussing."

"What's the shooting about?" Greer said, nodding his head up toward the twilight hills towering above Billy.

"Oh, come on now," Jack Williams said. "You boys know better than that."

Greer and Cameron smiled softly again.

"I don't care what those cattle and sheep people do to each other. They can kill everyone of themselves off if they're going to be that stupid, just as long as they don't do it in the streets of Billy."

"That county sheriff from Brooks. Up there's his problem. I don't think he ever gets off his ass, not unless he's looking for a piece of ass. Oh, God, I've done it again. Magic Child, when will this tongue of mine ever learn?"

Magic Child smiled up at Jack Williams. "I'm glad to be back." She touched his hand gently.

That pleased the town marshal of Billy whose name was Jack Williams and who was known far and wide as a tough but fair man.

"I guess I'd better get along now," he said. "Glad you're back, Magic Child." Then he turned to Greer and Cameron and said, "Hope you boys from Portland have a good time here but just remember," he said, pointing at the hills. "Up there, not down here."

· Ma Smith's Cafe ·

They had some fried potatoes and steaks for dinner and biscuits all covered with gravy at Ma Smith's Cafe, and the
people eating there wondered why they were in town, and
they had some blackberry pie for dessert, and the people,
mostly cowboys, wondered what was in the long narrow
trunk beside their table, and Magic Child had a glass of milk
along with her pie, and the cowboys were made a little
nervous by Greer and Cameron, though they didn't know
exactly why, but the cowboys all thought that Magic Child
sure was pretty and they'd sure like to fuck her and they
wondered where she had been these last months. They
hadn't seen her in town. She must have been someplace else

but they didn't know where. Greer and Cameron continued to make them nervous but they still didn't know why. One thing they did know, though, Greer and Cameron did not look like the kind of people who had come to Billy to settle down.

Greer thought about having another piece of pie but he didn't. It was a nice thought. He really liked the pie and the thought was as good as having another piece of pie. The pie was that tasty.

They heard half-a-dozen more gunshots back off in the hills while they were finishing their coffee. All the shots were methodical, aimed and well-placed. It was the same gun firing and it sounded like a 30:30. Whoever was firing that gun really thought about it every time they pulled the trigger.

· And Ma Smith ·

Ma Smith, a cantankerous old woman, looked up from a steak she was frying for a cowboy. She was a big woman with a very red face and shoes that were much too small for her feet. She considered herself big enough every place else without having to have big feet, so she stuffed her feet into shoes that were much too small for them. which caused her to be in considerable pain most of her walking hours and led her to having a very short temper.

Her clothes were very sweaty and stuck to her as she moved around the big wooden stove that she was cooking over on a night that was already hot enough by itself.

Cameron counted the gunshots in his mind.

1 . . .

2 . . .

3 . . .

4 . . .

5 . . .

6 . . .

Cameron waited to count the seventh shot, but then there was silence. The shooting was over.

Ma Smith was angrily fussing around with the steak on the stove. It looked like the last steak she was going to have to cook that night and she was very glad for that. She'd had enough for the day.

"I bet they're killing somebody out there," the cowboy said whose steak was being cooked. "I've been waiting for the killing to work its way down here. It's just a matter of time. That's all. Well, I don't care who kills who as long as they don't kill me."

"You won't get killed down here," an old miner said. "Jack Williams will make sure of that."

Ma Smith took the steak and put it on a big white platter and brought it over to the cowboy who didn't want to get killed.

"How does this look?" she said.

"Better put some more fire under it," the cowboy said.

"Next time you come in here I'll just cook you up a big plate of ashes," she said. "And sprinkle some God-damn cow hair on it."

· Pills' Last Love ·

They slept that night in Pills' barn. Pills got them a big arm-
load of blankets.

"I guess I won't be seeing you tomorrow morning,"
Pills said. "You'll be off at daybreak, huh?"

"Yes," Magic Child said.

"If you change your mind or you want some breakfast or
coffee or anything, just wake me up or come in the house and
fix it yourself. Everything's in the cupboard," Pills said.

He liked Magic Child.

"Thank you, Pills. You're a kind man. If we change our
minds, we'll come in and rob your cupboard," Magic Child
said.

"Good," Pills said. "I guess you'll work out the sleeping arrangements OK." That was his sense of humor after a few buckets of beer.

Magic Child had a reputation in town for being generous with her favors. Once she had even laid Pills which made him very happy because he was sixty-one years old and didn't think he'd ever do it again. His last lover had been a widow woman in 1894. She moved to Corvallis and that was the end of his love life.

Then one evening, out of the clear blue, Magic Child said to him, "When was the last time you fucked a woman?" There had been a long pause after that while Pills stared at Magic Child. He knew that he wasn't that drunk.

"Years."

"Do you think you can get it up?"

"I'd like to try."

Magic Child put her arms around the sixty-one-year-old bald-headed, paunchy, half-drunk keeper of strange horses and kissed him on the mouth.

"I think I can do it."

· In the Barn ·

Greer carried a lantern and Cameron carried the blankets and Magic Child trailed after them into the barn. She was very excited by the hard lean curve of their asses.

"Where's the best place to sleep here?" Cameron said.

"Up in the loft," Magic Child said. "There's an old bed up there. Pills keeps it for travellers to sleep in. That bed is the only hotel in town." Her voice was dry and suddenly nervous. She could just barely keep her hands off them.

Greer noticed it. He looked over at her. Her eyes darted like excited jade into his eyes and then out of them and he smiled softly. She didn't smile at all.

They carefully climbed the ladder up to the loft. It smelled sweetly of hay and there was an old brass bed beside the hay. The bed looked very comfortable after two days of travel. It shined like a pot of gold at the end of the rainbow.

"Fuck me," Magic Child said.

"What?" Cameron said. He had been thinking about something else. He had been thinking about the six gunshots off in the hills during dinner.

"I want you both," Magic Child said and passion broke her voice like an Aphrodite twig.

Then she took her clothes off. Greer and Cameron stood there watching. Her body was slender and long with high firm breasts that had small nipples. And she had a good ass.

Greer blew the lantern out and she fucked Greer first.

Cameron sat on a dark bale of hay while Magic Child and Greer fucked. The brass bed sounded alive as it echoed the motion of their passion.

After while the bed stopped moving and everything was quiet except for the voice of Magic Child saying thank you, thank you, over and over again to Greer.

Cameron counted how many times she said thank you. She said thank you eleven times. He waited for her to say thank you a twelfth time but she didn't say it again.

Then Cameron took his turn with Magic Child. Greer didn't bother to get out of bed. He just lay there beside them while they fucked. Greer felt too good to move.

After another while the bed fell silent. There wasn't a sound for a couple of moments and then Magic Child said, "Cameron." She said it once. That's all she said it. Cameron waited for her to say his name again or to say something else but she didn't say his name again and she didn't say anything else.

She just lay there affectionately stroking his ass like a kitten.

· The Drum ·

The slamming of screen doors and dogs barking and the rattling of breakfast pots and pans and roosters crowing and people coughing and grumbling and stirring about: getting ready to start their day beat like a drum in Billy.

It was a silver early-in-the-morning drum that would lead to the various events that would comprise July 13, 1902.

The town drunk was lying facedown in the middle of the Main Street of town. He was passed out and at peace with the summer dust. His eyes were closed. There was a smile on the side of his face. A big yellow dog was sniffing at his boots and a big black dog was sniffing at the yellow dog. They were happy dogs. Both of their tails were wagging.

A screen door slammed and a man shouted so loudly that the dogs stopped their sniffing and wagging, "Where in the hell is my God-damn hat!"

"On your head, you idiot!" was the female reply.

The dogs thought about this for a moment and then they started barking at the town drunk and woke him up.

· Welcome to the Dead Hills ·

They woke up at dawn the next morning and rode out on three sad horses into the Dead Hills. Their name was perfect. They looked as if an undertaker had designed them from leftover funeral scraps. It was a three-hour ride to Miss Hawkline's house. The road was very bleak, wandering like the handwriting of a dying person over the hills.

There were no houses, no barns, no fences, no signs that human life had ever made its way this far except for the road which was barely legible. The only comforting thing was the early morning sweet smell of juniper brush.

Cameron had the trunk full of guns strapped onto the back of his horse. He thought it remarkable that the animal could still move. He had to think back a ways to remember a horse that had been in such bad shape.

"Sure is stark," Greer said.

Cameron had been counting the hills as they rode along. He got to fifty-seven. Then he gave up. It was just too boring.

"57," he said.

Then he didn't say anything else. Actually, "57" had been the only thing that he'd said since they left Billy a few hours before.

Magic Child waited for Cameron to explain why he'd said "57" but he didn't. He didn't say anything more.

"Miss Hawkline lives out here," Greer said.

"Yes," Magic Child said. "She loves it."

· Something Human ·

Finally they came across something human. It was a grave.
The grave was right beside the road. It was simply a pile of
bleak rocks covered with vulture shit. There was a wooden
cross at one end of the rocks. The grave was so close to the
road that you almost had to ride around it.

"Well, at last we've got some company," Greer said.

There were a bunch of bullet holes in the cross. The
grave had been used for target practice.

"9," Cameron said.

"What was that?" Magic Child said.

"He said there are nine bullet holes in the cross," Greer
said.

Magic Child looked over at Cameron. She looked at him about ten seconds longer than she should have looked at him.

"Don't mind Cameron," Greer said. "He just likes to count things. You'll get used to it."

· The Coat ·

They rode farther and farther into the Dead Hills which
disappeared behind them instantly to reappear again in front
of them and everything was the same and everything was
very still.

At one time Greer thought he saw something different
but he was mistaken. What he saw was exactly the same as
what he had been seeing. He thought that it was smaller but
then he realized that it was exactly the same size as everything else.

He slowly shook his head.

"Where does Pills get these horses?" Cameron said to
Magic Child.

"That's what everybody wants to know," Magic Child said.

After while Cameron felt like counting again but because everything was the same it was difficult to find anything to count, so Cameron counted the footsteps of his horse, carrying him deeper and deeper into the Dead Hills and Miss Hawkline standing on the front porch of a gigantic yellow house, shielding her eyes against the sun with her hand and staring out into the Dead Hills. She was wearing a heavy winter coat.

· The Doctor ·

Magic Child was very glad to be home and she considered these hills to be home. You couldn't tell, though, that she was happy because she wore a constant expression on her face that had nothing to do with happiness. It was an anxious, slightly abstract look. It had been on her face since they had awakened in the barn.

Greer and Cameron had wanted another go at her but she hadn't been interested. She had told them that it was very important they get out to Miss Hawkline's place.

"911," Cameron said.

"What are you counting now?" Magic Child said, in a voice that sounded very intelligent. She was smart, too. She had graduated at the head of her class at Radcliffe and had attended the Sorbonne. Then she had studied to be a doctor at Johns Hopkins.

She was a member of a prominent New England family that dated back to the *Mayflower*. Her family had been one of the contributing lights that led to the flowering of New England society and culture.

Surgery was her specialty.

"Hoofsteps," Cameron said.

· The Bridge ·

Suddenly a rattlesnake appeared, crawling rapidly across the road. The horses reacted to the snake: by whinnying and jumping about. Then the snake was gone. It took a few moments to calm the horses down.

After the horses had been returned to "normal" Greer said, "That was a big God-damn rattler. I don't know if I've ever seen one that big before. You ever see a rattler that big before, Cameron?"

"Not any bigger," Cameron said.

"That's what I thought," Greer said.

Magic Child was directing her attention to something else.

"What is it, Magic Child?" Greer said.

"We're almost home," she said, now breaking out into a big smile.

· Hawkline Manor ·

The road turned slightly, then went up over the horizon
of a dead hill and from the top of the hill you could see a huge
three-story yellow house about a quarter of a mile away in
the center of a small meadow that was the same color as the
house except for close to the house where it was white like
snow.

There were no fences or outbuildings or anything human or trees near the house. It just stood there alone in the
center of the meadow with white stuff piled close in around
it and more white stuff on the ground around it.

There wasn't even a barn. Two horses grazed a hundred
yards or so from the house and there was a huge flock of

red chickens the same distance away on the road that ended at the front porch of the house.

The road stopped like a dying man's signature on a last-minute will.

There was a gigantic mound of coal beside the house which was a classic Victorian with great gables and stained glass across the tops of the windows and turrets and balconies and red brick fireplaces and a huge porch all around the house. There were twenty-one rooms in the house, including ten bedrooms and five parlors.

Just a quick glance at the house and you knew that it did not belong out there in the Dead Hills surrounded by nothing. The house belonged in Saint Louis or San Francisco or Chicago or anyplace other than where it was now. Even Billy would have been a more understandable place for the house but out here there was no reason for it to exist, so the house looked like a fugitive from a dream.

Heavy black smoke was pouring out of three brick chimneys. The temperature was over ninety on the hill top. Greer and Cameron wondered why there were fires burning in the house.

They sat there on their horses for a few moments on the horizon, staring down at the house. Magic Child continued smiling. She was very happy.

"That's the strangest thing I've ever seen in my life," Greer said.

"Don't forget Hawaii," Cameron said.

Book 2

· Miss Hawkline ·

· Miss Hawkline ·

As they rode slowly down the hill toward the house the front door opened and a woman stepped outside onto the porch. The woman was Miss Hawkline. She was wearing a heavy long white coat. The woman stood there watching them as they rode down closer and closer to the house.

It seemed peculiar to Greer and Cameron that she should be wearing a coat on a hot July morning.

She was tall and slender and had long black hair. The coat flowed like a waterfall down her body to end at a pair of pointed high-top shoes. The shoes were made of patent leather and sparkled like pieces of coal. They could easily have come from the huge mound of coal beside the house.

She just stood there on the porch watching them approach. She made no motion toward them. She didn't move. She just stood there watching them as they came down the hill.

She was not the only one watching them. They were also being observed from an upstairs window.

When they were a hundred yards away from the house, the air suddenly turned cold. The temperature dropped about forty degrees. The drop was as sudden as the motion of a knife.

It was like journeying from summer into winter by blinking your eyes. The two horses and the huge flock of red chickens stood there in the heat watching them as they rode into the cold a few feet away.

Magic Child slowly raised her arm and affectionately waved at the woman who returned the gesture with an equal amount of affection.

When they were about fifty yards away from the house, there was frost on the ground. The woman took a step forward. She had an incredibly beautiful face. Her features were clean and sharp like the ringing of a church bell on a full moon night.

When they were twenty-five yards away from the house, she moved to the top of the stairs which went down eight steps to the yellow grass which was frozen hard like strange silverware. The grass went right up to the stairs and almost up to the house. The only thing that stopped the grass from directly touching the house were drifts of snow that were piled against the house. If it hadn't been for the snow, the frozen yellow grass would have been a logical extension of the house or a rug too big to bring inside.

The grass had been frozen for centuries.

Then Magic Child started laughing. The woman started laughing, too, such a beautiful sound, the sound of them together laughing with white steam coming out of their mouths in the cold air.

Greer and Cameron were freezing.

The woman ran down the stairs to Magic Child who slipped like a grape peeling off her horse and into the arms of the woman. They stood there for a moment with their arms around each other: still laughing. They were the same height and had the same color hair and the same build and the same features and they were the same woman.

Magic Child and Miss Hawkline were twins.

They stood there with their arms around each other: laughing. They were two beautiful and unreal women.

"I found them," Magic Child said. "They're perfect," with snow piled up around the house on a hot July morning.

· The Meeting ·

Greer and Cameron got down off their horses. Miss Hawkline and Magic Child had exhausted their very affectionate
greeting and now Miss Hawkline had turned toward them
and was ready to meet them.

"This is Miss Hawkline," Magic Child said, standing
there and looking exactly like Miss Hawkline except that
she was wearing Indian clothes and Miss Hawkline was
turned out in a very proper New England winter wardrobe.

"Greer, Miss Hawkline," Magic Child said.

"I'm glad to meet you, Miss Hawkline," Greer said. He
was smiling softly.

"It pleases me that you're here," she said.

"And Cameron," Magic Child said.

"You please me also," Miss Hawkline said.

Cameron nodded.

Then Miss Hawkline walked over to them and held out her hand. They both shook hands with her. Her hand was long and delicate but the grasp was strong. The grasp was so strong that it surprised them. It was another surprise in a day full of surprises. Of course all that had transpired so far to surprise them was just a downpayment on the things that would happen before the day was out.

"1, 2," Cameron said, looking at Miss Hawkline and Magic Child.

"I'm sorry," Miss Hawkline said, waiting for Cameron to finish what he was saying. Cameron didn't say anything more.

"That means he's glad to meet you," Magic Child said, smiling at Greer.

· The Ice Caves ·

"Let's go inside the house," Miss Hawkline said. "And I'll tell you why Magic Child has brought you here and what you have to do to earn your money. Have you had breakfast yet?"

"We left at dawn," Magic Child said.

"It sounds as if breakfast is in order," Miss Hawkline said.

Greer and Cameron had noticed that the closer you got to the house, the colder the air became. The house towered above them like a small wooden mountain covered with yellow snow.

Greer saw something in a second-story window. It

floated like a small mirror. Then it was gone. He thought that there was somebody else in the house.

"You've noticed the cold, haven't you?" Miss Hawkline said as she led the way up the stairs to the porch.

"Yes," Greer said.

"There are ice caves under this house," Miss Hawkline said. "That's why it's cold."

· The Black Umbrellas ·

They went into the house. It was filled with beautiful Victorian furniture and very cold.

"This way to the kitchen," Miss Hawkline said. "I'll cook up some breakfast. You boys look as if you could use some ham and eggs."

"I'm going upstairs to change," Magic Child said. She vanished up a curved mahogany staircase into the upper reaches of the house. Greer and Cameron watched after her until she was gone. Then they followed Miss Hawkline into the kitchen. It was very pleasant trailing after her. She had taken her coat off and she was wearing a long white dress with a high lace collar.

She had exactly the same kind of body that Magic Child

had. Greer and Cameron could imagine her without any clothes on, looking exactly like Magic Child which was a very good way to look.

"I'll cook some breakfast and then tell you what we want done. It's a long trip here from Portland. I'm glad that you came. I think we'll all turn out to be friends."

The kitchen was immense. There was a large window and you could look out and see the snow and the frost on the ground. A hot fire was burning in the stove and it was warm and comfortable in the kitchen.

Greer and Cameron sat down in chairs at the table and Miss Hawkline poured them cups of strong black coffee from a huge pot on the stove.

Then she got a ham and sliced off some big pieces and got them cooking on the stove. Some biscuits were made very quickly and put into the oven to bake. Greer and Cameron couldn't remember anybody making biscuits that fast and getting them into the oven so quickly.

Miss Hawkline was very skillful with her kitchen as she was with all the things of her life. She didn't say much as she went about cooking breakfast. Once she asked them if they liked Portland and they said that they did.

Greer and Cameron watched her very carefully, thinking about her every move, wondering what was going to happen next, knowing that this was all the beginning of some pretty strange adventures.

They looked casual, relaxed, not in a hurry at all, as if what had happened so far and this strange house perched over some ice caves with frost on the ground in summer were every day occurrences with them.

Cameron had brought the trunk full of guns into the house with them. He had left the trunk in the front hall next to a large elephant foot full of black umbrellas.

· The First Breakfast ·

Just about the time breakfast was ready, Magic Child came into the kitchen. She was wearing exactly the same clothes that Miss Hawkline was wearing. Her hair was also combed the same way and she wore patent leather shoes that shined like coal. You could not tell the difference between Magic Child and Miss Hawkline.

They were the same person.

"How do I look?" Magic Child said.

"Fine," Greer said.

"You sure are 1 pretty girl," Cameron said.

"I'm so glad you're back," Miss Hawkline said, suddenly stopping breakfast to rush over and throw her arms around Magic Child again.

Greer and Cameron sat there, staring at these two identical visions of beautiful womanhood.

Miss Hawkline went back to the few minutes that took care of cooking breakfast and putting the food on the table where soon they were all gathered eating the first of many meals that they would eat together.

Book 3

· The Hawkline Monster ·

· The Death of
Magic Child ·

"Is anybody else going to have breakfast with us?" Greer said as he prepared to take his first bite of food. He was thinking about the flash of light he had seen in an upstairs window. He thought that the light was caused by a person.

"No," Miss Hawkline said. "There's nobody else in the house except us."

Cameron stared at his fork. It lay beside a plate that had a delicate Chinese pattern on it. He looked over at Greer. Then he picked up his fork and started eating.

"What do you want done?" Greer said. He had just finished swallowing a big mouthful of carefully chewed ham. Greer was a slow eater. He liked to enjoy his food.

"5,000," Cameron said. He still had some food in his mouth, so his words sounded a little bit lumpy.

"You have to kill a monster that lives under the house in the ice caves." Miss Hawkline said, looking over at Cameron.

"A monster?" Greer said.

"Yes, a monster," Magic Child said. "The monster lives in the caves. We want him dead. There's a basement with a laboratory in it above the caves. An iron door separates the laboratory from the caves and there's another iron door that separates the laboratory from the house. They're thick doors but we're afraid someday he'll break the doors down and get upstairs into the house. We don't want the monster running around the house."

"I can see that," Greer said. "Nobody likes monsters running around their house." He was smiling softly.

"What kind of a monster is this?" Cameron said.

"We don't know," Miss Hawkline said.

"We've never seen him," Magic Child said.

Ever since they had arrived at the house, Magic Child's personality had been changing. She was rapidly becoming more and more like Miss Hawkline. Her voice had been changing and the expressions on her face had been changing. She was growing closer and closer toward Miss Hawkline's way of talking and moving and doing things.

"But we can hear him howling in the ice caves and banging on the iron door with what sounds like a tail," Magic Child said, in a very Miss Hawkline manner.

Magic Child was becoming Miss Hawkline right in front of Greer and Cameron's eyes. By the time breakfast was over they were not able to tell the difference between them. Only their places at the table could tell who was Magic Child and who was Miss Hawkline.

"It's a terrible sound and we're afraid," Magic Child said.

Greer was thinking that as soon as they both stood up and you took your eyes off them for a second, you would not be able to tell which one was Magic Child and who was Miss Hawkline. He suddenly realized that Magic Child was going to die shortly in that kitchen and a second Miss Hawkline would be born and then there would be two Miss Hawklines and you wouldn't be able to tell the difference between them.

Greer felt a little sad. He liked Magic Child.

A few moments later, while they were all talking about the monster, both of the women got up and started moving around the kitchen, cleaning up after breakfast.

Greer kept his eye on the one that was Magic Child. He didn't want to lose her.

"We've never killed a monster before," Cameron said. Greer took his eyes accidentally off the women to listen to Cameron. Then he realized in horror what he had done and turned instantly back to the women but it was too late. He couldn't tell the difference between them.

Magic Child was dead.

· The Funeral of
Magic Child ·

"Which one of you is Magic Child?" Greer said.

The Hawkline women stopped their after-breakfast-kitchen-clean-up and turned toward Greer.

"Magic Child is dead," one of the women said.

"Why?" Greer said. "She was a nice person. I liked her."

"I liked her, too," Cameron said. "But that's the way it goes." Cameron had the kind of mentality that could accept anything.

"You die when you've lived long enough," one of the Hawkline women said. "Magic Child lived as long as she was supposed to live. Don't feel sad. It was a painless and needed death."

They were both smiling gently at Greer and Cameron. You could not tell the difference between the women now. Everything about them was the same.

Greer sighed.

"What about another name to tell the difference between you?" Greer said.

"There is no difference between us. We're the same person," one of the women said.

"They're both Miss Hawkline," Cameron said, to make it final. "I like Miss Hawkline and now we've got 2 of them. Let's call them both Miss Hawkline. Who gives a fuck in the long run?"

"That sounds fine," Miss Hawkline said.

"Yes. Just call us Miss Hawkline," Miss Hawkline said.

"I'm glad that's taken care of," Cameron said. "You have 1 monster in the basement. Right? And he needs killing."

"Not in the basement," Miss Hawkline said. "In the ice caves."

"That's the basement," Cameron said. "Tell us some more about this God-damn creature. Then we'll go down and blow its fucking head off."

· The Hawkline Monster ·

The two Miss Hawklines sat back down at the table with Greer and Cameron and started telling the story of the Hawkline Monster.

"Our father built this house," Miss Hawkline said.

"He was a scientist teaching at Harvard," the other Miss Hawkline said.

"What's Harvard?" Cameron said.

"It's a famous college in the East," Miss Hawkline said.

"We've never been in the East," Greer said.

"Yes, we've been there," Cameron said. "We've been to Hawaii."

"That's not East," Greer said.

"Don't Chinamen come from China which is in the East?" Cameron said.

"It's not the same," Greer said. "Saint Louis is in the East and Chicago. Places like that."

"You mean *that* East," Cameron said.

"Yeah," Greer said. "*That* East."

"The monster—" Miss Hawkline said, trying to get back to the original subject which was the monster that dwelled in the ice caves under their house.

"Yeah," Greer said. "How in the hell did we get to talking about Hawaii? I hate Hawaii."

"I mentioned it," Cameron said. "Because we were talking about the East. I hate Hawaii, too."

"Hawaii's a dumb thing to bring up in this conversation. These women have a problem," Greer said. "They paid us their money to take care of it and let's get on with it and I know you hate Hawaii because I was standing right beside you on the fucking place. I know you remember that because you remember every fucking thing."

"The monster—" the other Miss Hawkline said, trying again to get back to the original subject which was the monster that dwelled in the ice caves under their house.

"I think the problem is this," Cameron said, totally ignoring Miss Hawkline and the monster. "If Miss Hawkline had said, '*back* East,' then I would have known right away what East she was talking about. She said, '*in* the East,' so I thought about Hawaii where we just came from. See, it's all because she said, '*in* the East,' instead of '*back* East.' Every idiot knows that Chicago is *back* East."

This was a very strange conversation that Greer and Cameron were having. They'd never had a conversation like this before. They had never talked to each other this way before either.

Their conversations always ran along very normally except for the fact that Cameron counted the things that passed through their lives and Greer had gotten used to that. He had to because Cameron was his partner.

Greer broke the spell of their conversation by suddenly turning his energy away from Cameron which was a very hard thing to do, and saying to Miss Hawkline, "What about your father? How does he figure in with this monster you've got hanging around your basement?"

"It's not in the basement!" Miss Hawkline said, getting a little mad. "It's in the ice caves that are underneath the basement. We have no monster in our basement! We just have our laboratory there."

She had become infected by the just-finished conversation between Greer and Cameron about the East.

"Let's start all over again," the other Miss Hawkline said. "Our father built this house . . ."

· Hawaii Revisited ·

"He was teaching chemistry at Harvard and he also had a huge laboratory at home that he used for private experiments," Miss Hawkline said. "Everything was going along fine until the afternoon that one of the experiments got out of the laboratory and ate our family dog in the back yard. The next door neighbors were having a wedding reception in their garden when this happened. It was at this time that he decided to move to some isolated part of the country where he could have more privacy for his work.

"He found this location and built this house out here about five years ago with a huge laboratory in the basement and he was working on a new experiment that he called The Chemicals. Everything was going along fine until—"

"Excuse me," Greer said. "What about the experiment that ate your dog?"

"I'm coming to that," Hiss Hawkline said.

"I'm sorry," Greer said. "I was just a little curious. Continue. Let's hear what happened, but I already think I know what happened. Tell me if I'm wrong: one of the experiments ate your father."

"No," Miss Hawkline said. "The experiment didn't exactly eat our father."

"What exactly did it do?" Greer said.

Cameron was very carefully listening to everything.

"We're getting off on the wrong track again," the other Miss Hawkline said. "I don't know what's happening. This is very easy to explain but suddenly it's so complicated. I mean, I can't believe how strange our conversation has turned."

"It is sort of weird, isn't it?" Greer said. "It's like we can't say what we mean."

"I just forgot what we were talking about," Miss Hawkline said. She turned to her sister. "Do you remember what we were talking about?"

"No, I don't," the other Miss Hawkline said. "Was it Hawaii?"

"We were talking about Hawaii a little while ago," Greer said. "But we were talking about something else. What was it?"

"Maybe it was Hawaii," Cameron said. "We were talking about Hawaii. Isn't it a little bit colder in here now?"

"It does seem colder, doesn't it?" Miss Hawkline said.

"Yes, it's definitely colder," the other Miss Hawkline said. "I'll put some more coal in the stove."

She got up and went over to the stove. She opened the

lid on top to find the stove filled with coal because she had put some fresh pieces in just before she had sat down with her sister to talk to Greer and Cameron about the monster.

"Now, we were talking about Hawaii, right?" the other Miss Hawkline said.

"That's right," Greer said.

"It's a miserable place," Cameron said.

"I think we'd better go into another room," Miss Hawkline said. "This fire isn't warm enough."

They left the kitchen and went into one of the front parlors. They didn't say anything as they walked down the long hall to the parlor.

As soon as they stepped into the parlor, Greer turned to Miss Hawkline and almost shouted, "We were talking about the fucking monster, not Hawaii!"

"That's right," she almost yelled back and then they stood there staring at each other for a moment before Miss Hawkline said, "Something happened to our minds in the kitchen."

"I think you'd better tell us all about that monster right now," Cameron said. He looked grim. He didn't like his mind fucked around with by anybody, including monsters.

· The Chemicals ·

The parlor was exquisitely furnished in an expensive and tasteful manner. They were all sitting down in beautiful chairs facing each other except for Cameron who was sitting on a couch by himself.

There was a generous coal fire burning in the fireplace and the room was warm and cozy, far different from the kitchen and they all could remember what they were talking about.

"Where's your father?" Greer said.

"He disappeared into the ice caves," Miss Hawkline said. "He went down there looking for the monster. He didn't come back. We think the monster got him."

"How do we figure into this?" Greer said. "Why didn't you go for the marshal and have him come out here and take a look into this? He seems to be a good man and he has a lot of interest in one of you."

"There are too many things to explain and we're sure that our father is dead. That the monster killed him," Miss Hawkline said.

Cameron listened carefully from the couch. His gray eyes looked almost metallic.

"We were instructed to complete our father's experiment with The Chemicals," the other Miss Hawkline said. "He told us that if anything ever happened to him that we were to complete The Chemicals. It was his last important experiment and we are following his instructions."

"We cannot stand the idea of our father having wasted his life," Miss Hawkline said. "The Chemicals meant so much to him. We consider it our duty to complete what he started. That's why we didn't get the marshal. We don't want people knowing what we are doing out here. That's why we got you to help us. We cannot concentrate fully on The Chemicals until the monster is dead. It's distracting having that thing down there, trying to get out of the ice caves and into the house to kill us. So if you kill it for us, it will make everything a lot simpler."

"What happened there in the kitchen?" Cameron said. "Why were we talking so strangely to each other? Why did we forget what we were talking about? Has that ever happened here before?"

There was a slight pause while the two Miss Hawklines looked at each other. Then one of them said, "Yes. Things like that have been happening ever since our father added a few more things to The Chemicals and then passed electricity through The Chemicals. We've been trying to figure out a way to correct the balance of The Chemicals and complete the experiment. We've been following the notes that our father left behind."

"I like the way you say, 'behind,'" Greer said. "Behind meaning that some God-damn monster ate him in the basement."

"Not the basement, the ice caves!" Miss Hawkline said. "The laboratory is in the basement!"

Cameron looked at the two Miss Hawklines. Everybody stopped talking because they could see that Cameron was going to say something.

"You girls don't seem to have much grief about your father's disappearance," Cameron said, finally. "I mean, you're not exactly in mourning."

"Our father brought us up a special way. Mother died years ago," Miss Hawkline said. "Grief doesn't figure into it that much. We loved our father a great deal and that's why we are going to finish his experiment with The Chemicals."

She was a little mad about this time. She wanted to get onto the killing of the monster and away from superfluous conversations about things that she wasn't really that much interested in: like mortal grief.

"Tell us more about what happened in the kitchen," Cameron said.

"Things like that happen," the other Miss Hawkline said. "They're always strange occurrences and they seldom duplicate themselves. We never know what's going to happen next."

"Once we found green feathers in all of our shoes," Miss Hawkline said. "Another time we were sitting in a parlor upstairs talking about something when suddenly we were nude. Our clothes just disappeared off our bodies. We never saw them again."

"Yes," the other Miss Hawkline said. "That made me so fucking mad. I really liked that dress. I bought it in New York City and it was my favorite dress."

Greer and Cameron had never heard an elegant lady use the word fuck before. They would get used to it, though, because the Hawkline women swore a lot. It was something they had learned from their father who had always been very liberal with his language, to the point of being a legend at Harvard.

Anyway: on with the story . . .

"Has anything bad ever happened?" Cameron said.

"No, all the things that happen are like children's pranks except the child has supernatural powers."

"What does supernatural mean?" Cameron said.

The Miss Hawklines looked at each other. Cameron didn't like the way they looked at each other. All the fuck they had to do was to tell him what it meant. That was no big deal.

"It means out of the ordinary," Miss Hawkline said.

"That's good to know," Cameron said. He did not say it in a pleasant way.

"Are you ever afraid of what those chemicals might come up with next?" Greer said, taking over the conversation from Cameron and trying to put it on a more comfortable level.

The Miss Hawklines were relieved. They hadn't meant to hurt Cameron's feelings with the word supernatural. They knew it was a dumb thing that they had done, looking at each other, wishing they hadn't done it.

"They're never evil things," Miss Hawkline said. She

was going to say malicious, but she changed her mind. "Just very annoying sometimes like my favorite dress disappearing off my body."

"What are those chemicals supposed to do when they're finished?" Greer said. "And is this the same stuff that ate the dog?"

"We don't know what it's supposed to do," Miss Hawkline said. "Our father told us when The Chemicals were completed that the answer to the ultimate problem facing mankind would be solved."

"What's that?" Cameron said.

"He didn't tell us," Miss Hawkline said.

· The Dog ·

"You didn't answer the question about the dog," Cameron said.

"No, it wasn't The Chemicals," Miss Hawkline said. "They haven't eaten anything. They're just mischievous."

"Then what ate the dog?" Cameron said. He really wanted to know what ate the dog.

"It was an earlier batch of some stuff that Daddy had mixed up," Miss Hawkline said.

"Did it have anything to do with The Chemicals?" Cameron said. He had just picked up the habit of calling Professor Hawkline's last experiment The Chemicals.

Miss Hawkline did not want to say what she was about

to say. Cameron was watching carefully the expression on her face just before she spoke. She looked like a guilty child about to speak.

"Yes, it was an earlier stage of The Chemicals that ate the dog but Daddy took the stuff and flushed it right down the toilet."

Miss Hawkline was blushing now and staring down at the floor.

· Venice ·

Miss Hawkline got up from the chair she was sitting gravely
in like a captured child and went over to the fireplace to poke
the coal.

Everybody waited for her to finish and come back to the
conversation about The Chemicals, the dog being eaten,
etc., and what other topics that might be of interest on
July 13, 1902.

While they waited Cameron counted the lamps in the
room, 7, the chairs, 6, the pictures on the walls, 5. The
pictures were of things that Cameron had never seen before.
One of the pictures was of a street lined with buildings.
The street was filled with water. There were boats on the
water.

Cameron had never seen a street with boats on it instead of horses.

"What in the hell is that?" he said, pointing to the picture.

"Venice," Miss Hawkline said.

Having finished with the fireplace Miss Hawkline sat back down and the conversation was resumed. Actually, something they had talked about earlier was repeated and then they went onto something else.

· Parrot ·

"If The Chemicals can change your thoughts around in your head and also steal the clothes right off your body, I think you've got something there that could be dangerous," Greer said.

"It's the monster we're worried about," Miss Hawkline said.

"Which one?" Greer said. "I think you might have two of them here. And the one behind the iron door down there in the ice caves might be the one that will give us the least trouble."

"Let's go down and kill that fucker right now," Cameron said. "Let's be done with it and then we can think about other things if you want to think about them. I'm bored with all this talking. It's getting us nowhere. I'll go get the guns and then let's go down there and do the killing. Do you know what it looks like or how big it is or what the fuck it is, anyway?"

"No, we've never seen it," Miss Hawkline said. "It just howls and pounds on the iron door that's between the ice caves and the laboratory. We've kept the door locked ever since our father disappeared."

"What does it sound like?" Cameron said.

"It sounds like the combination of water being poured into a glass," Miss Hawkline said. "A dog barking and the muttering of a drunk parrot. And very, very loud."

"I think we're going to need the shotgun for this one," Cameron said.

· The Butler ·

Just then there was a knock at the front door. The knock echoed through the house and brought silence upon everybody in the parlor.

"What's that?" Greer said.

"It's somebody knocking at the door," Cameron said.

Miss Hawkline got up and started toward the parlor door that led into the front hall.

"It's the butler," the other Miss Hawkline said, remaining in her chair.

"The butler?" Greer said.

"Yes, the butler," the other Miss Hawkline said. "He's been up in Brooks getting some things we ordered from *back* East for The Chemicals."

They heard Miss Hawkline open the front door and then her voice and another voice talking.

"Hello, Mr. Morgan," she said. "Did you have a good trip?"

Her voice was very formal.

"Yes, madam. I got all the things that you requested."

The butler answered her with the voice of an old man.

"You look a little tired, Mr. Morgan. Why don't you go freshen yourself up and then go to the kitchen and have a cup of coffee. A cup of coffee will make you feel better."

"Thank you, madam. I could stand to get some of this dust off me and a cup of coffee would be most refreshing after my journey."

"How was Brooks?" Miss Hawkline said.

"Dusty and depressing as always," Mr. Morgan said.

"Was everything we ordered there?" Miss Hawkline said.

"Yes," Mr. Morgan said.

"Good," Miss Hawkline said. "Oh, before you go, Mr. Morgan. My sister is back from Portland and she brought some guests with her who will be staying here with us for a while."

She brought Mr. Morgan into the parlor.

He ducked his head when he stepped through the door and into the room.

Mr. Morgan was 7 feet, 2 inches tall and weighed over 300 pounds. He was sixty-eight years old and had white hair and a carefully trimmed white mustache. He was an old giant.

"Mr. Morgan, this is Mr. Greer and Mr. Cameron. They have come all the way from Portland and have graciously agreed to kill the monster in the ice caves."

"I'm pleased to meet you both," the old giant butler said.

Greer and Cameron told the giant they were glad to meet him, too. The Miss Hawklines stood there watching the meeting, looking quite beautiful.

"This is truly good news," Mr. Morgan said. "That thing down there is a regular nuisance, pounding on the door and making such terrible noises. Sometimes it's hard to get a good night's sleep around here. The demise of that beast would greatly help in making this house a bit more tolerable to live in."

Mr. Morgan had never really approved of Professor Hawkline's move from Boston to the Dead Hills of Eastern Oregon. He also did not like the site that the professor had chosen to build the house on.

He excused himself and left very slowly, because he was so old, ducking his head again to get through the door. They could hear him walking slowly down the hall to his room. The heavy sound of his footsteps was very tired.

"Mr. Morgan has been with our family for thirty-five years," Miss Hawkline said.

"His previous employment involved working with a circus," the other Miss Hawkline said.

· Getting Ready to Go
to Work ·

"Let's go kill the monster and be done with it," Cameron said. "I'll get the guns."

"As soon as you get the equipment that you need, we'll take you down there," Miss Hawkline said.

Cameron went out into the hall and got the long narrow trunk full of guns that was beside the elephant foot umbrella stand. He came back into the parlor and put the trunk down on a couch and opened it.

"We'll need the shotgun for certain," Cameron said. He took out the sawed-off twelve-gauge shotgun and a box full of shells. They were 00 buckshot. He loaded the gun and then he put a handful of shells in his coat pocket.

Greer reached into the trunk and took out a .38 revolver. He loaded the pistol and put it into his belt.

Cameron took out the .38 caliber automatic pistol that had previously been used to kill Filipino insurgents. He put a clip of bullets in the butt of the gun and then he snapped back and pushed forward the receiver sending a shell into the chamber. He put the gun on safety and slipped it into his belt.

"How big are those caves?" Greer said to the nearest Miss Hawkline.

"Some of them are big," she said.

Cameron put an extra clip of bullets for the automatic in his coat pocket.

"Let's take a rifle with us," Greer said, reaching down into the trunk for the Krag. "We've never tried to stop a monster before. He might give us some extra work, so let's be prepared for it."

He loaded the box magazine of the Krag with shells and then he pulled the bolt back and slammed a shell into the chamber with a very quick motion. It surprised the Hawkline women and then it pleased them, knowing that Greer and Cameron were very experienced at their work.

Greer put another shell into the magazine, replacing the one that had just gone like a-cat-catching-a-mouse into the chamber.

The Krag had a leather strap on it and Greer slung the rifle over his shoulder. Then he put a handful of shells in his pocket. He was ready to earn his living.

"One of us is going to have to carry a lantern," Cameron said. "So he's only going to have one hand free if something happens real quick with that monster. You carry the lantern and this Filipino bustin' gun and I'll do the shotgun."

He handed the automatic pistol and the extra clip of bullets to Greer while saying, "Give me that .38 there."

Greer gave him the .38.

"I can get this rifle working real quick if we need it," Greer said. "And if the son-of-a-bitch jumps us, we've got enough stuff here to turn it into sausage."

"Can we be of any help?" Miss Hawkline said.

"No, girls. You'd just be in our way," Cameron said. "This is our line of work. So you just keep out of the way and we'll kill your monster for you. Who knows? Maybe we'll eat it for supper tonight. It might be real tasty."

· Journey to the Ice Caves ·

The Hawkline women guided them down the hall to a flight
of stairs that led to the laboratory and the ice caves.

They were halfway down the hall when they heard a
heavy slow shuffling sound. It was the butler. He emerged,
head ducking through a door, into the hall.

"You're going to kill the monster," he said, in a very old
voice. His mouth moved and his voice seemed to come out
moments later.

He towered above them.

His hair was white like the frost on the grass outside
the house.

"The monster ate my master," the giant butler said. "If

only I were younger, I'd kill that monster with my bare hands."

His hands were huge and knotted with arthritis. Probably in their day they could have killed a monster but now they were in repose like old gray uneatable hams.

"You're going to kill the monster," the giant butler repeated. He was very tired from his trip to Brooks to pick up new things for The Chemicals. He was getting too old to make a trip that long.

The giant butler's eyelids were drooping.

"Thank God," he said. The word God almost lost itself in his throat. It sounded like somebody sitting down in an old chair.

· The Door ·

The door that led to the basement was a heavy iron door with two bolts on it. Miss Hawkline pulled the bolts back.

There was also a large padlock on the door. The lock was very impressive. It looked like a small bank. Miss Hawkline took a huge key out of her dress pocket. She put the key into the padlock and started to turn it when suddenly there was a huge crashing noise behind them.

They were all startled and turned around to see the giant butler spread out, over 7 feet and 300 pounds, on the floor. He looked like a stranded boat in the hall.

Miss Hawkline ran down the hall toward him. The other Miss Hawkline followed like a shadow in her footsteps. They crouched on their knees over the giant butler.

Greer and Cameron stood there looking down. They already knew he was dead while the two Miss Hawklines still searched for life in his body. When they discovered that he was dead, they both stood up. Their faces were suddenly very composed. There were no tears in their eyes though they loved Mr. Morgan like an uncle.

Greer was holding a lantern in his hand and he had a rifle slung over his shoulder and a large pistol stuck in his belt. Cameron was holding a sawed-off twelve-gauge shotgun in his hands. The giant butler lay dead on the floor. The two Miss Hawklines stood there silent, totally composed, looking unreally beautiful.

"What do we do now, young ladies?" Cameron said. "Kill the monster or bury the butler?"

· Thanatopsis Exit ·

"Do you know what I really want to do?" Miss Hawkline said.

"What?" Cameron said.

"I'd like to get fucked."

Cameron looked down at the giant butler and then at Miss Hawkline.

"I'd like to get fucked, too," the other Miss Hawkline said to her sister. "That's what I've been thinking for the last hour. It would be very nice to get fucked."

Greer and Cameron stood there with their guns while the giant butler lay there alone and forgotten with his death.

Greer took a deep breath. What the hell? You might as well do one thing as another.

"First things first," Cameron said. "Let's move this body out of the hall. Where do you want it?"

"That's a good question," Miss Hawkline said. "We could put him in his room or we could lay him out in a front parlor. I don't want to bury him now because I want to get fucked. I really want to get fucked. What a time to have a dead butler on your hands."

She was almost a little mad that the giant butler had taken this particular time and place to die. He looked awesome lying there in the hall.

"Hell, this is too much to think about," the other Miss Hawkline said. "Let's just leave him here for a while and take care of getting fucked."

"Well, you don't have to worry about him going any place," Cameron said.

So they just left the giant old butler lying dead on the hall floor and went off to get fucked, taking along with them a 30:40 Krag, a sawed-off shotgun, a .38 and an automatic pistol.

· Thanatopsis Exit #2 ·

Greer as he made love to Miss Hawkline kept thinking
about Magic Child. Miss Hawkline had a body that was exactly the same in its appearance and delightful movement
as Magic Child's.

They were making love in a beautiful bedroom upstairs.
The room had many delicate feminine things that were un-
familiar to Greer. The only thing wrong with the room
was the cold. It was very cold in the room because of the ice
caves under the house.

Greer and Miss Hawkline made love under many blankets in an incredibly ornate brass bed. Their passion had not
allowed time to be spent building a fire in the fireplace.

Greer kept wondering as they made love if this Miss Hawkline were Magic Child. At one moment he almost said the name Magic Child to see if she would respond, but then he decided not to because he knew that Magic Child was dead and it did not make any difference in which Miss Hawkline she was buried.

· After Making Love Conversation ·

After they finished making love, Miss Hawkline lay gently cuddling up against him and then she said, "Don't you think that it's kind of strange for us to be up here making love while the butler is lying down there dead in the hall and we haven't done anything about it?"

"Yes, it is a little strange," Greer said.

"I wonder why we didn't do anything about his body. You know, my sister and I are really very fond of Mr. Morgan. I've been lying here for the last few minutes thinking about why we haven't done anything about him down there. It's not a very gracious thing to go off fucking while your family butler, whom you love like an uncle, is lying dead in the hall of your house. That has got to be a very peculiar way to react."

"You're right," Greer said. "It sure is."

· Mirror Conversation ·

In a bedroom down the hall a similar conversation was taking place between Miss Hawkline and Cameron. They had just finished making some very enthusiastic love in which Cameron had not a single thought about this woman being Magic Child. He had really enjoyed their fucking together and had not allowed any intellectual process to cloud his pleasure. He used his mind for more important things: like counting.

"I guess we'll have to do something about your butler," Cameron said.

"That's right," Miss Hawkline said. "I completely forgot about him. He's lying dead in the hall. He fell over dead and we left him there to come up here and get some fucking in. It totally slipped my mind. Our butler is dead. He's down there dead. I wonder why we didn't do anything about his body."

"I asked you if you wanted to do anything about it down there but you girls wanted to come up here and get fucked, so we came up here and that's what we've done," Cameron said.

"What?" Miss Hawkline said.

"What do you mean what?" Cameron said.

Miss Hawkline lay very puzzled beside Cameron. There was a slight furrow between her eyes. She was in such a state of consternation that it was almost like slight shock.

"We suggested it?" she said, after a few moments of trying to figure out what events led them away from the body of their beloved dead giant butler and upstairs into the arms of love-making.

"We . . . suggested . . . it?" she repeated very slowly.

"Yes," Cameron said. "You insisted upon it. I thought it was a little strange myself, but what-the-hell, you're running this show. If you want to fuck instead of taking care of your dead butler, that's your business."

"This is very unusual," Miss Hawkline said.

"You're right there," Cameron said. "It ain't your ordinary run-of-the-mill thing to do. I mean, I've never fucked before with a butler lying spread-out dead in the hall downstairs."

"I just can't believe it," Miss Hawkline said. By now she had turned her head away from Cameron and was staring up at the ceiling.

"He's dead," Cameron said. "You've got 1 dead butler downstairs in the hall."

· Won't You
Come Home, Bill Bailey,
Won't You Come Home? ·

Meanwhile, down in the laboratory above the ice caves
everything was very quiet except for the movement of a
shadow. It was a shadow that just barely existed between
forms. At times the shadow would almost become a form.
The shadow would hover at the very edge of something
definite and perhaps even recognizable but then the shadow
would drift away into abstraction.

The laboratory was filled with strange equipment.
Some of it was of Professor Hawkline's invention. There
were many work tables and thousands of bottles of chemicals
and a battery to make electricity out here in the Dead Hills
where there was no such thing.

The laboratory was very cold. Actually, it was frozen because of its proximity to the ice caves underneath it.

There were some cast iron stoves around the laboratory which were used to thaw it out when the Hawkline sisters came down here to work, trying to unravel the mystery of The Chemicals.

Though there was no formal light in the room, there was still a slight portion of light coming from somewhere which for the moment wasn't actually a definite place. The light was coming from somewhere in the laboratory but it was not possible to tell where the light originated.

The light of course was needed to establish the shadow as it played like a child's spirit between object and abstraction.

Then the light became a definite place and the shadow was then related to the place where the light was coming from which was a large leaded-crystal jar filled with chemicals.

This jar of chemicals was the reality and mission of Professor Hawkline's lifework. The Chemicals were what he had placed his faith and energy in before he disappeared. It was now being completed by his two beautiful daughters who lay in bedrooms upstairs with two professional killers, and his daughters were wondering why they had gone off making love to these men while the freshly-dead body of their beloved giant butler lay ignored, unattended and not even covered up on the front hall floor.

The Chemicals that resided in the jar were a combination of hundreds of things from all over the world. Some of The Chemicals were ancient and very difficult to obtain. There were a few drops of something from an Egyptian pyramid dating from the year 3000 B.C.

There were distillates from the jungles of South America and drops of things from plants that grew near the snowline in the Himalayas.

Ancient China, Rome and Greece had contributed things, too, that had found their way into the jar. Witchcraft and modern science, the newest of discoveries, had also contributed to the contents of the jar. There was even something that was reputed to have come all the way from Atlantis.

It had taken a tremendous amount of energy and genius to establish harmony between the past and present in the jar. Only a man of Professor Hawkline's talent and dedication could have joined these chemicals together in friendship and made them good neighbors.

There of course had been the earlier mistake that had caused Professor Hawkline and his family to leave the East but that batch had been flushed down the toilet and the professor had started over again out here in the Dead Hills.

Everything had been fully under control with the ultimate results of his experiments with The Chemicals promising a brighter and more beautiful future for all mankind.

Then Professor Hawkline passed electricity from the battery through The Chemicals and began the mutation which led to an epidemic of mischievous pranks occurring in the laboratory and eventually getting upstairs and affecting the quality of life in the house.

It started off with the professor finding black umbrellas in unlikely places in the laboratory and green feathers scattered about and once there was a piece of pie suspended in the air and the professor took to thinking too long about things that were not important. Once he spent two hours thinking about an iceberg. He had never spent more than a few moments previously in all of his life thinking about icebergs.

This mischief led to the clothes vanishing off the bodies of the Hawkline women upstairs and other things too silly to recount.

Sometimes the professor would think about his childhood. He would do this for hours at a time and then afterwards not be able to remember what he had been thinking about.

Then one day a horrible monster started howling and banging on the iron door that separated the ice caves from the laboratory. The monster was so strong that it shook the door. The professor and his daughters didn't know what to do. They were afraid to open the door.

The next day one of the Hawkline sisters went down to the laboratory to bring the professor some lunch. When he was working hard he didn't like to come upstairs to eat.

Because of his immense dedication he continued working, trying to reestablish the balance of The Chemicals while the monster from time to time hollered and banged on the door with its tail.

His daughter found the door to the ice caves open and the professor gone. She went to the door and yelled down into the caves, "Daddy, are you in there? Come out!"

A horrible sound came from deep in the caves and started coming through the darkness of the caves toward the open door and Miss Hawkline.

The door was immediately locked and one of the sisters, dressed like and thinking she was an Indian, went to Portland to find men qualified to kill a monster but who also possessed discretion, for they wanted to undo the mistake their father had made without public attention and finish his experiment with The Chemicals in a way that he would have approved of for the benefit of all mankind.

But they did not know that the monster was an illusion created by a mutated light in The Chemicals, a light that had the power to work its will upon mind and matter and change the very nature of reality to fit its mischievous mind.

The light was dependent upon The Chemicals for sustenance as an unborn baby relies upon the umbilical cord for supper.

The light could leave The Chemicals for brief periods of time but it had to return to The Chemicals to revitalize itself and to sleep. The Chemicals were like a restaurant and a hotel for the light.

The light could translate itself into small changeable forms and it had a shadow companion. The shadow was a buffoon mutation totally subservient to the light and quite unhappy in its role and often liked to remember back to the days when harmony reigned in The Chemicals and Professor Hawkline was there, singing popular songs of the day:

"Won't you come home, Bill Bailey, won't you come
   home?
She moans de whole day long;
I'll do de cooking, darling, I'll pay de rent;
I knows I've done you wrong."

As he poured a drop of this and a drop of that into The Chemicals in hopes for a better world, little realizing that each drop led him closer and closer to the day when he would pass electricity through The Chemicals and suddenly evil mischief would be created and the harmony of The Chemicals would be lost forever and soon the mischief would be turned in all its diabolical possibilities upon himself and his lovely daughters.

A lot of the contents of The Chemicals were not happy with what had happened since the electricity had been passed through them and the mutation occurred that created evil.

One of the chemicals had managed to completely separate itself from the rest of the compound. The chemical was very unhappy with the recent turn of events and the disappearance of Professor Hawkline because it had wanted very much to help mankind and make people smile.

The chemical now cried a lot and kept to itself near the bottom of the jar.

There were of course chemicals who were basically evil in nature and glad to be free of the professor's good-neighbor policy who exulted now in the goofy terror the light, which was the Hawkline Monster, inflicted upon its hosts, the Hawklines, and anybody who came near them.

The light possessed unlimited possibilities and took a special pride in using them. Its shadow was disgusted with the whole business and trailed, dragging its feet reluctantly behind.

Whenever the Hawkline Monster left the laboratory, drifting up the stairs and then slipping like melted butter under the iron door that separated the laboratory from the house, the shadow always felt as if it were going to throw up.

If only the professor were around, if only that terrible fate had not befallen him, he would still be singing:

"Me and Mamie O'Rorke,
Tripped the light fantastic,
On the sidewalks of New York."

· The Hawkline Orchestra ·

Greer and Cameron and the Hawkline women, who were still mystified by their behavior, returned clothes to their bodies and all joined together in a music room on the same floor as the bedrooms that they had just finished making love in.

Greer and Cameron put their guns down on the top of a piano. Miss Hawkline went downstairs and made some tea and brought it back up on a silver platter and they all sat in the music room surrounded by harpsichords, violins, cellos, pianos, drums, organs, etc. It was a very large music room.

To make tea Miss Hawkline had to step around the body of the giant butler in the hall downstairs.

Greer and Cameron had never had tea before but they decided to try it because what-the-hell with all the things that were going on in this huge yellow house that was so weird that it almost breathed, straddling some ice caves that penetrated like frozen teeth deep into the earth.

Greer and Cameron had wanted to do something with the dead body of the giant butler as soon as they were finished with the living bodies of the Hawkline women, but the women insisted that they all have tea first before getting onto the disposal of the butler who was still sprawled out like an island in the hall.

A freshly-started fire was burning in the music room fireplace.

"Do you like your tea?" Miss Hawkline said. She was sitting beside Greer on a couch next to a harp.

"It's different," Greer said.

"What do you think, Cameron?" the other Miss Hawkline said.

"It doesn't taste like coffee," Cameron said. He counted all the musical instruments in the room: *18.* Then he said to the closest Miss Hawkline, "You have enough musical stuff here to start a band."

"We've never thought about it in that way," the Miss Hawkline said.

· The Butler Possibilities ·

"What are we going to do with the butler's body?" Cameron said.

"That is a problem," Miss Hawkline said. "We'll really miss him. He was like an uncle to us. Such a good man. Huge but gentle as a fly."

"Why don't we start by moving him out of the hall. It's hard walking around him," Cameron said.

"Yes, we should move him," the other Miss Hawkline said.

"Why didn't we do that before we sat down here and started drinking this stuff?" Cameron said, looking disdainfully at his cup of tea. It was very apparent that Cameron was not going to be converted to the geniality of tea drinking. It was, you might say, not his cup of tea.

"I think we should bury him," Miss Hawkline said, thinking for a few seconds.

"You have to get him out of the hall if you want to put him into the ground," Cameron said.

"Precisely," the other Miss Hawkline said.

"I think we'll need a coffin," Miss Hawkline said.

"2 coffins," Cameron said.

"Do you gentlemen know how to make a coffin?" the other Miss Hawkline said.

"Uh-uh," Greer said. "We don't make coffins. We fill them."

"I think it would draw too much attention to us if we were to go into town and have one of the townspeople make us one," Miss Hawkline said.

"Yes, we don't want anybody coming out here and investigating into our business," the other Miss Hawkline said.

"Definitely not," Miss Hawkline replied, taking a very lady-like sip of tea.

"Let's plant him outside," Greer said. "We'll just dig a hole, put him in it, cover him up and it'll all be taken care of."

"We don't want to bury him close to the house," Cameron said. "The ground's frozen hard around this place and I'll be fucked if I'm going to dig a hole that big in frozen ground."

"We'll dig a hole outside of the frozen ground and then drag him out of the hall and put him into the hole," Greer said.

"It's sad to think of our beloved butler Mr. Morgan

in these terms," Miss Hawkline said. "I knew he was getting along in years and that someday he would die because, as we all know, death is inevitable, but I had never thought about what a problem the hugeness of his body would make. It's just something you don't think about."

"You didn't think he was going to turn into a dwarf when he died, did you?" Cameron said.

· On the Way to a Butler
Possibility ·

As they started downstairs to take care of the butler which meant guiding him to his eternal resting place, a hole in the ground, they passed the open door of a room that had a pool table in it. It was a beautiful table with a crystal chandelier hanging above it.

The door had been closed when Greer and Cameron came upstairs to fuck the Hawkline women.

"Look, a pool table," Cameron said, carrying a shotgun. He stopped momentarily to admire the pool table. "Sure is 1 fine-looking table. Maybe we can play some pool after we bury the butler and kill the monster."

"Yeah, some pool would be nice after we finish our

work," Greer said, with a 30:40 Krag slung over his shoulder and an automatic pistol in his belt.

"That's a pretty lamp, too," Cameron said, looking at the chandelier.

The room was illuminated by sunlight coming in the windows. Light from the windows gathered in the chandelier which reflected delicate green flowers from the pool table.

But there was also another light in the flowery pieces of glass that hung like a complicated garden above the table. The light moved very subtly through the pieces of glass and it was followed by a trailing, bumbling child-like shadow.

Greer, for a second, thought he saw something moving in the chandelier. He looked up from the pool table to stare at the chandelier and sure enough there was a light moving across the pieces of crystal. The light was followed by an awkward dark motion.

He wondered what could cause the light to move in the chandelier. None of the pieces of crystal were moving. They were absolutely still.

"There's a light moving in the chandelier," he said, walking into the room to investigate. "It must be reflecting off something outside."

He went over to a window and looked out. He saw the frost around the house circling out for a hundred yards and then stopping as summer took over the grass and the Dead Hills beyond.

Greer could see nothing moving outside that could cause a light to reflect in the chandelier. He turned back around and the light was gone.

"It's gone now," he said. "That's funny. There was nothing outside to start it."

"Why all this attention to a reflection?" Miss Hawkline said. "We have a dead butler lying in the hall. Let's do something about that."

"Just curiosity," Greer said. "The only reason that I'm still alive is because I'm a very curious person. It pays to keep on your toes."

He looked again at the chandelier but the strange light was gone. He did not know that the light was hiding on the pool table, near a side pocket, and there was a shadow hiding there, too.

"That light seemed familiar," Greer said. "I've seen it someplace before."

The light and the shadow held their breath, waiting for Greer to leave the room.

· A Surprise ·

As they descended the spiral staircase to the main floor of the house, Miss Hawkline said to her sister, "The funniest thing happened a little while ago."

"What was that?"

"It's really strange," she said.

"Well, what was it?"

Greer and Cameron were trailing behind the Hawkline sisters. They moved so gracefully that Greer and Cameron were almost spellbound. The sisters moved without making a sound on the stairs. They moved in the same manner as two birds gliding slowly on the wind.

Their voices delicately punctuated the air like the invisible movement of peacock fans.

"I found some Indian clothes hanging in my closet. I didn't put them there," Miss Hawkline said. "Do you have any idea where they came from?"

"No," her sister said. "I've never seen any Indian clothes around here."

"It's really strange," Miss Hawkline said. "They're our size."

"I wonder where they came from," the other Miss Hawkline said.

"A lot of very strange things have been happening around here." Miss Hawkline answered.

Greer and Cameron looked at each other and they had something more to think about.

· The Butler Conclusion ·

When they finally arrived at the body of the dead butler, they really had a surprise waiting for them. One of the Hawkline women put her hand up to her mouth as if to stifle a scream. The other Miss Hawkline turned white as a ghost. Greer sighed. Cameron put his finger in his ear and scratched it. "What the fuck next?" he said.

Then they just stood there staring at the butler's body. They stared at it for a long time.

"Well," Greer said, finally. "It's going to make burying him a lot easier."

Lying on the floor in front of them was the body of the butler but it was only thirty-one inches long and weighed less than fifty pounds. The dead body of the giant butler had been changed into the body of a dwarf. It was almost lost in folds of giant clothes. The pant legs were barely occupied and the coat was like a tent wrapped around the corpse of the butler.

At the end of a huge pile of clothes, there was a small head sticking out of a shirt. The collar of the shirt surrounded the head like a hoop.

The expression, which was of quiet repose, gone to meet his Maker, as they say, on the butler's face had remained unaltered in his transformation from a giant into a dwarf but of course the expression was much smaller.

· Mr. Morgan,
Requiescat in Pace ·

It did make burying the butler simpler. While Greer dug a small grave outside the house, just beyond the influence of frost, Miss Hawkline went upstairs and got a suitcase.

· Prints ·

After the funeral with appropriate words of bereavement
over a very small grave and a little cross, everybody went
back into the house and gathered in a front parlor.

Greer and Cameron no longer had their guns with them.
They had put them away in the long narrow trunk which
was back beside the elephant foot umbrella stand. They
only carried a gun when they were going to use one. The
rest of the time the guns stayed in the trunk.

Cameron put some coal on the fire.

The two Miss Hawklines were sitting next to each
other on a love seat. Greer sat across from them in a huge
easy chair with a bear's head carved on the end of each arm-
rest.

Cameron stood beside the fire, after having helped it out, facing the room and the troubled eyes of his contemporaries. He looked over at a table that had some cut-crystal decanters of liquor and fine long-stemmed crystal glasses that were keeping company on a silver platter.

"I think we need something to drink," he said.

Miss Hawkline got up from the love seat and went over to the table and poured them all glasses of sherry which they were momentarily sipping.

She returned to the side of her sister on the love seat and everybody was exactly as they were before Cameron made the suggestion except they had glasses in their hands.

It had been a delicately choreographed event like making different prints of a photograph except that one of the prints had glasses of sherry in it.

· Magic Child Revisited ·

"I'd like to ask you girls a question," Greer said, but first he took a sip from his glass of sherry. Everybody in the room watched him carefully take his sip. He held the liquor in his mouth for a moment before he swallowed it. "Have either of you ever heard of somebody called Magic Child?" he said.

"No," Miss Hawkline said.

"The name's not familiar," the other Miss Hawkline replied. "It's a funny name, though. Sounds like an Indian name."

They both looked puzzled.

"That's what I thought," Greer said, looking over at Cameron standing beside the fireplace. The coal burned silently and smoke journeyed upward in departure from this huge yellow house standing in a field of frost at the early part of this century.

Greer as he looked over at Cameron suddenly noticed that part of the fire was not burning and part of the smoke just beyond it was not moving upward but was just hovering above flames of a slightly different color that did not burn.

He thought about the strange reflection in the pool-room chandelier. The fire that did not burn resembled that reflection.

He looked away from Cameron and back to the Hawk-line women sitting primly beside each other on the love seat. "Who is Magic Child and what does she have to do with us?" Miss Hawkline said.

"Nothing," Greer said.

· Return to the Monster ·

"I guess we should think about killing the monster down there in the basement, Cameron said and the Hawkline women didn't say anything. "We've been here all day and we haven't gotten around to that yet. So many things have been happening. I'd like to get that God-damn monster out of the picture, so we can get onto something else because there sure as hell seems to be something else here to get onto. What do you think, Greer? Time for a little monster killing?"

Greer looked casually over at Cameron but at the same time his vision took in the fireplace. The fire that did not burn and the smoke that did not move were gone. It was a normal fire now. He looked back at the Hawkline women and casually but carefully around the room.

"Did you hear me?" Cameron said.

"Yeah, I heard you," Greer said.

"Well, what do you think? A little monster killing?"

The Hawkline sisters were both wearing identical pearl necklaces. The necklaces floated gracefully about their necks. But some of the pearls were glowing more brightly than the other pearls and some locks of hair hanging long about their necks seemed slightly darker than the rest of their hair.

"Yes, we should get around to killing the monster," Greer said. "That's what we're here for."

"Yeah, I think that's what we should do," Cameron said. "And then find out what's causing all these crazy things to happen around here. I never saw a man buried in a suitcase before."

· Questions Near Sunset ·

The house was by now casting long shadows out across the frost as the sun was nearing its departure from the Dead Hills and Eastern Oregon and all the rest of Western America while Greer was asking the Hawkline women some last minute questions.

"And you've never seen the monster?" Greer said to Miss Hawkline.

"No, we've just heard it screaming down in the caves and we've heard it banging on the iron door that locks the caves off from the laboratory. It's very strong and can shake the door. The door's thick, too. Iron."

"But you've never seen it?"

"No, we haven't."

"And the door's been locked ever since your father disappeared?"

"Yes," Miss Hawkline said.

The pearls about the Hawkline sisters' throats had grown a little more intense in light, almost approaching a diamond-like quality. Greer saw a motion in the darkness of their hair. It was as if their hair had moved but it hadn't moved. Something had shifted in their hair. Greer thought for a second. Then he realized that it was the color of their hair that had moved.

"And sometimes you hear screams?"

"Yes, we can hear them all over the house and we can hear the banging on the iron door, too," Miss Hawkline said.

"How often?"

"Every day or so," Miss Hawkline said.

"We haven't heard anything," Greer said.

"Sometimes it's like that," the other Miss Hawkline said. "Why all these questions? We've already told you everything that we know and now we're telling it to you again."

"Yeah," Cameron said. "I want to get that monster out of the God-damn way."

"OK," Greer said. "Let's kill the monster," while letting his vision casually brush past the necklaces about the Hawkline sisters' throats.

The necklaces were staring back.

· What Counts ·

But now the sun was down and early twilight had sub-
stituted itself on the landscape and though everybody was
ready to kill the monster, they were also very hungry and
soon their hunger got the best of them and killing the monster was put off until after supper which the Hawkline
women returned to the kitchen to prepare while Greer
and Cameron stayed on in the parlor.

When the Hawkline sisters departed, the strange light
stayed on the pearls and the moving dark color remained
in their hair and they unknowingly transported them to the
kitchen which was fine with Greer because he wanted to
talk about them with Cameron.

Greer started to tell Cameron what he had seen but Cameron interrupted him by saying, "I know. I've been watching them. I saw them in the hall by the butler's body after it got changed into a dwarf person. They were on the shovel while you were digging the grave and I saw them when I was putting my clothes on after fucking one of those Hawkline women."

"Did you see them in the chandelier above the pool table?" Greer said.

"Oh, yeah. But I wish you hadn't been so obvious about going in there and looking for them. I don't want to make them nervous and know that we know about them."

"You saw them here in the room?" Greer said.

"Sure. In the fire. Why do you think I was standing over there? because I wanted a hot ass? I wanted a closer look. They're gone now with the Hawkline women, so what do you think? I know what I think. I don't think we have to go down in the ice caves to find that fucking monster. I think we only have to go as far as the basement and those fucking chemicals that their crazy father was working on."

Greer smiled at Cameron.

"Sometimes you surprise me," Greer said. "I didn't know that you were picking up on it."

"I count a lot of things that there's no need to count," Cameron said. "Just because that's the way I am. But I count all the things that need to be counted."

· But Supper First, Then the Hawkline Monster ·

Greer and Cameron decided to have supper first before they dealt with The Chemicals in the laboratory and search out what they thought would lead them to the Hawkline Monster.

"We'll just play like we're going down into the ice caves and blast out whatever, but when we get down to the basement we'll come up with some excuse to linger around down there and if we come across something interesting, maybe like The Chemicals, we'll shoot it," Cameron said. "But first let's enjoy a good supper and not let on at all that we know about that light and its shadow sidekick."

"OK," Greer said. "You've got it all pegged."

Then the Hawkline sisters came into the room. They had changed their dresses. They were now wearing dresses with very low necklines that accentuated beautiful young breasts. They both had tiny waists and the dresses showed them to advantage.

"Supper's ready, you hungry monster killers!"

The Hawkline women smiled at Greer and Cameron.

"You need energy if you're going to kill a monster."

Greer and Cameron smiled back.

The same necklaces were still about the Hawkline sisters' throats and the light and the shadow were still there. The light looked comfortable in the necklaces and the shadowy dark color that could move was at rest in their long flowing hair.

At least the Hawkline Monster has good taste, Greer thought.

· Counting the Hawkline
Monster ·

During supper Greer and Cameron casually watched the
Hawkline Monster about the throats and in the hair of the
Hawkline sisters.

The monster was very informal during the meal. Its
light diminished in the necklaces and the shadowy moving
color in the sisters' hair was motionless, fading almost into
the natural color of their hair.

The meal was steaks and potatoes and biscuits and
gravy. It was a typical Eastern Oregon meal and eaten with
a lot of gusto by Greer and Cameron.

Greer sat there thinking about the monster and thinking about how this was still the same day they had awakened

in a barn in Billy. He thought about all the events that had
so far transpired.

It really had been a long day with the prospects of much
more to follow: Events that would lead him and Cameron
to attempt to deprive the Hawkline Monster of its existence
and the strange powers that it possessed sitting across the
table from them, staring out of two necklaces about the
throats of two beautiful women who were completely unsuspecting, at faith with their jewelry.

Cameron counted random things in the room. He
counted the things on the table: dishes, silverware, plates,
etc. . . . 28, 29, 30, etc.

It was something to do.

Then he counted the pearls that the Hawkline Monster
was hiding in: . . . 5, 6, etc.

· The Hawkline Monster
in the Gravy ·

Toward the end of supper the Hawkline Monster left the necklaces and got onto the table. It condensed itself into the space of a serving spoon that was in a large bowl of gravy on the table. The shadow of the monster lay on top of the gravy pretending that it was gravy.

It was very difficult for the shadow to pretend that it was gravy but it worked hard at the performance and sort of pulled it off.

Cameron was amused by the monster getting on the table and he understood how difficult it was for the shadow to pretend that it was gravy.

"Sure is good gravy," Greer said to Cameron.

"Yeah," Cameron said, looking over at Greer.

"You boys want some more gravy?" Miss Hawkline said.

"It sure is good," Greer said. "What about you, Cameron, more gravy?"

The shadow of the Hawkline Monster was lying as flat as it could on top of the gravy. The monster itself was slightly uncomfortable in the spoon that had a little more reflection to it than it should have had.

"I don't know. I'm pretty full now. But . . ." Cameron put his hand on the spoon. He was now touching the Hawkline Monster. The spoon, though it was in a bowl of hot gravy, was cold.

Cameron casually thought about how in the fuck he could kill the monster but he couldn't think of a way to kill a spoon, so he just used the Hawkline Monster to put some more gravy on his potatoes.

The monster obliged and fulfilled the function of a spoon. The shadow squirmed off the spoon when Cameron lifted the gravy from the serving bowl and it fell very awkwardly back into the bowl.

The shadow was very uncomfortable, almost sweating.

Cameron put the spoon back in the bowl and again disturbed the shadow which was now on the edge of panic.

"How about you, Greer? You want some more of this good gravy?"

The Hawkline sisters were pleased that their gravy was getting such rave notices.

"No, Cameron. Good as it is, I'm just too full," Greer said. "I think I'll just sit here and watch you enjoy it. I like to watch a man eat who likes what he's eating."

The shadow thought that it was going to throw up.

· Parlor Time Again ·

After supper they retired to a front parlor leaving the Hawkline Monster dangling spoon-like in some gravy. There
was a large painting of a nude woman on the parlor wall.

Greer and Cameron looked at the painting.

The Hawkline Monster did not follow them into the
parlor. It went downstairs to the laboratory to get some
rest in The Chemicals. It was tired. So was its shadow.
Supper had been very long for them.

"Our father was fond of naked women," Miss Hawkline
said.

Coffee was served in the parlor with snifters of cognac
by the Hawkline sisters who looked even prettier if that were
possible.

Greer and Cameron kept looking at the nude painting of the woman and then at the Hawkline sisters who knew what they were doing but acted as if they didn't. They could have chosen a different parlor. They were excited by the situation. The only way they showed their excitement, though, was by a slight increase in their breathing.

"That's 1 pretty painting," Cameron said.

The sisters did not answer him.

They smiled instead.

Greer and Cameron while paying attention to the nude painting and the beauty of the Hawkline women had carefully gone over the entire room looking for the monster and it was not there.

They had a couple of cups of coffee and a couple of snifters of cognac as they waited to see if the monster would return but it didn't and their appreciation of Hawkline beauty increased some.

"Who painted that painting?" Cameron said.

"It was painted in France years ago," Miss Hawkline said.

"Whoever painted it sure knew how to paint," Cameron said, staring at the Hawkline sister who had just answered him. She liked the way Cameron was staring at her.

"Yes, the artist is very famous."

"Did you ever meet him?"

"No, he was dead years before I was born."

"That's a shame," Cameron said.

"Isn't it?" Miss Hawkline said.

· Soliloquy of the Shadow ·

The Hawkline Monster had returned to its jar of chemicals in the laboratory. It lay there in repose . . . strange sections of light not moving. These chemicals, the long and arduous work of Professor Hawkline, were the energy source, rejuvenation and place where the Hawkline Monster slept when it was tired, and while the monster slept, The Chemicals restored its power.

The shadow of the Hawkline Monster slept nearby. The shadow was dreaming. It was dreaming that it was the monster and the monster was it. It was a very pleasant dream for the shadow.

The shadow liked the idea of not being the shadow anymore but instead being the monster itself. The shadow did not like to sneak around all the time. It made the shadow nervous and unhappy. The shadow often cursed its fate and wished that The Chemicals had given it a better throw of the dice.

In the shadow's dream it was the Hawkline Monster and occupying a bracelet on the wrist of one of the Hawkline sisters. It was very happy in the dream and trying to please her by making her bracelet shine more brightly.

The shadow did not approve of the monster's tactics and was ashamed of the cruel things that the monster had inflicted upon the minds of the Hawkline sisters. The shadow could not understand why the monster did these things. If fate were reversed and the shadow changed into the monster, everything would be different around the house. These cruel jokes would come to an end and the monster's energy would be directed to discovering and implementing new pleasures for the Hawkline sisters.

The shadow was very fond of them and hated to be a part of the monster's sense of humor and wished only pleasure and good times for the Hawkline sisters instead of the evil pranks that the monster loved to play upon their bodies and their minds.

The shadow also strongly disapproved of what the monster had done to Professor Hawkline. It thought that the monster should have been loyal to him and not pulled such a diabolical prank on him.

The bracelet dream of the shadow suddenly dispelled itself and the shadow was wide awake. It stared down at the Hawkline Monster sleeping in The Chemicals. For the first time, the shadow realized how much it hated the monster and tried to think of ways to end its evil existence and take the energy of The Chemicals and change them into good.

The monster slept unsuspecting in the jar of chemicals. The monster was tired from a day of evil deeds. It was so tired that it was snoring in The Chemicals.

· Meanwhile, Back in the Parlor ·

It was now almost midnight and a Victorian clock was pushing Twentieth Century minutes toward twelve. Its ticking was loud and methodical as it devoured July 13, 1902.

Greer and Cameron casually but very carefully examined the parlor again to see if the Hawkline Monster had returned. It hadn't.

They of course did not know that it was sound asleep, snoring in a jar full of chemicals in the laboratory and they were all safe for the time being.

After they were certain that the monster was not about, Greer said to Cameron, "I think it's time we told them."

"Told us what?" Miss Hawkline said.

"About the monster," Greer said.

"What about it?" Miss Hawkline said.

Her sister had turned her attention from a cup of hot coffee in her hand to intently waiting for the next words from Greer.

Greer searched his mind to find the right words and a simple, logical sequence to tell them in. He paused a little too long because what he had to say was so fantastic that he could not easily find a simple way to say it. Finally the right words found him.

"The monster's not down in the ice caves," Greer said. "It's here in the house. It's been all over the place today. It spent a couple of hours sitting around your necks."

"What?" Miss Hawkline said, incredulously.

Her sister put her cup of coffee down.

They were both now in a state of amused shock.

"The monster's some kind of strange light that moves around followed by a goofy shadow," Greer said. "I don't know exactly how it works but it works and we're going to destroy it. We don't think there's anything in the ice caves that we've got to kill. The light has the power to change things and to think and it can get into minds and fuck 'em around. Have either of you noticed the light and the shadow that follows it like a dog?"

The Hawkline sisters did not say anything. They turned and stared at each other.

"Well?" Greer said.

Finally a Miss Hawkline spoke, "It's a strange light that moves around with a clumsy shadow following it?" she said.

"Yeah, we've seen it all over the place," Greer said. "It's been moving around with us, dogging us. For a long time this evening it was right there in your necklaces. It left a while ago and hasn't been back since."

"What you're describing is one of the properties of The Chemicals," Miss Hawkline said. "There's a strange light in the jar and a kind of swirly awkward shadow that stays near the light and follows it when it moves in the jar. The light is an advanced stage of The Chemicals. Our father told us before he disappeared that the light would eventually be changed into something that would be extremely beneficial for all mankind."

"We've needed some more chemicals to complete that change and those are the chemicals our poor butler brought us from Brooks. We were going to finish the experiment as soon as you killed the monster," the other Miss Hawkline said.

"I wouldn't finish anything," Greer said. "I think what you should do is to throw that batch of stuff out and start over again. You've got something that's out of control down there. I think that stuff killed your butler and is responsible for your father's disappearance and it also changed one of you girls into an Indian and has fucked with our minds, too."

The Hawkline sisters stared on, lost in deep silence.

"Let's go down and get that jar of fucking stuff and throw it out and then get a good night's sleep," Cameron said. "I could stand it. I've never buried a dwarf before and I'm tired. I've fucked so much today I'm afraid my prick's going to fall off."

"The Chemicals were our father's lifework," Miss Hawkline said, breaking silence desperately. "He dedicated his life to The Chemicals."

"We know that," Cameron said. "And we think the fucking chemicals turned on him. Bit the hand that fed them, so to speak. You saw what it did to your butler. It killed him and changed his body into a dwarf. The devil only knows what that fucking stuff is going to do next. We've got to throw it out before we're all changed into dead dwarfs. There's nobody to bury us in a bunch of suitcases."

· Meanwhile, Back in the Jar ·

The Hawkline Monster, a light in a jar full of chemicals, slowly turned over like a sleeping person and then turned over again.

God-damn it, thought the shadow and slowly turned over and then turned over again.

The monster was now uncomfortable in its sleep and moved again like a person on the edge of waking up and turned over again and *God-damn it,* thought the shadow and turned over again.

The Hawkline Monster was uneasy in its sleep. Perhaps it was having a bad dream or a premonition. It turned over again and *God-damn it.*

· A Man's Work Turned
to Nothing ·

"You mean you want us to destroy our father's lifework?"
Miss Hawkline said.

"Yes," Cameron said. "It's either that or have it destroy
you."

"There has to be another alternative," the other Miss
Hawkline said. "We just can't throw away what he spent
twenty years working on."

It was a minute before the hour of midnight. Miss
Hawkline got up and put a lump of coal on the fire. The
other Miss Hawkline poured Greer some more coffee. She
was pouring from a silver coffee pot.

Everything had stopped momentarily while the Hawkline sisters were thinking about what to do next. It was an enormous decision for them to make.

"And don't forget we think that fucking thing got your father, too," Greer said, as the clock began tolling midnight and changing the world into July 14, 1902.

"4," Cameron said.

"Give us a few more minutes," Miss Hawkline said, looking anxiously over at her sister. "Just a few more minutes. We've got to make the right decision. Once it's done, it's done."

"OK," Greer said.

"12," Cameron said.

· Waking Up ·

The Hawkline Monster continued stirring in The Chemicals. It was now almost awake. The shadow sighed as the monster hovered on the edge of waking. The shadow dreaded again being a part of the next thing the monster would think up. He did not approve of the way the monster fooled with the Hawkline women, making them do things that were completely out of character. The transformation of one Hawkline sister into an Indian, the shadow thought, was a very gross deed.

There was no way of knowing what the monster would come up with next. No thing was too terrible for the monster not to consider and of course its powers of dark invention had just barely been tapped.

The light which was the monster continued to toss and turn in The Chemicals as waking roared toward it like an early winter storm.

The shadow sighed again.

God-damn it.

Suddenly the monster was awake. It stopped stirring about and lay very quietly in The Chemicals. It looked over at the shadow. The shadow stared helplessly back, resigned to its fate.

The light looked away from the shadow. The light looked about the room. The light was anxious. It continued looking about the room, still a little sleepy but rapidly becoming energized. The light felt something threatening but it didn't know what it was.

Momentarily, it would be in full control of its powers.

The Hawkline Monster felt that something was very wrong.

The shadow watched its nervous master.

The monster's mind, like a tree in an early winter storm, shook off the leaves of sleep.

The shadow wished that the Hawkline Monster were dead, even though it would probably have to follow the monster into oblivion.

Anything was better than the living hell of having to be in partnership with the Hawkline Monster and do all these evil things.

The shadow remembered back to previous stages of The Chemicals and how exciting it was to be created by Professor Hawkline. At that time the light was benevolent, almost giddy with the excitement of having just been created. There was a future with the possibility of help and joy for all mankind. Then the light changed in attitude. The light concealed its personality change from Professor Hawkline.

The light started pulling little pranks that the professor let pass as accidents. Something falling over or something being changed into something else, so that the professor thought that he had made the mistake or something had been mislabeled and then the light found that it could leave the jar and move about and of course the poor innocent shadow of the light was forced to follow and become a participant-observer in pranks that gathered in momentum until they became acts of evil.

After while Professor Hawkline knew that there was something very wrong with The Chemicals but he kept thinking right up to the moment that the monster did that terrible thing to him that he would be able to correct the balance of The Chemicals and complete the experiment with humanitarian possibilities for the entire world.

But that was never to be because one afternoon when the professor was upstairs working on a new formula in his study the light pulled its most gross evil prank upon him.

The shadow shuddered to think about it.

The light was at last totally awake and knew that it was being severely threatened by the people upstairs and it had better take care of that threat right now.

The light crawled out of The Chemicals and balanced on the rim of the jar in preparation for departure and the shadow reluctantly prepared to follow.

· The Decision ·

"Yes," Miss Hawkline said, finally.

Her sister nodded in agreement.

"It's a difficult decision but it's the only way," Miss Hawkline said. "I'm sorry that this had to happen to our father's lifework but there are things that are more important."

"Yeah, our lives," Cameron interrupted. He was impatient. He wanted to go downstairs right now and throw that jar of stuff out and then sleep tonight beside the body of a Hawkline woman. He was tired. It had been a long day.

"We have the formula to The Chemicals," Miss Hawkline said. "Perhaps we can start over again or give it to some-body who might be interested in it."

"I don't know," the other Miss Hawkline said. "I'm a little tired of the whole thing, so let's not talk about the future now. Let's just pour the stuff out and get some sleep. I'm tired."

"Those are my feelings," Cameron said.

· Upstairs ·

The monster drifted off the lip of the jar and glided across the laboratory to land on the bottom step of the stairs that led upward to the house.

The shadow clumsily followed behind it, darker than the darkness in the room, more silent than complete silence and alone in the tragedy of its servitude to evil.

Then the Hawkline Monster flowed like a reverse waterfall up the stairs. It sparkled and reflected as it moved. The shadow followed behind it, a reluctant complement of darkness. The Hawkline Monster stopped at a dim space of light that shined under the laboratory door.

It was waiting for something to happen. The light of

the monster was now almost surgical in its perception. It looked under the door and down the hall.

The monster was anticipating something about to happen.

The shadow waited behind the Hawkline Monster. The shadow wished that it could look out underneath the door to see what was happening, but, alas, its role in life was only to follow and so it detailed itself right behind the ass of the Hawkline Monster.

· Whiskey ·

Everybody started to leave the parlor to go downstairs and pour out the Hawkline Monster but just as they reached the door and one of the Hawkline women had her hand on the knob, Cameron said, "Hold it for a second. I want to get myself a little whiskey." He walked over to the table where the liquor was in various cut-glass decanters.

He paused, trying to figure out which bottle was the whiskey. Then one of the Hawkline sisters said, "It's the bottle with the blue top."

That Miss Hawkline was carrying a lamp.

Cameron took a glass and poured himself a big slug of whiskey. Greer thought that this was strange because

Cameron never took a drop before a job and certainly the destruction of the monster was a job.

Cameron held the glass of whiskey up to his nose. "Sure smells like the good stuff."

Greer in sudden anticipation of killing the monster did not notice that Cameron, though he had poured himself a big glass of whiskey, did not take a drink from it. When they left the room, he was carrying the glass in his hand.

· Searching for a Container ·

Then a parlor door opened to the hall and one of the Hawkline sisters stepped into the hall, followed by another sister and Greer and Cameron who had a glass of whiskey in his hand.

The shadow could not see over the Hawkline Monster but the shadow heard the door opening and the people coming out into the hall. It wondered what was up, why the monster was so interested in the people at this time. Then the shadow shrugged. It was useless to continue with this line of thought for there was nothing that the shadow could do about it. The shadow could only follow the Hawkline Monster which it hated.

The Hawkline Monster watched them come down the hall toward the laboratory door. It waited, contemplating what form of action to follow next. It tried to realize a container, a shape to put its magic and its spells in and then to evoke that container upon these people who threatened its existence.

The shadow by now had given up trying to figure out what was happening. The shadow just didn't give a fuck anymore.

· To Kill a Jar ·

"Do you think we need a gun?" Greer said to Cameron.

There was no reply.

Greer thought that perhaps Cameron hadn't heard him, so he repeated the question.

"To kill a jar?" Cameron said.

The Hawkline women smiled.

Greer did not get the joke. He also did not notice that Cameron still had the glass of whiskey in his hand. Greer was unusually excited by the prospect of direct confrontation with the Hawkline Monster.

Cameron was carrying the glass of whiskey the same way he carried a pistol, casual but professional, waiting to be supereffective without any impression of menace.

Even the monster watching from underneath the laboratory door paid no attention to the glass of whiskey in Cameron's hand.

The Hawkline Monster had by now formulated a plan to take care of the threat to its life. The monster smiled at its own cunning. It liked the plan because it was so fiendish.

The monster suddenly backed its ass up and moved down a step toward the laboratory floor and knocked the unsuspecting shadow down two steps.

Fuck! the shadow thought and tried to regain some of its nonexistent dignity while keeping a close watch now on the Hawkline Monster, so that it could follow what the monster did next because that is the business of shadows.

· The Elephant Foot Umbrella Stand ·

As they walked down the hall, they passed the elephant foot umbrella stand and Cameron could not but count the umbrellas in the stand.

... 7, 8, 9.

Nine umbrellas.

Miss Hawkline paused beside the stand. There was something very familiar about it but she could not figure out what it was. There was just something very familiar. She wondered what it was.

"What is it?" Greer said.

Miss Hawkline was standing there staring at the umbrella stand. She thought that she had paused there for just a few seconds but it was longer than that and she did not realize it because she was lost in total curiosity.

She was holding up the possible demise of the Hawkline Monster.

"This elephant foot umbrella stand is very familiar," she said, addressing her sister. "Is it familiar to you?"

Her sister, who was also Miss Hawkline, took a look at it. Her gaze was suddenly equally intent. "Yes, it is familiar but I don't know what it is about it that is familiar. It almost reminds me of a person but I can't quite figure out who it is. It's somebody I've met, though."

Greer and Cameron looked at each other and then carefully around the hall. They were looking for the monster but they didn't see it. This conversation about the elephant foot umbrella stand had all the markings of the kind of stuff the monster would pull off.

But the monster was nowhere in sight, so they mentally put aside this Hawkline sister concentration as mere eccentricity.

"It certainly does remind me of somebody," Miss Hawkline said.

"Why don't you think about it later after we've finished off the monster? There'll be plenty of time for you to figure out who it is, then," Cameron said.

· The Hawkline Monster
in 4/4 Beat ·

The Hawkline Monster backed down the stairs to the laboratory, causing a shimmering flow of light like an ungodly waterfall. It also caused a confused inept shadow to bungle along in front of it.

The Hawkline Monster was now very confident. It knew how to handle things and looked forward in anticipation to the results of its power.

The Hawkline Monster had conceived of a diabolical fate for Greer, Cameron and the Hawkline women. It considered the plan one of the best things that it had ever come up with. It was the true amalgamation of mischief and evil.

The Hawkline Monster almost laughed as it strategically retreated down into the laboratory with its shadow scrambling awkwardly, tumbling goofily and carrying on in a demeaning, laughable manner as it tried to perform the perfunctory tasks of a shadow.

The Hawkline Monster was basking in confidence as it drifted and flowed down the stairs. What did it need to worry about because after all, did it not have the power to change objects and thoughts into whatever form amused it?

· Daddy ·

Miss Hawkline opened the iron door to the laboratory. She pulled back the two bolts and took the key from her pocket which soon released the huge padlock. All the time that she was opening the door, her mind was fixed on the elephant foot umbrella stand trying to figure out what person it reminded her of. The recognition of that person hovered right on the edge of her mind.

She pulled back the first bolt on the door. It was a little hard to get back, so she had to give it a good tug.

That umbrella stand was so familiar.

Who was it?

She pulled back the second bolt. It came back much easier than the first one did. She barely had to pull on it.

I've seen that umbrella stand thousands of times before but not as an umbrella stand, she thought, *but as somebody I know.*

She took a large key from the pocket of her dress and inserted the key into the huge padlock on the door and she turned the key and the lock fell open like a clenched fist and she took the lock off the door and hung it on the hasp.

Then she yelled, "DADDY!" and turned and ran down the hall to the elephant foot umbrella stand.

· A Harem of Shadows ·

The Hawkline Monster had found itself a good position of concealment in the laboratory and now just waited for Greer, Cameron and the Hawkline women to come into its domain.

The Hawkline Monster was so confident of their future that it was not even curious when it heard one of the Hawkline sisters scream and run back down the hall away from the laboratory door, followed by everybody else.

What difference did it make what they did up there for soon they would return and come down that flight of stairs and the Hawkline Monster would play with them a little bit. Then it would change them all into shadows and the monster would have five shadows following after it instead of one incompetent shadow.

Perhaps, these four new shadows would be skillful at playing the role the Hawkline Monster had devised for them. *Yes,* the monster thought, *it could stand a little competence in the shadow line.*

The Hawkline Monster had concealed itself behind some test tubes full of chemicals which were a rejected possibility of de-eviling The Chemicals that the professor had worked on for months before abandoning them as failures.

The shadow had concealed itself behind a clock on the table beside the test tubes. As soon as there was light in the laboratory the incompetence of its concealment would be revealed.

The shadow could not do anything right.

"Soon you will have playmates," the Hawkline Monster said to the shadow.

The shadow didn't know what the fuck the Hawkline Monster was talking about.

· Father and Daughters Reunited (Sort of ·

Miss Hawkline was on her knees and she had thrown her arms around the elephant foot umbrella stand and she was sobbing uncontrollably and saying over and over again, "Daddy! Daddy!"

The other Miss Hawkline stood there looking down at her sister, trying to figure out what was happening.

Greer and Cameron were busy looking around for the Hawkline Monster. Had they missed seeing it when they had looked for it before? Or had it come up behind them in the hall? They looked all over but they couldn't find the monster anywhere.

Then the other Miss Hawkline bent forward and looked very hard at the elephant foot umbrella stand.

Suddenly a huge flash of emotion exploded itself across her face and she fell to her knees beside her sister and said, "Oh, Father! It's our father! Daddy!"

The Hawkline sisters were not as emotionless as they thought they were.

Greer and Cameron stood there watching the Hawkline sisters hugging and calling an elephant foot umbrella stand Daddy.

· Marriage ·

Greer and Cameron left the Hawkline women with the elephant foot umbrella stand and walked back down the hall to the laboratory door. It was time to do something about the Hawkline Monster and right now. Greer and Cameron had had enough of its antics.

Greer was now carrying the lamp.

Cameron had a glass of whiskey in his hand.

Greer still had not noticed anything different about Cameron carrying the glass of whiskey. His mind was really someplace else because under any other conditions, he would have noticed the glass of whiskey. This was a first for him. Perhaps it was time that he should start thinking about retiring, about hanging it up and finding a good woman to settle down with.

Yes, that was probably a good idea. Maybe one of the Hawkline women. He of course had no way of knowing that the Hawkline Monster had already planned a sort of group marriage for them, anyway.

· Dream Residence ·

Greer went first. He opened the laboratory door and the light from the lamp in his hand illuminated the stairs and part of the laboratory. It was a very complicated place. Greer had never seen anything like it before. There were tables covered with thousands of bottles. There were machines that would have been at home in a dream.

"Go on, Greer. Let's go down and look around," Cameron said.

"OK."

The Hawkline Monster was watching them. The monster was amused by their helplessness. The women were not with them but the monster would take care of them after it had finished with Greer and Cameron. There was plenty of time for everybody.

The monster was so gleeful about the horrors that it was about to perform that it did not notice that a strangeness was being generated inside the shadow.

The shadow had been watching Greer and Cameron as they came down the stairs and then went over and lit three or four lamps, so they could see better, but then the shadow turned its attention to the Hawkline Monster and was staring at it and a strange for-the-first-time feeling was being born in the shadow as it continued to stare harder and harder at the Hawkline Monster.

A unique thought was now in the shadow's mind and the thought was linking itself up with a plan of direct action to take place when next the monster chose to move.

"This sure is a weird place," Greer said.

"It ain't any weirder than Hawaii," Cameron said.

· The Battle ·

Cameron had spotted the hiding place of the Hawkline Monster when he and Greer were halfway down the stairs. He saw strange sparks of light on a bench behind some funny-looking bottles. He didn't know what a test tube was.

"Why don't you light those lamps over there?" he said, motioning Greer over to a bench on the far side of the laboratory.

The Hawkline Monster was amused as it watched them. The monster was deriving so much pleasure from this that it decided to wait a few minutes before changing Greer and Cameron into shadows.

This was real fun for the monster.

Meanwhile, its current and only shadow waited for the monster to move so that it could put into action a plan of its own.

Cameron had also spotted a large leaded-crystal jar on a table in the opposite direction that he had sent Greer to light some lamps.

From the description that the Hawkline women had given him, he knew that this was the source of the Hawkline Monster . . . The Chemicals. He was standing about ten feet away from the jar. And the monster was "hiding" about five feet away from the jar.

Suddenly Cameron yelled, "It's over there! I see it!"

Greer turned toward where Cameron was yelling and pointing. He couldn't figure out what was happening. Why Cameron was yelling. This was not like Cameron but he turned anyway to the direction.

The Hawkline Monster was curious, too. What in the hell was happening? What was over there if it was over here?

So the monster moved . . . involuntarily . . . out of curiosity.

Cameron in the interim of artificial excitement moved over to the table where a jar called The Chemicals was residing and he was standing right beside it.

When the Hawkline Monster moved to get a better view of what was happening, the shadow, after having checked all the possibilities of light, had discovered a way that it could shift itself in front of the monster, so that the monster at this crucial time would be blinded by darkness for a few seconds, did so, causing confusion to befall the monster.

This was all that the shadow could do and it hoped that

this would give Greer and Cameron the edge they would need to destroy the Hawkline Monster using whatever plan they had come up with, for it seemed that they must have a plan if they were to have any chance at all with the monster and they did not seem like fools.

When Cameron yelled at Greer, the shadow interpreted this as the time to move and did so. It obscured the vision of the Hawkline Monster for a few seconds, knowing full well that if the monster were destroyed it would be destroyed, too, but death was better than going on living like this, being a part of this evil.

The Hawkline Monster raged against the shadow, trying to get it out of the way, so that it could see what was happening.

But the shadow struggled fiercely with the monster. The shadow had a burst of unbelievable physical fury and shadows are not known for their strength.

· The Passing of the
Hawkline Monster ·

Cameron poured the glass of whiskey into the jar of chemicals. When the whiskey hit The Chemicals they turned blue and started bubbling and sparks began flying from the jar. The sparks were like small birds of fire and flew about burning everything they touched.

"Let's get out of here!" Cameron yelled at Greer. They both fled up the laboratory stairs to the main floor of the house.

The Hawkline Monster responded to the whiskey being poured into the jar of its energy source by just having enough time to curse its fate

"FUCK IT!"

the monster yelled. It was a classic curse before shattering into a handful of blue diamonds that had no memory of a previous existence.

The Hawkline Monster was nothing now except diamonds. They sparkled like a vision of summer sky. The shadow of the monster had been turned into the shadow of diamonds. It also was without memory of a previous existence, so now its soul was at rest and it had been turned into the shadow of beautiful things.

· The Return of
Professor Hawkline ·

Greer and Cameron rushed up out of the burning laboratory and down the hall toward the Hawkline sisters. Just then the elephant foot umbrella stand changed into Professor Hawkline. He had been held prisoner in that form by a spell from the just-freshly-defunct Hawkline Monster who would now be at home in a jewelry store window.

Professor Hawkline was stiff and cranky from having spent long months as an umbrella stand. He wasn't as friendly to his loving daughters as he should have been, for the first words that came from his mouth in direct response to their cooing, "Daddy, Daddy. It's you. You're free. Father. Oh, Daddy," were, "Oh, shit!"

He didn't have time to say anything else before Greer and Cameron were upon him and his two daughters and hustling them out of the burning house.

· The Lazarus Dynamic ·

When they got outside they ran to just beyond the frost that encircled the burning house like a transparent wedding ring.

A few moments later they were all carefully watching the fire when suddenly the ground near them began to rumble and move like a small earthquake.

It was coming from the butler's grave.

"What the hell!" Greer said.

Then the ground opened up and out popped the butler like a giant mole covered with dirt and there were bits and pieces of a suitcase lying around him.

"Where . . . Am . . . I?" rumbled his deep old voice.

He was trying to shake the dirt off his arms and shoulders. He was very confused. He had never been buried before.

"You just came back from the dead," Cameron said as he turned back to watch the house burning down.

· An Early Twentieth-
Century Picnic ·

They stood there for a long time watching the house burn
down. The flames roared high into the sky. They were so
bright that everybody had shadows.

The professor had by now returned to a normal disposi-
tion and he had his arms affectionately around his daughters
as they watched the house go.

"That was quite a batch of stuff you mixed up there,
Professor," Cameron said.

"Never again," was the professor's response.

He had been introduced to Greer and Cameron and
he liked them and was very grateful for their having rescued
him from the curse of The Chemicals which could also be
called the Hawkline Monster.

Eventually they just sat down on the ground and watched the house burn all night long. It kept them warm. The Hawkline sisters changed the loving arms of their father for the arms of Greer and Cameron. The professor sat by himself contemplating the result of all his years of experimenting and how it had led to this conclusion.

From time to time he would shake his head but he was also very glad not to be an elephant foot umbrella stand any more. That was the worst experience he'd ever had in his life.

The butler was sitting there still dumbfounded and brushing the dirt off his clothes. There was a piece of suitcase in his hair.

The way everybody was sitting it looked as if they were at a picnic but the picnic was of course the burning of a house, the death of the Hawkline Monster and the end of a scientific dream. It was barely the Twentieth Century.

· The Hawkline Diamonds ·

By the light of the morning sun the house was gone and in
its place was a small lake floating with burned things. Everybody got up off the ground and walked down to the shores
of the new lake.

The Hawklines looked at the remnants of their previous
life floating here and there on the lake. Professor Hawkline
saw part of an umbrella and shuddered.

One of the Hawkline women noticed what had disturbed her father and reached over and took his hand. "Look,
Susan," she said to her sister and then pointed at a photograph floating out there.

Greer and Cameron looked at each other.

Susan!

"Yes, Jane," was the reply.

Jane!

The Hawkline women had first names and another prank of that damn ingenious monster had been dispelled.

Some of the house was still smoldering at the edge of the lake. It looked very strange. It was almost like something out of Hieronymus Bosch if he had been into Western landscapes.

"I'm curious," Cameron said. "I'm going to dive down into the basement and see if there's anything left of that fucking monster."

He took his clothes off down to a pair of shorts and dove into what just a few hours before had been a house. He was a good swimmer and swam easily down into the basement and started looking around for the monster. He remembered where the monster had been hiding before he poured the whiskey into The Chemicals.

He swam over there and found a handful of blue diamonds lying on the floor. The monster was nowhere in sight. The diamonds were very beautiful. He gathered them all together in his hand and swam upward out of the laboratory to the shore of the lake which had once been a front porch.

"Look," he said, climbing up onto the bank. Everybody gathered around and admired the diamonds. Cameron was holding them in such a way as for there to be a shadow. The shadow of the diamonds was beautiful, too.

"We're rich," Cameron said.

"We're already rich," Professor Hawkline said. The Hawkline family was a very rich family in its own right.

"Oh," Cameron said.

"You mean, you're rich," Susan Hawkline said, but you still couldn't tell the difference between her and her sister Jane. So actually the name-stealing curse of the Hawkline Monster really hadn't made that much difference, anyway.

"What about the monster?" Professor Hawkline said.

"No, it's destroyed. When I poured that glass of whiskey in The Chemicals, that did it."

"Yeah, it burned my house down," Professor Hawkline said, suddenly remembering that he no longer had a house. He liked that house. It had contained the best laboratory he'd ever had and he thought that the ice caves made a good conversation piece.

His voice sounded a little bitter.

"Would you like to be an elephant foot umbrella stand again?" Greer said, checking in with his arm around a Hawkline woman.

"No," the professor said.

"What are we going to do now?" Susan Hawkline said, surveying the lake that had once been their house.

Cameron counted the diamonds in his hand. There were thirty-five diamonds and they were all that was left of the Hawkline Monster.

"We'll think of something," Cameron said.

· Lake Hawkline ·

Somehow the burning of the house caused the ice caves to melt even down to their deepest recesses and the site of the former house became a permanent lake.

In 1907 William Langford, a local rancher, purchased the property from Professor Hawkline who had been living *back* East ever since his strange sojourn in the West.

The professor had given up chemistry and was now devoting his life to stamp collecting.

William Langford used the lake for irrigation and had a nice farm around it, mostly potatoes.

Professor Hawkline had been so glad to get rid of the property that he sold it for half of what it was worth but that didn't make any difference to him because he was happy to get rid of the place. It had a lot of bad elephant foot umbrella stand memories for him.

He never went West again.

And what happened to everybody else?

Well, it went something like this:

Greer and Jane Hawkline moved to Butte, Montana, where they started a whorehouse. They got married but were divorced in 1906. Jane Hawkline ended up with possession of the whorehouse and ran it until 1911 when she was killed in an automobile accident.

The accident had barely killed her and she was quite beautiful in death. The funeral was enjoyed and remembered by all who attended.

Greer was arrested for auto theft in 1927 and spent four years in the Wyoming State Penitentiary where he developed an interest in the Rosicrucian way of faith.

Cameron and Susan Hawkline were going to get married but they got into a huge argument about Cameron counting things all the time and Susan Hawkline left Portland, Oregon, in a huff and went to Paris, France, where she married a Russian count and moved to Moscow. She was killed by a stray bullet during the Russian Revolution in October 1917.

The diamonds that had formerly been the Hawkline Monster?

Spent long ago. Scattered over the world. Lost.

The shadow of the Hawkline Monster?

With the diamonds and blessedly without memory of previous times.

As for Cameron, he eventually became a successful movie producer in Hollywood, California, during the boom period just before World War I. How he became a movie producer is a long and complicated story that should be saved for another time.

In 1928 William Langford's heirs sold Lake Hawkline and the surrounding property to the State of Oregon that turned it into a park but being in a fairly remote area of Oregon with very poor roads, the lake never developed into a popular recreational site and doesn't get many visitors.

Richard Brautigan was born January 30, 1935, in the Pacific Northwest. He was the author of ten novels, nine volumes of poetry, and a collection of short stories. He lived for many years in San Francisco, and toward the end of his life he divided his time between a ranch in Montana and Tokyo. Brautigan was a literary idol of the 1960s and early 1970s whose comic genius and iconoclastic vision of American life caught the imagination of young people everywhere. Brautigan came of age during the Haight-Ashbury period and has been called "the last of the Beats." His early books became required reading for the hip generation, and Trout Fishing in America *sold two million copies throughout the world. Brautigan was a god of the counterculture, a phenomenon who saw his star rise to fame and fortune, only to plummet during the next decade. Driven to drink and despair, he committed suicide in Bolinas, California, at the age of forty-nine.*